SHANA GALEN

No Earls Allowed

CAN'T GET ENOUGH OF SHANA GALEN'S SPARKLING REGENCY ROMANCE?

PREPARE TO BE DAZZLED...

Covent Garden Cubs

"Smashing."
—*Fresh Fiction*

"Magical."
—*RT Book Reviews*

"Amazing."
—*Night Owl Reviews*

Jewels of the Ton

"Delicious."
—*RT Book Reviews*

"Captivating."
—*Night Owl Reviews*

"Superb."
—*Long and Short Reviews*

ISBN-13: 978-1-4926-3901-5

9 781492 639015

50799

EAN

No Earls Allowed

SHANA GALEN

sourcebooks
casablanca

Published by Sourcebooks Casablanca, an imprint of Sourcebooks,
Inc.
P.O. Box 4410, Naperville, Illinois 60567-4410
(630) 961-3900
Fax: (630) 961-2168
sourcebooks.com

Printed and bound in Canada.
MBP 10 9 8 7 6 5 4 3 2 1

One

London, 1816

NEIL WOKE AND GULPED IN AIR. THE ACRID SMELL OF cannon smoke burned his lungs, and the stench of burning flesh assaulted his nostrils. His hands fisted in the sheets on the bed, their softness reminding him he was not lying on a battlefield beside his dead brother but in his bed in his flat in London.

Without looking, he reached for the glass of gin on the bedside table. There was always a glass of gin on the bedside table. It wasn't a gentleman's drink, but here, in the dark, alone with his demons, Neil didn't want to be a gentleman. And so he bought gin for the nights when the dreams of battle haunted him. And when he drank the bitter brew, he tried to forget he was the son of a marquess.

He sipped the gin and lit a lamp, taking solace in the fact that his hands didn't shake. If he'd dreamed on, he likely would have woken with trembling hands and a scream echoing in his ears. For, as he'd lain beside his dead brother on that hill in Portugal, the smoke of the battlefield had coalesced around him, settling inside him. Instead of stifling him, the smoke caught the breeze and the flame of rage ignited within him. The fire built until it seared and burned, and he'd not been able to quench the heat until he rose and, with a roar, stumbled after the French soldiers the dragoons hadn't routed. Like a berserker, he'd cut every one of them down, even as they raised hands in surrender, even as they'd begged for quarter.

Neil had expected to be reprimanded for his behavior that day—behavior unbecoming an officer and a gentleman—but Draven had pulled him aside and given him a promotion of sorts.

If one could call leading a suicide troop a promotion.

The flame of rage had long been extinguished, and in its place lay a weight like a sodden mantle, bowing his shoulders. Neil could not shed it, no matter how hard he tried. Now he rose and pulled on trousers and a linen shirt. He didn't bother to tuck in the shirt or button it at the throat or sleeves. Instead, he padded to the window and pushed the heavy curtains open. He had a view of St. James's Street. He liked the sight of carriages and men coming and going from gambling hells or brothels. He liked the noise and the lights spilling from the establishments. It drowned out the sounds of battle that too easily plagued him in silence.

Neil stood and stared out the window for a long time before shoving his feet into boots and shrugging on a coat. His manservant would not arrive until later in the morning, so Neil managed the cravat on his own. As for his wild hair, he combed his fingers through it, pushing the sides out of his eyes.

He had no one to inform of his departure. He lived alone, a necessity when one woke screaming five out of seven nights of the week. He took his walking stick as a precaution against drunkards, who might be stupid enough to accost him, and left for his club.

Twenty minutes later, Porter greeted him. "Mr. Wraxall," the older, distinguished man said as he opened the door. "A pleasure to see you, sir."

Neil handed the Master of the House his walking stick. "Don't you ever sleep, Porter?"

Porter raised his brows, silver to match his hair. "Don't you, sir?"

"Not unless I have to. I know it's half past three. Is anyone here?"

"Mr. Beaumont is asleep in the card room."

No doubt Rafe had retreated to the Draven Club to escape some woman. Neil might have laughed if he hadn't come to escape his own demons. Not that the club didn't have its ghosts. His gaze strayed to the shield hanging directly opposite the door where no one entering could miss it. It was a silver shield bisected by a thick, medieval sword with a pommel shaped like a fleur-de-lis. Under the grip, the cross-guard was ornamented with a skull. It would not have been particularly macabre except for the eighteen marks on the flanks and base. Each fleur-de-lis, nine on the dexter side and nine on the sinister side, stood for a member of the troop of Draven's men Neil had lost during the war. Neil often felt he carried the weight of the enormous shield on his back.

"Anyone else here?" he asked the Master of the House.

"No, sir." Porter placed the walking stick in a stand, his wooden leg thumping on the carpet. "Would you care for a drink or something to eat, sir?"

Neil wanted more gin, if only to settle his nerves, but he could have drunk himself into a stupor at his flat. He'd come here to affect civility. He'd come here because it was the closest thing to home he'd ever known. "Brandy would suit me, Porter."

Though Neil could have found it blindfolded, Porter led him up the winding staircase and into the dining room. The five round tables in the paneled wood room were empty, their white linen tablecloths bright and clean and anticipating the next diner.

Neil chose a chair near the big hearth and settled back. The silence here didn't bother him. He could all but hear the echoes of his friends' voices—those who had survived—raised in song or laughter. He half expected to look to the side and see Ewan Mostyn—the brawny, muscled protector of the group—bent over a meal or spot Rafe Beaumont leaning negligently against one of the walls, under a sconce.

Neil never felt alone here.

Porter returned with the brandy on a silver salver. Neil had told the man a hundred times such gestures were unnecessary, but Porter believed in standards. Neil lifted the brandy, then frowned at the folded white paper that had been beneath it.

"I almost forgot, sir. This note came for you a few hours ago."

Neil lifted it and nodded to the silver-haired Master

of the House, who departed quite gracefully, considering he had but one leg. It didn't surprise Neil that correspondence meant for him had been sent here. He was here more than anywhere else, and anyone who knew him knew that. He broke the seal and opened the paper, recognizing the hand immediately. It was from the Marquess of Kensington. It said simply:

> Call on me at the town house at your earliest convenience. I have need of you.
>
> —Kensington

Neil folded the letter and put it in his pocket. It was not unusual for his father to request Neil's assistance with various tasks, from inspecting an investment opportunity to traveling to one of the marquess's many estates and assisting the steward with a duty or question. As a bastard, Neil had no social commitments and no obligations to the Kensington title as his elder brothers did. In Neil's opinion, acting in his father's stead was the least he could do, considering his father had claimed him, seen that he had been educated, and now granted him an allowance of sorts. The marquess would never have called it payment for Neil's services, but that was what it amounted to.

Neil bore his legitimate brothers no ill will, and they had always been civil to him. Especially Christopher. Neil and Christopher had been friends as well as brothers. The marquess's wife had always been coolly polite to him, though it must have chafed every time she encountered him. No doubt she wished Neil, not Christopher, had died in Portugal.

Neil was the product of Kensington's liaison with a beautiful Italian woman he'd been introduced to in London shortly after the birth of his second son. He'd been instantly smitten, and what ensued was a brief and passionate affair. The marchioness had looked the other way, suffering in silence as other women of her class had before her. The relationship might have gone on indefinitely if Neil's mother had not conceived a child and, after a difficult pregnancy, died of complications.

Neil had never known his mother. Instead, he'd been raised by a farmer and his wife who lived on Kensington's Lancashire estate. He'd been a small, dark child with startlingly blue eyes and a fondness for woodcarving, like his foster father, and horses, like his real father. Neil had always known the marquess was his real father. The giant of a man had come to visit him without fail once a month unless he was in Town for the Season.

At eight, Neil had gone to school—not Eton like his brothers, but a good school for middle-class children—and he'd learned reading and writing and arithmetic. He'd left school and his father had bought him a commission in the cavalry. On his own merits, he'd earned a position in the Sixteenth Light Dragoons, also known as the Queen's Lancers. He'd always been proud of his service as a member of the Sixteenth.

He was not so proud of the service he'd done afterward.

But his father did not want to speak to him about the war or how Neil had sold his soul to Lieutenant Colonel Draven on the same day Christopher had been killed. The marquess didn't blame Neil for Christopher's death.

Neil still blamed himself—for that death and those that followed—and he would spend the rest of his days in atonement.

He looked down at the note once again. Cold seeped along his limbs as he reread it. Neil had a feeling he wouldn't like what his father requested this time and not simply because he'd be expected to be sober when hearing it. With a sigh, Neil rose, threw the brandy in the fire, and prepared for the worst.

Two

LADY JULIANA, ONLY REMAINING DAUGHTER OF THE Earl St. Maur, could have screamed. She'd had a more abominable morning than usual, and that was saying something.

First, she'd been called away from the Duke of Devonshire's ball by the appearance of Robbie, one of the orphans from the Sunnybrooke Home for Boys. He'd told her she must come immediately. There was an emergency at the orphanage, and she'd made her excuses and run out, much to her father's annoyance. It probably hadn't helped matters that she'd taken the family coach.

Then she'd arrived at the orphanage just as the sun was rising to find that her cook was packing her bags to leave. Julia had known it would happen sooner or later; she'd simply hoped it would be later. Mrs. Nesbit had been complaining for months about the state of the kitchen, claiming she could hardly be expected to work in such conditions. Julia had agreed. The ovens smoked, the roof leaked, and the boys had stolen all the decent knives. Lately, Mrs. Nesbit had also complained the staples she stocked had been steadily disappearing as well—flour, cornmeal, potatoes, and garlic. Julia wondered if perhaps Mrs. Nesbit was cheating her and selling the stock on the sides, but she had no proof and couldn't afford to lose the cook. She'd begged Mrs. Nesbit to give her more time to ask the orphanage's board for money and make the repairs.

She'd thought she'd succeeded at persuading the woman, until, of course, the boys had thought it amusing to loose three tame rats in the kitchen as Mrs. Nesbit prepared breakfast. When Charlie had shown her the rats again, just to prove they were harmless, the poor cook had shrieked loud enough to wake the dead—or at least the dead tired, as Juliana thought of herself—and resigned effective immediately.

Which meant Julia had to cook the boys breakfast. One could not simply allow a dozen boys to go hungry, and she did not have the funds to buy them all pies from the hawkers' carts. Not when each boy ate as much as a horse.

And so, Julia had calmly collected the rats, placed them back in their straw-lined box with a bit of bread for their breakfast, and, in her jewels and dancing slippers, heated oats in a large pot she could barely move. She tried not to feel sorry for herself. Even as she rolled and kneaded bread until her arms ached, she pushed memories of walks in the promenade and ices at Gunter's Tea Shop aside. And when her once-lovely copper-colored ball gown was covered in flour and sticky pieces of dough, Juliana did not allow her thoughts to stray to all the lovely balls where she had worn the gown and danced with countless handsome and charming gentlemen.

Or at least she didn't allow her thoughts to stray much.

But no sooner had she placed the bread in the oven than Mr. Goring, her manservant, had knocked on the open door and informed her Mr. Slag was waiting for her in the parlor.

Julia had stared at the servant as though the man had gone mad. Sticky, white hands on her hips, she'd glowered at Mr. Goring until he'd lowered his eyes. "Why on earth did you seat Mr. Slag in the parlor?" She also wanted to ask where he had been when the boys he was supposed to be watching in her absence were foisting rats on the cook, but she couldn't afford to lose Mr. Goring too.

"There ain't nowhere else except the dining room, and the lads is in there making a racket about wantin' their vittles."

Julia had heard and ignored the noise. If the boys had wanted to be fed in good time, they shouldn't have taunted the cook with the rats. "What I meant, Mr. Goring," she clarified, though she knew he'd understood her perfectly, "is why did you admit Mr. Slag? I told you never to admit him. Not under any circumstances."

Goring scratched the sparse hair at the crown of his forehead. "Did you want me to close the door on him?"

"No." She spoke slowly and deliberately, as she often spoke to Charlie, who was four. "I wanted you to say what I told you to say."

"But, my lady, you *are* home."

"Not to him!" Defeated, she removed the apron that was supposed to protect her ball gown and tossed it on the worktable. She'd deal with Mr. Slag, then serve breakfast. Before leaving the kitchen, she closed the box with Matthew, Mark, and Luke and perched it under one arm. She did not want to risk the rodents escaping into the kitchen and causing more mayhem.

With a last look of annoyance at Goring, she marched toward the parlor, passing the dining room as she did so. She studiously avoided turning her head to look in. The boys were stomping their feet on the floor and banging their plates on the table. They needed a lecture, and she had no time at present to give it.

She wanted to be angry at Mr. Goring for admitting Slag, but she supposed Goring was as frightened of Mr. Slag as everyone else in Spitalfields. The crime lord ran the rookery, and his methods for dealing with those who displeased him were rather...harsh.

Julia was frightened of him as well, but she was able to mask her fear better than most. After all, she'd met other imposing figures—the King, the Queen, Wellington, and Brummell, to name a few. If she hadn't flinched when Brummell had scrutinized her dress with his quizzing glass, she would not flinch when confronted by Mr. Slag. And truth be told, until recently, he'd been no more than a minor irritation. But as she'd been forced to spend more time at the orphanage and less at her father's home in Mayfair, Mr. Slag had been harder to push to the back of her mind.

She opened the door to the parlor, and Slag rose immediately. He was a robust man and not very tall, only a few inches taller than she. He had mentioned on several occasions that he had been reared in a foundling house. She knew how cruel and heartless such institutions could be, which was one reason she was here and trying to improve the lives of the orphans under her care. But Joseph Slag had obviously found no such protector. He might have been a handsome man if not for the ravages of his brutal youth. His crooked nose, the deep lines around his eyes and mouth, and his cold, hard eyes were testament to the harsh life he'd led. Even dressed in fine linen and well-tailored clothing, he wore his low station like a permanent mantle. Joseph Slag was known to always carry an ebony walking stick with a golden handle in the image of a flame. The rumor was that he'd beaten more than one man to death with the stick.

Julia glanced at the stick now, leaning against the armchair Slag had occupied, and tried not to shudder. She pasted on a bright smile. "Mr. Slag, how lovely to see you this morning." She set the box of rats on the table just inside the room and curtsied prettily. Her mother would have been proud.

Slag bowed with some style of his own. "Lady Juliana, how kind of you to take time from your busy morning to see me."

He hadn't given her much choice, but she merely smiled and took the seat across from the one he'd occupied. "I'm afraid I am not at leisure to chat this morning, sir. My cook has given her notice, and as you no doubt can hear, I have hungry boys to feed."

"Ah. No wonder you look"—his eyes traveled down her dress, lingering a bit too long on her breasts, all but on display in the ball gown—"out of sorts. May I be of some assistance?"

"Do you cook?" she asked.

He gave her a look of appalled shock.

"Then I'm afraid not."

"What I meant, my lady, is that maybe I could find you a new cook. I'm well connected, I am. Maybe I'll hire a maid for you too." He didn't look at the dust covering the table near him, but Julia knew he'd seen it nevertheless.

"I thank you kindly, Mr. Slag, but I have a maid"— though she only came once a week—"and I already have another cook in mind." This was a blatant lie, but she knew that without a doubt it would be a mistake to put herself in Mr. Slag's debt. She'd made that mistake once before, and she would not repeat it.

"Then maybe I could make a donation to the orphanage. I know what hardships these boys face."

Julia raised her hand. "That is far too generous of you, Mr. Slag. I couldn't possibly accept any more of your charity."

He moved closer. "Then maybe you've given some consideration to my other proposal?"

The other proposal.

The proposal of… It hadn't exactly been marriage. Lord, she'd hoped he had forgotten about that. When he'd propositioned her last week, she'd pretended she hadn't understood what he meant.

Perhaps that tactic would work again. "I cannot recall another proposal at the moment, Mr. Slag, but I am ever so distressed this morning." She rose. "If you could call another time—"

His hand came down hard on her shoulder, and she flinched from the feel of his leather gloves on her bare skin. "Allow me to remind you, Lady Juliana. I offered you my protection."

"Thank you very much." She slid out of his grip. "Now, if you will excuse—"

"Stop playing games. I am a man of business, and you are not a stupid woman. There are dangerous men about, and you and the children who live here need a protector."

Julia didn't need to translate his words. *He* was the dangerous man.

"I am offering you my protection for a small fee."

Small fee? "I do believe you mentioned one thousand pounds, Mr. Slag. That is no small fee."

"Your father is an earl."

"Yes, and most of his money is tied up in lands."

"There is another option." He moved closer, his round belly brushing against her dress. "You can pay the fee by offering me a place in your bed. You're an attractive woman." His gaze slid to her breasts, making her skin itch. "And even the gentry like a bit of slap and tickle. What do you say, Julia?"

Though abhorrent to her, he made the proposal in earnest. He probably thought it more than fair, and if she had been another woman, she might have agreed without blinking an eye. Her father had tried to marry her off to men ranging from elderly to lecherous. What did Slag propose but a similar arrangement without the permanence of the vows?

But Julia had not come to Spitalfields to end up some man's plaything. She could have stayed home in Mayfair and become a kept woman. Which meant her answer to Slag was an unqualified *Never. No! Not ever.*

But one did not say such things to Mr. Slag and walk away with one's brains intact. Julia liked her head round, not smashed flat on the carpet. And so she smiled and chose one of the many phrases she knew and had used in the past on the sons of dukes and viscounts and lowly barons. "Sir, you flatter me with your proposal, but this is all so sudden."

"Then maybe you just need a bit of persuading." He reached for her, and she took a step back. Dear God. She dearly hoped this would not turn into him chasing her about the parlor. And why hadn't she seen this coming? The problem was that she spent only part of the week within the walls of the St. Dismas Home for Wayward Youth—er, rather Sunnybrooke Home for Boys, as she had renamed it. And during that time, she was so absorbed with the problems of the boys and running the orphanage, she had no time to consider how to deal with Mr. Slag. And when she might have snatched a moment to deal with the problem, she had to return to Mayfair to be thrust into the world of the *ton*, and then Slag and Sunnybrooke seemed so far away.

But Slag was not far away now. He was far too near and her strategy of ignoring him and hoping he'd go away would not work this time.

She took another step back, and he followed, but she was saved from running behind her desk when someone tapped on the parlor door.

"Come in!" she yelled. "Please!"

The door opened to reveal Mr. Goring.

"Sorry to interrupt, my lady."

"Not at all, Mr. Goring. Come in." She crossed to him and pulled him inside. "You should join us."

He frowned at her as though the ways of the upper

classes were foreign and mysterious to him. "You have another caller, my lady."

Julia frowned. Another caller? Who on earth would be calling on her here? Her friends had been forbidden to visit her here, and her father did not rise from his bed this early, and when she did see him, he preferred she go to him at their town house in Mayfair. It occurred to her that this caller might be one of Slag's men. In which case, she would be in worse straits than at present. "Do you know the caller?"

"No, my lady. He says it's a matter of—what was the word?—urgency."

He? Then the thought struck her. It was a representative from the bank. Perhaps the board had made good on its threat not to pay the mortgage and the bank had come to close her down.

"Tell him to come back later," Slag ordered.

"No!" Bank representative or no, whoever it was would be an improvement on Slag. "Show him in, Mr. Goring."

Goring looked from her to Slag.

"Go on, Mr. Goring," she said as forcefully as she could. "Show him in."

"Maybe I should come back at a more opportune time," Slag said.

"Please do, Mr. Slag. I am so sorry we were interrupted."

"May I call on you tonight?"

"Tonight? No. I'm very, very busy tonight."

He lifted his stick, then crossed to her and took her hand. At some point during their little dance, he'd removed his gloves, and as she'd removed hers in the kitchen, the press of his bare fingers on hers made her throat tighten.

"You can't put me off forever, Lady Juliana," he said softly. "Lest you forget, I'm a man who gets what I want. And the longer you make me wait, the more I want."

With that, he strolled out of the room, jostling the man entering. The two stopped, looked each other up and down, and then with a warning glare, Slag went on his way.

The other man watched him, then strode into the room. "Friend of yours?" he asked.

Julia let out a breath, then caught it again. She blinked at the man before her, but she had not dreamed him. He was better than any dream her mind might have conjured. It was as though he had just stepped out of a painting depicting a god or an angel. He was tall but not so tall she had to crane her neck to look up at him, and he had olive skin with a touch of gold. His thickly lashed eyes were the most beautiful shade of blue she had ever seen. She had never been to the Mediterranean Sea, but this was what she imagined the waters would look like. His hair brushed his collar, the thick waves falling about his face. With a cupped hand, he brushed them back in what must have been a habitual gesture, then, seeming to remember his manners, bowed to her.

His bow and the attention it drew to his clothing told her everything she needed to know. This man was no crime lord. He was of her father's ilk. Her ilk, when she was playing the part of Lady Juliana in Mayfair drawing rooms. His dark coat fit snugly over broad shoulders, his cravat was snowy white against bronze skin, and his breeches strained quite nicely over muscled thighs…

She tried to speak over the pounding of her heart. "You will forgive me, sir, if I do not recall having met you before." She hadn't met him. If she'd met him, she would not have forgotten.

"My lady," he said in a deep voice, "it is you who must forgive me." He had a cultured British accent with no hint of the Spanish or Italian that must run in his blood. "I'm sorry to call on you without notice. I do, however, have letters of introduction from your father and mine." He reached in the pocket of his waistcoat and withdrew a small packet of papers. He handed them over smoothly, his hand gloved hand brushing hers. Her heart thudded again, and she looked up at his face. He was perfect, so handsome that he did not seem real. If he'd asked her to dance a waltz, she'd have said yes and suffered her father's displeasure. What she wouldn't give to press against his strong, muscled body.

The man cleared his throat and raised his brows. Julia realized she had been staring too long and hadn't offered him a seat.

"Where are my manners?" she said, keeping her eyes down. He must think her a complete ninny. And she was! If she looked at him again, she'd probably start drooling. "Please sit. I should offer you tea, but my cook just—" Quite suddenly she remembered the bread and the oatmeal.

"Oh dear God." Dropping the letters, she hurried toward the door. Why hadn't she smelled the smoke earlier? Her bread was burning!

Unfortunately, her guest blocked the door, and she swerved to the side to avoid colliding with his shoulder. That sudden motion brought her hip in contact with the table near the door, which held the box of rats. She'd placed it precariously close to the edge—that was her fault—and at the collision, it tumbled toward the floor. Uttering a shriek, she bent and caught the box, but one of the rats—*Mark*, she thought—managed to catch his little paws on the edge and began to climb out. Julia shoved the box under her arm, caught the little creature before he could escape, tucked him in the small silk pocket tied under her gown, and raced for the kitchen.

Behind her, the visitor muttered, "What the hell?"

Julia didn't have time for explanations. She spotted Robbie's concerned face peering out of the dining room. At eleven, he was one of the older orphans and had stick-straight, brown hair framing a long, amply freckled face. The children's din had quieted now, as they had probably smelled the smoke as well and realized their breakfast was in jeopardy.

"My lady! I smelled—" Robbie began.

She raised a hand. "I am on my way, Robbie."

She burst through the door to the kitchen. Smoke filled the area near the oven, its acrid smell making her nostrils burn. She placed the box of rodents on a chair near the worktable and grabbed the first towel her hand landed on, a thin one for dish drying. Wrapping her hand, she used the towel to open the oven door. More black smoke poured out. Waving the towel to disperse the smoke and coughing so hard her lungs burned, Julia reached in and took hold of the bread. As soon as she had it free of the oven, she realized the towel was scant protection from the heat of the charred bread.

"Ow!" She tossed the bread in the air, catching it again so it would not land on the floor, just in case it was salvageable. She quickly dumped it on the work-table and frowned at the charred loaf.

"May I be of some assistance?" her too-handsome guest asked, stepping gingerly into the kitchen.

Julia refrained from moaning. She had no time to mourn the loss of the bread. She might still save the oats. A quick glance at the hearth showed the oats bubbling over the big black pot. Mindful of her raw hand, she took a moment to locate the thick, quilted mitten, slip it on her hand, and pull the pot away from the fire. She lifted the large spoon hanging nearby and stirred the oatmeal. The top layer of mush ceased bub-bling onto the floor, but the oats at the bottom stuck fast to the pot. Breakfast had been burned.

Tears stung her eyes.

"Is there anything I can do to help?" the visitor asked from the door.

She heaved out a sigh. "Not unless you can repair burnt oatmeal or bake bread."

"I confess I have no talent in either arena. Was that the children's breakfast?" Abruptly, the man took a step back. "Uh, I don't mean to alarm you, but you have a mouse in your pocket."

She looked down to where Mark's head poked out. "It's a rat," she said. *Think, Juliana. There must be something else you can prepare.*

If only she had restocked the larder, but the shelves were all but bare.

"My mistake."

Mark had wriggled to the edge of her pocket, and she caught him before he could make a bid for freedom. There had to be more oats, and she knew there were potatoes. Potatoes took so long to cook, though…

"Here." She held the rat out to her visitor absently. He took a large step back, his gaze telling her exactly how daft he thought her.

"Will you hold him for a moment?" she asked in exasperation. "I need to search for something to cook."

"No, I will not."

"Oh, don't be missish. He's harmless."

"Missish?" His blue eyes narrowed.

She shoved Mark into the visitor's hands. The visitor made a sound somewhere between a grunt and a curse, but he held the animal securely while she searched cabinets and shelves.

"If that was breakfast," the visitor said, "perhaps you could have the cook start on the noon meal. It's nigh eleven."

"I don't have a cook," she said, the feeling of hopelessness growing as she found nothing but empty drawers and bins. "She quit this morning."

Silence.

"Then perhaps your lady's maid—"

"She quit last week."

"Your manservant then. Allow me to send the man to fetch bread or pies from one of the street vendors."

She rose, wishing she could disappear, just for an hour, back to her Mayfair life, with its scones and drinking chocolate. "I would," she said with a sigh, "but I don't have the coin to spare."

"Then allow me."

She whirled to face him. "I cannot do that, sir."

"I would gladly pay the price if it meant I could relinquish my role as rat holder."

She almost laughed. "I do apologize." She took Mark from him and placed him in the box that served as the rats' cage. "My manners are sorely lacking this morning."

"You have nothing to apologize for." His gaze met hers, and she found it hard to breathe with those Mediterranean Sea eyes so focused on her. Had she ever known a man this handsome? She didn't think so, and she had known many handsome men. She'd had her share of Seasons and beaux over the years. She realized she'd once again stared at him too long when he lifted a brow.

"How many more of those are you wearing?" he asked with a nod at the box of rats.

"Just the one. There are three in total." She lifted the box so he could see, but he didn't even lean forward to catch a glimpse. "Their names are Matthew, Mark, and Luke," she said, knowing she was babbling now and wishing she would simply *shut up*.

"What happened to John?"

"We don't discuss John."

His eyes almost smiled at her then, though his mouth remained tight. "I understand. Give me a quarter hour, and I'll return with warm food."

"Really, Mr…sir. I cannot allow you to do that."

"Lady Juliana," he said, already starting for the door. "You cannot stop me." He paused and looked back at her. "And you look like you need all the help you can muster."

With that, he was gone. She sank into the chair and would have cried, except that she did need help and just the knowledge this man would take care of breakfast was one small weight off her shoulders. But that weight was quickly replaced by a glance at the state of the kitchen. It was in shambles, and without the cook here, she would be the one to clean it.

"My lady?" Robbie stood in the doorway.

"Yes, Robbie?"

"Who was that man?"

"I…" Good question. She'd never had a chance to look at the letters of introduction. "I don't know yet, but he's gone to fetch you and the other boys something to eat."

A roar sounded from the hallway, and she realized the other boys must have been standing behind Robbie.

"Before he comes back, will you please take your pets up to your room? They've caused enough trouble for one day."

Robbie looked chastened. Almost. "Sorry, my lady."

"I'm sure you are." The boys were always sorry after they'd done something wrong. For the life of her, she could not seem to teach them to think of the consequences *before* they acted.

Robbie took the box and, with a quick smile she could not quite resist, ran off. The other boys followed, all but James, who was about five and as blond as a Dutchman. "Is the man coming back?" James asked in his sweet, high voice.

"I should think so," she answered, tousling his pale hair affectionately. "And he'll bring your breakfast with him. Are you hungry?"

"Yes, my lady!" He nodded vigorously. "Will you fix yourself before he returns, my lady?"

Julia raised her brows. "Fix myself?"

"Aye, my lady. You look a fright, and we'll never find a father if you scare all the good ones away."

Julia opened her mouth to reply, but she was saved from saying who knew what when James scampered away. She stared after him, her eyes burning for another reason. In the few weeks she'd been here, some of the younger boys had become quite affectionate with her, even mistakenly calling her Mama. Most of the time it was when they were sleepy or needed comfort from a scrape or tumble. She had thought it an innocent mistake, but was it? Had the boys begun to think of her as their mother, and were they, as James suggested, looking for her to find them a father?

She would happily mother them all as much as she could, but she had seen all of marriage and fathers she could ever want. And yet clearly a house full of boys needed a man to look up to. She didn't even have a cook at present. Where would she find a man to guide a dozen orphans? How did one even advertise for a position like that?

Remembering James had said she looked a fright, she lifted one of the trays on the worktable. It was scratched and tarnished, but she could see well enough. Flour streaked her face and her coiffure was askew. She did look a fright. Normally, she wouldn't have cared a whit, but normally she didn't meet handsome strangers. Not that he had come to court her or any such foolishness. No, if her father had sent him, she had to consider him an enemy.

Still, she supposed it would not hurt to put her appearance to rights. And she would have done so if she hadn't heard the yell and the crash and had to run up three flights of stairs, yelling, "What have you done now?"

Three

Neil found a man with a cart selling some sort of freshly baked pies. The food smelled decent enough to him, but as he had no intention of hauling two-dozen pies back to the St. Dismas Home for Wayward Youth, he paid the man to bring the cart to the building.

When they arrived at the servants' entrance, he rapped on the kitchen door for a good three minutes to no avail. His father had said the earl wanted Lady Juliana to come home again and stop playing at her charity work. Neil had thought it would be a simple assignment—he'd be in and out. Apparently, he'd misjudged. So far, nothing about Lady Juliana had been simple. Least of all his reaction to her. He hadn't expected her to be so...so damned delicious. Even the smattering of flour and dough on what must at one time have been an expensive dress couldn't take away from the sensuality of her generous curves, the luster of her coppery hair, or the way her mouth turned up in just the barest hint of a smile.

He'd wanted to kiss that mouth to see if it was as

soft as it looked. From the way she'd looked at him, Neil didn't think she'd object to a kiss either.

Such thoughts weren't like him. He might no longer be a soldier, but he still considered Lady Juliana a mission. One did not kiss missions—unless one was Rafe Beaumont.

And Neil thanked God daily he wasn't Rafe Beaumont.

After another knock went unanswered, Neil supposed he would have to make the vendor drag the cart around to the front, but as he turned to give the directive, the kitchen door popped open. No one stood in the doorway, and when Neil leaned closer, he saw the latch was ineffective and the lock useless. Considering the look of the man Neil had encountered in the parlor earlier, he would have thought security a high priority for Lady Juliana. Anyone could walk in and steal from the orphans—or worse. And in Spitalfields, the *or worse* happened more often than not.

He'd made a mental list he'd titled *Problems and Dangers Relating to St. Dismas Orphanage*, and he planned to mention it to Lady Juliana at the first opportunity. Poor security would be at the top and the primary reason she should return to her father's abode immediately. In the meantime, he gestured to the pie man. "Bring the pies in here and set them on this table."

"Yes, guv." The man went to work while Neil looked in the hallway for any sign of Lady Juliana. She was nowhere to be seen, but the raucous sound of boys' laughter floated down from above. And then there was a thump and a cheer.

"Sounds like you got a full 'ouse, guv."

Neil looked up at the ceiling as the next thump sounded, then he handed the man a pound. "Come back tomorrow, and there will be another just like it."

The man's eyes grew large as he stared at his bounty. "I'll be 'ere, guv. You can count on Jacob, you can." He walked as if in a daze out of the kitchen.

Neil shut the kitchen door and studied the broken bolt just as another thump shook the house. This time it was followed by the unmistakable sound of a woman's voice. He'd have to leave the lock for later, so he shoved a heavy crate half-full of potatoes in front of the door and made his way through the building.

The building was large and, from what he could surmise, had probably once been the home of a well-to-do merchant. It was close to the large market in Spital Square that had operated there since King Charles II had granted its charter. But the building had not been the home of a prosperous merchant in some time. Neil knew little about fashionable furnishings, but everything he saw looked old fashioned and faded, like a painting left in the sunlight too long.

From what he'd seen so far, the kitchen, dining room, and a third room—probably a library or parlor—were on the first floor. He imagined servants' quarters were on the lower level and the drawing room and bedchambers on the second floor. He hadn't looked closely when he'd been outside, but he didn't think the building high enough for a third floor. Likely Lady Juliana had converted public rooms on the second floor into dormitories for the boys.

Neil found the stairs inside the small, dark vestibule.

He'd seen them when Goring, the manservant, had shown him in. As he stood at the base, more cheers rang out above him followed by groans. Lady Juliana's voice grew louder. Neil began to climb the rickety staircase, and when he reached the landing, he said a silent prayer that, whatever hell he was about to enter, it wouldn't involve more rats. He turned left, toward the noise, and stepped into a room with rows of four beds on either side. At the far end, a crowd of boys had gathered. Above their heads, he could just see Lady Juliana standing in the center, straining, her arms spread wide.

"Fight! Fight! Fight!" the boys chanted.

"There will be no fighting!" the lady said through clenched teeth. Neil realized she must have been holding two boys apart. He looked around for another adult who might be charged with supervising the children and saw no one. Was the petite daughter of the Earl of St. Maur the sole authority in an orphanage full of boys?

This was even worse than he'd thought.

Neil crossed his arms over his chest and cleared his throat just loud enough for the boys in the outer circle to hear him. One or two turned around, and eyes growing large as plates, they tapped the shoulders of their neighbors. Neil watched awareness ripple through the circle, and within seconds, the boys parted, leaving the two combatants and Lady Juliana exposed. Those three were so occupied they did not see him. The two boys—about eight years of age, if he judged correctly—swung at each other and tried to skirt around Lady Juliana. For her part, she ordered them to *Cease this instant* and *Do behave* while she danced between them and kept them apart.

He shouldn't have wanted to laugh. He never laughed anymore, and this situation was particularly unamusing because he had a feeling that the more trouble Lady Juliana faced with these lads, the more determined she would be to reform them. On the other hand, perhaps after this experience, she would have seen the futility of reform and would welcome being saved. That cheerful thought gave him pause to appreciate how utterly ridiculous—and, truth be told, adorable—she looked. She couldn't have been more than an inch or two over five feet and the curves her efforts exposed above the high waist of the voluminous gown were nicely rounded. Her coppery-red hair fell about her shoulders and her large, brown eyes flashed anger while the pale skin that often accompanied that red shade of hair was tinged pink with exertion.

With all the flour and dirt streaking her cheeks and arms, her wrinkled gown, and her hair flying in every direction, she should have looked as though she ought to be a resident of the orphanage. Instead, she brought to mind the image of a woman rising from rumpled sheets, skin pink from exertion—and pleasure.

He had heard his half brothers mention her name a time or two over the years. Lady Juliana was considered a beauty and had a dowry large enough to tempt one or two of them to court her, though it appeared no one had tempted her into marriage. Either that or her suitors had run screaming from the room at one flash of fire from her eyes. She did have expressive eyes. But he wasn't cowed, and unfortunately, neither were her charges.

Neil straightened his shoulders and marched forward to do what he'd come to do—save the day.

Standing before the threesome, he cleared his throat again. This time the three pairs of eyes darted to his face. Lady Juliana's gaze locked on his in horror, but the two boys were too enraged to take much note of him. Instead, they took advantage of the lady's momentary lapse of attention and tore at each other like rabid dogs.

With a screech, the lady jumped back and out of the way. And then, instead of doing what she ought and scampering to safety, she jumped between the two boys.

Neil was so completely surprised that he didn't move for a full three seconds. In that time, she almost parted the boys, but her skirts tangled about her feet and she ended up on her bottom.

"What the devil is going on?" Neil bellowed. "You, over there. You, on that side!" His temper began to simmer, and he pushed it back down, reminding himself these were children. He reminded himself as well that he'd sworn after that bloody day in Portugal he would never lose control again. Like a fist closing, he reined his emotions in and stepped forward. The two combatants scattered, and Neil held out a hand to Lady Juliana.

She brushed it away.

Confused, Neil continued to extend it, but she didn't take it. Instead, he stared in astonishment as she climbed to her feet unassisted. Then she pushed her hair out of her eyes and glared at him. She'd probably been glaring at him for several moments, but he hadn't been able to see for the profusion of coppery hair. "*You.*"

The one word was full of seething anger and condemnation.

What the devil was wrong with the woman? Perhaps she'd misunderstood. "I would have helped you to your feet, my lady," he said.

"Oh, I think you've *helped* quite enough for one day," she answered, her jaw clenched and her lips barely moving.

He stared at her and pointed a finger at his chest as if to ask whether she was referring to him.

She gestured to the pugilists. "I had the situation under control."

He let out a huff of laughter. She was obviously deluded. "Is that what you call it?"

She looked as though she had a ready retort on her lips, but he was saved from the tongue-lashing when one of the boys who had been fighting jumped forward. "Forgive me, my lady. I didn't mean to make you fall."

"Me either," the other one said, head hanging in a very good imitation of one shamed by his actions.

She gave the boys narrowed looks. "This wouldn't have happened if you had not been fighting. How many times have I told you fighting is not allowed?"

One of the boys with dark hair and freckles waved his hand and jumped up and down eagerly. "Ooh! I know! I know!"

She turned and sighed. "Michael?"

"One hundred and twelve times, Lady Juliana. I've been counting, I have!"

"I know you have, Michael. Your counting skills are quite extraordinary." She looked back at the combatants. "You would think after"—a glance at Michael—"112 reminders you would know the rule by now."

"I do, Lady Juliana, but he took my cards." This from what Neil had come to consider the older combatant, as he was taller and had a shaggy mane of brown hair.

The other, a bit shorter with curly, blond hair and a chubby face, which grew redder at the accusation, clenched his fists. "Did not. Those cards are mine!"

"Are not!"

"Are too!" countered the younger one.

Neil raised his brows at Lady Juliana as if to ask whether this was what she meant by *under control*. She glared right back at him, then held her hand out in front of the boy with the curly hair. "Give me the cards, George."

"But, Lady Juliana…" George whined.

"I told you there's to be no gambling."

"No fighting, no gambling. What type of establishment is this?" Neil drawled.

She turned her fiery, brown eyes on him. "And you, sir. I will speak with you in the parlor, if you would kindly wait for me there."

He gave her a mock bow. "Of course, my lady." But she would not win the field that easily. "The pies in the kitchen are growing cold."

"Pies!" That exclamation from every child in the room. And then he flinched as a line of boys, every bit as formidable as one of the French battalions, raced past him, thundered down the steps, and presumably landed in the kitchen.

The lady blew out an exasperated breath as though to indicate he had done something else of which she disapproved. "I'd better go down and make sure the little ones are given their fair share. There will be no practicing table manners this morning," she said, attempting to sweep by him as though her stained attire were a court-presentation dress.

He caught her arm, surprised by the warmth of her skin. "A moment of your time, my lady. I believe introductions are in order."

She sighed. "You are right. I've been terribly remiss. The morning has been rather hectic. I wish I could say it has been unusually hectic, but I'm afraid chaos has been the norm since I arrived."

He released her arm. "And when did you arrive?"

"Oh, almost three months ago. Or has it been four?"

The shock must have showed on his face because she quickly continued, "It used to be much, much worse. We actually have something of a routine now."

This was a routine?

A crash sounded from somewhere in the building, but before she could run off, he made a slight bow. "I am Neil Wraxall. My father is the Marquess of Kensington."

Her eyes narrowed. "Then you've come at my father's request. St. Maur and Kensington have been friends since their days at school."

He inclined his head. "As you say."

"And you obviously know I am Lady Juliana."

He would have made some nonsense remark about how he was pleased to meet her—although he hadn't been particularly pleased yet—but she held up a hand to stay his response.

"I see what this is about, and I regret to inform you that you are wasting your time. I have no intention of returning home until I have matters here in order. My father wants me to dance at balls and attend the theater. I ask you, how am I to attend the theater with all of *this* to think of?"

Neil knew an ambush when he saw one, and he remained silent.

"If my father sent you to convince me to return home, you are wasting your time, sir."

"I am not here to convince you to leave," he said. In fact, he'd intended to simply carry her out, put her in a coach, and send her home.

He saw now that while brute tactics might win the battle, they wouldn't win the war. She'd be right back here.

And then so would he.

This moment called for diplomacy, as Rafe would have called it. Ewan would have called Neil's next words by their true nature: a lie. "I am here because your father is worried for your safety. He asked me to put measures in place to ensure you are well protected."

She gave him a wary look. "My father said that?"

"I didn't actually speak to the earl, but that is my interpretation." A very loose interpretation.

"What sorts of measures?" she asked with narrowed eyes.

"I don't know yet. I'll need to do some reconnaissance before I make recommendations."

"Reconnaissance? Are you by any chance a soldier, Mr. Wraxall?"

"I was." Now would come the endless questions

about what branch he served in and the battles he fought in, and when she learned he was one of Draven's Dozen, she would probably press a hand to her chest and flutter her lashes.

He wouldn't mind that reaction, though he certainly would be no gentleman if he took advantage of her swoon to kiss her...

She turned her back on him and walked away.

Neil frowned. Where was the swoon and his ill-gotten kiss?

"Go ahead and do your reconnaissance, sir. You may note your recommendations when you are finished. I trust that will be shortly?" She paused at the door and looked over her shoulder at him. "We have no need for soldiers and military regimentation here."

Her skirts swished as she moved into the corridor and down the stairs. Neil could have imagined how lush her hips looked as she moved. He gritted his teeth and shifted his thoughts back to the mission. Clasping his hands behind his back, he surveyed the dormitory. A handful of buckets littered the floor, half-full of water from the rains the night before. He looked up at the leaky ceiling and noted the plaster was crumbling in more places than he could count. None of the boys' beds were made. Blankets and pillows were thrown on the floor as were articles of clothing. Dirty clothing, pamphlets, half-eaten apples, and decks of cards and dice littered the trunks at the end of the beds. No wonder the place had rats. He quickly found the box that housed the creatures near the window on the far side of the room. Even from this distance, he could see the latch on the window was broken. No doubt the boys were sneaking out at night and doing God knew what.

He had his work cut out for him, and this was but one room in what he estimated to be close to a dozen. One thing was for certain. Lady Juliana might not know it, but she needed military regimentation and a whole hell of a lot of it.

∽

Julia fumed all the way to the kitchen, and then she fumed more when she saw the state in which the boys had left it. She'd have to spend half the morning putting everything to rights. If her father wanted to help her, why didn't he send her a maid or a cook? She could sorely use one of each. Leave it to a man to send help in the form of one more inconvenience. On the other hand, if her father knew her lady's maid had resigned and the cook had fled and she was living here three or four days a week essentially unchaperoned, he would have come himself and dragged her home.

At least the boys would be busy for the next few hours. Mrs. Fleming should have arrived by now. The teacher would have had to begin her lessons late, but some education was better than the complete ignorance in which the boys had been living before she arrived.

Julia found the broom and sighed over the crumbs and smashed bits of food on the floor. If only Harriett could see her now. Her sister would have laughed at *dainty, little Julia* sweeping up after orphans. But then, her sister had always been laughing.

Harriett had been her best friend and closest

confidante. The sisters, only nineteen months apart, had behaved like twins. They'd always been so happy together. And who wouldn't have been happy when life was filled with nights at the theater, dancing under glittering ballroom chandeliers, and presentations at court? Their life had been exciting and beautiful and charmed. And when some small discomfort intruded, Harriett had made everything right again. She'd always been the strong, healthy one as well...until she wasn't.

Julia's eyes burned, and she closed them briefly. She was here because she'd already mourned Harriett and now she needed to do something besides embroider pillow covers and sip tepid tea at garden parties. The magic that had been her life in the *haute ton* had faded without Harriett, and each event seemed more dreary and tiresome than the last. Her father balked at the thought of his last remaining child running an orphanage. At one time, Julia would have balked too. Charities and benevolence societies were always Harriett's domain. She'd been a tireless supporter of this orphanage and several others. When she'd been confined to her bed, she'd asked Julia to go to the meetings in her stead.

And when she'd died, Julia had continued to go because she did not know how *not* to go. It had been painful enough saying goodbye to her dear sister and her best friend. The charities were one way to keep Harriett alive.

Davy had been another way.

But he'd been taken from her as well.

How could she sit in that too-silent town house and go on with her life as usual? Without Harriett or Davy, all that was left was a deep, dark hole. The day she'd walked into the St. Dismas Home for Wayward Youth, a ray of light had shone in the blackness threatening to engulf her life. She'd felt as though she belonged. She'd felt like this might be a place she could call home. She'd been delivering embroidered napkins, which anyone with half a brain could see was not what the orphans really needed, and she'd simply never left. First, she'd spent one day a week here, then two, then more. Now, she was all but splitting her time between her father's town house and the orphanage.

She felt close to Davy here. She felt closer to Harriett.

She felt...that something was not quite right.

She paused in her sweeping and cocked her head. It was too quiet, and she'd quickly learned when it was too quiet something was amiss. Laying the broom handle against the worktable, she left the kitchen and stuck her head in the hallway. The classroom was just up the stairs, in what had been a drawing room before the residence had been made into an orphanage. Shouldn't she hear the drones of Mrs. Fleming as she recited numbers or read aloud?

Instead, Julia heard...nothing.

She crept down the hallway and would have started up the stairs except she spotted Mr. Wraxall in the vestibule. She'd wanted to forget about him. She knew who he was as soon as he introduced himself. She'd never met him, but as she'd said, her father and his father had been friends for a long time. She knew about Kensington's bastard son. She'd only met the legitimate sons, of course, though the marquess claimed his bastard and had paid for him to be reared and educated.

Wraxall didn't look at all like his father and brothers, who were pale and slightly plump and who had inherited the crooked front teeth that were the hallmarks of the marquesses of Kensington from time immemorial. Wraxall must have taken after his mother, for he was not pale, not plump, and his teeth were white and straight.

She'd looked just a little too long at his mouth to pretend she didn't remember his teeth. Or his lips, which looked soft and yielding.

Except for his lips, everything about him was straight and proper and sober. He'd undoubtedly made a good soldier, because when he turned his gaze on her now, she almost felt as though she should stand at attention. She resisted the silly urge and then, because he made her nervous, she latched on to the first item she saw—other than his quite kissable lips. It was a small notebook and pencil he held in his hands. "What is that?"

He glanced down at the notebook as though just remembering he held it. "I'm taking notes, my lady."

"Notes, Mr. Wraxall? About the front door?"

He turned back a page. "I've already finished my notes on the dormitories. I didn't want to barge into unfamiliar rooms, and since I haven't been given a tour of the premises yet, I thought the front door seemed a good place to continue."

"Continue making notes?"

"As you see."

"Is there very much to note about the door, other

than it is rectangular, wooden, and sorely in need of paint?" Come to think of it, hadn't she asked Mr. Goring to paint it last week?

"It is all of those things, my lady, but I am also noting that the lock does not work."

"What?" She moved closer. "I lock it every night."

"I have no doubt of that, but the mechanism has been rigged so the bolt does not slide into place fully." He pushed the bolt into place, and then he tugged on the door and it came open easily.

"But how—"

"Here." He showed her the way the wood had been smoothed down in the casement so that it took only a little pressure to free the bolt from its mooring.

"Oh dear. I shall have to have that repaired." Once again she glanced about for the elusive Mr. Goring. She hadn't seen him since he'd shown Wraxall in.

"Did I imagine you had a servant earlier?"

Ah, then she wasn't the only one who hadn't seen him.

"I do."

"Just the one servant?"

"Could you show me the door again?" she said, hoping to distract him.

"What about a companion or a lady's maid?"

Curses. If word reached her father that she was here without a chaperone, all her plans would go to waste. "So the lock on the door is not working?" She bent to peer at it.

He pushed it closed. "Forget the door. Is there a female servant in residence?"

She had never been a good liar, but she did know

how to dance and how to sidestep. "By 'in residence,' do you mean on the premises?"

His eyes seemed to turn a darker shade of blue. "That is the usual meaning."

"Mrs. Fleming is here."

"The lady lives here?"

"She is in the classroom." She ought to play chess. That was a narrow escape.

"Mrs. Fleming is an instructor?"

"Yes." Distraction was the key, and Julia was already starting up the stairs, making her way around the boards that were weak and rotting.

"And where is this classroom?" He followed her, seeming not to have realized she hadn't answered his question. He trailed her closely, stepping where she did as though he too had seen the rotted wood.

She gestured to the top of the stairs. "In what was formerly the drawing room."

"Are you certain?"

"Of course I'm certain. See for yourself." She opened the drawing room doors and stared at the empty room. She looked right and then left.

No pupils. No teacher.

Wraxall leaned on the door beside her. "Impressive," he drawled.

She would have told him to shut up, but she was too angry to speak. She *knew* it had been too quiet. She had no idea where either the boys or their teacher had gone. That was if Mrs. Fleming had even come to work. The boys were not exactly well behaved, and Julia would hardly blame the woman if she sought employment elsewhere.

Then she heard it.

She hoped she imagined it, but when she looked at Mr. Wraxall, he too was looking at the front windows. With a sigh, Julia crossed to the windows looking out onto the street and parted the curtains. As the shouts and hoots of laughter she'd heard had indicated, there were the boys. It would have been bad enough to see them loitering in front of the orphanage and harassing passersby, but it was even worse to see them playing keep-away with Mrs. Fleming's reticule and books. The items were tossed from one boy to the next, just in front of Mrs. Fleming, but continually out of her reach. For her part, Mrs. Fleming stood with her hands on her bony hips, her square chin jutted out, and her eyes narrowed under her ugly hat.

First, her cook; now, her teacher. Julia was aware she should run downstairs, stomp outside, and end the nonsense below with all possible haste. But it wasn't even noon, and she had no more energy. Perhaps if she rested her forehead on the cool glass for a moment and gathered her strength…

She hadn't realized Mr. Wraxall had come to stand behind her until she felt the warmth of his body. She almost turned, but then his arm brushed against hers as he further parted the curtains she held. Her skin tingled beneath the silk of her gown, and she had the wanton impulse to rub against him again. She refrained, but she was not so angelic as to move to put some distance between them. She wanted him to touch her again. More than that, it was lovely to imagine, just for a moment, that she was not alone in all of this. His form felt solid and steady, and he smelled lightly of baked bread and coffee—smells, she imagined, that lingered from his earlier quest to find the boys food. She wanted to turn her head into his waistcoat and breathe him in.

Julia couldn't imagine where the idea had come from. Then her belly rumbled and she remembered she had not eaten at all today. That was it. She must have been half-mad from hunger.

She lifted her head, and her hand inadvertently slid down to where his rested on the edge of the curtain. At the feel of his bare skin against hers, she pulled away quickly, but not as quickly as he did.

"I'm terribly sorry," she sputtered.

"It was my fault." He shoved his hands in his pockets, presumably to keep them from ever touching her again. Clearly, she was the only one imagining his arms around her. And how could she blame him? She looked a fright and had acted like a shrew. Their gazes met, and his jerked quickly to the window. He couldn't even look at her.

"The woman is your teacher?"

"Yes. I had better go and save her." She was eager to be away. She didn't need to see him flinch away from her a second time. "And accept her resignation."

"You can't allow her to resign."

She raised her brows. "I don't see how I can prevent her."

"But the cook already resigned today."

"Yes, thank you for reminding me. I'd quite forgotten what a wretched day this has been."

He seemed to ignore the barb. "And we can't find your manservant anywhere."

Her brows lowered to a glower. "Yes, and my lock does not work, and the kitchen is a catastrophe, and I haven't eaten anything since supper at the ball last night. Make note of all of it in your little book and be sure to tell my father, will you?" It seemed the logical end to this horrendous day.

She started away, and he matched her stride. "I have no intention of telling your father."

She thought she heard a silent *yet* at the end of that sentence, and she didn't allow herself to feel relief.

"Then what *do* you intend?"

He seemed to falter, as though not quite certain himself, but then he was by her side again as she descended the stairway in the same careful way she had ascended it. "We divide and conquer," he said.

She saluted him. "Yes, sir."

"Mock me if you want, but rule and order would not go amiss with those boys right now. I'll take them and clean up your kitchen while you—"

She halted. "The boys will clean the kitchen?" she said, her tone disbelieving.

"Under my supervision, yes."

She barked out a laugh. "I have tried to make them sweep and mop before, and they made more of a mess than we started with."

He muttered something under his breath. They stood at the bottom of the steps, his face in shadow in the dark vestibule. Just beyond the front door, she could hear the boys' voices and knew their game continued.

"What was that you said?"

"Planned incompetence," he answered, articulating every syllable.

"What does that mean?"

"It means the boys made a mess of the chores you assigned them so you wouldn't ask them to do them again."

She inhaled sharply. "They wouldn't." But she knew they would. Of course they would. Why hadn't she thought of that before? "And what does one do about planned incompetence?" she asked.

"Oh, a night in the stocks usually takes care of it," he replied.

She stepped back. "Mr. Wraxall! These are children we're speaking of and—"

He held up a hand. "Save your ranting. I won't put anyone in stocks."

Was it her imagination or did he mutter *this time* after those words?

"Having me act as supervisor will be sufficient."

"And you know how to use a mop and broom?" she asked dubiously.

"I was a soldier. I know how to launder my own clothing and sew on a button too, Lady Juliana. You take the teacher and speak with her in the parlor. I'll take the boys and clean up the kitchen. While we're at it, they might as well straighten the dormitories."

"Good luck with that."

"I wish you the same in your endeavor to convince the school teacher to remain. Now that we both know our assignments…" He reached for the door. "Ready and"—he opened it—"charge!"

He strode out first and began bellowing orders. Julia held back for just an instant. Her life had become a whirlwind, but she couldn't allow herself to trust Mr.

Wraxall to do any more than pull her free momentarily. He might help her now, but he'd soon lose interest. She wouldn't make the mistake Harriett had and put her faith in him or any man.

Four

THE ORPHANS WERE NOT SO DIFFERENT FROM NEWLY enlisted soldiers. They were brash and bold on the outside, but inside they wanted direction and the comfort of having someone to tell them what to do.

Neil still thought a few hours in the stocks would have done several of them a world of good.

Neil dealt with the paltry resistance the boys put up when he told them to clean the kitchen. The younger ones followed the older boys, so when the first older boy, the tall one with shaggy, brown hair in his eyes who had been fighting, folded his arms and refused to pick up the broom, calling it woman's work, Neil got an apron and told the boy to put it on.

The lad folded his arms. "I won't!"

"Then you don't eat." Neil looked at all of the boys, meeting each one's gaze in turn. "Let me explain to you how life works. You either earn your keep or you have none. If you don't work, you don't eat."

"You can't keep us from eating," another of the boys, this one with straight, brown hair and freckles, said.

He would have had any soldier who challenged him

thus whipped. Instead, he gave the boy a dark look. "Can't I?" Neil asked, leaning close. "Would you like to test me?"

The boy's eyes grew wide and he stepped back.

"Since Lady Juliana has not yet hired a cook," Neil continued, "I will be providing dinner. Baked pies like you had earlier."

Some of the younger boys cheered. Neil ignored them.

"If you want a pie, you work. If you don't work, you make your own dinner." That was more than generous. He would have let grown men go hungry.

Neil leaned back against the wall and waited. If there was one thing he knew, it was men's—and boys'—stomachs. In about three heartbeats, every boy was sweeping, mopping, or washing dishes. Even the fighter with the hair in his eyes. Neil pointed to him. "You over there."

The one who liked to count—Lady Juliana had called him Michael—cleared his throat. "That's Walter, sir."

Walter scowled at Michael and did his best to ignore Neil.

"Master Walter," Neil said. "You said this is woman's work. So put on the apron."

"But—"

Neil raised a brow.

With a scowl, the boy yanked it over his head and went back to sweeping.

Neil heard a few sniggers. "First boy I catch laughing at him has to wear an apron too."

The laughter ceased immediately. Then one of the

little boys, a lad who couldn't have been more than four and who was attempting to sweep with his thumb in his mouth, toddled over. He tugged on Neil's coat. Neil almost bent down, but he resisted the urge. "What?"

The boy pulled his thumb from his mouth. "What if we want to wear an apron?" He blinked large, brown eyes up at Neil. Neil steeled his heart. He would not allow these children to worm their way into his affections. He was here to do a duty, nothing more. Once Lady Juliana was safe, he would be gone.

"What's your name?" Neil asked against his better judgment. It was better if he didn't know the children's names, but he couldn't go around pointing and saying *you there* for the next few days. And he'd seen enough of the orphanage to know he would be here for several more days to come.

"Sharee," the boy said, thumb back in his mouth.

Neil plucked the thumb from the mouth, dismayed to feel saliva on his fingers. "Say again?"

"Charlie," came the reply in the high voice.

"You want to wear an apron, Charlie?"

Charlie nodded fervently.

"Anyone else?" Neil asked.

Two more little boys who couldn't have been much older than Charlie jumped up and down and shouted, "Me! Me!"

Neil could only find one more apron so he fashioned aprons out of dish towels for the other two, whose names he discovered were Chester and Jimmy. Michael, eight-year-old fount of information that he was, informed him Charlie was four and a baby, Chester was five and his mother was a harlot, and

Jimmy was five too and not really an orphan. His parents were in debtor's prison.

"What's a harlot?" Chester asked when Neil had the dish towel secured around his waist.

"A harlot is—"

Neil gave Michael a quelling look. "Don't worry about it." Neil handed Chester a clean towel. "Wipe the table."

Neil stood back and surveyed his troops. They had done a decent enough job. He'd send half upstairs to clean the dormitory and keep the rest with him to finish down here. Lady Juliana hadn't eaten, and that had to be rectified as well.

"Michael," Neil said.

Michael straightened immediately. "Yes, sir!"

"Who is the oldest among you?"

"Robbie, *sir!*"

"Who's Robbie?"

A lad with freckles and straight, brown hair came forward. "I am. I'm probably eleven."

Neil nodded. "I need you to do a job for me, Robbie. Pick five men and go upstairs to straighten the dormitory."

Robbie frowned at him. "But there aren't any men here, save you, sir."

Neil stifled a sigh. "Pick five boys and straighten the dormitory. You are in charge, Robbie. I want beds made, clothes put away, and the entire place ready for inspection. So pick your boys carefully."

Robbie glanced at the other orphans. "I'll take Michael."

Robbie was no fool, Neil thought. Michael would

probably annoy every single one of them, but he'd do his job. "And? Four more."

Robbie's eyes passed directly over Walter. Again, Neil approved. Better to leave Walter with him. Robbie might be older, but he wouldn't be able to control Walter. Robbie pointed to the chubby boy with the blond curls. "I'll take George, Angus, James, and Billy."

Neil noted them each in turn. Angus was five or six with red hair. James was blond and small enough to be the same age as Charlie. Billy was quiet and kept to himself. He was the tallest boy, though, and probably as old as Robbie.

"Dismissed," Neil said. "I want that dormitory in perfect order in one hour."

"Yes, sir!" Michael said with a backward salute.

Neil thought about smiling. Instead, he looked at his remaining troops. He had Walter, a.k.a. Trouble; Charlie, thumb in mouth; Chester, what's-a-harlot; Jimmy, only about five as well; and two other boys who had been more or less pretending to be industrious.

"Who here can cook?"

Charlie's thumb came out of his mouth as he raised his hand high. Neil rolled his eyes. "Charlie, you can be the assistant. Walter, can you cook?"

Walter didn't look up from the spot he'd been sweeping for the past five minutes. "No."

"That's 'no, sir.' Get over here."

Walter glared at him. "I just said I can't cook."

Neil glared back.

"*Sir*," Walter added.

"Then this will be a lesson for you. Chester?"

The little boy looked up.

"You work with that one to wash the towels and dishes. What's your name, lad?" Neil asked the boy with a black eye and shorn, brown hair.

"Ralph," he snarled.

"Ralph, you and Chester wash."

Ralph made a growling sound.

"Jimmy, you and…"

"I'm Sean, sir," said the last boy, with a touch of Irish in his speech.

"Sean, you and Jimmy finish sweeping and mopping. Put all the dust and dirt in the rubbish bin." Sean flashed him a smile, and Neil decided he liked Sean. Sean reminded him a bit of his friend Rafe Beaumont, who could charm any woman, and almost any man as well, with his smile.

"Now, Chef Walter and Assistant Charlie, we will be preparing tea and toast for Lady Juliana." It wasn't fancy, but Neil figured he and the boys could manage it. "First, find the kettle and fill it with water…"

A half hour and two burned pieces of toast later, Neil carried a tray of hot tea and perfectly browned and buttered toast to the parlor. The door was closed, and he balanced the tray on one arm before tapping lightly.

No answer. Neil didn't wait and knock again. Between the miscreant he'd seen earlier, the missing manservant, and the lack of any real locks on the building, he feared the worst. He burst into the parlor then stopped short.

Lady Juliana was alone in the cold room, for the fire in the hearth had not been lit. She sat in what had once been a chair with rich blue upholstery at a small writing desk. Her head rested on the writing desk, one cheek pressed to several sheets of paper. One hand was thrown over the top of the desk and the other was tucked in her lap. The woman was breathing deeply, obviously sound asleep.

Neil placed the tray on the table set in the center of a small grouping of chairs and looked down at Lady Juliana. Her red-gold hair covered the papers she'd been looking at, papers filled with numbers. The orphanage's accounts?

Oh, how Neil wished he could go back to the early hours of the morning and pretend he'd never received his father's summons. If he'd known the sort of woman he would be dealing with, he would have found a way out of this mission. "Just take the gel home," his father had said. Clearly, his father had not known Lady Juliana either.

He'd have to find another way to convince her to leave. Neil liked plans. He was the one who generally made them, and he told himself all he needed now was a very good plan.

And a little willpower.

Because with her eyes closed and her mouth relaxed, Lady Juliana looked perfectly lovely. He had the sudden desire to caress one pale-pink cheek, smooth that tousled hair off her forehead, and run his hands down her back.

And if he did any of that, she'd wake up and slap him. She was an earl's daughter, and despite her current living situation, she was a lady. No lady wanted anything to do with a bastard. No, they married dukes, sons of viscounts, and foreign princes. They didn't look at bastards, even those whose fathers were marquesses.

And somehow knowing his father's station made the circumstances of Neil's birth worse. Why couldn't he have grown up the adopted son of a merchant or a farmer? He would never have had a glimpse into the world of the *ton*. He would never have had all the glittering wealth and beauty dangled before him only to be snatched away whenever anyone realized he was *that* son.

His father was a good man, but all that goodness hadn't done Neil any favors.

He cleared his throat in an effort to wake Lady Juliana without touching her. When that didn't work, he lifted the tray and set it down, rattling the teacup. She didn't even move. Had the woman had any sleep of late? She was obviously exhausted.

Finally, he leaned close. "Lady Juliana?" he said.

She took a deep breath and continued sleeping.

"My lady?" he said a bit louder. He didn't want to scare her, but he couldn't let her continue to sleep. It would be time for dinner soon, and he had questions for her before he left for the night. "My lady," he said a bit louder. He'd been surrounded by boys for the last hour, and she smelled nothing like *boy*. She smelled of freshly cut roses, a scent so light and pretty it reminded him of his father's country estate on a spring morning. Perhaps it was the soap she used to clean her hair. He leaned a bit closer to sniff it, and she opened her dark eyes and looked at him.

He pulled back immediately, standing at strict attention.

"Oh!" She sat straight and blinked as though she didn't know quite where she was. Then she lifted an arm and brushed the hair from her face. Neil could imagine her doing so when she first woke in the morning, and he had the sudden urge to be in her bed and see for himself. She'd changed out of her ball gown and now wore a muslin gown of yellow with reddish-pink flowers. The neckline was higher and the sleeves longer, so it didn't show as much flesh.

Not that he'd been hoping to see any. He looked away and then, because she wasn't Draven or Wellington, relaxed his posture.

"I apologize for startling you. The boys and I fixed you something to eat."

"You... I'm sorry. What did you say?"

He moved to the side and indicated the tray. "We made you tea and toast. It's not much, but I have limited resources."

In fact, he wanted to speak to her about the lack of any foodstuffs in the larder. But first, she needed to eat.

She stared at the tray, and he wasn't certain she'd heard anything he'd said. She rose slowly and stalked toward the tray as though she were a cat and it a dangerous, unidentified object. Finally, she stopped before the food and stared down at it. Then she looked up at him. "*You* made this?"

"Walter and Charlie made it. I supervised."

"Walter? How did you convince Walter to do anything but sulk?" She put a hand to her heart. "What did you do to him?"

"Not what I would have done had he been about five years older." He crossed his arms over his chest.

"The boys are fine. The kitchen is clean, and I am on my way to inspect the dormitories."

"You persuaded the boys to cook and clean?" She still hadn't so much as lifted the teacup.

"In a manner of speaking. Do you plan to drink that tea before it becomes cold?"

She looked down at the tray as though seeing it for the first time. Then she lifted the teacup and tasted it. She nodded her approval and nibbled on the toast, licking a drop of butter from her plump bottom lip. Neil gritted his teeth.

"This is very good. Thank you. I…I don't know what to say. I am certain neither your father nor mine intended you to cook for me or play nursemaid to a dozen orphans."

He shrugged. "I was in the army, my lady. I follow orders, and my orders were to make certain you are safe and well. If that means I feed you, so be it. I'm not helpless. I didn't have a batman for much of my service, so I learned to take care of myself. Not only can I cook and clean, I can also do laundry." He narrowed his eyes. "Though I'll want more than a thank-you if I have to wash the boys' drawers. Now, yours"—he winked—"I'll do for free."

Her cheeks turned a fetching shade of pink, and she took a rather large sip of tea. Fortunately, it had cooled and she didn't burn her mouth. "I have a washerwoman come once a week to wash the clothes and linens. Your services in that arena will not be required."

⌇

She would have thought he'd look more relieved, but he merely nodded. He had a way of nodding that made her feel as though she were a soldier. In fact, everything he did was done with precision and in an orderly fashion. He stood straight and tall, hands clasped behind his back in a not-quite-relaxed stance. He didn't so much as shift his weight as he stood. He was perfectly still, the occasional head nod or gesture done with a brusque authority.

With his sultry good looks and sea-blue eyes, had she met him on the street, she would never have guessed he was a soldier. But now she could hardly imagine him as anything else. Only that sweep of dark hair brushed back from his forehead suggested any tolerance for a lack of strictness and order.

"Did your teacher resign?" he asked, and she realized she'd been staring at him. Again! She wanted to sink onto the long, apple-green couch and wait for her wobbly knees to stop shaking. Instead, she studied her toast intently and tried to think of something besides running her hands through that thick hair. Teacher... He'd mentioned a teacher.

"Oh, Mrs. Fleming?" She glanced up at him, and he frowned.

"You had better sit down and eat more toast."

"I'm perfectly fine. I was merely thinking of... something else." Her lips on his temple, his eyes meting hers... She cleared her throat. "Yes, she did resign. But"—she raised a finger—"I have a plan."

One of his thick brows rose slowly. "Do you?"

"I have written to my former governess and asked her to come and help until I can find a permanent teacher. I thought if she could keep my sister and me in line, these orphans will be easy for her."

"I can well believe it."

Julia opened her mouth to assure him she really *had* been that bad, then realized what he'd said. "Sir, you are supposed to say that I was a perfect angel as a child."

"I don't believe that for a moment. If you were an angel, we wouldn't be here today. You're obviously stubborn and willful."

"You say it as though those are bad traits."

A hint of a smile touched his lips. "You'll need both to keep this orphanage going. So far you need a new cook and a new teacher."

She went back to her desk and lifted two letters. "I've written the advertisement for the cook and a letter to my former governess. I'll post both as soon as Mr. Goring returns and can escort me."

"Ah, the elusive Mr. Goring." His gaze traveled to the cold hearth. "And what exactly does he do here? He obviously doesn't cook or teach, do laundry or light fires. And considering the state of the building, he doesn't make repairs either."

All the warmth she'd felt for Wraxall earlier began to seep away. Who was he to challenge her? "Mr. Goring was actually quite industrious until a week or so ago. He told me his mother has been ill, and he's had to leave to care for her. But he usually tells me when he leaves. Perhaps he told me and in all the chaos today I didn't remember."

Mr. Wraxall looked skeptical. "And I have a feeling I will find him in the closest gin house."

"You don't have much faith in people, do you?"

"Not since I came back from the war, no." He held out his hand. "Give me the letters, and I'll post them for you. I'll find Goring and send him back too."

"But I can't ask you to do all that."

He waved a hand. "Orders. I need you to stay where you are safe"—he looked around—"relatively safe and can keep the boys from destroying the place. I'll be back in an hour. No more than two. I'll bring supper." He held out his hand, and she handed him the letters.

He started out of the parlor, and she followed him. "That's very generous of you, sir, but I cannot possibly pay you for all you have done. I have limited resources at present."

He didn't even look at her as he started for the steps to the second floor. "I don't want your blunt."

She lifted her skirts and followed him up the steps. "So this is about following orders then?"

"For the most part." He turned and began to ascend the next flight of stairs.

"Where are we going?"

"I told the boys I'd inspect the dormitory."

"I can do that."

He paused and looked over his shoulder at her. "I don't think so."

Her jaw dropped open as she watched his back. The man was certainly arrogant. She chased after him. "For your information, I am perfectly capable of ascertaining whether a bed is made and clothing articles put away."

"I would be inclined to believe you, except I saw the state of the rooms earlier."

"Yes, well, today has not been our finest. But I—"

His sharp whistle cut her off. It was so loud and shrill she actually flinched. When she opened her eyes again, he stood in the doorway of the older boys' room. Eight of the twelve slept in here, and when she peered around Wraxall, she saw all eight scrambling to attention at the end of their beds. The room was as neat as a fresh coiffure. The beds were made, the trunks were closed and presumably full of clothing, and the floors and bedposts gleamed.

"Attention!" Wraxall ordered. Julia almost squared her shoulders. Instead, she stayed in the doorway as he marched through the center of the room. His gaze seemed to miss nothing. Not a pair of breeches forgotten under a bed, a trunk not perfectly aligned with a footboard, not the collection of dirty dishes hidden behind a curtain.

"You've earned your supper, lads, but not any dessert. Next time, if your work is exemplary, there will be ices."

"Ices!" George said with a squeal. "I want ices!"

"There will be another inspection tomorrow. At ease." And he strode out the door and right past her.

"You will be back tomorrow?" she asked, following him. Why should the prospect of seeing him again make her heart thump harder?

"It appears that way." He stopped in front of the younger boys' room. This time she was prepared for the whistle and plugged her ears. "Attention!"

The little boys scrambled to their places, Chester and Jimmy on one side and James and Charlie on the other. They stood at perfect attention, except Charlie who had his thumb in his mouth. Wraxall cleared his throat, and Charlie put his hand at his side.

Julia didn't have to be in the army to see that this room would not meet Wraxall's standards. The beds were poorly made, the trunks had items of clothing peeking out, and the dusty furniture had the occasional clean swipe as from a rag. Julia cringed. If Wraxall made these little ones cry, she would have his head.

But he moved inside, his head nodding. "Good job, men."

"Is it good enough for a sweet?" asked little James.

"It's good, but not that good."

"Aw!" Chester and Jimmy groaned and sagged.

"Do you want me to show you what to do to earn a sweet tomorrow?"

"Yesth! Yesth!" Charlie jumped up and down, his thumb back in his mouth.

"We'll start with how you make a bed. Watch very carefully, lads. You want the corners tucked under like so."

Julia stood in the doorway for a good five minutes, watching as Wraxall showed the boys how to make beds, dust, and fold clothing. And then she had to walk away, because if she didn't, she feared she would forget she did not like him.

On the way back to the parlor, she had two questions.

Just who was this man?

And how much had her father paid him to put on this act?

Five

WHEN HE STEPPED OUT OF THE ORPHANAGE, NEIL FELT as though he could breathe again. The tightness in his chest finally lessened, and by the time he'd hailed the hackney and was away from Spitalfields, his shoulders had relaxed and his head ceased throbbing.

He didn't need to go to King Street in St. James to post the letters for Lady Juliana. He could have done it in Spitalfields, but he wanted to go to his club. He needed one hour there, just to remind him who he was. The orphans were not as bad as he'd first thought. It was fortunate none were older than eleven, or Lady Juliana would never have been able to manage them. As it was, she would need to watch Walter and Billy closely. Living in the midst of a rookery meant there were always gangs looking for cubs to train as thieves. Small hands were nimble hands, and the young were given lenient prison sentences and could be back to work within months.

Neil had told himself his work at St. Dismas Home for Wayward Youth was temporary. He had his orders—persuade Lady Juliana to return home. It hadn't taken a quarter hour for him to ascertain she would not be easy to persuade and that the situation was worse than he'd anticipated. She wasn't safe in the least, and as far as her well-being... Well, the rats with biblical names spoke for themselves. So he'd done what he always did when he assumed command: he handled the crises as they came. He'd fed the children and then handed them off so he could do the real work of identifying the threats to safety. But every time he thought he had the boys taken care of, they landed back in his hands.

And so he'd gritted his teeth and did what was required. He'd told himself he'd been assigned worse tasks than supervising a dozen orphans. He'd had to set up camp in Russia in the middle of winter, he'd had to order men to complete missions he knew were suicide, and he'd had to inform mothers and fathers that the sons they'd lovingly rocked in their arms as infants were dead.

Making tea and toast with orphans was—pardon the pun—child's play. Except it wasn't. Because every single time he looked into those boys' faces he saw himself. No, he hadn't been raised in an orphanage, but he was Robbie and Jimmy and Chester all the same. His mother had died in childbirth. His father had claimed him, but even that acceptance couldn't wipe away the shame of his birth. He was a bastard, and every look, every word exchanged, every moment spent with the orphans was a harsh reminder of his bastardy.

When the hackney stopped in front of the Draven Club, Neil almost sagged with relief. Here no one cared he was a bastard. Here he could forget that he was an outcast and that his own father didn't quite know what to do with him, and that father's wife would gladly have traded Neil's life for that of her beloved son Christopher.

There were days Neil would have traded himself for Chris too.

The Draven Club was a haven from the circumstances of his birth, and it was the one place he could go to remember the men he'd lost. Ewan and Rafe and he could reminisce about their fallen comrades and, in that small way, keep the men's spirits alive. It was the least Neil could do, considering he'd killed them. All eighteen of those lives were on his conscience.

He paid the hackney driver and walked briskly to the door of the club. Porter opened it as though he'd been expecting Neil at precisely this moment. "Hello, Porter."

"Mr. Wraxall, a pleasure to see you, sir."

Neil handed the Master of the House the two letters from Lady Juliana. "Would you post these for me, Porter?"

"Certainly, sir." He tucked the letters into a pocket and took Neil's greatcoat and hat. "Do you want dinner?"

It was still a bit early for dinner, and Neil wasn't hungry. The churning of his stomach from the reminders of his bastardy that had been thrown in his face all day had dampened his appetite. But he had promised Lady Juliana to deal with dinner for the children.

"I wonder if you could help me on that point, Porter," Neil said.

"Of course, Mr. Wraxall."

Neil explained his needs, and Porter assured him it

would be nothing for the cook to make another pot of stew and bake several more loaves of bread. The bounty would be ready in an hour, and Neil must take the club's carriage in order to convey the meal to the orphans and their mistress.

Neil made a note to mention increasing both Porter and the cook's salary when Draven's men next met to discuss club business. He'd also ask about the aforementioned conveyance. Why hadn't he known the club had a carriage and a coachman?

"Is anyone here at this hour, Porter?" Neil asked.

"Mr. Beaumont is in the Billiards Room, sir."

Neil nodded. No doubt Rafe was hiding from some woman who hoped to sink her claws in him for a night or two. Most men would have been happy to have Rafe's problems with women. Even Rafe had been happy to find himself a magnet to the female sex, until he'd realized that his love affairs often created more trouble than they were worth.

Neil ascended the stairs and leaned against the door, watching Rafe study the billiards table and position his cue, then, taking aim, knock two balls into the pocket.

"Nice shot," Neil commented.

Rafe turned smoothly. Neil had no idea if his presence had surprised Rafe. The man had a way of appearing smooth and unruffled no matter the situation. "I wondered when you would show your face."

"Tired of looking at your own?" Neil entered the room and stood at the other end of the table. He wasn't interested in billiards, but he liked to watch a man with skill, like Rafe, sink the balls.

"Who could tire of looking at my face?" Rafe asked, lining up another shot.

"I could name any number of husbands."

"I don't dally with married women," Rafe said. He hit the white ball, but his aim was off and it went wild, bouncing off the sides of the table.

Neil laughed. "Since when?"

"It has always been my policy." Rafe chalked the end of the leather cue tip. "I cannot be held responsible if some of those wives are extremely persuasive."

"No, I'm sure you can't."

"We could talk about me all day." Rafe lined up another shot.

"We usually do," Neil muttered.

"Where have you been? I thought your father had business for you and imagined you'd be riding to Hampshire or Dorset to oversee some agricultural fiasco."

"The business was actually closer to home."

"Oh?" Rafe took his shot.

"Spitalfields."

Rafe looked up sharply, ignoring the *thunk* of the white ball into the pocket. "What was that?"

"You heard me."

"There's no agriculture in Spitalfields."

"Not unless you count the growing of thieves and the multiplying of stolen wipes in shop windows."

Rafe studied the table again.

"I've been at the St. Dismas Home for Wayward Youth."

The table was forgotten, and Rafe stared at Neil with something like horror on his face. "*Why?* Did your father discover another offspring?"

"No. I think he learned his lesson after me. Not to mention Lady Kensington would probably castrate him if he showed up at her door with another bastard."

"Then... But you couldn't possibly have one there." The sentence was a statement. Still, Rafe gave Neil a questioning look.

Neil shook his head. "My feelings on that score haven't changed. None of the boys are mine."

"Then you are still..." Rafe gestured vaguely.

"A virgin? Yes, though with my experience I think one could hardly call me that."

"And yet I do enjoy it. Our Virgin Warrior."

Neil ignored the jibe. He was not so easy to bait. The men of Draven's troop had always called him the Warrior. It was only Rafe and a few other brave ones who dared add *Virgin* before it.

"And if you weren't searching for lost offspring, what were you doing at an orphanage?"

"Lord St. Maur's daughter has made the place her pet project."

Rafe blew out a breath. "Women and their charities." He rounded the table and began to collect the balls from the pockets. "I suppose your father asked you to make her see the error of her ways."

"Exactly. The situation is worse than I thought. She has no cook, no teacher, and her manservant is not to be found. Not to mention the place is about as invincible as the ladies in a Parisian brothel. If she will not return home, I may be forced to spend the night."

Rafe dropped the red ball with a heavy thud. "Then St. Maur's daughter is as beautiful as I've been told."

"What has that to do with it? Whether or not she's pretty, she must be protected."

A slow smile crossed turned Rafe's mouth upward. "So she *is* pretty."

"Who is pretty?" asked another voice. Neil glanced at the door and saw Jasper standing in it. He was removing the length of black silk that covered his hair and the half mask he wore when outside to conceal the scarred skin on his cheek. He dropped it in his coat pocket and rubbed his face, which was rather pink from the heat of the silk against his skin.

"No one," Neil said at the same time Rafe said, "St. Maur's daughter."

"Why do we care about St. Maur's daughter?"

"Neil cares," Rafe said, repositioning the balls for the opening shot.

"No, I don't. I am only following orders."

Both Jasper and Rafe groaned. Neil couldn't blame them. He'd said that phrase so often during their time on the Continent that even he'd wanted to groan when he said it.

"If I have to hear about orders," Jasper said, "I need a drink."

"No drinks." Neil spotted Porter entering with a decanter of amber liquid and waved him away. "I need you to do something for me."

"Of course," Jasper answered automatically. It never failed to amaze Neil that these men who had barely survived the war would risk their lives if Neil asked. He hadn't even had to give them orders. He'd done that initially, but after surviving a mission or two, the men formed a bond that went far beyond that of superior and subordinate. These men were his brothers. They'd saved his life and he theirs. They'd suffered victory and defeat together. They'd lost eighteen of their brothers, and they were the only men alive who knew what the last moments of those who'd been lost were like.

They were the only men alive who had gone to hell and come back again because the missions Draven had been taxed to give the troop dubbed the Survivors were not missions the men were expected to return from. Only men who had special skills, who were younger sons, and who had no dependents were chosen. Only men who answered no to Draven's infamous question were accepted.

Are you afraid to die?

Neil had answered no when he'd been asked shortly after Christopher's death. He'd wanted to die at the time, would have welcomed death to shut out the pain he'd felt. Maybe that was why Draven had chosen him as the group's leader. He was a warrior, a man who lived for nothing but combat.

He'd certainly had his share of war, and he'd managed to beat the odds and come home. He didn't want to fight anymore. And that was part of the problem. If he wasn't the Warrior any longer, who was he?

"I suppose you need me to play Runner," Jasper said when Neil didn't elaborate immediately. Jasper was the best tracker and scout among Draven's men. In fact, he was the best Neil had ever known. Now that he was in London again, Jasper often took work as a bounty hunter or assisted the Bow Street Runners. Despite what would have seemed a very conspicuous mask, Lord Jasper could slide in and out of places without ever being seen, and that was how Jasper liked it. The wicked scar of burned flesh on his face made him self-conscious everywhere but in the Draven Club.

Before the ambush where he'd been burned, Jasper, one of the higher-ranking men in the troop, had often attended social functions and was quite popular with the ladies. Now, he was never seen in public, and Neil suspected Jasper kept his distance from women too. He would have liked to tell his friend the scar was not as monstrous as Jasper seemed to think, but when he'd tried, Jasper argued that was because Neil was used to it.

"There's a man named Goring," Neil said. "He's employed as the manservant for St. Dismas Home for Wayward Youth, but he's a frequent deserter. Assuming he returns for dinner, I want you to watch him tomorrow and tell me where he goes and what he does. If he doesn't return, find him and report back."

Jasper shrugged. "Call Porter back with the brandy. I can finish this racket in my sleep. In fact, I don't even have to look for him to tell you where he is."

Rafe placed the cue balls on the baulk line for the lag. "Are you playing?" he asked Neil.

"No."

"Jasper?"

"Sure."

Rafe handed Jasper a cue.

"Where is he?" Neil asked Jasper.

"One of two places: drinking in a gin shop"—he watched as Rafe took aim—"or in bed with a woman. Probably a brunette with tits like…" Rafe looked over and his cue scratched the table. Jasper smiled and held his hand out. "Like billiard balls."

"Arse," Rafe muttered.

Jasper blinked innocently. "What? Do you like buxom brunettes?"

Neil rolled his eyes. Rafe liked every shape, size, and flavor of woman, but he had a weakness for dark-haired ladies with ample charms.

"Those are the logical choices," Neil said, watching Jasper circle the table.

"Then why do you need me?"

"Because despite that fact that St. Maur's daughter seems to have gone temporarily daft, risking her reputation and her safety to run an orphanage, she doesn't strike me as a lackwit. If Goring disappeared like this every day, she would have discharged him by now."

"So what changed?" Rafe asked, scowling as Jasper considered his next move.

"I don't know, but I'll know more when Jasper tells me where Goring has been all day and where he goes tomorrow."

Jasper lowered the cue. "Oh, now I have to find out not only where he goes, but where he's been?"

"Too difficult?"

"Nice try." Jasper was the least likely of his men to fall prey to goading, but Neil knew the man was proud of his skills and probably wouldn't hesitate at the chance to show them off.

"Mr. Wraxall," Porter said, leaning into the room. "The cook has your dinner ready. Would you like it loaded into the conveyance now, or would you prefer to keep it warm a little longer?"

Neil checked his pocket watch. It was growing late, and he had a dozen hungry boys waiting for him. "Now, Porter. Tell John Coachman I'll be there in a moment."

"Very good, sir." Porter nodded and was gone.

"What conveyance is this? Did you buy a coach?" Rafe asked. Then, "Hell's teeth, Grantham, will you take the shot already?"

Jasper ignored him.

"It's the club's carriage," Neil answered.

"The club has a carriage?" Rafe looked as surprised as Neil had been earlier. "Why didn't I know that? I could have been using it for nefarious purposes all this time."

"That's probably why you didn't know," Jasper answered.

"I didn't know either." Neil turned to Jasper. "But you did?"

"Of course." He leaned down and took a shot, striking Rafe's cue ball, then the red ball for a cannon.

Rafe groaned.

"I'm paid to know these sorts of things."

That was what Neil counted on.

❧

Julia finally tucked the last of the younger boys into bed, said prayers with them, and blew out the lamps. Carrying her lamp, she checked once more on the older boys. They were all in bed, but Robbie lay with his hands folded under his head, staring at the ceiling. He glanced at her when she peered in. "Is everyone in bed?" she whispered.

"Yes, my lady."

"And where are Matthew, Mark, and Luke?"

"In their cage, my lady. Charlie tried to convince us to let him sleep with them, but we told him you'd object."

"He does love those rats." Charlie could spend hours petting the creatures and giving them morsels of food. "Thank you. Good night, Robbie."

"Night."

She closed the door and paused at the top of the steps. She would have to go down to the parlor to speak to Mr. Wraxall, and she wanted to put that off as long as possible. The old Julia would have looked forward to spending time with such a handsome man. The old Julia would have flirted with him. The old Julia would have suffered apoplexy at the thought of sleeping with rats. Now, she only forbid it because she feared Charlie might roll over in his sleep and crush the little animals. Rats were actually cleaner and more companionable than she had known.

That was only one of the things the new Julia knew that the old Julia couldn't have fathomed.

She started down the steps, telling herself speaking with Mr. Wraxall was no hardship. He was quite pleasant to look upon and he had good manners, when he wasn't ordering everyone about. He was thoughtful as well. He'd provided two meals for the boys today. In fact, dinner had been absolutely delicious. She couldn't remember when she'd had such a tasty meal. But when she'd asked if the cook was looking for hire, he merely smiled and shook his head.

After dinner, he'd managed to organize the boys into washing, drying, and stacking teams. The dishes were clean and put away in far less time than ever before. He had a way of getting people to do what he wanted. He had a way of convincing her to do what he wanted. Look at what he'd done today. She'd planned to post the letters she'd written herself as soon as Goring returned, but Wraxall had held out his hand and she'd given them over without so much as a peep of protest.

How did she know he'd really posted the letters? It was no secret her father wanted her to give up the orphanage and come home. If she didn't have a cook or a teacher for the children, then her father might go to the board and persuade them to remove funding if she did not accede to his wishes. Wraxall was only her father's latest method to convince her she should return to Mayfair.

Well, Wraxall would have to return to her father in defeat. These boys needed her, and she would not abandon them. She would be the person to show them that there were good people, *reliable* people, in the world. She would be the person they could trust and count on.

She reached the parlor, and as the door was cracked, she spotted Wraxall inside. He sat at *her* desk…looking through *her* ledger book. Of all the nerve!

She shoved the door open. "What do you think you are doing, sir?"

He barely raised his eyes. "Looking through your accounts. Exactly how much of your own money have you contributed to the upkeep of St. Dismas?"

"It's Sunnybrooke Home for Boys. I renamed it."

He gave her a perplexed look. "*Sunny*brooke?"

"I've asked Goring to repaint the sign."

"Ah, that will cost more blunt. How much have you contributed again?"

"That's none of your business."

He glanced at the ledger. "Looks to be fifty pounds or more."

"And?" She crossed to the desk and snatched the ledger away, slamming it shut. "It's my coin."

He studied her for a moment with those eyes that were far too pretty to belong to a man. "Pin money?" he asked. It was a logical assumption, as a woman of her station wouldn't have any other means of income. "If you can spare fifty pounds, how much pin money does your father give you each month?"

"Not so much, but I preferred to save mine rather than spend it. I never needed for anything anyway."

Neither had Harriett, but she had spent hers every month regardless.

He stood, and she realized the room suddenly felt smaller. She moved to the corner of the desk, trying to make room for him. Trying to put distance between them. Then she looked down at her hands where they clutched the ledger. If she didn't look away, she'd end up staring at him like an infatuated schoolgirl.

"If you won't return home, I will have to sleep here tonight," he said.

"What?" Her gaze met his, and she forgot to be infatuated. "No, sir, you will most certainly not!"

"Yes, I will. My orders were to see you were safe and well."

"And I am both."

"You are not safe. I've done more inspecting while you were putting the boys to bed, and few of the windows and neither of the doors in this building are secure. Anyone could enter during the night and steal, commit murder, or attack you."

Her cheeks heated because she knew by *attack* he meant *rape*. "I understand your concerns, Mr. Wraxall. I have my own concerns, which is why I employ Mr. Goring. As you saw at dinner, he has returned. I will lock my bedchamber door, as I do every night, and rely on Mr. Goring to keep us safe, as *he* has every night."

"At least your bedchamber door has a solid lock."

"You checked my bedchamber?" Her skin prickled with heat.

"I like to be thorough. And if your cheeks are pink because you left that scrap of lace on the floor, I assure you I was thinking only of my orders." But his smile said otherwise.

He had seen her undergarments! Her cheeks were not simply pink but burning hot. "You, sir, are impertinent."

He laughed. He actually laughed!

"I've been called far worse. I would rather be impertinent and see you safe than reverent and see you come to harm."

She crossed her arms. "Lovely sentiments, but you cannot stay under my roof. We have no chaperone. I know it may seem to you that I am throwing my reputation to the wind, but I'd rather not have my neighbors mistake me for a woman of loose morals." Mr. Slag's face floated into her mind just then. No, she definitely did not want him to form any more ideas about her.

"I assure you I would prefer to sleep in my own bed tonight," Wraxall said.

"Good. Then go home and sleep well. I shall see you out, sir."

He shook his head. "I shall see you home. The only way I leave you here alone tonight is if you go to your father's house."

Her shoulders and her hopes fell. "Mr. Wraxall, I love my father. He and I have no quarrel. He supports my work at Sunnybrooke." That was partly true. He did support her philanthropic endeavors, but he did not support her moving into the orphanage. "Nevertheless, the boys here need me. I cannot leave them."

"Mr. Goring is here."

She scoffed. "Mr. Goring is not to be relied upon. The last time I left him in charge, Mrs. Nesbit gave her notice. Not to mention Mr. Goring knows nothing about the needs of small children. What if Charlie wakes with a nightmare or James needs a drink of water?"

"You are not their mother."

"I am the closest they have right now, and that is another reason you cannot stay. The more you are here, the more attached the boys will become. They need a father figure in their lives, but if that is not to be you, it's best the boys do not become attached at all."

Mr. Wraxall's face seemed to have paled, and he made an odd sound in the back of his throat. "Me? Their father?"

"Father figure," she clarified. "And yes, they could use one. The only men they see here are thieves and criminals. I'd like them to have a man with some morals to look up to."

Wraxall seemed to shrink away from her. "I am not that man. I'm no father and certainly no model of good behavior."

She frowned in disappointment but not surprise. She had known he would not want to become more involved. He was here temporarily, and as far as she was concerned, the more temporary, the better. "Then you should go home."

He pressed his fingers to his eyes and then dragged his hands over his face. His jaw was lightly stubbled, now that it was the end of the day, and his hair was more tousled. "Madam, as I have already explained, I cannot go home if you do not." He raised a hand before she could object. "And do not tell me you are already home. You know my meaning."

"Then we are at an impasse," she declared. "You cannot stay here, and I will not go home."

"You forget I was a soldier. I have faced impasses before, and the way to resolve them is that one side must give ground."

"And I suppose I am the one to give ground?"

He shrugged. "It's for your own safety."

Her chin notched up. She would give ground, all right. Let him see just what kind of ground she would give him. "Unfortunately, I have no bed for you. The boys and I occupy the second-floor rooms, and Mr. Goring has the only bed in the servants' quarters. The former cook occupied my room when I was at my father's town house, and Mrs. Fleming did not sleep here." She indicated the parlor with its dainty furniture. "You are welcome to sleep here, although I am not certain you will fit on the couch."

He didn't even blink. "I have slept in worse places, and I don't intend to sleep much. I'll keep guard."

"How gallant of you." Julia did not think she would sleep much either if she thought much about him a floor below her, awake and keeping watch. He would probably loosen his cravat and unfasten his shirt, exposing the bronze skin of his chest...

She closed her eyes and prayed for strength. If this was a battle, now was the time for a retreat. "Good night, sir."

"Good night."

And she left him in the parlor. When she reached her bedchamber, she found the fire in her hearth stoked and her underclothing picked up from the floor and draped over her bed. She locked the door, then hastily removed her clothing and pulled her nightgown on. It was silly, she knew. She was in the privacy of her own room, but she couldn't help feel strange having a man—an attractive man—so close by.

She took her hair down, brushed it, and performed her nightly ablutions. Then she climbed into her warm bed and tried, desperately, not to imagine his hands on the lace at her breast.

Six

THE QUIET KNOCK CAME A LITTLE AFTER MIDNIGHT. Neil had been sitting cross-legged on the floor on the entryway, waiting, but now he rose stiffly and crossed to the door. He hadn't bothered locking it—a child could have forced that lock—and he opened the door and stepped outside to meet Jasper.

"Well?" he asked without preamble.

"He spent most of the day in an alehouse called the Ox and Bull."

"Not a gin house or a brothel?"

Jasper made a noncommittal sound. It was too dark for Neil to see his expression, and he wouldn't have been able to read it anyway, as Jasper wore his head covering and mask. "I'm not certain what the place is."

"Not merely an alehouse?" Neil asked.

"There's something more there. I'd like to watch the place again tomorrow. Your cull was already back here by the time I tracked him to the Ox and Bull. I'd be interested to see what he does if he goes back and who he sees."

"So would I." But Neil was aware he no longer commanded Jasper. "I would consider it a favor if you did this for me, Grantham, but I know you have other obligations."

In the darkness, Neil could feel Jasper's scowl. His shoulders straightened, and he became Lord Jasper—a man Neil rarely saw. "After all we've been through, you think I'd put tracking some petty rogue before your concerns?"

"I don't even know if I have any concerns. Goring may be straight as they come."

"I'm not ready to vouch for that. I'll take another day to observe, if that's agreeable to you." His voice dripped with sarcasm.

"You don't owe me anything, Jas. I don't want you to feel as though you owe me anything."

Silence broken only by the distant sound of a baby squalling and the twang of someone playing a stringed instrument.

"Neil, you're an even bigger arse than I thought. Of course I owe you. I owe you my life. But"—he held up a hand—"if you think I do this out of some sense of obligation, you're an idiot and an arse. I do it because you're my friend. My brother."

Neil raked a hand through his hair. "I am an arse. I don't know what I'm saying."

"I do. You feel guilty because you gave the orders that ended men's lives."

"Now, wait—"

"Don't bloody argue, Neil. We all know it eats you up inside. We also know that every single one of us joined Draven's troop voluntarily. And when Draven asked if we were afraid to die, we knew what we were up against. Your orders brought twelve of us back, so start looking at the men you saved and stop looking back at the men we—all of us—lost."

Neil wished it were that simple. He wished he could close his eyes just once and not hear Bryce screaming as he burned alive or watch Guy's eyes go flat as the blood poured from the gash in his belly.

"I'll look into this Goring not because I owe you, but because I have your back. I'll always have your back."

"And I have yours, Jas. You know if you ever have need of me, you have but to say so."

"I know." He gripped Neil's shoulder with one hand. And as he walked away, Neil heard him murmur, "Unfortunately, no one can give me what I need."

❧

The chair in the entryway needed new stuffing, but despite his aching back, Neil dozed. He didn't dream. He'd become an expert at keeping his sleep light enough that he did not dream. He had no desire to wake the boys with his screams.

And so it was with some shock that he came awake suddenly at the sound of a blood-curdling scream.

Not his.

One of his men, then. The camp was under attack.

He reached for his pistol, then realized he wasn't wearing it. He wasn't in camp. He wasn't a soldier any longer. The curving staircase of the orphanage's entryway rose before him and the back of the chair rested against the front door. The door hadn't opened or he would have been jarred.

He heard the scream again—a child's scream. He grabbed the fireplace poker leaning against his chair and took the steps two at a time. When he reached the second floor, he first passed Lady Juliana's bedchamber. Her door stood open, and one glance inside told him she had fled her bed in a hurry. The door to the older boys' dormitory was closed, but across the way, the younger boys' door was open.

Neil went directly to it and stepped inside, squinting at the light from a lamp set on a table. "What the devil is wrong?" he demanded.

"Shh!" came the response from the far corner, where Lady Juliana sat on the edge of one of the beds. "You'll wake the whole house," she chided him.

"*I'll* wake the house?" *He* hadn't been the one screaming.

He saw who it was. It was the dark-haired boy, Chester. Tears streamed down his face before he buried it once again in Lady Juliana's shoulder. She was dressed all in white, a long robe of muslin draped over the bed and trailing to the floor. But the material didn't hide her bare feet. Neil could only be glad she'd taken a moment to don the robe. Over the course of the long night, he'd entertained several fantasies about seeing her in various states of undress, and it was better for everyone if she stayed well and truly covered.

He would have followed the same principle, except he'd forgotten to pull on his coat and now stood in shirtsleeves. She had been right to worry about the lack of a chaperone. If anyone saw the two of them, she'd be as good as ruined and he'd be forced to ask her to marry him.

Neil looked about the room and saw James rubbing his eyes sleepily. Meanwhile, Charlie lay on his side, thumb tucked securely in his mouth. Jimmy slept too, his arms flung upward as though in surrender.

"You can go back to bed," Lady Juliana said, glancing at him over her shoulder. "It was only a nightmare." Then, looking back at the boy in her arms, she said, "You're safe, Chester. No one will hurt you here. I won't let anyone hurt you."

Neil must have looked dubious because James propped himself up on his elbows. "No need to worry, sir. He does this all the time, he does." He nodded to Chester. "No one but me wakes up anymore."

Neil looked back at the weeping boy, whose sobs and shudders were slowly subsiding. Why would a boy of five have frequent bad dreams? What had happened to him before he'd come here?

"Good night, then, lad. I'll wait outside the door until everyone is settled again." He said it more for Lady Juliana's benefit than anyone else's, but she ignored him and went on cooing to young Chester.

Neil stepped outside and leaned against the wall. He was tired and his body ached from the uncomfortable position he'd occupied for the last several hours. He missed his bed, and though he rarely had an uninterrupted night of sleep, at least in his flat there was a chance of it. He ran his hands through his hair and rolled his neck to work out the stiffness. Then he paced up and down the corridor. The third time he passed Lady Juliana's chamber, he slowed and peered inside. He'd seen it earlier, but then the bed had been made—hastily so, but made nonetheless. He could see the slight indentation where her body had lain before she'd been awakened by Chester's screams. He wondered if her pillow smelled like flowers or perhaps something a bit more sultry...

Neil made himself walk on. Another few passes and he craned his head to see into the dormitory. Lady Juliana stood beside Chester's bed, looking down at him. The long robe gave her an ethereal quality, and the straight fall of her coppery hair down her back looked like a river of lava. Finally, she bent and kissed the boy's forehead. Neil tried not to notice her rounded backside when the fabric of her robe tightened over it.

She turned and started for the door, pausing to kiss James as well. Neil moved out of the doorway and stood at attention. A moment later, she emerged and quietly pulled the door closed. She'd tugged her hair over her shoulder, and when she faced him, it fell between her breasts. They were generous breasts. The robe had opened enough for him to see the edges of the lace cupping her form. At his glance, she pulled the fabric closed, holding it securely with one small, white hand.

"You could have gone back to bed," she told him in a whisper.

"I don't have a bed," he whispered back.

"That's your choice. As you can see, I'm needed here."

He did see that, although if he could hire the right people, that wouldn't be the case. "James says the lad often wakes screaming."

She nodded. "He dreams of men yelling and hurting him. I don't know what his life was like before he came here. He says he doesn't remember in the daylight. I think he must have been born in...well, a place no child should be born."

"A brothel?" Neil didn't frequent them, but he'd seen his share on the Continent. They were places men gathered, which made them good places to gather information. Neil hadn't been interested in the services the ladies were selling. When he looked at the women, he saw frightened or numb girls forced to sell the only commodity they possessed—themselves. He'd seen the children too. Boys and girls as young as three or four, not peddling their bodies, but fetching and carrying and witnessing all sorts of lewd behavior.

If what Chester said was true and his mother was a harlot, it was likely he'd seen all sorts of activities he didn't understand and that might frighten a toddler.

Juliana lifted the lamp and motioned him away from the closed door, closer to her room. "That is what I suspect, although I don't know for certain because the woman who ran the orphanage before I took over kept very poor records. Only a few of the boys—Robbie, Billy, and Jimmy—have any sort of file with information as to when and why they were left here. Some of the boys, like Ralph and Sean, have nothing at all. I have no idea how long they've been here or if those are really even their names."

He wanted to ask her if that was why she'd come to live at the orphanage, to straighten out paperwork, but that didn't really matter to him. What mattered was convincing her to leave so he could complete his mission.

He should have told her good night then, but he waited too long, his gaze fixed on the copper trail of silky hair winding through the valley of her breasts. He would have liked to brush it over her shoulders and brush the robe off in the process. By the time he met her gaze again, she was looking at him expectantly. He cleared his throat, searching for something to say. "And is it true about Jimmy then?"

"That his parents are in debtor's prison? That is what his file says and what he claims as well. I'm sure they will be back for him, but of course, they have to find a way to pay the debt first." She stepped back, closer to her open door. "If you'll excuse me, Mr. Wraxall, I'll say good night again. The boys are awake early, and I'd like to rest a few more hours before I attempt to make them breakfast."

"I'll take care of breakfast," he said before he could stop himself. He should quit making her life easier. Yesterday, he hadn't known the situation he'd stepped into. Now, he did. She had made her bed. Why not let her lie in it?

"I couldn't ask you to do that, sir."

He frowned. "You didn't ask. I offered." And he'd be damned if he would retract his offer now. The pie man would be back, and to supplement, they had a whole house full of able-bodied children. "Besides, the boys should learn some self-sufficiency."

Her dark eyes rounded. "You intend to have the children cook their own breakfast?"

"Why not? I did it during the war." If he could do it, so could these boys. More to the point, if a man like Rafe Beaumont, who could charm a woman into pretty much anything and probably never had to cook or sew or even shave himself before joining Draven's men, could cook his own porridge, so could these boys. Even little Charlie would do a better job than Rafe's first laughable attempt.

"It must bring back fond memories," she said. When he raised a brow, she added. "You're smiling."

"Just send the boys to me when they wake," he told her. "I'll take care of breakfast."

The look she gave him was one he could only characterize as confusion. "Why are you being so nice to me?"

He let out a choked laugh. "You think I'm nice?" If only she had even an inkling of what he'd done during the war, she would probably run from him, screaming all the way. Shaking his head, he strode down the stairs, back to his hard chair and his cold post.

❦

In the morning, Julia did as Wraxall had suggested and sent the boys down to the kitchen. With Wraxall in charge of the boys—and the scent of something cooking—she had extra time in the morning for the first time since she'd come to the orphanage. She took her time washing all over with the cold water in her basin, dressed carefully in the best of what she thought of as her work dresses. Those were the ones she had pulled from her dressing room and taken with her— she swallowed the lump in her throat—when she'd come here.

Her work wardrobe amounted to four or five dresses, although she had finer garments here as well.

She could not return to Mayfair dressed like a maid. Of course, now that she no longer had Mrs. Nesbit to help her dress, she was rather limited to what she could manage to don without assistance. The dress she wore—a pale-blue muslin day dress with pink roses on the hem and bodice—was probably too fine for the orphanage. The material was too light in color and would show every stain. It would probably be soiled by midmorning. She'd have to tie an apron over it. And, Lud, but she hoped her mother did not look down from above and see her dressed in an apron.

Julia often tucked her hair in a mobcap, but though it was practical and modest and kept her hair out of the way, she could not make herself do it this morning. She didn't want to think too much about why she wanted to look pretty. She didn't want to think about who she was trying to look pretty for because the boys certainly didn't care what she looked like.

She braided several sections of her hair and was almost done winding them into a simple but elegant coiffure when she heard something crash. She dropped the hairpin she'd held delicately between two fingers and listened for more crashes.

None came.

She also didn't hear any yelling.

Whenever one of the boys had been responsible for a mishap in the kitchen previously, the cook had screamed with the full power of her well-developed lungs. Now, she heard nothing more than a pause in the murmur of voices and then their resumption.

Interesting. So Wraxall was not the sort of man who lost his temper easily. Not the sort of man who yelled and bellowed at others—or at least not at children. She lifted the pin from the floor and frowned at herself in the small oval mirror. The man was too good. She'd find him out today.

When she'd finished her hair, she gave herself a slight nod in the mirror. She looked more presentable than she had in weeks. She took the servants' stairs to the kitchen, wanting to see what exactly Mr. Wraxall had the boys doing, but she was met at the closed door by Charlie, thumb in his mouth.

"Youangoinere," he said around his thumb, holding his free hand up for emphasis.

Julia smiled. "Charlie, I can't understand you with your thumb in your mouth. Do take it out."

He did, keeping the wet, wrinkled digit at the ready. "But, my lady, it's clean and everything. The major made us wash our hands and faces." He wrinkled his nose. "With soap."

"The major? Is that Mr. Wraxall?"

"Mmm-hmm." The thumb had gone back in his mouth.

"And he made you wash with soap?"

"Mmm-hmm."

She tugged the thumb out gently. "And why do you call him the major?"

"Robbie asked… I forgot what he asked, but Mr. Wraxall said 'major.' So now we all call him the major." His thumb went back into his mouth like a spoon into a plum pudding. Julia stared at the kitchen door and pressed her lips together. This would not do at all. She did not want the boys giving Mr. Wraxall nicknames and growing close to him. He would not be staying.

But when she stepped forward to try again to enter the kitchen, Charlie held up his hand. He pushed his thumb to the side of his mouth, stretching his face almost comically. "I'm supposed to take you to the dining room, my lady."

She raised her brows. "Oh?"

He offered her his arm. It took a moment for her to realize she was supposed to take it, but when she did so, he led her back upstairs, then down again via the formal stairway. Mr. Goring skulked outside the dining room, but when he saw her, he straightened and removed his cap. "Will there be anything to break our fast this morning, my lady?"

Julia looked down at Charlie. "I understand they are hard at work in the kitchen."

"Who? Them boys?"

"Unless you have seen them elsewhere, Mr. Goring, that seems to be the case."

He stuck out his lower lip. "If you don't mind, my lady, I'll find my own breakfast. Can I have leave?"

"Certainly. But don't be gone too long, Mr. Goring. I may have need of you later. Mr. Wraxall has pointed out several places in need of repair."

He doffed his cap and was gone.

Charlie opened the door to the dining room and led her inside. The two tables that stood side by side and ran the length of the room had been set with the mismatched dishes she'd found when she came here. Prior to her arrival, the boys had served themselves from a communal pot, but Julia thought it important to eat meals seated together like a family. She'd also intended to teach the boys some table manners, although she had not been overly successful in that endeavor. Yet.

Her mind flashed back to all of the house parties she'd attended at country estates. When she'd come down to breakfast at ten or eleven in the morning, not seven or eight, the tables had been covered in expensive linen and set with the best china, silver, and crystal. A footman would pull out her chair and pour her chocolate, and she'd serve herself from a sideboard laden with so many delectable dishes she had difficulty choosing. As she ate, she'd listened to discussions of poetry, literature, and music. And she'd faced windows that overlooked rolling hills and fabulous gardens.

Now, her standards were simpler. Today, she was pleased to see the dishes set at each chair, the cheap silverware beside them and laid straight, if not necessarily on the correct side. The curtains had been parted to let in the morning light. One of the four windows had broken and been replaced by a large board some time ago, but the others were moderately clean and the light filtering through them created a patchwork of squares on the wooden floor below.

"Am I to sit and wait?" she asked Charlie.

He nodded, then ran off in the direction of the kitchen. Julia sat in the chair at the head of the table where the younger boys ate. Mrs. Fleming had eaten at the table with the older boys when she'd stayed for meals, but Julia supposed Mr. Wraxall could take that seat—for today only.

It had been some time since Julia had had any time to herself to think or reflect, and as she looked about the room, she remembered the improvements she'd planned. She'd wanted that window replaced, new curtains, and tablecloths for the tables.

The cook had told her there were tablecloths in a storage room, but she'd advised against using them, since it would mean more washing. Though Julia now had a maid coming once a week, and a few tablecloths would not add too much to her load. If only she could squeeze a few extra pounds from the board of directors, she might be able to have the maid come twice a week. Except the board was made up of a half-dozen titled men whose wives had cajoled them into serving and who had very little interest in the orphans or Sunnybrooke. Since she'd taken over, the board had only met once and that was to accept her donation to the orphanage and to ensure she had her father's permission to concern herself with matters in the orphanage.

Her father had written the check that would ensure the St. Maurs were the leading benefactors of the orphanage and thus had some say in its day-to-day operations, and he'd reluctantly given his consent for her to live there a few days a month. She'd never forget his pale, drawn face as she'd stood in the grand vestibule of their town house in Mayfair, waiting for the coachman to finish loading her things and drive her to Spitalfields.

"Julia, it has been six months. You cannot think Harriett would want you to leave your family and go to live with orphans."

They'd had the argument before, and she'd said all she wanted to say. She wasn't leaving because Harriett was dead or because her mother was dead or because the house was silent as a tomb. She was leaving because Davy was *not* dead, and she couldn't stand to be in the place where everywhere she looked she thought of him. But she would never see him again, and she could only think of one way to fill the ragged hole in her heart, and that was to take these little orphan boys under her wing and do what no one else in the world seemed to want to do—love them.

And so she'd straightened her back and looked her father in the eye. "An empty town house is not a family. There's nothing to keep me here, Father. I'm three and twenty, well past my majority. If I want to ruin my chances at marriage by concerning myself with the upkeep of an orphanage, then I hurt no one but myself."

She didn't want to wound her father, but she also did not want him to hold out hope she would return to her life before. She did not expect him to come after her. Her father spent all his time at his club or in the Lords. Anything else, he delegated to others. If he could have delegated his need to use the chamber pot to a lackey, the Earl of St. Maur would have done so. Thus, it did not surprise her that he had sent someone to fetch her home. The fact that it was a former soldier was a bit unnerving. Perhaps her father was more serious about her returning home than he had been in the past.

Her thoughts were interrupted by the scuffling of feet in the corridor, and a moment later, Robbie opened the door to admit Michael and George carrying one large pot and Angus and Sean carrying a smaller one to the sideboard. Ralph entered next with a basket, followed by Walter and Billy, who carried teapots. The younger boys carried serving utensils and the whole lot of them were talking all at once in an excited cacophony.

"We're having porridge, my lady," Jimmy told her.

"And toast," James added.

"And Major says we're to eat like the nobs do," Robbie added. Then he smacked Angus on the back of the head. "Get your fingers out of the porridge. We have to pray and then Lady Juliana eats first."

Angus sent up a loud protest, but it was interrupted—as was the rest of the commotion—by the arrival of Mr. Wraxall. He didn't say a word or do anything more than step into the room, and the boys fell silent. Robbie gazed at him with something like adoration while Walter's lip curled in a sneer. Julia rather thought her own gaze must have mirrored Robbie's. Wraxall looked devastatingly handsome this morning. In a coat, breeches, waistcoat, and cravat, he made quite the contrast to the boys in their untucked shirts and frayed trousers. Charlie had said Wraxall had made the boys wash, and Julia could also tell some of them had brushed their hair. Wraxall had also tended to his own toilette. His face was freshly shaven and his dark hair brushed back. His blue eyes regarded her from under thick lashes.

He gave her a slight bow. "My lady."

Her heart might have stopped if the boys hadn't distracted her by copying him and bowing themselves—all save Walter and Billy. She blinked in surprise at the greeting. Then she remembered herself and rose. "Good morning, Mr. Wraxall and…gentlemen." She had been about to call them boys, but she knew it would please them more if she called them gentlemen, especially as they were acting so gentlemanly. "Master Charlie tells me you have prepared a feast to break our fast."

"It's just porridge and toast, my lady," James said, ever truthful.

Julia smiled. "Yes. A feast. Shall we say grace and then eat?"

"Aye!" George said. "I'm fair starving."

Julia was thankful for the distraction of the boys. She had something to look at besides the imposing form of Mr. Wraxall. As she folded her hands, she spared him another look. He had a wry smile on his face. "Mr. Wraxall, would you like to do the honors, or shall I?"

He inclined his head toward her. "I wouldn't dream of taking your place, my lady."

She nodded, then lowered her head and closed her eyes. Usually, she kept one eye open and trained on Walter or Ralph, but today, she didn't worry. She thanked God for the meal and the service of the young gentlemen, and when she finished, the young boys were beaming. Then at a nod from Wraxall, the boys took their seats and Charlie escorted her to the sideboard. As the plates were already on the table, she carried hers with her. When they reached the sideboard, Wraxall was there.

"What do I say again?" Charlie asked him.

"Ask if you can be of any assistance."

"Can I be of any assistance?"

"No, thank you, Charlie. You may sit down." She opened the towel keeping the toast warm and used tongs to place one on her plate. It smelled fresh and yeasty, and she gave Wraxall an approving smile. "I must say I'm impressed, Mr. Wraxall. This looks quite delicious." She lifted the lid of the larger pot of porridge and spooned some into her bowl. Porridge was one of her least favorite foods, but she would eat every last bite because her boys had made it.

"The boys are good at following orders," he said, taking her plate and handing it to Walter. "Take this to Lady Juliana's seat."

Walter took it and mumbled something.

"What was that, Walter?"

"Yes, sir," he said more loudly. Clearly Wraxall understood, as she had quite early on, that keeping Walter busy meant keeping him out of mischief.

"You are good at giving orders," she said, adding a meager helping of sugar to her tea. It was a luxury and she used it sparingly.

"I've had practice."

"And your skills have proved quite useful. Do you think you will be able to finish securing the orphanage by the end of the day? I'm certain that applicants for the position of cook will arrive tomorrow, and I can handle breakfast for one morning. We can't expect you to stay another night."

His eyes narrowed. "I'll stay as long as necessary."

It was a generous offer, and she wanted to be appreciative, but every time she looked at him, she felt an unwanted tug of attraction. And every moment she was with him was one more chance for him to show his true nature.

You think I'm nice?

She had to remember he was a man. Everything he did was for his own selfish reasons. She could not fathom what those might be, but she did not trust him.

Seven

Neil needed a drink. He hadn't had so much as a sip of wine since he'd arrived at the orphanage. Without drink to smooth the edges, he felt his emotions too keenly. Since coming back from the war, Neil had learned that feeling anything was dangerous. He didn't want to relive the anguish he'd felt when his brother had died or when Draven's men had been killed. He'd felt it all too powerfully, and he'd been powerless to do anything about it.

Now, the rawness of the pain and loss he'd suffered seeped in again. And with those emotions came others. Neil couldn't have said why, but when he'd heard Lady Juliana's voice on the other side of the kitchen door, in reply to Charlie, his chest had tightened and his heartbeat quickened. He'd been eager to see her, anticipate the look on her face when she saw the meal he'd helped the boys prepare.

And then he'd seen her—her body wrapped in the long, flowing lines of the dress and her hair perched delicately on her head, making the graceful nape of her neck appear porcelain against the blue of the dress.

He'd been momentarily stunned by how much he wanted her approval of the breakfast. And then when she'd given it, he wished all the boys would disappear so he could take her in his arms and…

What would he have done? Kiss her? To what end? She was an unmarried lady, not a widow or an actress. He could be attracted to her, but he couldn't act on it. And that was for the best, because while he was here, he had to maintain strict control. He had his orders. Today he would make sure the building was secure for the boys' safety. She'd taken steps to hire a new cook and a new teacher. Once those servants were here to take care of the orphanage, she'd have to admit she was not needed here.

When all the boys had finished ladling porridge into their bowls and each taken two rolls from the basket, he filled his own bowl and took a seat at the head of the older boys' table. He couldn't think for all the noise the lads made, and he sent a look down the table that had the effect of stopping the conversations in midstream. The little boys quieted, and Neil looked at Lady Juliana, whose eyes were wide at the sudden silence.

"My lady," he said, "have you seen Mr. Goring this morning?"

She sipped her tea and replied, "I have, Mr. Wraxall. He stepped out for a moment to fetch his own breakfast."

"But why?" Robbie interrupted. "We made enough for him."

Neil gave the lad a long look, and Robbie bowed his head. "Sorry, Major. I didn't mean to interrupt."

"It's fine, Robbie," Lady Juliana said.

Neil frowned again. The lad would never learn discipline if she didn't correct him.

"I believe Mr. Goring wasn't certain whether enough had been prepared for him. He did not want to assume."

Neil could tell she was lying because she didn't want to hurt the boys' feelings. Goring probably hadn't believed the boys could cook a decent meal. Hell, Neil wasn't sure he'd believed it either. But Neil suspected wherever Goring went he had a reason for going other than fear over lumpy porridge. Jasper would be watching, and Neil would know soon enough.

"Since we don't know when Mr. Goring will return, I'll need you boys to help me with some of the tasks I had planned," Neil said.

Most of the younger boys cheered while the older boys looked wary.

"What sorts of tasks, Mr. Wraxall?" Lady Juliana asked.

Neil took a bite of his roll. Considering the limited ingredients he and the boys had had to work with, it was not bad. "Securing the locks, mending broken stairs, and the like."

"Oh, but those are Mr. Goring's responsibilities. I am certain he will return within the hour."

Neil was far less certain. He didn't think the man would be back until midday, if at all. But that wasn't the point. "My lady, may I speak with you privately?"

Her brows rose. "Of course. We can speak in the parlor after breakfast."

Neil rose. "We'll speak now."

Her brows lowered again, and she gave him a

poisonous look. Slowly, she rose and placed her napkin in her chair. "We will be back in a few minutes, children."

The boys nodded, keeping their heads down. All except Walter, who grinned as though he expected his headmistress to be scolded and enjoyed the idea.

Lady Juliana swept out of the room, and Neil followed her. She went directly to the parlor and held the door open until he crossed the threshold. Then she closed the door quietly and marched to stand before him. She was petite and she had to look up at him, but that didn't seem to cow her.

"I don't know what you are used to in your everyday life, Mr. Wraxall, but let me make one thing clear—you do *not* give *me* orders."

Neil felt the prick of heat that indicated she'd fired his temper. He pushed it down. "Someone needs to."

Her dark eyes grew round with an emotion somewhere between surprise and fury. "I assure you, sir, that *someone* is not you. I have been running this orphanage for several months now, and in that time—"

"In that time, you're lucky it hasn't fallen apart or worse." He inclined his head. "I suppose I should not interrupt you, either, but I don't have time for social niceties."

"You, sir, are no gentleman," she said, then immediately covered her mouth. "I do apologize. I should not have said that."

It was one of the worst insults a lady might mete out, but Neil would not allow it to faze him. "No, you are correct, my lady. I am no gentleman. I'm a bastard, as you must know, and I promise you that I no more want to surround myself with a dozen boys who remind me of my own bastardy every time I look at them than you want to look at me yourself."

"That's not what I—"

"But I have my orders, and I will follow them. As you have no teacher for the boys yet, I will keep them employed with assisting me by making repairs around the orphanage." He began to pace. "The smaller ones can fetch and carry, while the older ones can do most of the work. By the end of the day, I expect the stairs will be sound, the windows and doors secure, and all the chimneys clean so they are not a fire hazard."

"I'll allow that." Her voice made him stop in his tracks. "On one condition."

"*You* will allow it?"

"Yes. I am headmistress of this building, and I am responsible for the welfare of these children. That is not a question legally. The board of directors has put me in a position of authority."

Neil folded his arms over his chest. "Is my father on the board?"

She advanced on him. "Is that a threat, Mr. Wraxall?"

"Clearly. And I do not make frivolous threats. I would prefer to complete my orders by sending you home to your father. Since you won't comply with that directive, then my only choice is to do what is necessary to ensure your safety and well-being on these premises. If you attempt to hamper my efforts, I will take whatever measures necessary to defeat you."

"Am I an opponent to be defeated?"

She was angry. He could see the stains of pink on her cheekbones, but it was better they have this conversation now and put everything out in the open. He could do what was necessary more quickly then, and she'd know her place. "You tell me," he answered.

"I will tell you, Mr. Wraxall." She poked him in the chest. "You *are* a bastard, but not by virtue of your birth. No. In that way, you have no right to compare yourself to these children, who bear no shame for the sins of their parents. You are a bastard because you think you have the right to come in here and throw your power around just because you see me as a defenseless woman in charge of defenseless children." She poked him again. "I have news for you, Wraxall. I have known men like you, and I am far from defenseless. You have today and today only to complete your sacred orders, and then I want you out. If you don't leave, I will have you physically thrown out, and I'll make certain both my father and yours know of your unpardonable behavior."

Neil felt heat creep along the back of his neck. What she threatened would indeed cause him no end of explaining and probably anger his father and St. Maur. She wasn't worth it, and neither was the orphanage.

"That won't be necessary, my lady. I will finish today and be gone tonight."

She nodded once. "Good."

"Is that all?" he asked.

"Yes."

"Good." He opened the parlor door and stormed out.

❦

Julia's legs felt wobbly as she reached tentatively for a chair. Finding one of the armchairs, she lowered herself into it slowly and took a shaky breath. How dare he threaten her! How dare he speak of her boys as bastards! He did not want to look at them? Fine. She didn't want to ever see his face again.

She didn't go back to the dining room. She was too angry, and she knew her feelings would show on her face. If one of the boys were to ask what the matter was, she'd probably burst into tears. Not because she was weak. No. Because she was so angry that all she could think to do was wail with fury. She busied herself in the parlor with the account books, answering correspondence, and studying lists of inventory the cook had made up before she had left.

By the time she glanced at the clock again, it was almost eleven. She'd been aware of the sound of the boys' voices and the tapping of hammers and louder banging on occasion, but now she realized she hadn't been bothered once all morning. For all that Mr. Wraxall was an arse, he seemed to have the children well in hand. They would probably be hungry for lunch, and she would make sure all was well before making sandwiches for the midday meal.

She opened the parlor door and made her way into the entryway. She stopped at the opening and stared at the activity. Boys sat on the stairs, hammers in hand, nailing boards down. The younger boys stood ready with nails, while the older boys pounded or ripped out rotten boards and called for younger boys to bring new pieces of wood. At the door stood Mr. Wraxall with Walter and Robbie. He was showing the two how to install a new dead bolt. Outside the open door, two of her boys painted the steps leading up to the orphanage door. And since the door was open, she could see the dark clouds gathering behind them. It would rain this afternoon and the rain would likely be heavy. It was a good thing she did not need pots and pans to make sandwiches.

"It looks as though you have been working very hard, boys." She did not look at Mr. Wraxall, but she could feel his gaze on her, and it made her want to shuffle her feet. She forced herself to stand still.

"We have! We have!" James told her, his high voice even higher with excitement. "Come and try the steps. They don't creak anymore."

"I shall try them when you have finished. In the meantime, I thought I would make sandwiches. You must have worked up an appetite."

There was a chorus of ayes and hurrahs.

"Good. Then I will call you when the meal is ready."

Still without looking at Mr. Wraxall, she made her way to the kitchen, laid out bread and sandwich items, and put together two dozen sandwiches. It took her three trips to carry all the sandwiches and the pitchers of lemon water to the dining room, but when she'd finished and set the tables, she called the boys. The sound of their progress was what she imagined a stampede of wild animals in Africa must sound like, and she quickly moved out of the way lest she be trampled. It wasn't until after the boys were all seated with food and drink and had said a prayer that she noticed Mr. Wraxall had not come to the dining room.

"My lady," Michael was telling her, "did you know we used one hundred and twelve nails so far today?"

"Goodness. That many?" She spied Charlie stuffing part of a sandwich crust in his pocket. "Charlie, what are you doing?"

"I thought I'd feed this to Matthew, Mark, and Luke."

Of course. The cook usually gave the boys scraps from the kitchen for the rats. "You go ahead and eat that," she told Charlie, "and I'll bring them an apple, cheese, and a piece of bread after lunch."

"All that?" Charlie smiled. "They won't be able to finish it."

"Then they will have the leavings for dinner." She scooted Charlie's plate closer to the edge of the table so fewer crumbs would fall on the floor. Charlie's and the other young boys' eyelids drooped. She'd have to encourage them to nap after lunch. "Michael, where is Mr. Wraxall?" she asked.

"With that man," Michael said.

Julia glanced at the older boys' table. At her look, several of them nodded. "What man?" she asked.

"He wore a mask," Michael said. "Like a highwayman."

Sean nodded. "It's true. And he seemed to come out of nowhere. Ralph and I were painting outside, and he wasn't there. Then we looked up, and he was right before us."

"He was like a spirit," Ralph said. "He didn't even walk up the steps. We would have seen him."

Julia stood. "Robbie, make sure all the boys finish their lunches and then take their plates back to the kitchen. I need to speak with Mr. Wraxall."

Robbie was on his feet. "Yes, my lady."

She started for the doorway, and when she reached it, she noticed Robbie was still standing and Billy had joined him. "Why are you still standing?" she asked.

"The major says a gentleman stands when a lady stands."

"Too bad you're no gentleman," Walter muttered loudly enough for her to hear.

"Well, I think it shows very good manners."

Michael and Sean jumped up too.

"Thank you, gentlemen."

She left the dining room and closed the door behind her. As much as she wanted to dislike Major Wraxall, he was making it more and more difficult. But she'd see what this meeting with the masked man was all about.

Wraxall was not in the entryway, which smelled of freshly cut wood and wet paint. She was about to check in the parlor when she heard a murmur of voices outside the door. The new bolt had been installed, but it was not in use. Quietly, she pulled the door open.

And came face-to-face with a man in a black silk mask.

His hair was covered by a length of black silk tied at the back of his neck, and he wore a black mask that covered most of one side of his face and the upper portion of the other. Behind the mask, eyes the blue of the sea before a storm looked at her. "Who are you?" she blurted out, putting a hand to her pounding heart.

"This is a friend of mine."

She turned to see Wraxall moving closer to her. She hadn't even noticed him when she'd stepped outside.

The wind blew fiercely, making the branches of the birch tree bow and wave. "I see. What is he doing here?"

"He's good at finding people. I asked him to look for Mr. Goring."

"Mr…" Belatedly, she realized she hadn't seen him all morning and hadn't even thought to look for him. With Wraxall nearby, she hadn't needed the servant, though he certainly could have made himself useful lighting fires in the grates or carrying the trays into the dining room for her. How long had she been relying on herself and not noticing the manservant's absence? "Mr. Goring hasn't returned then."

Wraxall shook his head. "I think he's long since had his breakfast."

"Oh dear. I hope nothing has happened to him."

"He's perfectly well. I have just come from him," said the man in the mask, his voice a deep rumble. "He is sitting at the Ox and the Bull."

"What is that?"

"An alehouse nearby," Wraxall told her. "One Slag and his gang frequent."

A shiver of unease ran up her spine. Goring had been the one to tell her to keep her distance from Mr. Slag. He'd been the one to tell her Slag's gang ran all Spitalfields. Lately, Slag had been paying more attention to her, and Goring hadn't been able to keep the crime lord out. But she couldn't think of any reason Goring should wish to spend any time in Slag's establishment.

"I don't understand," she said. "Is Mr. Slag keeping Mr. Goring there against his will?"

"No," the masked man told her. "Your servant seems quite content to partake of Mr. Slag's hospitality."

"What of his duties here?"

"Lord Jasper and I believe your servant may have found a new master," Wraxall told her.

Julia stared at the masked man. He was a lord?

"We think Slag is paying Goring for access to you," Wraxall continued.

A thousand possibilities flew through her mind in that moment, swirling about like the leaves dancing in the wind along the street. She knew exactly why Slag wanted access to her. He wanted her father's money or her as his mistress. "But Mr. Goring warned me away from Mr. Slag. Why would he do that if he was working for the man?"

"Perhaps he wasn't working for him initially," Wraxall said, "but every man has his price. Whatever the case, Goring is working for Slag now."

"Then I shall dismiss him immediately."

Wraxall held up a hand. "Not so quickly. Take away Slag's perceived pathway to you, and he'll be forced to find another or do something more dramatic. Now that we know of Mr. Goring's duplicity, we can watch him and discover Slag's plans."

"And then what?" she asked.

"And then we persuade Mr. Slag you are not worth the trouble."

"That sounds like a job for the Protector," the masked man said. "If you have no more need of me at the moment, I'll take my leave. I think I've scared enough women and children for one day."

"You didn't frighten us," Julia lied. "I was not expecting you."

The masked man's eyes met hers with a penetrating

stare. "Would you like me to scare you?" He touched his mask. "The few women who've looked on me without my mask have either screamed or fainted. Which would you be?"

Julia caught her breath, and Wraxall moved in front of her. "You're dismissed." Wraxall put a hand on his friend's shoulder. "And thank you."

Lord Jasper shrugged. "You would have done the same for me." And then just as Ralph had described, the masked man seemed to all but disappear into the growing darkness and the bustle of people looking for shelter before the storm.

"Is he one of your men?" she asked Wraxall, forgetting for the moment that she didn't wish to speak to him. "One of the soldiers you served with?"

"He is."

"Is his face that awful? Is that why he wears a mask?"

"He was burned in a fire during an ambush. He's lucky to be alive, but he's self-conscious about the scar."

Julia noticed he didn't answer her question about the gruesomeness of the burn. "He should be proud of it. He's a hero."

Wraxall gave her a wry smile. "I don't think any of us feel much like heroes, my lady. Come inside before we're blown away."

But before they could close the door, another figure fought the wind to start toward the orphanage. Wraxall stepped in front of her, probably to protect her, but there was no need. She recognized the livery the man wore immediately as that of the Earl St. Maur. Julia put a hand on Wraxall's arm, then just as quickly removed it. She'd felt the hard solidity of his muscle beneath her hand.

"It's one of my father's footmen," she told him, avoiding looking into Wraxall's face.

"My lady!" the footman called over the wind. "I have a message from your father."

She held out a hand to take the folded paper. "Won't you come in and have some tea in the kitchen?"

The footman shook his head. "I had better get back."

"Very well." When he turned to leave directly, she called, "You do not need a reply?"

"No, my lady. The earl said none was required."

Julia stepped inside, and Wraxall closed the door and pushed the bolt home. Annoyingly, he stood and waited for her to open the letter. She gave him a glare, but it didn't seem to deter him. She might have scolded him if she hadn't been distracted by the contents inside the envelope. The only item inside was an invitation to Viscount Sterling's ball that evening. Scrawled across the invitation, in her father's spiky hand, were the words *Your attendance is required.*

"Oh no," she muttered.

"Oh yes," Wraxall answered, reading over her shoulder. "You will attend if I have to escort you myself."

She narrowed her eyes at him. "And if I attend this ball, who will take care of the children?"

Wraxall opened his mouth, paused, then smiled. "I have just the person in mind."

"Who?"

"Leave that to me. You will attend that ball."

"And what about the situation with Mr. Goring?"

"He can float away in the deluge for all I care. You and I will go."

"Go where?" Michael asked. Julia turned to see about half of the boys crowding into the entryway.

Julia folded her hands and smoothed her expression. "Go upstairs to put you boys down for a nap."

"Not me!" Michael said, shaking his head violently.

"Not I," Julia corrected.

"I won't make you take one, if you don't make me, my lady."

Julia laughed. "You don't need a nap, Michael, but Charlie, Chester, Jimmy, and James do."

"I'm not tired, my lady!" James said.

"Me either," Charlie said, his eyelids drooping.

"Nevertheless, a little rest is just the thing." She bundled the four boys together and pushed them toward the stairs.

"Lady Juliana," Wraxall said from behind her. "You are taking a third of my workforce."

"Well, perhaps now is a good time for all of you to rest. These are boys, sir, not soldiers. They should have some time for recreation."

She glanced down from the steps and saw him frowning at her. Before he could argue, the first clap of thunder sounded and a steady rain drummed on the roof. It was the sort of day she'd always loved when she'd lived in Mayfair. It was less comforting here. "Robbie, you and Billy get the buckets. Walter, will you and Michael get the pots and pans? Ralph, go and cover Matthew, Mark, and Luke's enclosure. You know the rain makes them nervous. Best they feel snug and secure so we don't have to spend the rest of the afternoon searching for them."

There was a chorus of "Yes, my lady," and then

she shuttled the little boys upstairs again. Wraxall was right behind her.

"What the devil is this?" he asked.

"Sir, watch your language around the children."

The little boys giggled as she herded them into their room and pulled the curtains closed. The room was already dark, but this made it feel cozier. "Off with your shoes, boys. Then climb under the covers."

Wraxall stood in the doorway. "What the *deuce* is this?"

"Nap time," she answered.

"No, I meant with the buckets and pots and pans."

"That's to catch the water," Jimmy told him, hopping into bed. "Don't forget our bucket, my lady."

"I won't." She tugged it from the corner and placed it between Chester and James's beds, where water had already begun to leak from the roof.

"Do you mean to tell me the roof leaks?" Wraxall asked.

"I hadn't intended to tell you at all, but I suppose it's quite apparent now. We have plenty of buckets to deal with the leaks."

"If we use the pots and pans too," James said. "But that doesn't work so well when it's dinnertime."

"Shh." Julia placed a kiss on James's forehead then went to Jimmy and Charlie. Chester was taking his time. "Chester, nap time."

"I'm not tired." He yawned. "That wasn't a yawn. I was stretching my mouth."

"You don't have to sleep," Julia told him, pulling back the blanket on his bed. "Just rest. I will come and get you up in an hour."

"Major doesn't need to rest."

Julia glanced at Wraxall. Now was the time for him to either help her cause or hurt it. If he hurt it, she would be plagued by tired, cranky boys all evening.

"Actually," Wraxall said, "I think Lady Juliana makes a good suggestion. We should all rest, and when you wake, we'll be refreshed and ready to begin anew."

"So you won't work on the steps without us?" Chester asked.

Clearly Wraxall hadn't anticipated having to make that sort of promise. Julia raised her brows. He sighed. "No. We will wait until nap time is through. You'll miss nothing."

"Promise?" Charlie asked sleepily.

"I do."

"My parents promised to come back for me," Jimmy said. "But they still haven't."

Julia sighed. Her heart broke for Jimmy, who couldn't possibly understand that his parents either could not come for him or did not have the money to support him if they did. These poor children had learned not to trust adults. She'd been steadily earning their trust, but they hadn't chosen to test her now. They'd chosen Mr. Wraxall.

She looked at the major, not certain whether to interrupt or let him answer. For a long moment he stood uncertainly in the doorway, then he strode into the room and went to Jimmy's bed, sitting on the side. "When I make a promise, I keep it. No work will be done on the house while you rest. I'm certain your parents will keep their promise too. They are in a difficult situation. Give them time, and they will come for you."

He brushed the boy's dark hair back from his forehead. "Sleep now." He looked at the other three boys. "That's an order."

"Yes, sir," they said in unison, though Charlie's reply was garbled as his thumb was already in his mouth.

Julia stepped outside and closed the door when Wraxall followed her. "Thank you," she said. "I know you meant what you said, and it's so important to the children that they have adults in their life they can count on."

He had moved away from the room and closer to her bedchamber. Though the little ones could likely not hear, she had lowered her voice as she followed him.

"I agree. That's why I'm surprised you haven't done more to show them they can count on you."

Julia glared at him. "What precisely do you mean by that, sir?"

"I mean that you have them living in a place where they aren't safe. What will you tell them when someone breaks in and hurts one of them or you?"

"I don't have to worry about that anymore. You have fixed the locks."

His light eyes bored into her. "Then what will you tell them when the roof collapses on their heads?"

"I've asked the board of directors for more funds and instructed Mr. Goring to begin work on it."

"The same Mr. Goring who sits at Slag's alehouse all day?"

Oh yes. She'd forgotten she would have to let the servant go. "I'll hire another manservant then."

"And how will you be certain he isn't also in Slag's pocket? That man wants you. You won't be safe until he's dealt with."

"Yes, well, I'm certain half the residents of Spitalfields wish he would be, as you say, 'dealt with,' but so far we are not so lucky." She took a deep breath and squared her shoulders. "In any case, it is not your concern. We had an agreement. You would leave at the end of the day. I expect you to keep your word to me."

He gave her a long look. "You know I can't do that. There's the ball tonight."

She blew out a breath. "I am no child who needs your supervision, Mr. Wraxall. Nor do I need my father's lackey to serve as a nurse."

"I am not your father's lackey. I don't stay for money."

"Well, you aren't staying out of the goodness of your heart." She paused, almost hoping he would contradict her. But he didn't.

"No. As I told you before, I don't have a weak spot for orphans, but I do have my—"

"Orders," she said before he could. "Is that all you care about? Orders?"

"No," he said quietly. "I have found at least one more item to care about lately."

And to her complete shock, he reached up and ran a finger down her cheek. His touch was light and fleeting, but it seemed to burn a path into her delicate skin. She stood rooted in place, all but paralyzed by his touch, but instead of touching her again, he gave her a nod and moved away and then down the steps.

Slowly, Julia raised a hand to her cheek. Why had

he touched her so intimately? Did he mean to imply he cared about her? They hardly knew each other. The thought had made her cheeks heat and her heart thud heavily in her chest. For a moment, she wondered what his lips might feel like on her cheek.

She closed her eyes, imagining the light touch of his lips and the rasp of his dark stubble, and then a cold drop landed on her arm. Julia glanced up and saw a new leak had begun outside her door. With a sigh, she entered her room and collected a vase to catch the water. The activity helped clear her brain, and she was thankful for the interruption of her daydream.

He'd almost fooled her. Julia had always wondered how Harriett could have been taken in by such a lying, cheating rogue as the man she'd married, but now she had firsthand experience.

Men could be charming to have their way. Wraxall had all but made her forget he was only here to report back to her father what a disaster she'd made of running the orphanage. Soon he'd try to persuade her to leave.

He was not her ally. He was not here to help her or the boys. Julia simply had to bide her time until he proved it.

Eight

THE DELUGE OF THE AFTERNOON HAD GIVEN WAY TO A light sprinkle, and Neil stood in Lady Juliana's parlor watching the rivulets of water run down the window. He'd sent for his evening clothes and now wore the dark coat and breeches required for a ball. His silk waistcoat was dark blue, and Neil supposed that was to add color to his otherwise somber appearance.

The last thing he wanted to do tonight was attend a ball. Ordering boys around all day was far more taxing than ordering soldiers about. Neil had never known children had so much energy. They didn't ever tire of bouncing up and down or asking questions. Thank God they had gone up to bed—

A scream shattered his quiet, and he raced into the vestibule to find Lady Juliana brandishing a fan. The boys clambered down the stairs in various states of undress, presumably to protect her. "Who are you?" she demanded of the tall, platinum-haired man standing just inside the doorway. Instead of speaking, the man cut his gaze to Neil.

"Protector," Neil said. "Good to know you haven't forgotten how to make an entrance."

Ewan scowled. He was muscular and broad-shouldered and more than a little intimidating. "Good to know you haven't forgotten how to give orders." His voice was low and his speech slow, giving weight to each of his words. "I'm here. Who do you need me to kill?"

Lady Juliana gasped and jumped in front of the boys, shielding them from the perceived harm.

Neil held up a hand. "He's not serious."

At least Neil didn't *think* Ewan was serious.

"Lady Juliana, may I present Mr. Ewan Mostyn."

Her wary, brown eyes cut to Ewan then to him.

"Mostyn is a friend of mine. I trust him with my life. And so I thought it only reasonable that I might trust him with the lives of the children while we are out."

"What?" Juliana and Ewan said together.

Lady Juliana recovered first. "You cannot possibly expect me to leave the children alone with—with *him*. No offense, Mr. Mostyn. You simply do not look like a nursemaid."

Ewan waved away her apology. "My job is to kill people. If you need a nursemaid, call Rafe."

Juliana's eyes grew wide, and Neil yanked Ewan out of the vestibule and into the privacy of the corridor. Rather, Ewan allowed Neil to lead him. If Ewan didn't want to be moved, nothing and no one would budge him.

"Stop talking about murdering someone. You are scaring the lady."

Ewan flashed a quick grin. The arse was having fun with his role as brute. "I'm no nursemaid."

"Of course not. The boys will be in bed shortly. I need you to protect the orphanage from anyone attempting to break in."

Ewan lifted a brow.

"Yes, I know. People usually try to get out of orphanages, but there's a crime lord who has recently taken an interest in the lady. All you have to do is sit here and keep watch."

Ewan narrowed his eyes. "What if the boys get out of bed?"

Neil shook his head. "Order them back to bed." He paused. "In a nice way. You don't want them to start crying."

Ewan's expression turned fearful. "They cry?"

"No. They don't cry. Lady Juliana and I will return in a few hours." He clapped a hand on Ewan's shoulder. "I need you, Protector."

"If there's crying, there will be hell to pay."

"Understood." Neil led Ewan back to the vestibule, where Lady Juliana still stood in front of the boys. "Has your father's carriage arrived yet?"

"You cannot possibly think to leave?"

"I have my orders. Mr. Mostyn has his. The boys will be fine." He pointed to the lads on the stairs. "Go back to bed. Mr. Mostyn will watch over the orphanage until we return."

"What if he murders us in our sleep?" James asked in his high voice.

"Mr. Mostyn wouldn't murder you. He would never commit murder. Right, Mostyn?"

Ewan just stared at him. Neil stared back. Finally, Ewan nodded. "Right."

Juliana furrowed her brow. "That wasn't very convincing."

Neil took her arm. "The sooner we leave, the sooner we return home." He all but dragged her away from the children. Finally, at the door, she turned back. "Go to bed, boys. I'll kiss you good night when I return home."

"Blech." That from some of the older boys. Neil heard the distinct sound of sniffling from a few of the younger boys. Ewan threw him a panicked look, and Neil pushed Lady Juliana out the door.

It wasn't until they'd arrived at Viscount Sterling's ball that Neil had a chance to look at Lady Juliana— really look at her. And then he wished she'd stayed in the darkness of the carriage. In the glittering lights of the Sterling's foyer, her rose-colored gown seemed to shimmer. The designs at the hem and the bodice were simple and wrought in silver thread that matched the silver combs in her hair. Pink as it was, the gown should have made her look young and innocent, but the way her breasts pushed at the bodice and the slight cling of the fabric to her rounded derriere did not bring to mind debutantes and prim misses. Perhaps if she hadn't had that fiery hair swept up and caught by the combs, he might have been able to look away. But all he could think of was freeing the fire and pressing his lips to the smooth, exposed skin of her back while the coppery tresses brushed against his face.

He wasn't the only man who noticed her either. As they moved through the foyer and up the stairs to the ballroom, Neil noted men's heads turning. If Lady Juliana noticed, she gave no indication. In fact, her eyes were slightly unfocused as though she were deep in thought.

"Is your father here already?" he asked her.

"Pardon? Oh, Papa? Yes, I am certain he came early and then sent the carriage for me. He would have wanted to discuss politics with Sterling." They paused to allow the couple in front of them to be announced. "I hope the boys are in bed asleep," she said.

So that was what occupied her mind. "I'm certain they are. I kept them busy today, and I imagine they are more fatigued than usual."

"And your friend is completely trustworthy?"

"As I said, I'd trust him with my life."

They moved forward, and Neil handed both of their cards to the butler. "Lady Juliana St. Maur and Mr. Neil Wraxall."

Neil felt his cheeks heat. He hated having all eyes on him like this, especially the eyes of the *ton*, men and women who thought they were above him simply because of an accident of birth. He never felt more like a bastard than at moments like these. Lady Juliana, on the other hand, glided into the room as though she had been born to do this. And, of course, she had. But what surprised Neil was the ease with which she transitioned from the orphanage to the ballroom. Was there anywhere she felt out of place?

A few minutes later, he had the answer. St. Maur intercepted them as they made a circuit of the ballroom. "Step outside with me, darling," he said, taking his daughter's arm. "You too, Wraxall."

Neil followed the man. He was only an inch or two taller than his daughter but walked with a regal bearing. At one time he'd had bright-red hair, but most of it had faded to white. His green eyes were still sharp and alert, and as soon as they were outside, he turned them on his daughter. "What is this nonsense I hear about not coming home?" Before Juliana could answer, he pointed to Neil. "And you, your father said you would have her home within the hour. It has been much longer than an hour, sir."

"Yes, my lord." Neil stood straight. St. Maur was right to chastise him. He had failed in the mission.

"Papa, I'm hardly a child to be called home on your whim. The orphans need me."

"Well, they shall have to get on without you. I let you play at this game because I know how devastated you were at your sister's death." His voice softened, and Neil caught a glimpse of the man who had indulged his daughter. "But the time for all that is over."

Lady Juliana raised her chin. "We had an agreement, Papa. I attend events during the Season and you leave me alone to do my work at Sunnybrooke."

"I want to change our agreement. It's past time you married. If something were to happen to me, you would be all alone in the world."

"I'd rather be all alone than stuck with a husband." She said the last word as though it were a curse. "As I told you before, I will never marry."

"Yes, you will. Not all men are like Lainesborough."

Her gaze bored into her father. "No. Some are like you."

"Excuse me, but I see a friend of mine—" Neil

began, thinking now would be a very good time to escape this family feud.

"Mr. Wraxall, won't you dance with me?" Lady Juliana said suddenly, turning to face him.

"I don't—"

But she took his arm and steered him to the end of a line of dancers.

"I will see you at the Darlington musicale!" her father called after them.

On the dance floor, Neil panicked. He would rather face a line of French infantry than this line of dancers. He knew the steps well enough to avoid making a complete fool of himself, but that did not mean everyone would not discuss him. He had heard it all over the years.

Just like his tart of a mother.

He conducts himself well…for a bastard.

Has his father no shame? Flaunting his by-blows in public!

Neil avoided the *ton* and their social events religiously. Even after he'd returned from the war a hero and everyone wanted to throw fetes in his honor, he declined. As far as Neil was concerned, Rafe could represent them all.

But here he was, in full view of his critics, about to dance with one of the most beautiful ladies in the peerage. The two lines of dancers came together, and Lady Juliana pressed her hand to his and circled. "Why are you scowling?" she murmured. "You are supposed to be having fun."

"Why are you scowling?" he shot back. "Aren't you having fun?"

"No. I'd rather be back at Sunnybrooke, but I can't leave until I've danced at least two sets. That is my father's rule, although it seems the rules are changing. Where would you rather be?"

They parted, and Neil danced with a blushing blond girl, then he was beside Juliana again. "A pit of vipers? A French dungeon?"

"You hate it that much?"

"I'm a bastard. We are not supposed to show our faces in polite society."

They parted again, and Lady Juliana stared at him intently across the path for the dancers. Then it was their turn to promenade. "I suppose you expect me to apologize."

"You are not that predictable, Lady Juliana."

"Good. Because I will not apologize. You are every inch the man any legitimate son is, and you have nothing to be ashamed of. I am glad I asked you to dance."

"That makes one of us."

"We can show everyone what a gentleman you are."

"I think all we will do is give everyone a new topic for gossip. The set is ending, my lady." He bowed and kissed her gloved hand.

"We must take a turn about the room."

"Forgive me if I do not take part in that spectacle."

"I will not." She linked her arm with his, and he was forced either to make a scene or promenade her about the ballroom. As much as he hated the attention he garnered and the false smiles and too-slight bows of the nobility, he could not pretend he did not like having her beside him. She smelled of fresh roses, and when the crowds swelled, she was pushed against him, giving him the impression of lush curves and round softness.

"My lady." A young man stepped before them. To Neil he looked barely out of the schoolroom. "May I have the next dance?"

"No," Neil said at the same time Juliana said, "Yes." She glared at Neil, then looked back at the boy. "Lord Peter, have you met Mr. Wraxall?"

Peter bowed. "An honor, Mr. Wraxall. I studied your accomplishments on the Continent at university. You are a true hero."

"Thank you," Neil said, feeling like an old man.

"He is a hero," Lady Juliana said. "In so many ways." Her dark eyes met his, then she looked back at the boy lord. "Shall we, my lord?"

Lord Peter bowed again and took Lady Juliana's arm, leading her back to the dancing. Neil wished he were on the battlefield. He would have shown Lord Peter a thing or two.

"Didn't expect to see you here."

Neil turned to see Rafe sipping a glass of champagne. He raised it to Neil. "To what do we owe this honor?"

"To the fact that my latest mission is proving more difficult than I expected."

"Ah, yes. The Lady Juliana. Since our conversation in the Billiards Room, I have done a bit of investigating."

"Why?" Neil drawled, watching Juliana laugh and twirl with Lord Peter. Where had Rafe acquired that champagne? Neil needed a bucket.

"Because I am curious by nature. Aren't you the least curious as to what Society says of Lady Juliana?"

"No." It was a lie, but he knew Rafe would tell him anyway.

"She is stubborn and willful, but those qualities can be forgiven because she is so generous and kindhearted. Some say too kindhearted. It is difficult for her to see the bad in anyone. That is a boon for you, is it not?"

Neil cut Rafe a look. "Isn't there some chit looking to toss her skirts up for you?"

"Definitely, but this is vastly more entertaining. I have never seen you jealous."

Neil stiffened. "I am not jealous."

"Then why are your hands balled into fists, and why are you glaring at the Duke of Preston's youngest son like you want to sever his head from his body?"

Neil forced his fists to open. It did not matter to him who Lady Juliana danced with. In a day or so, she would be home and he could forget about her. She was not even his responsibility at the moment. Her father was here. Let him deal with his daughter. "I need a drink," Neil said.

"Words I long to hear. This way, old boy." And Rafe led him toward the card room, where women were in short supply and the brandy was overflowing.

∽

Julia exited the ladies' retiring room, where she had hidden to escape Lord Peter, and moved stealthily toward the ballroom. She had danced her two sets and wanted to return to Sunnybrooke before the terrifying Mr. Mostyn ate the children for a midnight snack. She peered through a crack in the door but didn't spot Mr. Wraxall. And she did not think he would be difficult to spot. In his evening clothes, he had looked even more handsome than usual, a feat she had not thought possible. The black of his coat made his hair look even darker, and the blue of his waistcoat gave his eyes even more depth. He'd secured his hair in a short queue, leaving his cheeks exposed. The chiseled planes were square and strong. If there was a more beautiful specimen of masculinity, she had not found it.

So where had he disappeared to? She was tempted to leave without him, but she did not relish the lecture he would probably give her later.

She shifted slightly to view the room at another angle and collided with a large shape. She stepped back and stared into the smiling face of Mr. Slag.

"What—?" she began, then stopped as she saw all too clearly how he had managed to gain entry to the ball. He was dressed in Viscount Sterling's livery and had probably entered unnoticed by either the guests or staff as the viscount had certainly hired additional servants for the evening.

"Lady Juliana, so good to see you." He took her hand and kissed it. Julia was relieved she wore gloves so she did not have to feel his lips on her skin.

"Mr. Slag, forgive me if I am surprised by your appearance here."

"You thought with that watchdog in your bed, you were safe from me." Slag's lips thinned. "But you won't get away so easily." He might have been smiling, but she could see the flush of color in his cheeks. He was angry. Gone was the pleasant man from her parlor. The man before her was the crime lord, and he was not pleased.

Julia took another step back. Just a few feet away, hundreds of people danced and chatted. And any moment a lady would pass this way to visit the retiring room or a servant would happen by. All she need do was scream, and she could be rid of Slag.

For the moment.

"If you scream now," he murmured as a lady passed them, "I will give you a real reason to scream later."

Julia swallowed the bile in her throat.

"How about a knife in the belly for that little boy who always has his dirty thumb in his mouth? Or maybe a good beating for the tall one with the freckles?"

Charlie and Robbie. Slag was threatening them.

"What do you want?" she asked, her voice steely.

"An answer to my proposal, my lady. Nothing more. Well, that and the head of your soldier on a pike, but all things in time."

"I don't have the money," she said.

"Then I'll join you in bed tonight. Get rid of your soldiers or face the consequences." He stared away.

"Wait!" Julia cried, running after him. A lady returning to the ballroom gave her a disapproving glare. Julia ignored her. "Mr. Slag!"

He turned.

"I will get you the money."

"Tonight?"

"No, I…I need more time."

"At the Darlington musicale. I know you will be there. That's your last chance." He moved closer, his breath on her cheek, smelling of stale onions. "Do not cross me or the little ones' blood is on your hands." He walked away, disappearing through a servants' door that opened out of a panel in the wall.

Julia stood rooted in place, her hands shaking and her knees wobbling.

"Juliana? Is that you?"

Of course her father would find her now. She pressed her lips together, forced a smile, and turned.

"Yes, Papa."

"Are you well?"

"Just a little tired. I hoped Mr. Wraxall could take me home."

"Home?" Her father's eyes lit with hope, and Julia felt like the worst villain extinguishing it.

"I meant the orphanage."

"Ah." Her father's face fell. "Won't you ever come home, Julia? I worry for your safety."

Not he missed her, not he cared for her—he worried for her safety. He was far too busy with his own pursuits to waste time on love or affection. Of course, he was right to worry for her safety when one of the most dangerous crime lords in the city had threatened her. But what was she to do? Slag wanted a fortune. Her father did not have it. She'd managed his household for years, and most of his money was tied up in land and repairs to his various properties. If she told him she needed money, he would only force her to return home, and then who would protect the children?

"I cannot come home right now, Papa. The children need me. And anyway," she said with what she hoped was a bright smile, "Mr. Wraxall is making certain we are safe and secure. Have you seen him?"

"He is in the card room. I will fetch him for you. You will be at the Darlington musicale?"

"Of course," she said. What other choice did she have?

In the carriage, Wraxall watched her. Julia stared out the window, but she could feel his gaze on her. She wanted to ignore it, but she had shouldered the weight of Slag's threats on her own long enough. She needed help, and Wraxall was all she had.

"I have a problem," she said, glancing at him.

"Just one?"

She glared at him. "If all you want to do is mock me…"

He crossed to sit beside her, which made her all the more aware of his solid form and the delicious scent of him. "I apologize. What is troubling you?"

"I saw Mr. Slag at the ball."

Wraxall showed no reaction. "Go on."

"He was dressed as a servant, and he made…certain threats."

"What does he want?"

"A thousand pounds."

"I see. Have you asked your father for it?"

She blew out a breath. "He doesn't have it."

"And even if he did, he would lock you up rather than give it to you."

She turned to him, her knees colliding with his. "Yes! And then what would happen to the boys?"

"What will Slag do if you do not give him the blunt? Or is there another way to pay him?"

She looked up and into his eyes. The carriage was dark, but the lamps showed her enough. Wraxall knew Slag had given her another option. "How did you know?"

"One look at you and how could I not know? He wants you in his bed."

She nodded, feeling her cheeks heat. "I have to give him the money at the musicale or he will…." She gestured vaguely.

Wraxall caught her hand. "He will never touch you, Lady Juliana. Never." He pulled her closer so she was almost flush with his chest. "Do you hear me?"

"Yes." Her voice sounded faint and her breath came in quick snatches. Wraxall's breath had quickened as well. Her gaze lowered to his lips, and she wondered what it would be like if he touched her. If he kissed her.

The carriage stopped, and she lurched against him. Wraxall caught her, his touch on her lingering, and then, quite suddenly, he released her and, opening the door, leaped down. Julia took a shaky breath and gave him her hand as she descended.

The rain had begun again, and she hurried toward the orphanage door. The coachman gave Wraxall an umbrella, and he used it to shield her from the worst of it. A moment later, they stepped into the dark vestibule.

It was empty.

Julia looked about. Everything seemed in order. "Where is Mr. Mostyn?" she asked, removing her cloak. She looked everywhere but Wraxall's face, not wanting the feelings she'd had in the carriage to rush back at her.

"Stay here," Wraxall ordered her. He moved toward

the dining room and parlor, and she followed. With a scowl, he looked over his shoulder. "I said, *stay*."

"I am not a dog!"

"A dog would have more sense."

"If you wake this child, I will break both of your necks," came a low rumble from the parlor. Julia grabbed Wraxall's arm, but he just grinned.

"It's Mostyn."

Julia was not so relieved. She stayed close, following Wraxall into the parlor. There, on her couch, sat the big brute of a man, Charlie curled up in his lap. Julia blinked, not certain whether she should believe her eyes.

"Ewan, this is a side of you I had not seen," Wraxall said.

The blond man narrowed his eyes. "He said he needed a hug to fall asleep." Mostyn's voice was as hard as rock. "He looked like he might cry. I did what was necessary under the circumstances."

Julia had to bite her lip to keep from smiling. Mr. Mostyn was not so bad after all. Surely he could have put Charlie to bed after the boy had fallen asleep. She was willing to wager he had not minded hugging the boy as much as he pretended.

"You're a good man, Protector," Wraxall said. "A fine soldier."

"Can someone take this…child now?" Mostyn looked down at Charlie pointedly.

Julia stepped forward and gathered the boy in her arms. "I will put him to bed. Good night, Mr. Mostyn. Thank you."

He made a rough noise, and she left the men to themselves as she carried the warm bundle to his bed.

Nine

JULIA USUALLY SLEPT LIKE A CAT SNUGGLED BESIDE THE fire when it rained. She didn't understand why people said *slept like a baby*, as little Davy had shown her that babies were not good sleepers by any stretch of the imagination. They awoke at all hours and slept only in short bursts.

Still, she wouldn't have traded her time with Davy for all the sleep in the world. If she could only see him once more, she would have consented to a lifetime of restless sleep. But as the devil hadn't yet approached her with that offer, she usually slept well. Charlie or the younger boys sometimes woke her when they had nightmares, but no one had called out tonight. Everyone slept peacefully while the rain tapped a lulling beat against the roof and windows.

So why was she lying awake, eyes wide open, in her bed?

"Wraxall," she muttered. This was his fault. She couldn't sleep because she kept thinking of the way he'd touched her in the carriage. She kept imagining him kissing her. Had he stayed at the orphanage tonight or gone home? He wouldn't have left her alone after Slag's threats. Would he? Perhaps she would tiptoe down and check.

Julia talked herself out of leaving her room and her warm bed and then talked herself back into it again before finally tossing off her counterpane, pulling on her robe and slippers, and cracking her door open. She held a candle with one hand and kept her hand on the latch with the other. The corridor was dark and deserted. What had she expected? Wraxall prowling outside her room or that of the boys? A small voice inside her head warned her to go back to sleep. If she did find Wraxall, he would only want to discuss Slag's ultimatum more, and she didn't have any answers or solutions. She could not go home, and she could not stay here.

Perhaps she should be certain Wraxall was still here. She did have a responsibility to keep the boys safe from Slag. Pulling the door open farther, she stepped into the corridor and shone the light on the pail outside her room. It was only about a quarter full of water, which meant someone had emptied it recently. The older boys usually took turns checking the pails, pots, and pans when it rained, but she hadn't reminded them tonight. Had they done it of their own volition or had Wraxall ordered them to empty the water buckets? Perhaps he had done them all himself, which meant he'd been right outside her room recently.

And why should that thought make her belly jump and flutter?

Seeking Wraxall out was a bad idea. The way he'd looked at her in the carriage, the way her breath caught when he came around a corner, the way her heart melted when she saw him showing one of the boys how to use a tool or make a repair—these were all warning signs that she should keep her distance. She, of all women, knew what villainy men were capable of. Why would she open herself to more pain than she'd already endured?

Because she was a fool, just as Harriett had been. Julia held the candle with one hand and her robe with the other as she descended the back stairs that led to the kitchen. But she was an even bigger fool than Harriett, because Julia knew the dangers awaiting her while Harriett had not.

The kitchen was empty, as expected, and Julia moved silently into the main wing of the building, passing the dining room and parlor doors. When she reached the entryway, it was empty. Mr. Wraxall was not keeping vigil over the front door. She turned in a circle, making certain to search the dark corners. Perhaps he had returned home after all.

What should she do? What if Slag was outside right now? Had Wraxall fixed all the door and window locks? She would check on the children. She would make sure all of them were safe in their beds, and then she would find a large blunt object and keep watch herself. She was about to ascend the main stairway when it occurred to her that when she'd passed the parlor, a faint light had spilled from the doorway. Wouldn't he have banked the fire before leaving? The fire shouldn't have still burned unless...

Julia tiptoed back the way she'd come, pausing right before the doorway of the parlor.

Please not Slag, she prayed. *Please.*

She leaned forward, inching closer to the open seam. She could almost see inside. The fire was still burning—

"Come in, Lady Juliana."

Julia jumped and almost dropped the candle she held. She fumbled, barely catching it, but managing to blow it out so at least if it fell it would not catch the rug on fire. Her heart raced but not from fear. That had not been Slag's voice.

She took her time righting the candle, and when she had secured it again, and then again, she swallowed and looked up and into the parlor. In the firelight, she could make out the outline of the man seated in a chair before the fire, his legs stretched out in front of him, his coat, waistcoat, and neckcloth removed.

"No, thank you," she said hastily. "I thought I heard a noise and came to check all was as it should be."

"You heard nothing of the sort. All has been quiet as a graveyard. You came looking for me."

She stood in the doorway, wishing he hadn't chosen to sit before the fire. She couldn't see his expression. "Not at all. Why would I look for you?"

"You tell me." But he must have already known.

She should return to bed. She should definitely not continue with this conversation. But then she said, "Very well. I wondered if you had gone home."

"You are not so fortunate."

Julia stepped into the room and saw that not only had he removed his coat, but he'd also rolled his sleeves to the elbow. His face was such a lovely, sun-kissed shade of bronze, and as the firelight played off the bronze skin of his arms, she wondered if the rest of him was that color as well.

And that was a thought better not explored further.

"Won't you try and sleep?" she asked. He looked tired, his face drawn and his eyes heavy-lidded.

"No. The pails should be emptied about once an hour."

"The older boys can take turns doing that. All of us, except the little ones, have taken a turn in the past. If we all take one hour, no one is disturbed more than once."

Wraxall shook his head. "The boys worked hard today. They need their sleep, as do you."

Julia moved closer to him. "You worked equally hard, and you did not sleep last night."

"Leave it be, my lady," he said, his tone one of warning. As if to emphasize his point, he pulled his legs in and sat forward.

"Perhaps I should keep you company. How am I to sleep when you sit up and keep watch?"

He blew out a breath and raked his hands through his hair, pausing to hold his head in his hands and shake it. "Why can't you be one of those biddable females? Why don't you do as you're told or, better yet, stay in your room?" He looked up at her. "You shouldn't be in here with me, alone, and in only your nightclothes. Aren't you concerned about propriety and your reputation and all the other rot you females hold so high?"

"Why can't you be one of those charming gentlemen who allows a lady to help him so she *can* return to her room and observe propriety?"

"Because I'm not!" He stood and stalked toward her. "I'm a soldier, and I'll always be a soldier. I don't need help or company. I will do my duty until you come to your senses and return home."

But he knew as well as she that she could not return home. Perhaps he felt the same anguish she did, the same tearing of loyalties. He loomed over her, and though she refused to step back and show her trepidation, she did lower her voice. "I thought you sold your commission. You are no longer a soldier. Is it possible you are here because you want to be here, not out of duty? Perhaps you are coming to care for the children too."

He laughed, a bitter laugh that made her shiver. "If you mean do I pity them, you have it correct. I pity them and every bastard ever born."

She stiffened. Why must he behave this way? Why could he not see that the circumstances of his birth did not define him? "Then go home. I don't want your misplaced sense of honor."

His fists clenched and his jaw tightened. If he'd been another man, she might have been frightened, but she knew he would never hurt her. "I will not leave you until you do," he said through clenched teeth.

"Then at least sleep."

"Go back to bed."

"Why won't you sleep?"

"Good God, woman! You are every bit as stubborn as they say."

She put her hands on her hips. "I prefer the term 'persistent.'" She bit her lip. "Is it Slag? Is that why you won't sleep? You think he will come here tonight?"

He closed his eyes as though in surrender. "No." His voice sounded weary and ragged. "No. It's not

Slag or the rain or a sense of duty. It's here." He tapped on his head. "Here is where the problem lies. You see, my brainbox remains firmly entrenched in battle, and I'd rather not wake the whole building with my shouts and screams. Is that answer enough for you?" He turned his back on her, staring into the fire.

Julia pressed her hands over her mouth. "Oh, Mr. Wraxall." She reached for him—to do what she was not certain—but he moved out of her reach.

"I don't want your pity." One hand went to the back of his neck. "God, but I need a drink. I'm too damn sober, and everything is too damn sharp and clear."

"I might have some wine in the kitchen—"

He held his hand up to stay her flight. "If I want a drink, I can procure it myself. If I can't go a few days without a bottle of Blue Ruin, then I'm a sadder case than even Rafe makes me out to be."

"Who is Rafe?"

He turned to look at her, seeming almost surprised she was still in the room. "Go to bed, Lady Juliana, before I say or do something else I regret."

"You've done nothing to regret, Mr. Wraxall. I am glad you confided in me. If you have nightmares, why not try some warm milk? My governess used to—"

The look he gave her made her close her mouth. "Do you think these are the stuff *warm milk* will cure? These aren't mere whimsy. I relive battles and ambushes and slaughter in my dreams. My mind doesn't conjure these horrors. The blood and the carnage were quite real."

"And you wake screaming?" she asked, her voice barely more than a whisper.

"I'm not the ideal houseguest."

"Certainly you don't have these dreams every night."

"No, but I'd rather not risk it tonight."

Julia stepped back, startled at his abrupt answer. "Why—"

He turned his back on her. "Go to bed, my lady."

She almost marched out of her room and back to her own chamber. Let him stay awake all night. He deserved his exhaustion if this was how he showed gratitude. But she didn't leave. Her feet stayed rooted in place, her hands clenched tightly at her sides.

"Of course you won't go," he said. "I would have had more success if I'd asked you to stay." He glanced at her over his shoulder.

She lifted her chin, refusing to back down. "If you don't want to sleep, that is fine, but I will stay and keep you company. It's the least I can do when—" She broke off.

He rounded on her. "When I am the only thing keeping Slag from coming in here and doing whatever the hell he likes to you?"

"I don't want to talk about him tonight."

"We are both speaking of things we would rather not, it seems." He stalked toward her, forcing her to back up until she was flush against the wall beside the door. "But understand this. I will never allow Slag to touch you. Never. I will do whatever is necessary to protect you from him, from your soft heart, and even from me."

"You?" she breathed. She could barely say the words. Her heart pounded and her lungs struggled to take in air. He was so close, his eyes so blue, his body so large and so warm and so close.

"Yes, me. At the moment, I have a tenuous hold on my control at best. Leave before I do something we will both regret. The very thing we both wanted in the carriage."

"What is that?" she asked, her breath catching in her throat.

His eyes blazed, and she realized she had challenged him yet again. Before she could take the words back or even flee the room, Wraxall put both hands on the wall behind her, effectively pinning her in. Taking another step closer, his body pressed against hers with a delicious warmth that made her realize exactly how cold she'd been before he'd touched her.

"I have wanted to kiss you since the first time I saw you." His finger traced her cheek. "You had flour here." He trailed to her chin, the pad of his finger burning a path along her skin. "Porridge here." He looked down, his finger flitting down her neck with a slowness that made her tremble. "And your dress…"

Julia closed her eyes. She was so warm that if he touched her body, she feared she might spark and flare like a newly lit candle. But his hand stopped at the vee of her robe.

"I looked a mess," she whispered.

"You looked irresistible." His mouth lowered toward hers, and she knew he would kiss her. She'd been kissed before, and she could easily avoid this kiss by turning her head and offering her cheek instead. Wraxall gave her plenty of time to avoid the kiss, taking his time and making his intention clear.

Julia knew she should turn her head. Better yet, she should shove him back and chastise him for daring to take such liberties. That was exactly what she had planned to do if a man ever attempted to kiss her again.

But for some reason, she could not turn her head. She could not make her legs run away. She could do nothing but look into his bluer-than-blue eyes and hold her breath.

When his mouth finally met hers, it was with a soft, tentative brush. Oh, there would be no denying she had known his intentions or not wanted his kisses. He gave her every opportunity to refuse.

"Slag will never touch you like this," he murmured.

"No," she agreed. Her lips tingled as he swept his mouth over hers, then pressed more firmly. One of his hands slid down the wall and came to rest on her waist. He made a sound low in his throat as his hand touched the silky material of her robe, and then he cupped her and pulled her flush against him.

"Or like this."

Julia gasped as her body pressed against his hard lines. She had known he was not a man who'd spent his life in idleness, but now she could feel the evidence of his exertions in every hard ridge and plane of his muscled torso.

His mouth teased hers as he explored her lips with his. He sucked and nipped and finally his tongue slid along the seam of her lips, coaxing them open. Julia tried to pull back. She had been kissed, but this was more than kissing. This was far too intimate.

"Kiss me back," he murmured, his warm breath tickling her cheek. "Show me what you like. What Slag will never taste."

She didn't know what she liked. No man had ever

asked, and she'd not thought it mattered. She did like the press of his lips on hers, not rough and demanding but coaxing. His question both thrilled and terrified her. "I don't know," she whispered.

"Then let me show you what I have been wanting to do for two days."

"I shouldn't."

"No. You shouldn't." His voice was black velvet caressing her as surely as the hand on her lower back made soothing circles, branding her through the thin layers of her robe and night rail. "You really shouldn't."

And that was all it took. Her father had always called her obstinate and headstrong in part because her first reaction when someone told her no was to raise her chin and do whatever it was she'd been ordered not to do anyway.

She might be three and twenty now, no longer a child, but she still could not abide being told what she should and should not do. Something defiant and rebellious took her over when she heard those words. Instead of doing what she had planned—pushing him away—she brought her hand up from where she'd clenched it at her side and fisted it in the hair at the nape of his neck.

His hair was surprisingly soft and silky, and she twined it around one finger, pulling his head down and closer to hers. Then she kissed him back. First she simply pressed her lips to his. He made no objection, though she'd felt him stiffen slightly, as though in surprise. He didn't even move to kiss her back. He made no move at all, except that after her lips joined his and they stood there, joined, his hand curled against her back.

The pleasure of that simple movement rushed through her, and she wanted more. She wanted to be closer to him. She wanted both his arms around her, holding her, touching her.

Her mouth moved against his and then parted slowly. He seemed to hold his breath until she screwed up her courage and touched his lip with the tip of her tongue.

And then everything seemed to happen far too quickly.

Ten

Neil had held himself so still and so tightly he was all but vibrating. When the woman had slid her hand into his hair, tickling the back of his neck, he had almost pounced on her. And then when she'd kissed him, he'd wanted to devour her. He'd held himself in check, not wanting to scare her, until she'd darted that small pink tongue out and slicked it against him.

That was when he lost all control. No man could have controlled himself under those circumstances and with that sort of temptation. He held her ripe body in his arms, nothing but thin layers of silk and lace—and God, he knew what that lace looked like—between them. She was soft and warm, and she smelled sweet and clean. Perhaps if he buried himself in her, he'd forget the stench of cannon smoke and burning flesh.

He lifted her off her feet and pressed her hard against the wall as his mouth came down to claim hers. He'd been playing with her before, giving her a chance to flee, giving her a taste of danger, but he was through with games. He took her mouth as a parched man takes his first sips of honeyed water. His mouth all but invaded hers, not softly or lovingly but with a need that was almost more than Neil could control.

How long since he'd felt such a need for a woman? Had he ever felt this ferocity of need? He slanted his lips over hers, invading her mouth with his tongue. He'd been half-afraid she'd fight him, but her tongue lashed his right back. Her lips met his with an ardor that mirrored his own. Her grip on his hair was so tight it hurt, but he welcomed the pain. It kept him centered, kept him from losing himself completely.

He might want her with a fierceness for which he had no compare, but he still had his limits. He was no Slag. He would not take her. If she was a virgin, he would not be the one to rob her of her innocence.

Their mouths met again and again, and Neil could not seem to have his fill of her. He was a man who had perfected the art of kissing. For most men it was an appetizer, but for him it had often served as the main course. He knew how to tease and tantalize with his mouth and his tongue, but he could not seem to control his movements. He could think nothing of skill or giving pleasure; he could only take and take and take from those sweet, supple lips. He tried to slow the kiss, to draw it out, to pull away from her lips so he might kiss her throat or the hollow behind her ear. No matter how he tried, he could not make himself leave her lips. He told himself *One more kiss, one more kiss* a dozen times and still his mouth sought hers.

Finally, she was the one who pulled away. His vision was blurry, but he could see the color high in her cheeks and the way her breath hitched in her throat. Slowly he became aware that he'd forced her into the position of wrapping her legs about his waist so she might keep from falling. His erection was cradled between them, and though he had no intention of freeing his cock from his trousers, if he had, he would have easily been able to thrust into her.

He looked down at their joined bodies and immediately wished he hadn't. Her robe had fallen open, and the lace across the bodice of her night rail concealed very little. Her pale breasts spilled from the lace, the pink nipples pressing their hard tips against the intricate pattern.

"I can't breathe," she whispered. "I can't think."

Neither could he, but he couldn't seem to find the words. Nor could he drag his gaze from the lovely expanse of flesh where her robe had opened.

"Put me down," she ordered.

Neil gritted his teeth, but he obeyed both out of respect and out of habit. He forced himself to step back and to separate his body from hers. It proved harder than he'd expected. Far from feeling sated after touching her, kissing her, and feeling her skin beneath his fingers, he only wanted more of her.

Lady Juliana slid toward the door, and Neil took another step back, proving he would not snatch her back into his embrace. "I didn't think my touch so distasteful to you, my lady," he said as she all but stumbled over her feet to move out of his reach.

"It wasn't distasteful at all." She pulled the edges of her robe together, covering herself. Neil felt the loss of the sight of those perfect breasts acutely. "That's the problem."

"It is a problem," Neil agreed.

"It cannot happen again." She kept her hand at her throat, clutching her robe as though it might shield her from her attraction to him. And that was what it was. He knew what he'd felt when he'd kissed her. What he'd felt when *she* had kissed *him*. She was attracted to him and desired him as much as he wanted her.

"How do you think to prevent it? There's obviously some sort of"—he gestured to the space separating them—"pull between us."

She straightened her shoulders. "Well, we shall simply have to ignore that…pull, as you call it. We are both adults. I am a lady and you a gentleman. Surely we can control our baser instincts."

When she spoke like that, so haughty and self-righteous, he felt he would rather strangle her than kiss her. But when he looked down to avoid glaring directly at her, he noticed she had lost her slippers and stood barefoot on the carpet. Her toes were small and round and peeking prettily out from under the white folds of her robe.

And just like that, he wanted her again.

"We should set an example for the children," she said, warming to her topic. "Surely they have seen the worst in humanity. We should strive to show them the best and the purest."

Neil looked up at her, one brow rising. "If you are looking for a paragon of virtue, I am not he."

Her mouth turned down. "I only meant—"

"I'm a former soldier, my lady. I only survived because of my, as you put it, baser instincts. I'm not proud of all I've done, but neither do I feel like I have to pretend to be something I am not so that children who are unlikely ever to overcome the stigma of their birth can be presented some unattainable myth of morality."

She drew in a breath, and Neil steeled himself for the lecture to come. But instead of railing at him, she seemed to deflate as quickly as a punctured balloon. "You are correct. None of us is perfect. You are a hero and—"

Neil laughed. "Hero? What do you know of me that you think I am a hero?"

She gave him an annoyed look. "I did read the letters of introduction my father sent. You served in the war against Napoleon. My father said you were instrumental in his defeat and showed uncommon valor. Those were his exact words. My father is many things, but he is not the sort of man to give praise lightly."

"What do you know of the war?"

She paused, not seeming to know where to begin.

"Have you ever heard of Lieutenant Colonel Draven?" he asked.

She shook her head.

"The Survivors?"

"The Survivors? It sounds like a name people might give to the boys here."

It did at that, and it would have been no less accurate for these unwanted children than it had been for his troop of younger sons of nobility. "It's what we called ourselves." Neil moved closer to the fire. Without her body pressed against his, he suddenly felt chilled. He could see her shivering and gestured for her to come closer.

She did, but she moved warily, as though he might pounce on her at any moment. Or perhaps she feared she would pounce? He could only dream.

He leaned against her desk and she sat in the chair closest to the fire. When he was warm again, he cleared his throat, trying to decide how much to tell her. "We started out as a troop of thirty. We were chosen by Lieutenant Colonel Draven. He selected me first and asked me to lead. I picked some of the other men, men I knew or had served with, and others he chose because they had special skills. He'd been asked to form a troop like ours weeks before he ever tapped me, and he'd been watching and making lists of men who would serve our purposes."

Her brow wrinkled. "A troop like yours? What sort of troop was it?"

"A suicide troop," he answered baldly. "Draven looked for the best, the brightest, and the expendable. None of us were expected to survive the first mission, much less the entire war."

She stared at his face. "But why would any man agree to serve in such a group?"

"Not every man Draven or I asked agreed. All of the men who did agree had one response in common."

"What was that?"

"Draven began every interview with the same question: *Are you afraid to die?* The men who said no, the men who had the skills we needed, were the men chosen."

She looked away from him and into the fire, seeming to consider all he had said for some time. The fire popped and crackled, and Neil began to think she wouldn't respond at all. But then she looked up at him. "And you answered no? Is it true? You aren't afraid to die?"

Neil gave her a wry smile. "Oh, I'm afraid to die. I've seen men die in the most horrible ways you can imagine. I'd be a fool not to fear death after what I've seen."

"But you said—"

"I never said I wasn't a fool. More accurately, I was half out of my mind. When Draven approached me about leading the troop, I was half-mad with grief and rage. I wanted to die. He saw that."

She shot up quite suddenly. "And so he used that grief against you and sent you to your death?"

Was she indignant on his behalf? Neil wasn't certain how to respond. No one had ever become indignant for him before.

"You have it wrong, sweetheart," he said. "Draven didn't send me to die. He gave me a reason to live."

Neil had never thought of it this way before, but it was true. Draven's missions had given Neil new purpose, new focus. He'd been able to think of something beyond the death of Christopher. He had still wanted to avenge Christopher's death, but he'd also wanted to keep his men alive. The more he'd come to know the men of his troop—Ewan, the Protector; Rafe, the Seducer; and the others like Jasper, Phineas, Duncan, and Nash—the more he'd wanted to keep them alive. Draven had saved Neil, even when Neil hadn't wanted to be saved.

But it begged the question, the one Neil asked when he was sober and sweating from the nightmares: What had Draven saved him for?

"Don't call me sweetheart."

Neil cut his gaze to her. He'd almost forgotten she was there. Almost. "My apologies, Lady Juliana."

"Julia," she said, shuffling uncomfortably. "I suppose if we are to live so closely for the next few days, you should call me Julia."

He nodded. "Julia suits you." It did. With her wild, copper hair—the wildness being partly his fault—her deep-brown eyes, and her wide smile, Julia had an informal and nurturing sound that fit her. "But paragon of virtue that you are, I'll continue to refer to you as Lady Juliana."

She scowled at him. "I simply thought we might be friends."

He raised a brow. "I have friends. I don't want to kiss them." And that was the least of what he imagined doing with Juliana. No, he did not feel *friendly* toward her at all.

"Thank you for telling me about your part in the war. The boys are fortunate to have you here. They need a father figure."

Neil held up his hand. "Don't imagine my presence here to be any more than it is. I am here to keep you safe from Slag and to bring you home to your father. That is all."

She took in a breath. "No, I wouldn't want you to do any more than what my father hired you to do." She tried to walk past him, but he grabbed her arm. That was a mistake. The softness of her skin and the feel of her warm flesh beneath his reminded him he wanted to kiss her again. But she did not turn to look at him, her gaze fixed on the door.

"I am not a servant to be hired. I'm here as a favor because your father and mine are such good friends. And if you want the truth of it, I would prefer—I think we would all prefer—you simply go home."

She turned to look directly at him then. "I am never going home. *This* is where I belong. These boys need me." She pulled her arm away, cradling it as though he had burned her.

"Do they need you or do you need them?" Neil asked.

Without an answer, she swept out of the room.

Neil was left to his own thoughts and desires. The empty room seemed larger without Julia in it. He sat back on the couch and stared at the fire. Why the devil had he kissed her? He was a man in control of his passions, so why had he allowed them to get the better of him tonight? Yes, she was attractive. Yes, she made his blood thrum when she was near. Yes, he wanted to both throttle her and trace her curves with his hands, but that didn't mean he should act on those impulses. Her father had asked Neil to keep her safe, not seduce her.

If Neil could just convince her to go home to her father, this would all be over. She felt some loyalty to the boys. That was understandable, but they could find another woman—or, better yet, a man—to run the orphanage. She could go back to…whatever it was she did before, and he could go back to…

What the hell did he have to go back to? Nightmares? Playing billiards with Rafe? Having the occasional meal with Ewan and telling war stories with Jasper? And what else was he supposed to do?

He couldn't go back to the army, and he wasn't suited to the clergy. Besides, the allowance his father gave him was enough to support Neil twice over. As long as he didn't see the need to become an icon of fashion or gamble excessively, Neil would never have to work again.

Which meant he was still thirty and completely without purpose.

He sat up straighter. But that did not mean this orphanage was his purpose. He'd rather face the French army again than spend the rest of his days tucking children in for naps and ensuring the pet rats were where they ought to be. And yet he couldn't deny that in only two days, he'd stopped looking at the boys as a passel of bastards and saw them more as individuals. He no longer remembered his own shame growing up every time he looked at them, but neither did he want to adopt any of them.

Except possibly Charlie. He liked that boy. He'd never seen anyone able to do so many chores one handed, since his thumb was always in his mouth. Neil remembered sucking his thumb when he'd been young. But long before he was four, he'd had his knuckles bruised and cut every time his thumb snaked its way into his mouth. He remembered being woken in the middle of the night to have his knuckles rapped once because his thumb had sneaked into his mouth when he'd been asleep. It had all been done by his father's order, and it certainly hadn't made Neil love the man, who was a stranger at best and a tyrant at worst. He might have been raised in a home and given all the food, clothing, and education necessary for a boy, but Neil hadn't grown up with any more of a family than these orphans.

His thoughts were interrupted by the squeak of one of the boards on the stairs. He'd been up and down those front stairs enough to know every sound the boards made. He'd repaired the rotting boards, but he hadn't fixed any of the squeaks on the sound planks. One never knew when one might need advanced warning.

Rising silently, Neil moved out of the parlor and into the entryway. He kept to the shadows, his back against the wall as he watched the lone boy make his way down the steps. The boy was stealthy, no doubt about it. He'd made the error of stepping on one creaky stair, but he didn't repeat his mistake. Neil watched as he carefully skipped or sidestepped other creaky stairs.

It was the shaggy mane of hair that finally identified Walter, even in the low light. Neil had known it wasn't the tall boy—whatever his name was—but he thought it might be the helpful one. Except that one had straight hair that looked to have seen a barber at some point recently. Neil should have known it was Walter. The boy had been trouble from the first.

Walter jumped off the last stair, obviously elated that he'd made it, and made straight for the front door. Before he could reach for the new bolt, Neil cleared his throat.

Walter froze.

"Where do you think you are going?" Neil asked, moving into the entryway, which was periodically lit up from the bolts of lightning outside.

Walter spun around. "Nowhere." He started back

for the steps, obviously intending to pretend the whole incident hadn't happened and he was going back to bed.

"Hold it." Neil's voice was all it took for the boy to freeze. "I asked you a question, and I want an answer."

The boy stood in front of the stairs, head down and shoulders hunched.

Neil moved closer. "I'm interested in where a child of eight—"

"Nine," Walter corrected.

"—nine then. Where a child of nine thinks to go in the middle of the night and during a rainstorm. Why aren't you sleeping?"

"The thunder woke me." The answer was given quickly. Too quickly.

"And so you decided to take a stroll in the storm?"

"I was…I was walking in my sleep."

Neil nodded, coming to stand in front of Walter. "Amazing how you can avoid the stairs that creak even when you're walking in your sleep."

Walter's head jerked up. "Fine. So you caught me. It's not a crime to go for a walk."

"No, but it seems to me you are asking for trouble if you go out in the middle of the night in London, especially in this area of London."

"I can take care of myself."

"And how will you do that?"

"I can fight."

Neil nodded. "Let me see."

Walter frowned. "What do you mean?"

"Imagine I walk up to you and threaten you. What do you do? Run?"

"I don't need to run." He pulled a knife from his pocket.

Neil eyed it, unimpressed. "So that's where all the knives in the kitchen have gone."

"I didn't take them all!"

"Who else has one?"

Walter looked away. "I'm no snitch."

"No, you're a fighter. You know how to use that knife?"

"I can hold my own."

"Show me."

Walter stared at him, uncomprehending. In the distance, thunder boomed again.

"Defend yourself with the knife," Neil said.

"But—"

"I give you leave. Cut me, prick me, do your worst."

Walter narrowed his eyes. *Clever boy*, Neil thought. He knew there was a condition coming. "But if I manage to come away unscathed—"

"Un…?"

"Unhurt. Untouched. If I come away intact *and* I am able to take the knife away from you, you tell me where you were off to."

"Sure." Lightning flashed, the light illuminating Walter's cocksure expression.

"The truth, Walter. Give me your word."

"You'll never get this knife away from me."

"Then you have no reason not to swear to me."

Still Walter hesitated, which Neil took as a good sign. The boy considered his word to be binding. He was not yet beyond reform.

"And if I do cut you? If I keep the knife?" Walter asked.

"Then you're free to go. No questions asked and no retribution."

Walter frowned at him.

"That means I won't try and hurt you. No revenge. Agreed?"

Walter nodded.

"Then go ahead. Come after me."

Walter took a moment to study him—another good sign in Neil's opinion. The boy didn't lunge or act without thinking. There was hope for him yet. And then Walter seemed to back away, almost as though he would run. Instead, he pivoted and slashed out at Neil. It was a good move. A good bluff.

But not good enough.

Neil stepped to the side, easily avoiding Walter's strike. When Walter's arm jabbed at the air where Neil had been, Neil reached out, twisted Walter's wrist, and the knife dropped neatly into Neil's other hand. Neil twirled the knife and pocketed it.

Walter stared for a long moment. "You cheated."

Neil crossed his arms. "That's a serious accusation. I'd think before making it if I were you."

Walter opened his mouth as though to protest again, then closed it. He muttered something that sounded like *You didn't cheat*, then lifted his face to glower at Neil. "How did you do that?"

"Maybe I'll teach you some day. But right now, you owe me an answer."

"I don't have to tell you anything." Walter crossed his arms over his chest.

"You gave me your word."

Walter seemed to consider this. Neil waited. Neil felt a growing sense of anticipation. He didn't know why he should care whether the boy honored his word or not, but he wanted Walter to do the noble thing.

Finally, Walter let out a huff of air. "You won. Fair and square. I'll tell you that I was on my way to the Ox and Bull."

Slag's place. Neil tensed. Had Slag not only recruited Goring, but the children as well?

"Are you part of Slag's gang?"

Walter shrugged.

"You want to be."

Walter looked up at him. "People are afraid of Mr. Slag. If I work with him, he'll keep me safe. I'll be one of his boys."

Neil nodded. He and Walter had more in common than Neil had expected. Both of them longed for family. Joining Slag's gang of criminals wasn't the way to find it.

"And what sort of work would you do for Slag? Pick pockets? Pilfer shops? I'm sure he has a dozen rackets for a boy of your age."

"He can use me."

"And that's exactly what he'll do. You steal for him, and if you're caught, you suffer the consequences while he gets rich."

"I'm young. The judges are lien…lenen… They go easy on you if you're young."

"They might not give you as much jail time, but you'll find yourself in Newgate for a few months. Do you have any idea what happens to young boys like you in Newgate?"

Walter swallowed.

Neil nodded. "So you have an idea. It's not a place you want to spend even one dark night, much less sixty of them."

"Maybe I'm willing to take my chances. What have I got to lose?"

Those were words Neil knew well. How many times had he said them? Thought them? At his lowest, his most hate-filled, Neil hadn't thought he had anything to lose. But that was before the nightmares and the skittishness every time someone shot a rifle. Neil hadn't realized he'd lose the men he counted as close as brothers. He hadn't counted on losing pieces of his heart, bloody shard by bloody shard, every time one of his men died.

"Look around you," Neil said, his voice hoarse from emotion. Walter didn't seem to notice. Neil put his arm around the boy's shoulders, turning him so he could catch a glimpse of the orphanage. "This is what you have to lose."

Walter snorted. "A leaky, old building filled with a bunch of smelly boys? I say good riddance."

Neil held Walter in place when the boy would have shrugged him off. "You're not looking hard enough, Walter."

Walter stilled and looked around again. "I don't see anything special."

"I do. You are fortunate to have a roof over your head."

"A leaky roof."

"Not when I am through with it, but I promise you there were nights during the war I would have given all the coin in my pocket for a leaky roof or any sort of roof. You know what else?"

"What?"

"I would have given a month's wages for a bed and a blanket and food in my belly. You have all that."

"They give you some of that in the army, don't they?"

"Of course, but I wasn't in the regular army. I was part of a special troop, and we had to travel light. We slept under the stars or in the rain or in the cold. We didn't have a supply cart to provide us provisions. We bought what we could, begged for some, and stole the rest."

"You stole?"

Neil released Walter and sat on the second to bottom step. Walter sat next to him.

"I stole food, weapons, clothes—whatever I could from the enemy. War doesn't feel quite so honorable when your belly is empty and your feet bare. But you know what got me through?"

"The battles? All the explosions?"

"No." Neil gave him a long look. "My friends. There were thirty of us to start, but only twelve came back. A dozen men, just like you have here."

"Aw, most of these orphans are crybabies. They aren't men."

"Then show them how to be strong. Be a leader. One day they will be men. One day you'll be out of this place. You'll want friends you can trust. Friends who will have your back no matter what happens."

"Do you have friends like that?"

"Absolutely. You met Mr. Mostyn already. When I'm in a scrape, Mostyn and my other friends are the first to come to my aid."

Walter seemed to consider this. "You were the leader? What did they call you? Major?"

Neil shook his head. What had ranks meant when the men died side by side? Neil might have given the final orders, but he dug the graves of the men they lost right beside the rest of the men. "They called me the Warrior."

"Why?"

"Because I had been a soldier before and because…" He considered how to explain the lust for revenge he had felt when he'd first formed the troop. "I was the most devoted to war."

"I could be a warrior," Walter said. "I can fight." He jumped up and moved his feet like a boxer, holding his fists up in front of his face.

"If you want to be a soldier, you'd better stay out of trouble and get an education. Lady Juliana will have a new tutor for you soon."

"Reading and writing and numbers? I don't need any of that."

"Then how do you think to read your orders or write reports or plan troop movements?"

"I don't want to do any of that. I just want to fight."

"Ah, so you want to be an infantry man. I always preferred the cavalry. I was in the Sixteenth Light Dragoons. They're known as the Queen's Lancers." Neil scratched his jaw thoughtfully. "Nothing like riding a horse into the heat of battle and saving the day for the infantry. But you need some education to be a dragoon." One needed money too, but if Walter ever made something of himself, Neil would make sure he was able to buy the commission of his choice. It was the least he could do for a child who understood what it was like to grow up without a family.

"I'll think about it," Walter said, apparently unwilling to commit verbally.

Neil knew the look in the boy's eye. He was intrigued and won over by the image of himself on horseback, charging heroically into battle. "Then back to bed with you. You'll need your rest, because tomorrow, we repair the roof."

Walter pulled a face. "Aww."

"And I'll teach you and the other lads how to behave like soldiers—how to salute, stand at attention, how to march."

"Really? I can't wait!" Walter ran up two steps, then ran back down two and hugged Neil hard. Neil raised his arms but couldn't quite make himself return the embrace. The boy didn't notice. He scampered back up the steps and down the hallway.

Neil didn't think he'd have any more trouble with Walter tonight, but he knew this was only the first sally. And there were more truculent foes to consider too. The tall, sullen boy, to begin with. Billy? Was that his name? He might not give Neil trouble outright, but that was because Billy was still sizing him up.

Neil was sizing him up as well. And Billy wouldn't give up his knives so easily.

Eleven

JULIA DUCKED INTO THE SHADOWS OF THE DRAWING room at the top of the stairs as Walter raced by her. The boy hadn't even known she was there, and neither had Wraxall. Or perhaps she should think of him as the Warrior. She'd gone back to her room after their kiss, and she hadn't been able to calm herself enough to lie down.

No wonder, as she'd never been kissed like that in her life. None of the kisses she'd received previously could even compare, and she would have remembered. Her body still vibrated from the feel of his hands on her. Her lips still tingled. Her heart had continued thumping hard in her chest. No, she would not soon forget the Warrior's kiss. She would still remember how it had made her feel when she was an old, old woman.

She wouldn't have heard the noise if she hadn't still been pacing her room. But she'd heard the voices and crept out, half-afraid Mr. Slag had returned. And despite all her protests about Wraxall's presence here, she was certainly happy he was nearby in that moment.

Except, it hadn't been Slag at all. It had been Wraxall and Walter. Julia had ducked into the drawing room so she wouldn't be spotted. She'd almost revealed herself when Wraxall had challenged Walter to stab him, but she should have known a former soldier could handle a mere boy.

What she couldn't have known was how the boy and the man would melt her heart. She'd never particularly liked Walter. He wasn't sweet like James or adorable like Charlie. He wasn't smart like Michael or helpful like Robbie. And he certainly didn't want her love like Sean or Chester. Walter had always pushed her away. No matter which method she employed to get to know him, he'd wanted nothing to do with her.

But he'd embraced the Warrior. Julia wouldn't have believed it if she hadn't seen it. She almost hadn't, as she should have been hiding and not sticking her head out to watch. What made it even worse was all the weeping. When Wraxall had talked about his friends, tears had streamed from her eyes. She could hear the sorrow in his voice and knew that though he made war sound heroic and glorious to Walter, the Warrior found it anything but.

And that could only mean one thing—Wraxall cared about these children. He might say he couldn't look at them. He might dislike that the orphans reminded him of the circumstances of his own birth, but they were winning him over. Just as the boys had won her over—not that she had been a difficult case. She could grudgingly admit she had a soft heart.

Unfortunately, Wraxall was winning her over too. He'd touched her heart tonight when he'd told

Walter to look around and to think what he had. The man really did see and understand what she was trying to do here and what she wanted to give these boys. And the way he'd put his arm about Walter, the way he'd spoken to him softly but firmly, the way he'd counseled him had melted her heart—Wraxall reminded her of her own father before her mother had died. Then he had been a different man, one who had always taken the time to listen to Julia's stories and praise her childish drawings and encourage her in piano and singing, even though every instructor had declared she had no musical talent.

Not all men were kind like her father, though. She'd come to think of him as the exception, not the rule. Damien Holbrook, Viscount Lainesborough, had showed her what most men were truly like. And who was to say the Warrior was not the same as Lainesborough once the layers were peeled back? Hadn't Damien been charming and kind when he'd courted Harriett? Hadn't he been everything genteel and charming even after they married? Then he'd grown tired of his new wife and Harriett had come home, weeping and inconsolable because the man she'd fallen in love with was not the man she'd married. The man she'd married was selfish, callous, and lecherous. He'd gone to Town for the Season, leaving her at his country home because she had been too ill with the first symptoms of pregnancy to join him at routs and balls.

Instead, he'd found a mistress and all the papers had reported their great love affair, making Harriett look like a complete fool.

And yet, Julia might have forgiven him that behavior. She was not the sort of person to hold a grudge. But she could never, ever forgive what he'd done after Davy had been born.

And now, Julia was tempted to trust this Warrior, this Mr. Wraxall. Though she feared she would be making the same mistake Harriett had made. The sisters had grown up in the *ton*. They had been weaned on scandal, raised on gossip, and educated early as to the differences between rumor and innuendo. That men— and women—were often unfaithful in their marriages was no surprise. Their father had not been quite as censorious with the papers as he ought to have been, and so Julia and Harriett always knew when the Duke (or Earl or Marquess) of Somewhere and the new actress from Drury Lane (or the new opera singer or the new viscountess) took up together, leaving their respective spouses to hold their heads high and ignore the liaison.

It was simply that Julia and Harriett had always considered that sort of behavior to belong to *other* people. Never in their wildest imaginings did they suppose the men they married would be the one to flaunt his paramour. And when Harriett came home in just such a situation, Julia was not as shocked as her sister, but it didn't make the blow any less painful.

If only she'd known that wasn't the worst outrage her brother-in-law would perpetrate on the family.

Wraxall might not look as though he was made from the same cloth as Viscount Lainesborough, but how could she be certain? She'd known him but two days, and she could not allow one dizzying kiss to completely addle her brain and weaken her resolve.

With that thought in mind, she retired to bed. Unfortunately, she did not sleep well, and she was still rather groggy the next morning when Mr. Wraxall knocked on her bedroom door at barely half past seven.

She'd been finishing dressing her hair and thought it must be Charlie, as he was always awake first. "Charlie?" she asked through the door.

"It's Wraxall."

Julia closed her mouth. She'd been about to invite Charlie in, but she could not extend the same invitation to Wraxall. "One moment." She gave her image reflected in the cheval glass an annoyed frown, then hurried to the door, her hair pinned on one side and loose on the other. "Yes?"

Wraxall stared at her. "Is that a new style?"

She blew out a breath. "You know very well it is not. I supposed you had come to my room with a matter of some urgency. If the matter can wait—"

He stuck his hand in the gap between the door and the casement, stopping her from closing the door. "It is a matter of concern. You have a line of women at the kitchen door. As the rain hasn't slowed, I told one of the boys to let them in. They're currently dripping on the kitchen floor."

Julia stared at him. "A group of women in the kitchen?"

"Yes."

"They stood outside in the rain?"

"That's what I said. They're here for the cook's position. What do you want me to do with them?"

The cook's position! Of course. The advertisement must have run in the *Times*. "Send them to the parlor."

He frowned. "Then they'll drip on the rug."

She waved her hands. "Then keep them in the kitchen."

"How do we prepare breakfast?"

Julia let out a huff. Men and their stomachs. But she could hardly be annoyed when Wraxall was apparently prepared—again—to cook the morning meal.

"Very well. What do you suggest we do with them?"

"Put them in the entryway. There aren't any rugs, and they'll be out of the way."

"Fine." She stepped out of her room and closed the door. "You send them to the entryway, and I'll bring the first one to the parlor to interview." She started down the stairs to the kitchen with Wraxall right beside her. Finally, they would have a cook. One of her problems would be solved. She would not think of the other half dozen she faced—namely, what she would do when Slag confronted her at the Darlington musicale.

They reached the bottom of the staircase, but before she could push the door open, Wraxall pulled her back against the wall. Julia caught her breath. She had never thought about how narrow the servants' staircase was or how enclosed and private. She could hear the prospective cooks' voices on the other side of the door, but in the stairwell, she and Wraxall were quite alone.

"What are you doing?" she whispered. Did he think to kiss her again? Her heart clenched with hope while her belly fluttered with fear. She did not want him to kiss her again. Did she? Certainly not here and not now? But her gaze drifted to his mouth and her lips suddenly felt quite dry. She licked them, and

Wraxall's hand, which had been reaching for her, paused in midair.

"Don't tempt me," he murmured, low enough for her to hear but not loud enough to carry over the din in the kitchen. His voice slid over her like warm velvet.

"Tempt you?" she hissed. "If you think I *want* you to kiss me, you are sorely mistaken."

"I don't think you want me to kiss you," he answered.

Well, that was good then. She had at least made one point clear to him the night before.

"I *know* you want me to kiss you."

Julia sputtered, too shocked to form a coherent thought or sentence.

"But that is not my intent." He reached for her again, but this time she caught his wrist.

"Do not touch me."

He lowered his hand and shrugged. "Fine. Go in like that."

"Fine." She turned to the door, then looked back at him. "Like what?"

He twirled a finger, indicating her head. "With that new style in your hair."

Julia gasped, her hands flying to her head. She'd completely forgotten her hair was only half-pinned. And she'd thought he wanted to kiss her. No doubt he wanted to laugh just looking at her in all her ridiculousness.

She moved back from the door, but he anticipated her. "There's no time now," he said and reached for her again. This time, she didn't move quickly enough, and his hand slid into her hair. She stiffened, unable to move as his fingers searched deftly for the pins she'd slid into the mass to secure it. Her scalp tingled as, one by one, he removed the pins, dropping them into his hand. Her hair fell down about her shoulders. When she glanced at him again, she felt very young and somehow more vulnerable with her hair loose.

"That suits you better. You look too matronly with your hair wound on top of your head."

There were more flattering styles, but one needed a hair dresser to achieve those, and before he'd come, Julia hadn't cared what her hair looked like as long as it was out of her way.

"I am the matron of this house, in case you've forgotten."

"Oh, you wouldn't allow me to forget that point. And as such, you cannot interview these ladies with your hair undone. You need...something..." He tapped his finger on his lips. "Ah!"

This time, she swatted his hand away when he reached for her bosom. "What are you about, sir?"

He caught her hand and smiled at her. It was a rogue's smile if she'd ever seen one. She knew she should not have trusted him.

"Not what you are thinking, though you seem to have found a way to make even drab gray look enticing."

She looked down at her muted dress, a dress she had put on without much thought this morning. "What do you—"

He reached for the bodice again, but when she would have slapped him away, he murmured, "Trust me."

Those were exactly the words that should have sounded the alarm in her head and her heart. Instead, she stood completely still while his fingers caught hold of the dark-blue ribbon adorning the dress's bodice. The bodice did not have a particularly low neck, but it was a dress suitable for multiple occasions. As it was morning, and she was supposed to be the head of the orphanage, she had tucked a thin, gauzy fichu in the bodice to cover the modest flesh exposed by the rounded style. Wraxall's fingers crushed the flimsy material as he pulled the ribbon from its bow and gently tugged it free from its moorings.

Julia could not have breathed if she'd wanted to. His fingers, though not straying from their task, burned her flesh wherever they touched. The feel of the ribbon being pulled free made Julia all the more aware that Wraxall might move his hand but a tiny fraction and he would be cupping her breast. She found, inexplicably, that she wanted to feel his hands on her. And the more she imagined his hands on her, the heavier her breasts felt and the more her nipples hardened until the peaks strained against the light fabric of her chemise.

She gulped in a deep breath, feeling much like a fish that's been tossed on land. Horrified, she couldn't help but notice that when she breathed in, the tops of her breasts rose from the dress's bodice and encountered Wraxall's warm fingers. A gentleman would have pulled his hand away. Wraxall didn't move any part of himself, except for his eyes, which lifted from their focus on the ribbon to meet her gaze.

Those eyes, usually so blue and clear, were the color of a stormy sea. Heat seemed to burn off the man, radiating in waves and washing over her. He nodded slightly, and Julia felt as though some agreement had been made between the two of them, some promise that would be honored later. She did not know precisely what it might be, but her body seemed to understand it. Her body swayed closer to him even as her mind cautioned her to flee.

She might have run back up the steps too if he hadn't put his arms around her. They didn't go around her exactly, but he reached behind her, gathering her hair into a long tail. Her whole body came alive as little frissons of pleasure trailed from her scalp to her neck and all the way to her toes. He looped the ribbon about her hair and tied it into a bow. Then slowly— far more slowly than necessary—he stepped back and away from her.

She still could not catch her breath, and she knew her chest rose and fell as she gulped in air. His eyes assessed her, initially inspecting his handiwork but then drifting to the motion of her chest and then to the folds of her skirts where her legs formed a vee. Oh yes. She was warm there too. Moisture had gathered and with it a ripple of awareness. But he couldn't know what she felt at the juncture of her thighs.

Could he?

"You had better go in now."

She nodded. And stood motionless. In one smooth movement, Wraxall pushed the door to the kitchen open and extended an arm in invitation. Julia closed her eyes to clear her head, then marched through the kitchen to the vestibule, smiling broadly at the potential cooks waiting for her.

❧

After Neil had moved Lady Juliana's applicants to the entryway, he corralled the orphans upstairs. There was no point in scaring the cooks away before they'd even interviewed. He'd planned to repair the roof today, but a steady drizzle interspersed with heavier deluges thwarted his plans. Perhaps that was for the best. He was so weary he would probably fall off the roof if he attempted to repair it. One of these nights, he would have to sleep. And at some point, he hoped he would be able to go home. He'd sent for clean clothing and washed in the servants' quarters, so at least he was clean and properly attired. He'd also managed to waylay Goring, who had returned this morning with a story of a sick relative. Neil intended to keep the manservant close and Slag uninformed.

When he had all the children gathered in the older boys' room, Neil issued his orders. "We can't work on the roof this morning and you still have no teacher for lessons—"

A resounding shout drowned him out. Neil ignored it. He raised one hand, and the din quieted. "So we will make use of our time by cleaning your quarters."

"Boo!" was the response.

Neil crossed his arms over his chest. "Gentlemen, when I want your opinion, I will give it to you. In the meantime, strip the beds, push all the furniture to one corner, get the broom, find a mop and bucket, and start cleaning." He turned to the four younger boys. "Mr. Goring will help you."

Goring frowned. "I ain't a maid, sir."

"You are today, Goring. Be thankful you don't have to do it all on your own."

The four younger boys scampered off, full of excitement, and Neil turned back to the chaos in the older boys' dormitory. Before he knew what had happened, the red-haired boy pushed a box into his arms. "You'd better hold on to these, Major, or they're likely to get free."

Neil looked down at the three rats, who blinked up at him. He took a deep breath. He'd never cared much for rats. He'd encountered them plenty of times on missions when he'd had to camp in dark cellars or fetid alleys. These rats were certainly cleaner and tamer. One of them rose up on its hind legs and sniffed at him with its little, pink nose. Neil didn't shudder, but he wouldn't go so far as to call the creature cute.

He resolved to build a proper cage for the little beasts, but until then, he took the box and placed it inside Lady Juliana's room. He made a point not to look around, not to imagine her in that silk nightgown he'd seen snatches of last night.

Leaving the rats, he returned to the dormitory in time to see the tall boy who kept to himself shove something under his mattress. "You." Neil pointed.

"That's Billy," Michael told him. "He's eleven."

Neil had already learned that Michael enjoyed numbers. He counted everything he could.

"What do you have there, Billy?" Neil made his way over.

Billy didn't look him in the eye. "Nothing, Major."

"What did you hide under the mattress?"

Billy's dark eyes rose and settled on Neil's face. Billy had a maturity beyond his years, and Neil knew that before he'd come to the orphanage, Billy had seen plenty on the streets of London.

"Let's see," Neil said.

Still looking at Neil, Billy lifted the mattress. Underneath, six kitchen knives gleamed. Immediately, the other boys in the chamber found themselves engrossed with other tasks.

"That's quite a collection," Neil remarked. "What do you need the weapons for?"

"Defense."

Neil looked about the room. "Against these lads? You're bigger than all of them. It seems to me if you had trouble, you could use your fists."

"I'm not worried about these lads."

Neil nodded. "Then who?"

Billy shrugged. "If there's any trouble, I like to be ready."

"I'm here," Neil said. "If there's any trouble, I'll handle it."

Billy nodded. "How long are you here?"

It was a good question. It was a question Neil continued to ask himself. He'd intended to be here a few hours. Then one night. Now, he'd been here two nights, and those would undoubtedly turn into three. But he didn't plan to stay after that. He didn't want to run an orphanage. He'd deal with Slag, see Lady Juliana safely home, then say his goodbyes.

That would be little consolation to Billy, though. A new thug would move into Slag's place or a thief desperate enough would find a way to break into the orphanage, and the boys and Lady Juliana would have no one to defend them. No wonder Billy wanted the knives.

Neil held out his hand. "Before I go, we'll find a way for you to defend yourself, if there's still a need. In the meantime, the new cook will want these."

Billy scooped the knives up in one large fist and handed them over. Neil nodded. "I have Walter's knife." He looked at the room of boys who were still pretending not to listen. "Who else has a knife or a weapon? Turn them over now. If I find them during my inspection later, you won't like the consequences."

By the end of the hour, Neil had collected three more knives, two bricks, a sharpened stick, two candlesticks that probably belonged in the dining room, and a half dozen hairpins that Lady Juliana was probably missing. The younger boys had their share of weapons too. Jimmy had a needle he'd swiped from Lady Juliana's sewing box, and Chester had taken a small pan from the kitchen.

By the time Neil disposed of or returned the items and inspected the boys' chambers, it was noon and no one had eaten. He made his way to the parlor, through the now-empty entryway. The parlor door was open and an appetizing smell drifted from the kitchen. He stuck his head in the door, finding Lady Juliana with her head bent and a quill in her hand. She was writing quickly, her lip caught between her teeth as she worked.

Neil cleared his throat. She looked up at him and her cheeks flushed. Just as quickly, she looked down again. He would have bet she was remembering their shared kiss.

"What is it, Mr. Wraxall?"

She was all business, but Neil wasn't put off.

Something about the sight of her with her copper hair spilling over one shoulder and that full lip between her small, even teeth made him want to kiss her again.

"I wondered how the interviews had gone, and the boys wondered when they might eat."

Her head popped up. "Oh no! They haven't eaten at all this morning, have they?" She rose, dropping her quill. "How could I have forgotten?"

Neil raised a hand. "I've kept them busy in their rooms, but as the weather is still unfit for travel, I haven't been able to go out and procure any food-stuffs. Does that appetizing smell mean you hired a new cook?"

"Yes, a Mrs. Koch. Appropriate, isn't it? Her husband fought in the Colonial War, and after his death, she settled in England. She has nine grown children and is used to cooking for a crowd, so to speak."

"She sounds perfect."

"Yes. I'll ask if she can have something ready for a noon meal."

"Good. If you need me, I'll be in the servants' quarters. I have a project I'd like to begin."

She frowned. "What sort of project?"

He felt like an idiot telling her he planned to build a cage for the pet rats. He should have been ordering her to release the rodents. But he knew she would refuse. The boys had become attached to the creatures, and they seemed harmless enough. "It's a surprise for the boys. I'll take Goring with me. If you would be so kind, send something down for us."

"Very well." She moved in front of the desk, looked toward the door, then leaned toward him as though telling a secret. "You are keeping an eye on Mr. Goring."

"I don't want Goring running to tell Slag what we're up to."

She furrowed her brow. "We aren't up to anything."

"I told you last night." He moved closer, lowering his voice. "Slag will not touch you. I'll bring several of my men to the musicale, and we will deal with Mr. Slag."

"You plan to kill him?" She put her hand to her heart.

"There are worse fates than death. The prison hulks come to mind."

"But—"

He held up a hand. "Leave it to me. And without Slag in command, his gang will falter. The last thing the men will care about is you or the orphanage. They will be too busy killing each other to determine the next arch rogue. You can go home."

"I told you. This is my home now."

Neil closed his eyes. Why had he gone to see his father? Why had he agreed to help St. Maur? *It will take an afternoon*, his father had said. *A piece of cake for a man like you*, his father had said. Neil, for one, would have been pleased never to set eyes on cake again.

"You cannot save this orphanage, Lady Juliana."

"I beg to differ. You just said with Slag gone, the orphanage would be the least of the gang's concerns."

"Until there's a new leader who takes an interest."

"And then we will have our foodstuffs stolen again."

Neil waved a hand. She still did not understand. "Turnips and flour are not the real valuables here."

"Then what is? We have little else."

"You're wrong. You have a dozen boys who would make perfect thieves and pickpockets."

"I won't allow that to happen. When I came here, I vowed to keep these boys safe. I won't let them go the way of so many of the former residents."

"You cannot stop it. You are one woman against deadly criminals and impossible odds."

Her gaze met his. "You faced death and impossible odds, and you came home a hero."

"I came home a ghost. I should have died with the men I sent to their deaths."

"Have you ever considered there's a reason you survived? What if you were spared because I needed you? What if you lived to save these boys—bastards like you but just as deserving of a chance in this world?"

Neil felt cold seep through his veins. He was no hero. He was not the man to save these children, not the man Lady Juliana seemed to want him to be. "I have one mission, Lady Juliana, and that is to return you home."

"I told you," she said tightly. "I *am* home, and I will never give up on these boys or Sunnybrooke."

Neil couldn't help but admire her spirit, misguided as she was. She was stubborn and idealistic, a dangerous mixture. And one he couldn't quite seem to resist.

Twelve

She didn't know where Mr. Wraxall disappeared to after their conversation. He'd gone out in the rain and hadn't returned by dinner. She and the boys had enjoyed a delicious meal together, and Julia had initially been happy it would be just her and the boys at dinner. It would be like old times again—before Wraxall had come.

Except it wasn't.

The boys had talked of little else throughout dinner. No one could say enough about when Major had done this or when he'd said that or how he'd promised to build Matthew, Mark, and John a new enclosure. Julia had tried to steer the conversation away from Wraxall, but the attempt had been only halfhearted. The truth was that Sunnybrooke wasn't the same without him. She didn't know how that was possible when he'd only been there two days, but in that time, they'd all become used to him and come to rely upon him. Now, there was more than an empty chair where he usually sat. There was an empty spot in the boys' hearts. In hers as well, though she told herself it was a small spot that could be easily filled.

The danger was in allowing the little piece of her heart he'd claimed to grow larger. She had to stop the attachment she felt from becoming any stronger. No more long conversations. No more nighttime eavesdropping. And no more kisses. Definitely no more kisses.

In that spirit, she'd tried not to think of him the rest of the evening as the boys had played games or listened to her read, then complained when she made them wash faces and brush teeth and climb into their beds— beds that had clean linen in rooms that were spotless.

But she would not think of that because noticing all of the changes would only lead to thoughts of Wraxall.

Finally, all the boys were tucked in. Julia checked with the new cook, who looked to have the kitchen in order and everything ready for the morning meal. Julia sent her to bed and told Mr. Goring he could retire. Part of Goring's job was to lock all the windows and doors at night, but considering what she knew about Goring, she checked everything again. All was secure. Was it possible Wraxall had been wrong about Goring? After all, with the major away, now would have been the perfect time to send Mr. Slag word she was alone and vulnerable. But Goring had stayed close all evening and locked everything up tightly.

In fact, she was left with a dilemma. She was ready for bed, but Wraxall still had not returned. He'd given her no information as to where he'd gone or when he'd be back. She did not want to leave the door open, but neither did she want to lock him out. Finally, she decided she would give him until midnight. If he hadn't returned by then, he was obviously not returning until the morrow. She built up the fire in the parlor and looked over correspondence and ledgers at her desk, but soon her eyes drooped and since she only had an hour until midnight, she decided to rest on the couch.

She opened her eyes what seemed like a moment later and screamed at the man standing above her. Before much more than a squeak left her lips, his hand came down and covered her mouth.

It was Slag, and he would kill her. Why hadn't she locked the door?

"If you scream, you'll wake the children."

She stilled and stared up at the man, whose face was in shadow. He removed his hat, and she instantly relaxed. It was Wraxall. Then anger replaced fear. She wrenched his hand from her mouth. "Just what are you about, sneaking in here and scaring me to death?"

"Sneaking in? I walked in. The door was open—a matter I'd very much like to discuss with you."

She sat and pushed her hair out of her eyes. "Oh, don't blame me for that. That is your fault, sir. I had no idea if you would return or not, and I did not want you banging on the door and scaring everyone to death when you returned to find the door locked."

"Give me more credit than that." He moved away to stand by the fire, and in the light, his features looked weary and a bit haggard. The man was exhausted.

"Very well." She lowered her voice. "You probably would have behaved like an idiot and sat outside all night, keeping vigil or some such nonsense. It's still raining, and you'd catch your death of cold. I don't want your death on my conscience."

He grinned at her. "Your concern is touching."

"I hope so. Where have you been all night?" She was aware she sounded more like a wife than she ought, considering he was under no obligation to tell her anything.

"At my club."

"Drinking?"

"I wish. No, I've been talking with friends of mine about the situation with Mr. Slag."

"What sort of friends?"

"The sort who can help me rid you of him permanently. Do you mind?" He pointed to the couch.

"Mind?"

"If I join you." He didn't wait for an answer. Instead, he sat heavily beside her. She almost fell into him but managed to scoot over toward the arm and thereby maintain some space between them. Julia marveled at how small the couch seemed once he sat on it with her. She had considered moving it out of the parlor several times, as it was rather large for the small area, but now it felt decidedly too small.

Julia also marveled that she was still seated beside him. Why hadn't she stood up?

He laid his head on the back of the couch and closed his eyes.

"You should sleep, Mr. Wraxall. You look terrible."

He smiled without opening his eyes. "You do know how to give a compliment."

But she didn't know how else to describe him when he had the shadow of a beard on his jaw, dark circles under his eyes, and a pallor under his bronze skin.

"You can go to bed now," he said. And how was

she supposed to sleep when all she could think of was kissing him again?

"I have a bit more work to do." She stood and moved to the desk. As soon as she was away from the couch, she felt colder and missed his scent of coffee and baked bread. "Why don't you rest for a few moments while I finish?"

"I know what you're about," he said, his eyes still closed. "I'm perfectly fine. You can go to bed."

"I have no idea what you mean." She sat at her desk and tried to look busy. "This letter to the prime minister will not write itself. I promise to rouse you when I am finished and retire. In the meantime, I assume you trust me to keep vigil."

"Not a chance."

"Mr. Wraxall, surely you assigned watches when you were in the army. You had to sleep at some point. Why not give me the watch for an hour and then I promise to hand it back for the rest of the night."

One eye opened. One bloodshot eye. "Fine. But if you don't wake me— -"

"Yes, yes. The full power of your mighty wrath will fall upon me and my entire household. I will wake you, sir."

He opened the other eye and gave her an assessing look. Then with a nod, he fell, rather than lay, on his side and was snoring softly within seconds. Julia stared at him, rather awed at his ability to fall asleep so quickly. She usually had to read for at least an hour, then toss and turn until the bedclothes were perfectly arranged and fluff her pillow at least five times before her mind would quiet enough for her to consider drifting into slumber.

Wraxall seemed to need only to close his eyes.

In case he was only pretending, she did write the letter she'd mentioned. Her father had told her about a bill he supported to give more aid to homes for unwed mothers. If the bill passed, Julia hoped more women would have the resources to keep their babies, rather than give them up. She could not vote, of course, but she had been writing the prime minister weekly to express her support for the bill and to urge him to take up her father's cause.

She finished her letter and, having penned a rather passionate epistle, did not feel at all tired. She checked the clock on the mantel and saw it was nearing one. Surely she could give the major another half hour of rest. She sorted through more correspondence and made notes in the boys' files, then finally had to admit her eyes would no longer stay open. Though she thought it ridiculous that Wraxall insisted on staying awake, she had promised to rouse him before going to bed.

She bent over the sleeping figure on the couch and looked down into his face. He looked so peaceful when he slept. He never looked thus when awake. Now that she had an idea of the demons that plagued him, she could understand why. But she hoped, for the past ninety minutes, his mind had been weary enough to give him nothing but blackness.

"Mr. Wraxall," she said quietly. "I am retiring now."

He did not move.

Julia considered leaving and telling him she'd tried to rouse him but that he would not wake. But she had promised. And she had not tried very hard.

"Mr. Wraxall." She shook him a bit. "I am retiring now." Nothing from him. Not even a change in his even breathing. Goodness but his shoulder was firm. Her hand wandered down his bicep, and even under the thick wool of his coat, she could feel the hard outlines of his muscles.

"Mr. Wraxall." She sat on the edge of the couch and bent closer. "Major?" That did it. He made an unintelligible sound and his hand reached out and wound about her waist. His eyes still did not open.

Julia tried to pull away, but he was holding fast and she feared if he let go suddenly, she would fall to the floor. "Major," she tried again. "Wake up."

"Not now, sweetheart," he muttered. With a shock, Julia realized he must think she was some sort of...*trollop*. He must think she was in bed with him and wanted him to wake for...carnal activities. "Lie down."

He tugged her, but she resisted. "Major, it is I, Lady Juliana. Wake up. I am going to bed."

He moved, turning more fully on his side. The action pulled her down, and when she got her bearings, she was tucked against him on the couch. Her back was to his chest, her legs dangling over the side, but his arm was clamped around her middle.

"Sir!" she hissed. When there was no response, Julia thought about elbowing him in the abdomen. That would surely wake him—but then she stilled. Why exactly did she want to wake him? No one could argue she hadn't tried to wake him. If she stayed here, he would get more sleep. If she stayed here, she could spend a few hours being held by a man and no one would ever be the wiser. It wasn't likely she'd ever have this opportunity again. After the business with Viscount Lainesborough, she knew she would never marry. And for a woman like her that meant chastity. When would she ever have the chance to lie in a man's arms after tonight? When would she be able to feel the steel of his muscles wrapped around her or the solid warmth of his chest?

He would relax in a few moments and release her. Then she could move safely away, and he need never be the wiser. No one need ever be the wiser. The parlor door was closed and the entire house was sleeping. She'd done nothing for herself since Harriett had come home. Couldn't she be forgiven for giving in to this one small urge?

Julia closed her eyes and snuggled back against the man holding her. Just for a moment, she pretended he loved her and that he held her thus every night. She imagined this was their house and the children here their children. It was a house filled with laughter and happiness and family. She'd had a life like that once. She'd had a family—before it had been ripped away from her not once but twice.

All she could do was imagine what it would be like to have that again. Of course, she knew she could never have it with Wraxall. What did an illegitimate son know about family? He was as unlikely as she to ever marry or become a parent. The difference was he did not want a family. He'd made it clear from the beginning that he saw her and the boys as a burden. She would always mourn what she could not have.

His hand tightened around her middle, and she closed her eyes and allowed herself to sink into his warmth and security.

The sound of the cannons firing was relentless. Portugal. That's where he was. A well-aimed cannon blast shook the hill and Tiberius reared as dirt flew at them from a few feet away. Neil lost his hold and toppled from the saddle, landing on his side and rolling to stand again. He slapped the horse's rump, a signal to depart, then pulled his pistol and fired at the first French soldier coming for him. With no time to reload, he raised his saber and charged into the thick of the French infantry.

As the First and Second Dragoons crested the hill, the French fought harder, knowing to give any ground would mean retreat.

It seemed hours had passed as Neil fought. His sword arm ached, his shoulder screamed, and he blinked blood out of his eyes. He wasn't certain if the blood was his or the spray from one of his casualties, and he didn't take the time to wipe it away. Every fallen redcoat might be Christopher. He took foolish risks, looking down at the bodies instead of in the faces of the enemies. Fatigue weighed on him like a waterlogged greatcoat, pulling him down and down.

The Sixteenth is coming. The Sixteenth is coming.

He had to hold out until the rest of the regiment arrived.

Finally, when Neil feared he could not raise his arm one more time, he could not cut down another living, breathing man, he heard the roar of hoofbeats. The ground shook beneath him. The French commander called for retreat, and Neil sagged as the enemy melted away.

The dragoons thundered past him. Neil stumbled to a man wearing the insignia of the Second Brigade. "Lord Christopher. Is he alive?" he panted, his breath burning in his lungs.

The man—more of a boy, really—shook his head. "I don't know, sir. I haven't seen him since we last stormed the hill."

Neil stumbled away, his eyes on the fallen infantry, looking for Christopher's golden-blond hair. Men with brown hair, black hair, gray hair, and dark-blond hair lay with unseeing eyes or clutching bleeding arms or legs. One man held a hand over a gash across his middle, keeping his intestines from spilling out. Neil couldn't let himself see this. Couldn't allow himself to believe any of it was real, else he'd lose his breakfast and his faltering courage. Neil trudged through the pools of blood, halting at the bright cap of blond hair lying in one of the bloody puddles.

His breath caught and his belly tightened.

"Chris," he said hoarsely, turning the man over. His heart pounded wildly, his vision dimmed, but when he opened his eyes again, the man he touched was not Christopher, not his brother.

"Water," the man croaked. With shaking fingers, Neil unfastened his canteen and pressed it into the man's hands. He moved on, moved down the hill, his eyes scanning for that crown of bright curls.

Please, God. No.

He almost passed another man with blond hair. This man's cap was still on his head, his face obscured because he lay facedown on the hill. Neil did not want to do this. Did not want to see the dead face. But he had to know. He'd go mad otherwise. Neil got behind the body, dug his heels into the steep slope for purchase, and flipped the man over.

Shock and pain stabbed through him as he stared at the face of Christopher Wraxall. He hadn't really expected it to be him. He hadn't been ready.

One green eye stared up at him, seeing nothing. The hole where a musket ball had entered stood in place of the other eye. Neil turned to the side and retched quietly, then he sank to his knees and lay in the mud and the gore beside his fallen brother.

How he wished the dead man had been himself.

Neil knew it was dream, but he couldn't seem to wake, couldn't seem to rouse himself from the soft, warm bed. It was like climbing out from under a mountain of blankets. Finally, he forced his eyes open and frowned in confusion at the unfamiliar room. Then he looked down at the unfamiliar body pressed against him. It was female. He knew that much, but he wasn't in the habit of spending the night with women. He tended to wake screaming, and guests seemed to find shrieks in the night off-putting. The smell of roses and the copper hair spilling over his chest left no doubt as to who he held in his arms. As soon as he realized Lady Juliana—he had certainly earned the right to call her Julia now—was sleeping beside him, he remembered his trek to the Draven Club the night before, returning to find her waiting for him, and that she'd promised to wake him after an hour.

The weak light slanting through the windows of the parlor told him what he already knew. He had slept all night, not merely an hour. Had she slept here with him? And what the devil was that pounding?

"Juliana Rose, open this door right now!" said a voice from the other side of the door.

The aforementioned Juliana Rose faced him, her cheek buried against his chest. She stirred and then snuggled closer to him. Neil had the mad urge to tell the person at the door to go away. But that would only cause more trouble, and he knew there would be trouble. No one but someone familiar with Lady Juliana would refer to her as Juliana Rose. That meant it couldn't be the cook or the maid, and Neil wouldn't be able to dismiss the intruder and make this all go away.

"My lady," he said, voice low. "You have a visitor."

She murmured something unintelligible and closed her fingers around a button on his coat. How had he slept so bloody well when he still wore his coat and boots? He'd barely loosened his cravat, and he couldn't have had more than four or five hours of sleep, but those hours had been some of the most restful he'd had in months. He hadn't dreamed of the war or of his missions until the pounding on the door reminded him of cannon fire.

"Juliana Rose!" came the impatient woman's voice.

"One more minute," she groaned.

"In another minute she will knock the door down and the situation will be far worse," Neil observed.

"Whose voice is that? Who is in there?"

Something she heard must have finally penetrated her brainbox because she started like a frightened fawn and tried to sit but ended up falling off the couch. Neil winced when he heard the thump. He probably should have caught her, but he rather thought he'd held her enough for the time being.

She popped up again, pushing her tousled hair back from her face. She looked at him. "Oh no." Then she looked about the room. "Oh no." Then she looked at the door. "Oh no!"

"Juliana Rose, if you do not open this door this minute, I will have this man—What is your name, sir?" There was a muttered reply. "This Mr. Goring knock it down."

"Mrs. Dunwitty?" Juliana asked more to herself than anyone else.

"It is I. You did write to me, did you not? And *this* is the welcome I receive!"

Her gaze met Neil's, and there was the panicked-fawn look again. "She cannot find us here together."

Neil's brows drew together. "Do you want me to hide like some sort of rake?"

"No, of course not." She looked wildly about. "I want you to escape through the window."

"With whom are you speaking, Juliana? I know there is someone in there with you. Open this door."

"Just a moment, Mrs. Dunwitty!"

"Who is Mrs. Dunwitty?"

"This is no time for questions!" She rose, grasped his hands, and yanked him up. His back protested, but he stood anyway.

"Jump out the window," she demanded, rushing across the room and yanking the draperies back from the rectangular window looking out on the street, obscured somewhat by a light fog. At least the rain had ceased.

She tried to push the sill up, her face turning as red as her hair as she strained.

"I cannot jump out the window."

"This is the first floor," she said between clenched teeth. "You won't be hurt."

"What I mean is the window is sealed."

She slumped down, breathing heavily. She was dressed in her robe and night rail again. The robe had come open, exposing the vee of her breasts, and though Neil had been trying to keep his eyes on her face, all of those heaving breaths made it difficult to act the gentleman.

She gave him a pained expression. "Why is the window sealed?"

"I sealed all the windows whose locks were broken beyond repair."

"And what shall we do if there is a fire?"

"Break the window or use the door." The pounding on the door to the parlor resumed. "Speaking of breaking doors, you should probably let her in."

"I can't do that! Do you know who she is?"

"No. You said there was no time for questions." Neil crossed the room. Apparently, he would have to admit the dragon, else he would be repairing this door later, and God knew he had enough on his hands with patching the leaky roof, building a rodent enclosure, and keeping Slag away from Juliana. Neil opened the door. He spotted Mr. Goring right away. The servant looked as though he would rather be anywhere else. Behind him, every boy in the orphanage, in various states of dress—or undress—had lined up to gawk at the newcomer.

Neil had to look down to address her. She was easily the most petite woman he had ever met. He doubted she was five feet in pattens. She wore all black and her small face looked up at him from under a tiny hat perched on a tower of white hair. He remembered reading that Marie Antoinette had worn towering wigs with birds and ships and probably whole pleasure gardens depicted in them. This woman's hair was not a wig, but it was piled high enough that a nest of birds could inhabit it. He couldn't help but wonder how she kept the hat pinned in place.

"Who are you?" she demanded.

Neil had never been called charming. He was a soldier through and through, better with orders and strategies than charisma. Rafe was the charming one, but at that moment, Neil would have traded places with his friend. He bowed, giving the gesture a flourish he'd seen Rafe make many times. "Major Neil Wraxall at your service." He never used his rank any more, but he needed all the fortification he could in the face of this tiny tyrant.

Mrs. Dunwitty put her hands on her tiny waist. "And what were you doing in the parlor with Lady Juliana, Major?"

The lady certainly did not have a small voice. Neil was fairly certain all of Spitalfields had heard the question. He held his hands up defensively. "Nothing."

Her eyes narrowed. "Then why was the door locked?"

"For…safety?"

Juliana rushed out of the room then, and Neil wished she had taken a moment to right her appearance. Not that he minded her rumpled hair or her gaping robe.

But he minded Mrs. Dunwitty the Terrible seeing her thus. Mrs. Dunwitty's large, green eyes widened behind her spectacles. "Lady Juliana! What on earth!"

Neil glanced at Mr. Goring, who quickly looked at the ceiling as though something up there interested him greatly. "Perhaps we should discuss this in private," Neil suggested.

Mrs. Dunwitty glanced behind her, seeming to notice the audience of orphans for the first time. "Boys," she said, her voice full of authority. "March right back upstairs. I want you in the dining room in twenty minutes—beds made, teeth brushed, hair combed, and dressed impeccably." She clapped her hands. "Off with you!"

To Neil's astonishment, the boys scattered, running like squirrels when a carriage approached. He could have used Mrs. Dunwitty in the dragoons. As the boys retreated, he heard Charlie say, "What does 'peccably' mean?"

"I don't know," Robbie answered. "But we'd better do it."

"And *you*." Mrs. Dunwitty looked at Mr. Goring. "Do you not have duties to attend to?"

"Yes, madam. I'll see to them right away."

Then she turned her gaze on him. "If you would, Major." She gestured to the parlor. Juliana scurried in and Neil followed. Mrs. Dunwitty closed the door with a thud behind them. "Now, I think we all know what happened here."

Juliana shook her head. "No, madam, you do not. Nothing happened."

"Do not talk back to me, young lady. I may not be

a woman of the world, but I am not a fool. A man and a woman alone in a locked room is bound to lead to frolics."

"Madam," Neil said as seriously as he could, "I vow there was no frolicking between Lady Juliana and me."

She glared at him. "And even if I believe you, sir, what does that matter? It is the *appearance* of frolicking that is the problem. You have ruined the lady whether you had your wicked way with her or not."

"My wicked way?" If he wasn't afraid she'd smash him over the head with her cane, he might have protested further. How fitting that he, of all men, should be accused of deflowering the lady.

"I am not ruined, Mrs. Dunwitty. Not that it matters. I told you that I will not marry. Regardless, Mr. Wraxall did not compromise me. He arrived late last night and fell asleep on the couch in the parlor. I... accidentally fell asleep too."

Neil studied her expression. There was more to the story, but he would wait until he was alone with Lady Juliana to hear it. He rather wondered how the lady had come to be asleep in his arms this morning.

"Do you expect me to believe that?"

"It is the truth."

Mrs. Dunwitty looked at Neil, and he nodded his agreement.

"Very well," said Mrs. Dunwitty, seating herself in one of the armchairs. "I will accept that explanation for the time being. But we have not finished our discussion of this matter. However, I see there may be more pressing matters to discuss. You wrote that you needed a teacher?"

"Yes. Have you come to help?"

So this was Lady Juliana's former governess. It all made sense. No wonder she played the overzealous chaperone. And no wonder Lady Juliana had asked for her assistance. If anyone could teach these boys, it was obviously Mrs. Dunwitty the Terrible.

"I will stay and teach until you can find a replacement. I'm far too old and feeble to take the position permanently."

Neil covered his laugh with a cough.

"Are you quite well, Major?" Mrs. Dunwitty asked.

"Actually," he said, clearing his throat, "I have a few matters to attend to. If you will excuse me."

"Of course." She dismissed him with a wave of her hand. A knock sounded on the front door, and Neil knew he was saved.

"What sort of matters?" Lady Juliana asked, her eyes flicking to him as if to beg him not to desert her.

"That is not our concern," Mrs. Dunwitty told her former charge. "Now, tell me what the boys have learned thus far."

Neil waved as he left the parlor, only to almost trip over the new cook, who had been standing just outside the room. "Mrs. Koch, was there something you needed?"

She put her hands on her hips. "Yah. If you vant me to cook the breakfast, then I don't have the time to answer the doors."

"Of course. You needn't answer the door." That was his excuse for escape. "Where is Mr. Goring?"

"I don't know vhere that man vent, but he vent in a hurry."

Bloody hell. Neil knew exactly where Goring had gone.

"You have a guest, yah?" She nodded to Neil and then pointed to the entryway.

Neil pointed to his chest as if to verify it was he who had a guest. When the cook nodded, Neil moved down the corridor and into the entryway and found Jackson suspiciously eyeing one of the buckets collecting rain.

The valet was tall and almost gangly with thinning, black hair that he combed over the bald spot on the top of his head. He had large eyes that reminded Ewan of a puppy's, along with a bulbous nose. But Jackson was good at his job. He did not dress Neil to within an inch of his life, as Rafe's valet did Rafe, but he made sure Neil was somewhat fashionable and that his clothing was well-maintained.

Jackson frowned with disapproval when he spotted Neil. "I see I was right to come."

It had obviously been a mistake to stop at his flat the previous day before visiting the Draven Club. "No, you were not. I didn't ask you to come here. I asked you to send clothing and toiletries."

A thud came from upstairs, and Neil realized it had been quiet for too long.

Jackson's puppy eyes widened with pleading. "Sir, I apologize for my behavior yesterday. I promise it will never happen again."

Neil moved toward the stairs. "What behavior yesterday?"

Jackson loped after him. "My gross inattention to my duties. Please do not dismiss me, sir."

Neil paused outside the drawing room at the top of the stairs. "You mean, when I found you napping?"

Jackson's face turned pink and he hung his head. "It will never happen again. I swear on my mother's grave."

Neil held up both hands. "I have no intention of sending you packing."

Another sound came from above, but this time, it was more of a crash.

"Go back to my flat and sleep all you want." Neil raced up the next set of stairs. "This torture can't last much longer."

"I cannot do that, sir," Jackson said, racing after him. "I have come to prove my indispensability."

Neil heard the shouts and the thumps from behind the closed door of the older boys' dormitory. Chester and James stood in the doorway of the younger boys' chamber, eyes wide with concern.

"What is this about?" Neil gestured to the closed door.

Chester shook his head. James just stared, wide-eyed.

Neil lifted the latch, but the door didn't budge. The boys must have put something against the door to prevent entrance. He tried shoving it open with his shoulder but made little progress. "Open up!" He pounded on the door. "Open up or I'll send all of you to a workhouse!"

The ruckus inside continued, and the door stayed closed. Neil pounded on it again.

"If you will excuse me, sir," Jackson interrupted. "Might I have a try?"

Neil stared at the valet. "Why not?"

Jackson cleared his throat. "The first boy to open the door will receive a shilling to buy a sweet."

Michael opened the door. "Where's my shilling?"

Neil pushed past him and into the center of the room where Billy and Robbie were circling each other, fists raised. Robbie's nose bled freely, flowing over his mouth and down his neck. Billy's cheek was red and his lip was split, but he was certainly winning the match.

"What the dev…deuce is this about?"

The boys ignored him as Billy struck at Robbie with an impressive left hook. Neil stepped between the boys and pushed them apart. Robbie lowered his arms immediately, but Billy resisted. When he tried to throw a punch at Neil, Neil used the back of his arm to push Billy up against a wall. "You want to think long and hard before you try to punch me again, lad. Hit me and I'll have you in a workhouse before noon."

"No, you will not!" came Lady Juliana's breathless voice. She ran into the room, her cheeks flushed and her eyes wide. "Robbie! Oh no! Billy, do stop."

The boys moved aside to allow her to enter. She rushed straight to where he held Billy. "Let him go, sir."

"My lady," Neil said, "with all due respect, I believe I am better suited to handle this situation."

"I don't need your kind of help," she argued. "How dare you come in here and threaten to take my boys away?"

Neil gaped at her. "This"—he inclined his head toward Billy—"is no *boy*. He's practically a man, and he doesn't need a hug. He needs another man to tell him what is and is not acceptable."

"I don't have to listen to you," Billy muttered.

"Let me talk to him," Juliana said.

"No. Go tend to Robbie. His nose may be broken."

She glanced quickly at Robbie, then back to Billy.

"Lady Juliana." Mrs. Dunwitty stood outside the room, her hand on her heart and her walking stick clutched in a small hand. "Listen to the major. Not only is that other boy injured, but the little boys are scared. They need you far more than that one."

Juliana looked from Billy to Mrs. Dunwitty to Robbie. Jackson had given Robbie a handkerchief, and the boy had it pressed to his nose. "I will tend to the young master," Jackson said, "if you want to see to the little ones, my lady."

"I'll help with the little ones," Michael said. "Then can I get my shilling?"

Juliana finally nodded to Mrs. Dunwitty and gave Neil one last look. "We will discuss this later," she said, then moved toward the youngest of the orphans.

Neil nodded. "Count on it."

Thirteen

Julia calmed the younger boys, then ordered all the boys except Robbie and Billy to tidy their rooms and dress for the day. Mr. Wraxall's servant had been more helpful than Julia might have anticipated. She had found time to change into a light-green dress with fairer green piping while Jackson tended to Robbie. When she had pulled her hair into a simple tail and come down to eat, the valet had informed her the boy's nose was not broken. It seemed he'd managed to restore order to the chaos of the morning, leading the boys to breakfast in the dining room in an orderly fashion and then to the drawing room for their first lesson with Mrs. Dunwitty.

Wraxall had shown up at the end of breakfast without Billy, and when Julia had asked where he was, all he'd said was, "We'll discuss it later."

Her stomach had cramped in fear. What if he'd already sent Billy away? What if it was too late and Billy was lost to her forever? Her hands had shaken so badly she could not manage to lift a spoon to eat her own porridge, even if she had been able to keep food down.

When Jackson took the boys to the drawing room, Julia had her first moment alone with Wraxall. "Where is Billy?"

"He's thinking about his behavior this morning." Wraxall ate a piece of bread.

"He needs breakfast."

"He needs someone to give him some hard and fast rules. He's like an untrained soldier—dangerous."

"Billy is not dangerous. He just needs someone to love him. He's been at the orphanage for years and seen adults come and go. His life has been full of unpredictability."

Wraxall tried his porridge, nodded, and ate another spoonful. "Exactly. Now we give him predictability. If he breaks another boy's nose, there's a consequence."

"Thankfully, Robbie's nose isn't broken, just badly bruised."

"That's not for lack of trying."

"Listen, Mr. Wraxall, you were sent here to persuade me to return home. I have told you that this is my home now. I have authority from the board of directors. You have no right to tell me how to raise the children."

The look he gave her was one she imagined he gave to the enemy before coldly bayoneting him through the heart. He stood slowly. "Listen, my lady—"

Jackson cleared his throat. "I am sorry to interrupt, but now that the boys are at their lessons, I wondered if there was somewhere I could unpack your things, sir, and perhaps ready water and your razor for a shave?"

Wraxall rubbed the bridge of his nose. "I have spare

shirts in one of the servants' rooms. I suppose you could unpack there."

Jackson stared at him. "You have been sleeping in the servants' quarters?"

"I haven't really been sleeping at all, but those are the only unoccupied quarters."

"I see."

Julia heard the note of disapproval and did not blame the man. Wraxall did not belong here, but she was in the uncomfortable position of needing him. What made her dependence even worse was that she no longer needed him only to protect them from Slag or to see to the roof repairs; she seemed to need his help with the boys as well.

He was becoming the father the boys so desperately needed, except that Wraxall, like most fathers she'd known, was destined to let the children down.

"I won't need a shave," Wraxall told his servant. "I plan to climb onto the roof and assess the damage."

"The roof, sir?"

"I've been on roofs before, and if I'm not mistaken, Jackson, you have been around children before."

Julia cocked her head. "You do seem to have a way with them, Jackson. I herd them like blind mice, but you managed to move them in an orderly fashion from the dormitories to the dining room and thence to the classroom." She had no concerns about the boys now that they were ensconced with Mrs. Dunwitty. Her former governess was stern but kind and a gifted teacher. Despite their best efforts to remain ignorant, Harriett and Julia had always managed to learn something under Mrs. Dunwitty's tutelage.

Jackson's shoulders seemed to straighten. "I have had some experience with children, my lady. I am the oldest of fourteen."

"Fourteen?" Wraxall sputtered.

"Your poor mother," Julia said.

Jackson shook his head, unperturbed. "She is still strong as ever. She bore nineteen children in all. Fourteen of us survived."

"I never knew this about you, Jackson," Wraxall said.

"You never asked, sir."

"How are you with roofs?"

"Somewhat less skilled, sir."

"Then I'll go alone." He looked at her. "If Mr. Goring returns, tell him I want to see him immediately."

"I will. Are you certain you should go on the roof by yourself?"

"I'm a man of many talents, Lady Juliana." And with that he strode out of the room. Jackson followed.

Jackson called after him. "Sir, when you have a moment, I do need to speak with you alone."

"That will have to wait, Jackson," he said, his voice trailing away.

She wished the room did not feel so empty without him. She wished she didn't have the urge to stand outside and watch him up on the roof. Mostly, she wished she could send him away and never look at him again, because every moment she spent with him made her long for more.

She had to keep busy. Clearing the dishes, she brought them to the kitchen and spent an hour with Mrs. Koch, making lists of foodstuffs to stock the empty larder. Julia knew she would have to write to the board and ask for funds. They would want to know what had happened to the food she had bought last month, and she would have to explain it had been pilfered. That would certainly not make her look a very good steward. What if the board denied her request? How would she find the funds to feed the children? She couldn't ask her father for more money, and the majority of her pin money was gone. It also looked as though she'd have to pay for roof repairs. With a sigh, Julia made her way to the parlor to begin her letters. If there was one thing she missed about her life in Mayfair, it was never giving a thought to money.

As soon as she unlocked the parlor and stepped inside, Billy jumped to his feet. He might have bloodied Robbie's nose, but Billy had taken a few hits too. One cheek was red and swollen and his lip had been split. Julia sighed. "Oh, Billy. Look at you."

"Robbie looks worse."

"Robbie is your friend. Why were you fighting him?"

Billy looked down at his scraped hands. Julia moved into the room and closed the door behind her. "I don't understand. You and Robbie never seemed to have a problem before."

Billy's shoulders hunched. "You wouldn't understand, my lady."

"You could try telling me."

He shook his head firmly. "No, my lady."

"Very well. I imagine you are hungry. Go to the kitchen and tell Mrs. Koch I said to give you something to eat. When you've finished, join the other boys in the drawing room with Mrs. Dunwitty."

"Yes, my lady. Is Mrs. Dunwitty the small lady with the poof of hair?"

She smiled. "Yes, but one thing I learned from Mrs. Dunwitty is that though someone may be small in stature that does not make them weak. Don't test her, Billy. You will not win."

"Yes, my lady."

He lumbered off, and she sat at the desk and put her head in her hands. Perhaps Robbie would tell her what had happened between Billy and himself. She lost herself in writing letters and detailing expenses, so much so that when Wraxall pushed her door open, so that it thudded against the wall, she nearly jumped out of her seat. "What is wrong?" Blood marred the white of his shirt, trailing down one sleeve. She jumped to her feet. "You are hurt, sir!"

He glanced at his arm seeming to discount the injury. "It's a scratch. You, my lady, may not come away so unscathed."

"What on earth do you mean?" She moved closer to him, her eyes widening as she saw how soaked the shirt had become with blood. "Oh, never mind. You really must have that seen to. Where is Jackson?"

"I sent him to fetch my evening clothes. The Darlington musicale is this evening."

Her heart seemed to thud painfully in her chest. "I'd forgotten." She'd hoped she would have more time.

"That seems a recurring theme. I also told you to leave Billy locked in the parlor."

"I did leave him here, but I had work to do, and he was hungry and has his studies."

Wraxall stalked toward her. "Did you ever stop to think there might be a reason I told you to leave him in the parlor?"

"Did you ever think to tell me what it might be?"

He glared at her, and she glared back, but as she did so a drop of blood fell from her hand onto the carpet. She'd had enough. "Sir, you will come with me immediately. I insist on seeing to your injured arm."

"I told you it was a scratch, and I haven't finished this discussion."

"Then by all means, we may continue it in my bedchamber."

He started to protest and then closed his mouth. Julia did not know if she should take that as a good sign or a bad. She did want to treat the wound before he bled to death before her eyes, but she wasn't certain she wanted him so eager to join her in her bedchamber.

Or perhaps it was she whose heart beat a little faster at the thought of him in her room, alone and shirtless.

"After you," he said, drawing her attention to the fact that she was still standing in the middle of the parlor.

She clenched her hands together and walked past him, trying very hard not to notice how, without his coat, the tight fit of his trousers was more apparent and his thin linen shirt did little to hide his muscled chest beneath.

In the corridor she hesitated, not certain whether she should take the servants' stairs or the main stairway. She decided on the main stairway so she would not have to explain herself to Mrs. Koch. All the boys and Mrs. Dunwitty were still at their lessons. Mr. Goring and Jackson were absent, which meant it would be her and Wraxall alone together. She lifted her skirts and started up the stairs, feeling his presence right behind him. Since he'd eschewed shaving thus far today, he had a dark shadow on his jaw. His work on the roof had left a smudge on his cheek and several more on his hands. The overall effect was one of danger.

The fact he stalked after her like a leopard hunting prey did not calm her nerves.

Finally, they reached the second floor and she led him into her chamber. She wisely left the door open as she rummaged on her dressing table for the kit she kept of basic medical supplies—bandages, strips of cloth, cotton, and spirits to clean a wound if need be. She found it, then turned to see him standing beside her bed, looking about her room with keen interest.

Too late, she realized she had been in a hurry when she'd dressed this morning—after the embarrassing incident with Mrs. Dunwitty catching them in the parlor—and she had left all of her underthings strewn about. Not to mention her bed was unmade and her night rail lay on top of the coverlet.

His gaze met hers, and Julia swallowed at the heat she saw in his eyes. She had to say something— anything—to ease the tension they both felt.

"Take off your shirt."

Quite possibly, that was not the correct phrase for this exact moment.

He raised a brow, probably considering all the naughty things he might say next. She cut him off. "I need to see to your injury."

"It's not an injury. It's a scratch. What we really need to discuss are Billy and Walter."

"Walter was not even involved in the incident this morning," she protested.

"That's because he and Billy are working together." He moved closer, his gaze locked on hers. "For Slag."

She remembered the conversation she'd overheard between Wraxall and Walter. Not Billy too. She shook her head. "Billy isn't working for Slag."

"I can't prove it. Not yet, at any rate. But all the signs are there."

This could not be happening. These were her boys. Slag could not have them. "I won't let Slag turn my boys into criminals."

"How will you stop him? It won't be long before these boys are bigger and stronger than you, and then they'll go where they like, when they like. I'm fairly certain Billy could best you."

"He would never hurt me." She knew Billy, knew that underneath his aloof exterior was a boy who just needed to be loved. She had to find a way to reach that boy and to show him that she would love him.

"My lady, forgive me, but I have fought with thousands of men and commanded hundreds. I know something about my own sex. All Billy knows is violence. He might not want to hurt you, but if you stand in his way, he will do what he knows best."

"And your solution is to condemn him to life in a workhouse?"

"Never. It was a threat, but the idea behind it is sound. If he is a threat to the other boys, then you owe it to them to send him away."

"No." Her chest tightened, and she struggled to draw a breath. "I will never let you take him away. I won't allow you to take any of them. They are mine, and you can't take them from me." To her shock, tears appeared in her eyes.

"Even if it's for the best?" he asked.

"It's best that they stay here with me." He was not Lainesborough, she told herself. *Not Lainesborough*. But it was too late. She could not calm herself.

He leaned down so their eyes were level. "You are not Billy's mother."

"I am the closest thing he has to a mother, and I will not allow you to rip him out of my arms as he cries in fear because he's being taken from the only people and the only place he's ever known."

She'd said too much. She knew it too late, and she pressed a hand to her mouth, but Wraxall's shrewd gaze missed nothing. Instead of replying, instead of asking her what the devil she was talking about, he stepped back, turned, and walked to the bedchamber door.

She closed her eyes. He would leave now. He would go to her father and tell the earl to send footmen to drag her back to the town house or, worse yet, an asylum. Perhaps he'd even warn the board she was not sane enough to hold this position.

She heard the door click closed and opened her eyes. But he wasn't gone. He regarded her as he leaned on the closed door. "Perhaps it's time I allowed you to tend to my injury."

She sniffled. "I thought it was merely a scratch."

"Yes, well, even a scratch can become infected and fester if not properly treated."

She nodded. Were they still talking of wounds or was he being metaphorical? And then she forgot her name, much less worrying about literal versus figurative language, when he moved away from the door, pulled his shirt tails from his trousers, and yanked the shirt over his head.

∽

Neil had never been tempted to break his vow to abstain from coitus until he stood half-naked in Lady Juliana's bedchamber and watched her brown eyes darken with desire when he removed his shirt.

She made him want to throw caution to the wind and take the chance that he might father a bastard.

His iron grip had always been steady and solid, even when he had a woman naked and willing in his arms. He'd always been able to give and receive pleasure without that one dangerous act, and though some women tried to entice him, he was steadfast.

Lady Juliana was doing nothing to entice him, and yet he felt himself harden. In his mind, images of her lying beneath him, crying his name as he drove into her, came again and again wholly unbidden.

He told himself this was not the time to give in to temptation. She was visibly upset—about Billy, yes, but about something far more traumatic. She needed a distraction and consolation. She did not need a man who could think of nothing but deflowering her.

Her pink tongue darted out to lick her bottom lip in a gesture that was obviously innocent but which fired his blood nonetheless. Abruptly, he sat on the bed and balled his shirt over the tent in his trousers, lest his arousal become patently obvious.

That seemed to compel her to action. She gathered her medical supplies and placed them on the bed next to him, then poured water from the ewer into a basin. "You are right, of course," she said, her voice a little wobbly but growing stronger. "The reason we came in here was to tend to your wound."

He glanced down at the scratch on his arm and resisted pointing out it really did not qualify as a wound. Distraction was key at present. When she had recovered herself, he could bring up the topic of Billy again. As to the other matter she had mentioned, he was curious, but to ask her about it would be a mistake. He was already in too deep here at the orphanage and with her. He could not encourage confidences. He could not allow emotions to whirl about them and spin a web binding them together.

Unfortunately, he was feeling some rather strong emotions when she knelt on the bed beside him and began to clean blood from his arm with a clean strip of linen.

Why the hell had he sat on the bed? She had a chair at the dressing table. Why hadn't he sat there instead of this bed that conjured images of the two of them entwined together even before she knelt beside him on it? Some of the blood on his arm had dried, and she lightly gripped his arm as she attempted to clean it. He clenched his jaw in an attempt not to notice the softness of her fingertips, the swell of her breasts against the light-green fabric of her dress, or the tempting fragrance of roses that scented her hair.

"Am I hurting you?" she asked.

"No," he said, not unclenching his teeth. "Why?"

"You seem rather tense."

Was it his imagination or did she sound as breathless

as he felt. He turned his head to look at her, then thought better of. If he looked at her, he'd only notice the way the light made her coppery hair look as though it was aflame or the pale translucency of her skin or the fullness of her mouth.

Stop it. Think of… He struggled to imagine something or someone unattractive. *Porter! Think of the Draven Club's Master of the House. There was absolutely nothing remotely arousing about Porter.*

"There, that's clean. Now, where is the bandage?" She leaned forward to look for it, pressing her breasts against his bicep. Neil closed his eyes, but he couldn't imagine Porter's wrinkled face. All he could imagine were the soft curves of those breasts as they strained within the confines of the lace night rail. He gripped the bedclothes with his uninjured arm and could almost feel the silk of the night rail against his palm.

Opening his eyes, he realized his hand had landed on the damned night rail. How the devil was any one man supposed to stand strong in the face of these temptations?

"Here it is." She sat back again. Neil thanked God only her hands touched him again. His nose caught the sharp smell of spirits right before she pressed a cloth soaked in whatever it was against his scrape.

"Bloody hell!" he swore. "You could warn a man."

She looked up at him, eyes wide. "Did that hurt?"

Not so much as the straining of his cock, but he couldn't do anything to ease that discomfort. "A little sting," he said, his voice clipped.

"I'm almost done."

He watched as she wound the bandage around his bicep. He was not about to take his eyes off her—not after she'd almost caused him to squeal like a child. She moved with grace and efficiency, and the scratch was covered in clean linen in no time. She tied it off, but having a difficult time making sure the knot was secure, she used her teeth to pull one end of the knot she made so she could keep the finger of her other hand in place.

Good God but he would embarrass himself in a moment. He could hardly stop himself from imaging those small, white teeth moving just a fraction to the left and scoring his bare chest.

Unfortunately, she chose that moment to glance up at him. "All done." Her smile faded when she saw the look on his face. "What's wrong?" she asked.

"I'm sorry," he grit out, leaning toward her and wrapping his good arm around her waist. When she gasped in surprise, he said again, "I'm sorry." His mouth took hers in a fierce kiss. She stiffened in his arms, her lips tight and unyielding. But as the kiss deepened, she became more pliant. Her body melted against his, and her lips softened. She returned the kiss tentatively at first and then she was kissing him back, her passion as hot as his. He growled and pulled her closer, needing more of her, wanting all of her. When that didn't satisfy, he lifted her and hauled her onto his lap.

Her hands dragged through his hair, and his hands held her waist and splayed upward until the tips of his fingers brushed the swell of her breasts. He waited for her to protest, but she only continued to kiss him, her tongue delving into his mouth and twining with his. And then as though the decision was made for him, she leaned into him and her breasts filled his hands.

What was a man to do? He cupped them, moving his thumbs until they traced the points of her nipples through the thick fabric of her gown. He traced the nipples, still kissing her, until he felt them pebble and harden. With a moan, she leaned back and looked at his face. Her breath came fast and hard, and her face flushed when she looked down at his hands, moving in circles over her rounded flesh.

She did not tell him to cease, and Neil had the impression that he might not be the first man she'd allowed this liberty. She was an earl's daughter. She'd been to balls and fetes and soirees. More than one man had probably pulled her into a dark alcove to kiss her, then try for more.

Her eyes closed briefly as his thumbs brushed her nipples. "You like this," he said quietly.

"I shouldn't."

"You were made to experience pleasure."

"I have a house full of orphans to care for. I don't have time for pleasure." She began to wriggle off his lap, which only made him want to keep her there.

"You can make time."

"No."

He had to allow her to pull away. He'd been raised as a gentleman. He knew when a lady resisted, a gentleman released her. He also knew he would not have this chance again, and whereas before, one woman was the same as another, now this woman was the only one he wanted.

And of course this was the woman who did not want him.

Neil released her, disappointment surging through

him. He hadn't expected to feel such fierce regret at having to let her go. In the past few days, he'd seen her frustrated, angry, amused, and nurturing. He'd also seen her aroused, and that was the look he liked best on her.

He held his arms out, a gesture designed to prove he would not attempt to keep her against will. Instead of pushing away from him, she sat motionless on his lap.

Was it his imagination or did she hesitate? Perhaps she was not so certain she wanted to be free of his embrace.

"Wait," she said, her voice quiet and hesitant.

Neil's heart began to pound, and he had to hold his arms at his sides to keep from wrapping her in them once again. She did not move, and after three thudding heartbeats, Neil swallowed. "Wait?"

She shook her head. "I was right to begin with. Stop." But she didn't rise or make any move to pull farther away from him. Instead, her gaze met his. He saw a wariness there he'd seen in her eyes when she'd looked at him before.

"Who hurt you?" he said, thinking aloud, the words free before he could rein them in.

"No one," she said immediately.

"Did some man force you? Did he physically hurt you?" His arms circled her, the gesture purely protective. "Tell me his name, and I will see that he receives the punishment he is due."

She gave him a sad smile. "Thank you, noble knight, but I wasn't accosted. There's no one who hurt me."

Neil could see in the way she shifted her gaze that she lied. And whatever it was she hid, that was the key to everything.

Fourteen

SHE WASN'T BEING COMPLETELY HONEST. SHE HAD BEEN hurt. Her heart had been torn from her body and stomped on not once but twice. But that pain, that injustice, was not of the kind he spoke of. He thought some man had forced unwanted attentions on her. That wasn't it at all, though she was not so innocent that she didn't know some men would take as much as they could if given a chance. Even gentlemen were not averse to demanding that pleasure bestowed be repaid.

"But you don't trust me."

She looked up from where her hands had fisted in the material of her day dress. She was painfully aware she still sat on his lap, painfully aware she should not be there, painfully aware of the hard length of him waiting to press against that most intimate part of herself if she only scooted forward slightly.

"Trust you how?"

"To stop when you ask me to stop. To release you when you say no."

Her cheeks heated. "We should not be discussing this." And yet she could not make herself move away from him. His arms still encircled her, and she loved that he held her. She wanted to move closer, put her head on his chest, press her lips against his bronze skin because of one thing she was certain—he was absolutely magnificent. When he'd removed his shirt, her legs had gone weak at the sight of all that perfect, golden skin. His shoulders were impossibly broad, his waist flawlessly tapered, his chest tightly muscled, and his abdomen taut and flat. He looked every inch the knight, the warrior of the storybooks.

"And yet you do not move away from me."

She might have moved away then, but as soon as the words were spoken, he leaned forward and nuzzled her neck. Small tendrils of pleasure curled through her. She sighed and put her hands on his shoulders, feeling the heat of him all but pulsing under her fingertips.

"Do you know why you don't move away?" he asked, his breath hot on her skin.

"Why?" she murmured, angling her head to give him better access to that one spot just below her earlobe. She would end this in a moment. She would tell him to cease and mean it.

"Because you like this. Because all day, you take care of everyone else, and right now, you have a moment to yourself, and you deserve pleasure. You *need* pleasure."

It was true. It had been so long since she had done anything for herself—read a book, taken a walk, lain abed and slept all day. Her life was all duty and responsibility—to the children, to her father, to the board. Wraxall's mouth moved over her skin so lightly and with such skill that she could not stop the shivers racing down her spine. She could have given herself to his lips all day. She needed nothing but the feel of his stubble tickling her skin and the brush of his mouth tantalizing her flesh.

"The children," she murmured.

"Are with Mrs. Dunwitty." His hands moved up her back, pulling her closer until she was pressed against the warm skin of his bare chest.

"And if she releases them?"

"We'll hear them." His mouth traced her jaw. "They are louder than a cavalry regiment." His mouth took hers in a long, lazy kiss. Her breasts felt heavy and ached for his touch. She pushed them harder against his chest, but her need went unfulfilled.

"I should see to the noon meal."

"Let me see to you, and Mrs. Koch will see to the kitchen."

Before she could protest—not that she intended to—his hands cupped her face, and he kissed her with such a thoroughness she could think of nothing but lips, and tongues, and teeth. Her hands explored the long, lean planes of his back, holding on tightly when she feared she had grown so light-headed she might fall.

"Juliana," he murmured between kisses.

"I like the way you say my name," she said. "You make it sound so exotic." She'd always preferred Julia to Juliana, which sounded so formal. But when Wraxall said her name, it sounded soft and sensual.

"Let me show you pleasure, Juliana."

Yes. That was what she wanted. More of this. More

of him. More of those heart-stopping, head-lightening kisses that made her forget empty larders and leaky roofs and scheming crime lords. "Just for a moment," she told him, but she knew she was his for as long as he continued this persuasive assault.

He pulled her even closer, and she felt the bulge of his erection pressing deliciously against the juncture of her thighs. Her skirts and his trousers were between them, but the feel of the material separating them did nothing to diminish the knowledge that he desired her. He wanted her, even after seeing her at her worst. His mouth continued to worship hers, and she wriggled on his lap, trying to relieve the ache growing between her legs.

He groaned, and she stilled. "Did I hurt you?"

"It's an exquisite pain," he said through clenched teeth. "I find that an apt descriptor."

"Exquisite pain. What does that mean?"

"I'll show you." His hands circled around her ribs, coming to rest just beneath her too heavy breasts. With a slowness that made her catch her breath, his fingers skated upward until they caressed the dark-green ribbon that lay just beneath her bosom. His hands traced her curves, stroking and cupping her, until her breathing had grown from quick to panting.

"Please," she said. Her eyes widened. "I did not mean—"

He put a finger to her lips. "Yes, you did. And I know what you want." His hand went back where she wanted him and then his thumbs moved toward the center of the orbs, brushing lightly over her nipples. She jumped as sensation flashed through her. His fingers caressed the hard pebbles again, circling them until they grew harder.

"More?" he asked.

Of course there was more. She knew there was more. It was simply that she had never allowed any man to go any further than this. To do so now, with this man who made her feel what no other man had ever made her feel, was surely madness. And yet she would be mad to tell him to stop.

She was beginning to understand what he meant by exquisite pain. She yearned and ached, but she never wanted that sensation to cease.

"Trust me," he said. His hand moved to where she'd pinned her bodice, and he slowly removed first one pin then another. He stuck them into the coverlet on the side of the bed, where they would not be lost, and he moved to unpin the other side of her bodice.

She couldn't trust him. She couldn't trust any man. She knew what they were. She knew they were selfish creatures who cared only for their own pleasures, but as this man lowered her bodice, she watched his gaze turn reverent. His fingers brushed lightly over the swell of her breasts at the edge of chemise and stays.

"Your skin is as beautiful as it is soft," he murmured. "Let me see you."

No man had ever seen her. She'd never imagined she would allow a man that liberty. After all, why give a man that privilege, satisfy his selfish desire? But this did not feel selfish at all. This felt altogether different. He was not using her to satisfy himself, but worshipping her, giving her pleasure.

One hand swept into the valley of her breasts and tugged at the knot keeping her stays tightly laced. Since she had no one to help her dress, she had to lace them in front, and now he loosened them easily and pushed them down and out of his way.

"You are exquisite," he said, his gaze going to her face and then back to her all-but-translucent chemise. She looked down and could see the pink of her aureoles and nipples through the fine fabric. He bent his head, pressing his warm mouth against one breast. His breath was hot, and the shot of pleasure went straight to her core. Wet heat dampened her sex as his tongue darted out to dampen the linen on her shift. He took her nipple through the fabric, sucking it and rubbing it with his tongue. The feel of the fabric scraping against her already-turgid flesh was more than she could resist. She moaned softly, and he stilled.

She opened her eyes—belatedly realizing she'd closed them—and looked at him to find his lovely eyes focused on her face. "I want to hear you do that again. Before we're through here, you'll moan my name, Juliana."

His mouth took her other nipple, and she closed her eyes. "Wraxall," she moaned.

"Neil," he said, his mouth still on her. And then she felt the knot of her chemise loosen and the cool air on wet skin. He parted the fabric, and his bare hands touched her bare flesh. She trembled, and the hard points of her nipples seemed to grow even fuller. She needed his mouth on her there, though she knew it would not give her the relief she sought.

This was what he had meant by exquisite pain. She

wanted more, burned for more, and when he gave it to her, her need simply grew.

His mouth pressed on the slope of one breast while his hand cupped the other. When he ran a thumb over that nipple, the rough pad of his finger on that tender bud, she moaned without restraint. His mouth moved lower, heat making a fiery path to the place she wanted him. "Please," she whispered. "Yes," she said when his mouth brushed over the stiff, throbbing point. His hand plucked at her flesh as his mouth teased her, and then he closed his hot lips over her, and she bucked at the pleasure. Her back arched, and she knew she had surrendered to him completely.

One hand wrapped around her, holding her steady, holding her sex against the hard length of him, while his mouth teased and tantalized. The more his mouth worshipped her, the more she wanted. She could not stop her moans and pants of pleasure, and if that behavior was not indignity enough, her hands fisted in his hair and all but pushed him into her chest.

And then his hands grasped her hips, and he groaned her name. "I shall embarrass myself if you keep this up."

For a long moment she did not know what he meant. The panting? The hands in his hair? And then she realized he held her hips—hips that wanted desperately to move. Good Lord, she had been grinding against him. She was little better than a dog in heat.

"No," he said, his hand cupping her chin and forcing her to look at him. "You've done nothing wrong. Your movements are perfectly natural. Let me give you what you want."

She nodded because she wanted so much, and he—he seemed to know exactly what it was her body yearned for. He lifted her, hands under her bottom, then laid her on the bed gently, on the side away from the pins. She looked up at him, feeling suddenly more exposed as she lay on the bed with her bodice open. Which was ridiculous. She had been just as exposed on his lap.

He sat on the bed beside her and one warm hand came to rest between her breasts. She might have turned into that touch if she hadn't felt his other hand on her ankle. That hand moved upward inch by provocative inch, exposing her ankle. She opened her mouth to protest, and his large hand closed over one breast. And then he bent over her, his mouth on the other. Her hands gripped the bedclothes as his hot breath made her quiver and his hand on her calf made her itch to move, to squirm, to…something.

And then his hand was on her knee, and she knew she must stop him. He sucked her nipple into his mouth, the pressure harder than before and that much more exquisite. At the same time, he pushed her knees open.

And she allowed it. She did not want him to stop. She wanted his hand on her thigh and higher—in that private place only she had ever touched. His hand slid upward, tickling the inside of her thigh. He raised his head, his eyes as blue as the sea when he looked at her.

"Are you wet for me?"

"Yes," she said, too aroused to be embarrassed.

"Will you let me touch you? I want to feel how wet you are."

"I can't," she said, the words so filled with regret she all but cried them. "I cannot risk a child, a pregnancy."

He shook his head. "You misunderstand. I won't take you—not like that. I won't touch you with anything but fingers." His fingers moved higher, and she widened her legs, despite knowing she should end this. The children could be through with their lessons. She had lost control. There was a midday meal to consider.

"And hands." He shifted on the bed, his hands pushing her skirts up until she was exposed to him. She almost grabbed them, to lower them again, but his hands slid over her pelvis and across her sex until they rested between her legs, those skilled fingers teasing her by inching higher and retreating over and again.

"You see? Only fingers." His finger brushed against her and she gasped. "And hands." He cupped her, and God help her, she pressed against his hand. "And perhaps my mouth."

She froze. Her gaze darted to his, and he gave her a wicked grin. "If you want me to stop, all you need do is ask." His palm pressed against her again, giving her the pressure she wanted just as one finger delved down and parted her flesh. "You are wet," he said. "But I want you dripping."

His finger entered her then, and she stiffened with surprise and pleasure. He stroked in and out, all the while his palm pressing where she most needed him. Her hips wanted to move, and she closed her eyes and arched them so they rubbed against his palm. He made a sound of approval, and then he entered her again, this time with two fingers.

"Oh yes," she moaned. Then "No!" when he moved his palm and slid his fingers out.

"Impatient, aren't you?"

One of his fingers caressed her as it moved upward to part her flesh and then circle the small bud of pleasure hiding in her folds. The world went black for a moment as she caught her breath at the unfathomable sensation. She had never felt pleasure like this, and yet she knew there was more. That finger continued to spread wetness over the sensitive bud, circling it and tapping it. Pleasure built. Heat built. Need built. Julia opened her eyes. Her breasts were bare, her skirts hiked to her waist, her legs spread. Neil Wraxall straddled one of her legs, his eyes seeing her more intimately than anyone else ever had.

And she did not care. She only cared that he never stop.

"Let go," he murmured, his intense gaze on her face. "I want to see you come."

She didn't know what he meant, but she knew that was the aim of the tension she felt. His gaze touched her breasts, making her nipples pebble with yearning. And then he gazed at the place where his finger touched her, and the look of desire she saw in his eyes undid her.

A wave of pulsing sensation flooded through her. She gasped and pressed hard against his hand, then fell back with a shuddering breath as a delicious warmth spread through her. He was correct. This was what she had needed. The tightness in her temples and shoulders had eased, and she felt relaxed for the first time in recent memory.

And then he leaned over her, and the warmth of the pleasure ebbed away. He kissed her lips, exploring her mouth. She had been kissed enough to judge, and he was an excellent kisser. But she could not enjoy the kiss. She knew what would come next. Men were selfish and calculating. She knew it, and she should not have allowed this interlude with Neil—Wraxall, rather—to go as far as it had. He would want to take his pleasure. She was a virgin and intended to remain so. Even if the thought of lying with him thrilled her, she had to think of the children and her responsibilities here. She could not risk a pregnancy or being found alone with him.

His mouth slanted over hers in a long, lovely kiss, but she forced herself to push him back. "You should dress and go."

A look she could only describe as shock crossed his face. He recovered quickly, raising one brow in amusement. "Am I to be so summarily dismissed?"

She threw her skirts down over her legs and pulled her bodice up, holding it with both hands. "I should never have allowed the events of this afternoon to progress as far as they did. I know you have expectations, and I am sorry to have to disappoint you."

She pushed to the edge of the bed, but before she could rise, he slid his arm over her, effectively blocking her and holding her in place. "How do you know my expectations?"

She risked a look at him and immediately wished she hadn't. He was so incredibly handsome, with his dark hair falling over his forehead and amazingly blue eyes bright against his bronze skin. She would have loved to trace his face with her fingers, to run her hands through his silky hair, to kiss his full lips. But she could not afford to dally with a lover. She had an orphanage to manage and children who needed her. "You are a man," she said. "Any girl who has been to a half dozen balls or an equal number of theatrical productions knows what men want from women."

"I see," he said, but he didn't move his arm. "So my plan is to debauch you. To have my way with you. To… What's another polite term? Ah! Ruin you."

"I did not say that was your plan, but now that you have given me pleasure, I assume you expect to be repaid in kind."

"Repaid? Do you think I view what just happened as a business transaction?"

Had she offended him? Should she apologize? Perhaps that was also part of his plan to seduce her. "I—" she stuttered. "Very well, then. How do you view our…liaison?"

He leaned closer until his mouth brushed her ear. She tried not to shiver. "As something I have wanted to do since almost the moment I met you."

"And how does that not prove my point?" she asked, her voice breathy.

"Because the more I have come to know you, the more I wanted to taste your lips, touch your skin"—he exerted gentle pressure with his arm and she gave in, lying back—"see your cheeks rosy with pleasure. I like you, Juliana. Our liaison is the physical evidence of my regard for you."

He was very close to her, looking down at her, one hand stroking the hair back from her face. "And I suppose you wish to show me more of your regard."

"I do, yes, but not in the way you mean."

She narrowed her eyes. "You don't want to lie with me?"

Still holding a lock of her hair between two fingers he looked at her. "If you mean do I want to strip bare, throw up your skirts, and thrust inside you, the answer is yes. There's nothing I want more. It's pure instinct for a man when he is aroused, and you most definitely arouse me." He rubbed her hair between his two fingers. "But I am not a man ruled by instincts. My father was such a man, and I don't intend to follow in his footsteps. I will father no bastards."

"I imagine most men don't want bastards, and yet the orphanages are full."

He dropped her hair and his gaze became serious. "Many men don't care and others don't care enough to do what is necessary to prevent a bastard from being born. I think you of all people know how I feel about bastards."

Julia considered this. There was only one way to ensure a child did not result from a tryst. "Are you saying you have never... I mean, that you are..."

"A virgin? Yes. Does it shock you?"

Beyond words. In her experience, men wasted no time divesting themselves of their virginity. Men of the nobility seemed to pride themselves on sowing wild oats, which meant leaving a trail of prostitutes, actresses, and barmaids in their lascivious wake. Even if she could believe Neil had retained his virginity, despite being a soldier and the son of a wealthy marquess, she could hardly believe it after what he had just done with her.

"You are shocked," he said, scrutinizing her. "You also seem dubious."

"I wouldn't dream of questioning you." She tried to sit.

He stalled her with one finger. "But?"

She looked askance. "You seem to have some experience."

"And you have none? I'll wager you've been kissed before."

"Yes, but not—" Her cheeks felt hot, though why she should feel at all embarrassed after lying half-naked and exposed before this man was a mystery. "Not the way you kissed me."

"I kissed you in an unvirginal manner?"

He'd raised her ire. "'Unvirginal' is not a word, but to answer your question, you kissed me like a man who has kissed many women. Like a man who knows how to kiss, how to enjoy it, and how to make certain I enjoy it."

She realized what she'd said too late and sighed at the wide smile on his face. "So you enjoyed my kisses. What else did you enjoy?"

"You know the answer to that."

The finger that had rested on her shoulder slid down. "The way I touched your breasts?" He pushed her hands aside with lamentably no resistance on her part and moved the material covering her. His hand stroked over her skin, just as she'd hoped he would. "The way I suckled your nipples?" He bent and lapped at one hard tip with his tongue, and she put an arm around his neck as though to keep him there. What was she doing? She couldn't trust him, couldn't trust men, and yet this man was not at all like any other man she'd known.

"But I think what you really enjoyed was my hand between your legs."

"You shouldn't say such things."

"My darling, Juliana, what you don't seem to understand is that I may be a virgin, but I'm no priest. Just because I haven't ever"—he seemed to be thinking of the way to put it—"known a woman in the biblical sense doesn't mean I haven't *known* women."

"I see." Her voice was barely a whisper as one of his hands trailed a lazy path down her abdomen.

"I don't think you do. I don't think you know all the extremely pleasurable, but very naughty, things we might do without there ever being any chance of a bastard."

"No, I don't." She gasped as his hand stroked over her center.

"Shall I show you another? That had been my plan before you accused me of all manner of nefarious plots."

"And how do I know you don't have nefarious intentions now?"

His hand fisted in the fabric of her skirts and began pulling it higher, revealing more and more of her legs. "Oh, I do. I intend to behave most wickedly, all in the name of giving you pleasure. But, Juliana." She opened her eyes at the demanding tone in his voice. "I do this because I want to, not because I expect anything in return. The day you give me more than the pleasure I take from watching you climax and hearing you moan and feeling your body writhe beneath my touch is the day you offer, freely and willingly, to pleasure me. Do you understand?"

His hand was between her legs again, and she couldn't possibly answer him. Her body was already tightening in anticipation of the feelings she knew he could give her. Though she could not manage to find words, she understood something very well. She had found a man who was, ostensibly, far less selfish than she because she planned to take what he gave and give nothing in return.

He moved over her, less tender now, and lifted her by the waist until she was farther back on the bed. He settled himself between her knees and spread them wide. Julia reached to cover herself, but he caught her hands. "I only want to look at you, to see what I will taste."

"Taste?" she squealed.

"I promised nefarious activities, didn't I?" His gaze went back to her core. "Perhaps I wasn't entirely honest earlier. Seeing you like this—lovely and pink and wet for me—is more than enough payment."

"I didn't mean—"

"Shh. I know what you meant, and I don't fault you. You'd be a fool to trust most men, most women too. And you are no fool. No." He bent and brushed his stubbled cheek along her inner thigh. Julia jumped. "You are brave." He kissed her thigh. "Determined." He kissed the other, this time a bit higher. "Intelligent." His lips brushed her curls. "Caring." His mouth brushed against that innermost part of her and she gasped. "And beautiful. So beautiful."

His mouth settled against her and then she felt his

tongue stroke and part her. The little bud he had teased with his hands earlier tightened and strained and was finally rewarded with a lick from his tongue. Julia moaned. He licked her again, his tongue lazy and inquisitive, rubbing against her until pressure began to build.

This pressure was unlike what she had felt last time. That had been pleasant and warm. This was more grasping, more desperate. As much as she had enjoyed the pleasure he'd given her before, this time she knew it would be more.

His hot breath feathered over her swollen flesh. "Do you enjoy my tongue here?"

She nodded.

"I can't hear you all the way down here." He blew a breath of cool air over her and she let out a small cry. "Do you like this?" He laved his tongue over her, and her hands fisted in the bedclothes. "Or this?" He flicked the tip of his tongue across her, and she cried out.

"Yes! Oh yes!"

"Good." His tongue returned, grating and tapping against her until her whole body strained toward something indefinable. The entire experience wasn't even pleasurable. It was agony, but the sweetest sort. She would have killed him if he had stopped, and she wanted to kill him for making her feel this way.

And then with a growl he pushed her legs wider. One finger slid inside her while his tongue kept up that exquisite torture. Then another finger slid inside her, stroking her, moving in and out as his tongue lashed at her. White spots blurred her vision and her entire body tensed. Then he did something. She could not have said whether it was his tongue or his fingers in the end, but everything inside her broke free. She felt as though her body was the fluffy dandelion seeds, blown apart by a wild gust of wind. Ecstasy rushed through her, making her cry out at its intensity. It twirled and danced and blew where the breeze would take it. And when it finally ebbed, she could only gasp in a breath and lay in an exhausted heap of feeling.

She managed to open her eyes and found him beside her, looking down at her with an expression she couldn't quite place. Tenderness? Affection? Desire?

"What are you doing to me?" she murmured.

"I think the better question is, what are you doing to me?"

❧

Several hours later, when he'd bathed, shaved, and changed into his evening clothing, Neil could admit he had not been entirely honest with Juliana. He'd been honest that he was, in the strictest sense, a virgin, but he was no sexual martyr. It was true that when he took a woman to his bed, he enjoyed giving her pleasure. Certainly, there had been times when, after the heat of battle, he needed a quick release and a woman willing to give it to him. For the most part, he was a considerate lover who gave as much as he took. The truth of the matter was that he did take. Juliana had been right to assume he would—any man would—seek his own release after giving her one.

But for the first time, his pleasure hadn't been paramount. For the first time, he wanted only her fulfillment. She deserved an hour of joy in an otherwise difficult day. What to him seemed like a stream of difficult days. Putting her pleasure above his didn't mean he didn't enjoy her. She was a beautiful woman, despite the drab gowns and mussed hair. And she was even more beautiful in the throes of passion. He was still aroused from their encounter, and Neil wasn't certain how he would manage to keep his hands off her the rest of the night.

Fortunately, the Earl St. Maur solved that problem. He arrived with the coach at half past eight, and soon, Neil and Juliana were inside with her father. Though her father attempted to appear interested in the orphanage by asking about the boys and the repairs, his questions were polite and his responses noncommittal.

For her part, Juliana sat stiffly and spoke only when spoken to. She was a vision in a white dress ornamented by sparkly gold flowers. She shimmered in the dark of the carriage, looking like a queen. Neil's gaze continued to drift to her lips, still swollen from his kisses. What he would have given to kiss them again.

St. Maur's next words reminded him, however, that this was the end of his association with Lady Juliana.

"And have you given any more consideration to my request you come home? I'm afraid if you are away much longer, people will begin to talk."

It was not an idle observation. People would talk, if they hadn't already, and then she would be ruined beyond repair.

"Papa, I told you, I don't care about what people say. The orphanage *is* my home."

"And what if I care? What if I do not want our family name dragged through the muck and mud?"

Juliana sighed. She could hardly argue against duty and honor.

"Fortunately, the way for Lady Juliana to return home should clear after tonight," Neil said. "The last of the major obstacles should be dealt with."

From across the carriage, Juliana glared at him. Her father, however, clapped his hands. "Capital! That is the best news I have had in weeks."

Neil barely paid attention to the receiving line or the performers at the musicale. His attention was focused on the guests and the servants. Slag was here somewhere, and Neil intended to find him before he found Juliana. He spotted Rafe at one end of the large music room. A brunette woman was on his arm, staring up at him adoringly. Rafe nodded to Neil and made a cut with his hand, indicating he had not spotted Slag yet. On the other end of the room, Ewan stood, all foreboding blond menace. His wife, Lady Lorraine, whispered to him. She was one of the most verbose women Neil had ever met, and he didn't expect an opera singer's aria was enough to silence her, even for a few minutes. Despite the distractions, Ewan caught Neil's eye and shook his head.

Juliana leaned toward Neil. He was seated on her right while her father sat on her left. "Do you think he is here yet?"

"If he is, no one has spotted him," Neil murmured back.

"Should I excuse myself and walk about? Perhaps that might lure him into the open."

Neil tensed. Was the woman mad? Why would she risk herself like that? "No. Under no circumstances should you be alone. Stay beside me or your father at all times. We will find Slag and deal with him."

"I hope this works," she said, sounding doubtful.

A woman behind them shushed them, and Neil focused his attention on the soprano again. Her high notes grated on his nerves almost as much as the stiff material of his cravat. Jackson, excited to have a reason to dress Neil in his best, had tied the damn neckcloth too high, not to mention starching the thing within an inch of its life.

After what seemed an interminable length of time, their host announced a brief intermission. Footmen in crisp, blue livery circled with wine and champagne, and ladies fluttered their fans and waxed poetic on the musical talent. Many of the men approached the soprano, who was young and pretty and spilled out of her bodice. Neil escorted Lady Juliana and her father toward one of the open windows and then excused himself. He headed toward Rafe, but he made certain to give Juliana a warning glance as he strode away. If she took even a step away from her father's side, he would have her head.

He'd taken no more than a few steps himself when he felt his arm entangled with another. He turned to face a woman who was familiar but whose name escaped him. "Mr. Wraxall," she cooed, drawing him close to her circle of three other ladies. "I have not seen you in ages."

"Ladies," he said with a quick bow. It must have been ages because he barely remembered her—Lady Sutcliffe perhaps? She had been one of the ladies vying for his oldest brother's hand in marriage. She had not been successful. "Lady Sutcliffe, how is your husband?" he asked, peering about and finding the older man leering down at the opera singer's chest.

"Tedious." She waved her fan. "Do you know Lady Marsh? And this is Mrs. Kemp and Miss Elliott." She made the introductions and Neil bowed, but his gaze sought Rafe. Ewan had joined Rafe, and the two watched him with undisguised amusement.

"It is a pleasure to meet all of you, but if you will—"

"Why do you not go into Society more often, Mr. Wraxall?" Lady Sutcliffe asked with a pout. "You are a war hero, and I, for one, know how to treat our heroes." She gave him a wink, and Neil had an inkling how Rafe must feel.

"I will endeavor to be more social," he said, knowing he would do nothing of the sort.

"Please do," Mrs. Kemp said. "There are no dashing young men to dance with at any of the balls. I imagine you…dance very well, do you not, Mr. Wraxall?"

At any other time and place, Neil would not have minded this feminine attention. Now, he could all but feel Lady Juliana's eyes boring into him. He glanced over his shoulder and saw her glaring across the room.

Seeing the direction of his gaze, Miss Elliott stepped forward. "Are you courting Lady Juliana? You were with her at the Sterling ball, were you not?"

"Her father and I are acquainted," Neil answered.

"She is a curious one, is she not?" Lady Marsh added. "I don't know why the men seem to fall all over her. She has that awful hair and spends all of her free time with dirty orphans."

"No wonder all her dresses are from last season!" Lady Sutcliffe laughed.

Neil turned and met Juliana's gaze again. "I can tell you why men fall all over her," he said. "She's the most beautiful woman in this room." He looked back at the four women surrounding him, all of them scowling. "And not just on the outside. She has the kindest, most forgiving nature of any person—man or woman—I have ever met. You would be lucky to have half of her courage, spirit, or compassion. If you will excuse me." And he strode toward Rafe and Ewan, leaving the women sputtering behind him.

Fifteen

Julia wondered what Wraxall had said to the women to cause them to glare at her with such malice. She had been giving him warning looks from the moment Lady Sutcliffe waylaid him. The quartet of ladies were overly fond of gossip, and they were not overly concerned as to whether the gossip was true. The last thing she needed was Wraxall making the wrong comment about where she had been living or where he had been sleeping. She could no longer claim—to herself, at least—that she and Wraxall were not involved romantically, or at least physically, but she had no desire for that knowledge to become public.

She let out a relieved breath when he finally reached his friends—the big blond soldier and a handsome man who dressed better than she did.

"Is everything all right?" her father asked.

Julia quickly pasted on a smile. "Of course. Why do you ask?"

"You seem tense." His kind green eyes assessed her. "I worry about you, Juliana. That is why I want you to come home."

"Papa, please. Not tonight."

He sighed. Julia hoped the discussion was over, but her father spoke again, his eyes on something across the room. "I am sorry, you know."

"Sorry?" she asked.

"For my neglect of you and Harriett after your mother died. I should have been there for you both, but instead I retreated into the only thing I knew—work."

"I suppose we all must cope with tragedy in the best way we can. Harriett and I never doubted you loved us."

He looked at her, his eyes bright. "Don't you see? That was the exact cause of my anguish. I loved your mother. Not when I married her." He waved a hand. "I barely knew her, but I grew to love her. When she died, it was so sudden. One day a fever and the next she was gone. Julia, I never told her."

Julia blinked in shock. He had never told her mother how much he loved her? "I am certain she knew, Papa."

"Are you? I am not. And not a day goes by that I don't wish I had but one more hour, one more minute with Mary so I might be certain she knew how I felt."

Julia took his hand, squeezing it tightly. "She knew, Papa. Harriett knew you loved her, and I know you love me."

"I only want the best for you, my darling. I only want another chance to be the father I should have been. Will you please consider coming home?"

Julia wished she could tell him yes, but she could never go back to the life she'd lived as an earl's daughter. The orphans needed her, especially now with Slag threatening them all. She could not leave them. "I will consider it, Papa," she said, but the way he looked at her told her he knew she did not mean it.

"Lady Juliana?" A servant appeared at her elbow with a silver tray holding a slip of foolscap.

"Yes."

"This came for you, my lady. A man delivered it and said it was urgent."

Frowning, Julia lifted the paper off the tray and opened it. Her hand shook as soon as she saw the words.

> I propose a trade. Your Billy for my blunt. The price is now two thousand pounds and a month in my bed.
>   Don't keep me waiting or the boy suffers.

"What is it?" Neil asked. She could not stop staring at the letter, and she had not even noticed that he'd crossed the room to her or that everyone was taking their seats for the next performance.

"Billy," she whispered, her throat feeling as though it was choked by sand.

Neil took the letter from her hand.

"What is wrong?" her father asked. "What is this about?"

Neil looked from the letter to Julia and then to the earl. "My lord, I must go, and I expect your daughter will want to come with me. There is a problem at the orphanage. May we have use of your coach?"

"Not this again."

"My lord, I promise that after tonight, there will be no more urgent summons from the orphanage."

Her father looked at Julia. "Will you make that same promise?"

She nodded, not at all certain it was a promise she could keep.

"If you don't mind, my lord, take your seat and pretend nothing is amiss. I will escort Lady Juliana to the orphanage and send the coach back."

"Very well." He pointed a finger at Neil. "I am relying on you to settle this, Wraxall."

Neil nodded. When her father turned away, he took Julia's arm, squeezing it reassuringly. "Mostyn and Beaumont are here. I'll bring them back with us. Make no mistake. *I* will bring Billy safely home."

Julia had not trusted a man in years, but in that moment, she had never believed in anyone more.

❧

Neil found the orphanage to be surprisingly quiet when he, Julia, and Rafe walked in. He had sent Mostyn ahead to Slag's flash ken, and he had to deliver Julia to Mrs. Dunwitty before he would follow. Julia had not ceased folding and unfolding Slag's missive all the way back from Mayfair. She hadn't spoken. There was nothing to say. Even Rafe had been uncharacteristically quiet.

"This is…charming," Rafe said, his tone of horror belying his words. "How very… Help me here, Wraxall."

"Shut up."

"Yes."

Jackson rushed in. "Sir, I am so relieved you have returned. We cannot find Master Billy."

"Slag has him," Neil said without preamble. "How long has he been gone?"

"According to Master Michael, at last reckoning it had been one hundred and eight minutes. Sir, your cravat—"

Neil shoved his hand away. "The Ox and Bull is a flash ken, not a royal residence. No one will care what my neckcloth looks like."

"As you say, sir." But Jackson's mouth drew down into a grimace.

Neil turned to Rafe. "Beaumont. I need you to stay here with Lady Juliana. If this is some sort of trick to leave the orphanage undefended, I will need you to protect the ladies and the children."

"What?" Rafe and Juliana said in unison.

"I am not staying behind," she said, stepping forward.

"Neil, you cannot possibly expect me to wait here. There are children and…and those hideous wall hangings," Rafe said.

Neil ignored him. "Keep the doors and windows locked and the boys inside." He cocked an ear, then looked at Jackson. "Where are the lads now?"

"In their rooms," the valet answered.

"Why is it so quiet?"

"Mrs. Dunwitty has given them one hour of independent study. The little boys have fallen asleep—they are exhausted from their lessons—and the older boys are pretending to comply."

Julia stepped between the men. "I am not staying behind. Slag has Billy. *My* Billy."

Jackson cleared his throat. "Perhaps I should take a tour of the dormitories and see if any of the children need help with his lesson."

"Good idea, Jackson." Neil gave the valet leave, but he hadn't waited for permission. Rafe didn't move. "Beaumont, don't you have something else to do?"

"No. I want to go too."

"You are staying and that is—"

Rafe raised a hand. "An order." He sighed. "Lady Juliana, where are the children?"

She pointed to the stairs. "On the second floor, sir. That way."

"Good." Rafe walked in the opposite direction. When they were alone, Neil spoke low. "If Slag has Billy, I will bring him back."

"And you think Slag will simply let you take him?"

Neil smiled. "Mostyn specializes in convincing men to do things they do not always want to do."

"I have no doubt, but I will go with you." She started for the door, but he stepped in front of her.

"No. You are staying here, where you will be safe."

"Billy is not safe. He needs me."

"The eleven boys here need you."

She moved around him and lifted a dark-green cloak off the rack, lying the thin shawl she had worn to the musicale in its place. "Jackson, Mrs. Dunwitty, and your pretty friend are here. The boys are in good hands." She fastened the cloak at her throat, and the green accented her dark-brown eyes. "I am ready."

"No, you are not. If you come with me, you only endanger yourself and me. I'll have to watch you instead of focusing on Slag, and that makes you a liability."

Her eyes narrowed. "Who said you need to take care of me? I can take care of myself."

"You stay."

She jerked her chin up. "I go." Then she stepped closer and lowered her voice. "I thought we were on the same side. Did this afternoon mean nothing to you?"

He could see what it cost her to mention their liaison. Her cheeks flamed red, making a lovely contrast to her copper hair. Neil reached out and touched one of those rosy cheeks. "It meant everything to me. That is why I want to keep you safe."

She moved out of his reach. "And if I wanted to be safe and locked up tightly, I would have stayed home in Mayfair. I will have my way in this. Either I go with you or I follow behind. I think it safer if we go together."

Neil saw the truth of her words in the hard set of her mouth and the lift of her brows in a slight challenge. He had been fighting for days to control his temper, but she'd finally cut the last tether. "Bloody hell, woman! Do you *want* to die?" he yelled.

"Watch your language, sir."

"I bloody hell won't." He grabbed her shoulders, not roughly, but firmly enough that she couldn't shake him off. "I am trying to keep you safe."

"And who do you think kept me safe before you came?" She pointed at her chest. "Me. I can take care of myself, and I won't have you coming in here and taking over."

This wasn't worth a raging tirade. Neil released her and clenched his fists. "If you want to die, fine. Let's go."

"Fine, let's go." She unlocked the door and pulled it open.

"After you," he said, and she marched out the door. Neil had never wanted to throttle a woman so badly.

Sixteen

Julia shuddered at the dark street, which seemed menacing tonight and such a contrast to the warm, comforting hand on her shoulder. Neil took her arm then and led her away from Sunnybrooke and into the heart of Spitalfields.

"I know you are angry," she said, as they stepped into the street, keeping to the side and out of the way of any carts and horses. She glanced at Neil, but his face was stoic and unreadable. He had a look of menace, a look of danger that was probably intended to keep criminals at bay.

"That is not the word I would use," he answered.

"Furious? Enraged? I know you are worried, but you cannot expect me to stay home."

He slanted her a look. "This won't be a garden party, sweetheart."

"I am well aware, sir, but neither must it be the battle you have made it out to be. Perhaps my presence might have a positive effect on the negotiations. At the least, we can all behave civilly."

Neil laughed, and she huffed and looked away from

him. She would reason with Slag, to buy them all more time. Perhaps if she gave him part of the money, he would be mollified.

Fall was upon them, and the days had begun to grow shorter. Men and women made their way through the streets, ostensibly to homes where they would see family and eat a meager evening meal. The beggars sat on every corner and every stoop, hands out, eyes pleading.

Julia looked down. The children were the ones who tore at her heart. When she had first come here, she had tried to take some of them in. For her efforts, she'd been chased away and accused of kidnapping. She'd quickly learned the children's parents—at least that's what the adults had claimed to be—benefitted from the pitiful, little beggars and were not eager to part with them.

The sad-eyed dogs and skinny cats were as omni-present as the dirt and the smell of burnt onion. She would have liked to rescue them if she could ever gather the funds for some sort of kennel.

Prostitutes were another staple of the streets. Julia had learned stay away from them. She'd always thought them poor women forced into selling their bodies for blunt. Perhaps that was true, but they were not kind—at least not to her. She had the sense most of them would slit her throat and rob her blind before they'd ever consider any charity from her.

Not that she could blame them. A hard heart kept them alive in the rookeries of London. They could not afford to trust anyone.

Julia kept her head down and avoided the

malevolent stares of the prostitutes, the pleas of the children, and the whines of the dogs. Neil must have known where the alehouse was located because he walked confidently past wipe shop after wipe shop—all selling stolen handkerchiefs. Julia clutched her own handkerchief—in her hand and ready should she need to cover her nose—tightly.

Finally, Neil stopped, and she squinted up at a low, dark building that looked to have been built at least two hundred years before. The small windows were grimy and the building's paint had chipped off. The sign out front must have portrayed proud illustrations of an ox and a bull once, but they had faded to almost unrecognizability.

It was the sort of establishment Julia would have crossed to the other side of the street to avoid. Too late now. She swallowed. "Are we going inside?"

"Not yet."

To her relief, Neil waited for a passing cart, then led her across the street. As she was about to inquire where he was taking her, a tall, fair-haired man with pale-blue eyes stepped into view. Mostyn. Julia could not have said where he had been a moment before, but his height and Nordic appearance made him stand out in the crowd of stoop-shouldered, dirty passersby. She had the sense that she would not have seen him until he wished to be seen. Clearly that was now, as Neil was leading her directly for him.

When they reached Mostyn, Julia looked up to meet his eyes. "Thank you for coming, Mr. Mostyn."

He nodded at her, not speaking. In fact, he barely glanced at her before he returned his attention to Neil.

"Report," Neil said, sounding very much like she imagined a general on the battlefield might sound.

"No one new in or out since I've been here," Mostyn answered.

"The boy is still inside."

Mostyn lifted a shoulder. "I can't see the rear exit."

Neil looked at her. "Then I suppose there is only one way to be certain. You have my back."

It wasn't a question, and Mostyn didn't dignify the remark with an answer. But when Neil turned to lead Julia back toward the alehouse, Mostyn stepped in front of them. They had no choice but to pause. To do otherwise would be to attempt to walk through a stone wall.

"The lady," Mostyn said.

Neil sighed, sounding weary. "I cannot leave her alone outside, and she refused to stay at the orphanage."

Mostyn's gaze flicked to her, then back to Neil. Whatever he saw when he looked at her must have convinced him persuading her to return to the orphanage was not an option. "I can go in alone," he said.

Neil shook his head. "I considered that on the way here, but I want to attempt negotiation first. You are not known for your skills in that arena, my friend."

"Why bother?" Mostyn asked. "Give Slag all the words you want. It will end the same way."

"Are you implying violence is inevitable, Mr. Mostyn?" Julia asked.

He looked at her. "I never imply."

"True enough," Neil said. "But you have your

orders." He looked at Julia. "Revised somewhat, but basically the same. Are you ready?"

"I have my dancing shoes on," Mostyn replied.

Julia wondered what that was supposed to mean. But she had no time to ask as, a moment later, she was ushered inside the Ox and Bull. It was even darker inside than she had anticipated, and it was rank with the smell of urine, smoke, and the odor of unwashed humans. She put her handkerchief to her nose, but even the rose fragrance she dabbed on the cloth could not disguise this stench. She coughed and attempted not to wretch. The sound seemed unbearably loud because as soon as they entered, all conversation ceased.

Julia looked at the low-ceilinged room packed with small tables and chairs. At each table sat men who looked more dangerous than the last. She suddenly regretted her decision to come along. That regret intensified when the barkeep called from the back of the room, where he stood behind a scarred and battered wooden partition, "We don't serve your kind. Get out."

"Want me to kill him?" Mostyn asked so low only she and Neil could hear.

"Not yet," Neil said. Then louder, "I wish to speak with Mr. Slag."

Julia was relieved Neil could speak. She could not move, much less form a coherent sentence.

"What do ye want with 'im?" a lad of no more than fifteen asked from the table closest to them. A weak lantern sat on top of that table beside several empty mugs, but the light did little more than illuminate the boy's small features and dirt-streaked face.

"It's a private matter," Neil said.

"Oh, a private matter," an older man said in a tone meant to mock Neil's upper-class accent. "Well, la–di–da. I 'ave a private matter I'd like to discuss with your wench." He grabbed his crotch, and Julia's face flamed.

"Want me to kill that one?" Mostyn asked, this time his voice a bit louder.

"Yes, and slowly." He raised a hand when Mostyn began to move forward. "But not yet." Neil looked around the room. "If Mr. Slag won't come out, I can only assume he is afraid to face me."

Julia's heart froze at those words. She knew men liked to taunt each other, but a remark like that seemed purely suicidal. Perhaps she would fare better outside with the rabid dogs and the greedy prostitutes. But as her gaze swept the room, taking in the angry looks of the patrons, one face looked back at her with fear.

"Mr. Goring?" she said. Her voice was loud enough to carry and, as it was a female voice and quite proper in tone, the rumbling rolling through the room died and every man to a one followed her gaze to the back table where her servant sat, head down, shoulders hunched over his ale.

"Is that you?" she asked. She forgot her fear for a moment. "I did not want to believe Mr. Wraxall when he said you were a patron here, but I see I have been deceived and betrayed."

Goring looked up then back down. "I apologize, my lady."

"You have a lot more to apologize for than this. It was you, was it not, stealing from the larder?"

Goring didn't answer.

"Shame on you," she said, directing the comment to the room at large. "Stealing from poor orphans."

"Cry me a river," one man called.

"I was an orphan, I was, and no one gave me so much as a crumb. Bollocks on orphans."

Too late, Julia realized her mistake. She'd let her emotions get the better of her and forgotten her audience. These men didn't care a whit for orphans. She took careful step back and her back collided with Neil's chest. He caught her and held her in place. "Is this the bit where you inspire civility?"

"Shut up," she said through clenched teeth.

"Perhaps we might engender more goodwill if you keep quiet and let me speak."

She doubted it.

"Not another word."

Now was not the time to point out that she didn't take orders from him.

"Protector," Neil said, as the group of men began to rise and move toward them. "It might be time to start dancing." He backed up, taking her with him, and then stopped just as abruptly. She felt Neil stiffen, then heard Mostyn growl.

"So nice of you to call on us, Mr. Wraxall and Lady Juliana and…friend. Won't you join me for a drink?"

Julia closed her eyes as Neil turned, moving her in the process. She knew what she would see—the harsh, cold stare of Mr. Slag.

❧

Neil had known this was a mistake. It was a mistake to go after Billy, a mistake to give Slag the advantage of choosing the battlefield, and a mistake to refrain from tying Juliana up and locking her in her room. The situation—two dozen angry men behind them and one homicidal monster in front of them—looked bad. In fact, the situation looked *very* bad. But he'd been in bad situations before, and he and Ewan had always gotten out alive.

I have my dancing shoes on.

But this was one devil even Neil did not want to dance with.

"Finally someone who understands the meaning of hospitality," Neil said. Ewan growled his disapproval of Neil's flippant tone, but Neil felt levity was the key now. "I find I am quite thirsty. You, Mr. Mostyn?"

"Parched."

"And you, my lady?"

"Not really," she squeaked. He squeezed her arm reassuringly. It was too late to give in to fear. The feeling was useless and dangerous. She would have to show some of that backbone he'd seen in her time and again.

She cleared her throat. "Tea would be lovely. Thank you, Mr. Slag."

Slag gave her an amused look, then inclined his head toward the rear of the alehouse. "Join me in my private chambers then, won't you?"

The men in the room parted, like the Red Sea before Moses's staff.

Slag moved first and Neil followed. He worried he might have to drag Julia with them, but she walked on her own, head held high and looking every inch the earl's daughter. Ewan followed, of course. Neil could always count on Ewan at his back.

Slag's ebony walking stick thumped on the floor as he led them past the bar and into a dark corridor. If the crime lord had an ambush planned, this was the time and place for it. Behind him, he heard Ewan's steps slow as the Protector prepared for an ambush. It didn't come. Instead, Slag opened a door and led them into a room lit with lamps and made cozy by a crackling fire.

Though perhaps *cozy* was not the correct word. The furnishings were comfortable enough—several chairs and a couch set on a large, colorful rug and visible by the light of lamps on scattered tables—but the ceiling was low and there were no windows to speak of. To Neil, the place felt like a well-appointed prison.

"Take a seat, won't you?" Slag pointed to the couch and chairs, but he remained standing, positioning himself near the fire.

"I prefer to stand," Neil said. Ewan leaned on the wall beside the door and crossed his arms over his broad chest. Julia sank into one of the chairs, looking as though she was only now realizing her mistake in coming. Good, perhaps in the future she would be less likely to rush headlong into danger, although judging from her past behavior, he doubted it.

"It will be difficult to drink tea standing," Slag said.

"You can drop the ruse, Mr. Slag," Neil said. "You know why we are here. Let us waste no more time. Give us the boy, and no one will get hurt."

Slag's gaze drifted slowly to Juliana. She was peering about the room and missed his look. A small mercy that, for the crime lord's leer turned Neil's stomach.

"Give me my blunt or, better yet, the chit, and you have a deal."

"Out of the question," Neil said.

Juliana turned back to them. "Where is Billy? Have you hurt him?"

"Hurt him?" Slag laughed. "The lad came of his own free will. I offered him shelter."

"Shelter? He was quite safe at Sunnybrooke," said Juliana.

Slag shook his head. "That was not the tale he told, my lady. And the bruises on his face seem to imply he has recently been involved in a violent exchange."

Neil did not know much about criminals. He knew they were usually caught, if not right away, eventually. He knew they were usually hanged. He knew that the large numbers hanged or transported or tossed in prison hulks did nothing to deter criminals. By necessity, he had associated with criminals on the Continent. He had no trouble deducing why they were usually caught. Most criminals were not very intelligent.

But Slag was no ordinary criminal. He had managed to survive the underworld and to come to dominate his small patch of it. Neil hadn't investigated Slag's criminal record—he was no Bow Street Runner—but he imagined if he had, he would have seen prosecutions for a several petty crimes when Slag had been young. Before he had learned to either evade the authorities, bribe them, or, as he did now, send others to do his dirty work.

Slag had probably grown up in Spitalfields, but he had enough wits to learn to speak properly, dress properly—if a bit garishly—and act cunningly. All of this information did not bode well for the rest of the interview.

"He and another boy had a dispute," Juliana said. Neil had known she would not heed his directive to cease speaking. "But that is none of your affair. I would like to see Billy."

"Absolutely," Slag said, though he made no move to call for the boy. "And if he wishes to go back to the orphanage, I will not keep him here."

Juliana was no lackwit either. She knew Slag would not give Billy up so easily. "But..." she hedged.

"But." Slag spread his arms as though the situation were out of his control.

She swallowed. "I don't have all the money. But what if I gave you some of it? I could get a hundred to you tomorrow."

Slag wrinkled his nose, and Neil clenched his fists. Was she really attempting to bargain with a crime lord?

"I'd rather the full amount. If you don't have it, then I am willing to accept substitutions."

She exhaled and glanced in Neil's direction. Clearly, she was considering accepting Slag's offer. The fear in her eyes and the rigid stiffness of her shoulders told him what he already knew—she would do anything to save the orphans she loved.

"She won't have you," Neil said before she could answer.

Both Slag and Juliana glared at him. Neil was pleased to see the leer on Slag's face had been wiped away.

"So you won't have me?" Slag said, the look in his eyes murderous but his voice deceptively calm.

"I wouldn't have put it that way." Juliana stood, sensing as they all did that a storm was about to break. "You see, while I am indeed honored by your, uh, proposal, I fear we are too different to make a successful match—"

"Enough!" Slag roared. He thumped his stick on the floor.

"You should have left it," Neil said, moving to block Juliana from Slag's wrath.

But even as he moved in front of her, the door behind them burst open and four of the largest men Neil had ever seen lumbered inside. Two of them even made Ewan look puny, and that was no easy feat. Julia gawked at them, and Neil thought he might be gawking too before he recovered himself.

"Wait!" he said even as Ewan moved into a defensive stance. "I am certain we can come to some sort of arrangement."

Slag stared at him.

"I have a proposal of my own."

"Go ahead."

"You tell these men to go back to whatever hole they crawled out of and give us Billy."

"And in return?"

"We won't completely destroy you."

Slag stared at him for a long moment. Even Juliana turned to stare at him, her face clearly betraying her thoughts—he was completely and utterly mad.

And then Slag began to laugh, and Ewan had a moment when he thought, *Bloody hell, it might all work out after all*. He laughed too, and even Ewan curved one corner of his mouth upward.

But then Slag, still smiling, slashed his walking stick through the air and said, "Kill them all."

Seventeen

Julia had not intended to scream. She liked to think she would not have screamed if she hadn't been tossed onto the couch and told to *get down and stay there*. That was an order Julia had no trouble following. She had seen and done a great deal in the time she had dedicated herself to the orphanage. More than 90 percent of what she had seen and done were not the sort of things ladies should ever see or do. She had broken up fights, cleaned up vomit, nursed sick children, buried the carcasses of dead animals who had chosen the orphanage's stoop as their final resting place. She had endured hunger, cold, lack of sleep, and what she had thought of as fear.

But now she realized that she had never before known real fear. Real fear struck her when she watched Neil hurtle himself across the room and slam into Slag. The two men fell back against the hearth, Neil narrowly missing being thrown into the flames. She tore her gaze away from Neil at a loud crash behind her. One of the tables had fallen, and it was no wonder, as the four thugs had encircled Mr. Mostyn, hiding him from view. She only knew he was still on his feet and fighting because she caught flashes of his light hair.

And then one of the thugs stumbled back and toppled onto a chair, crushing it, and Mostyn slid through the opening, grasped the table in one hand, broke off a leg, and brandished it at the other thugs. One didn't move quickly enough and took a crack to the head. He fell back, crashing into the couch and almost falling on top of her.

It was then she decided that perhaps she might be more out of the way if she climbed under the couch. She scooted under the furnishing just as the thug *did* tumble onto the couch, causing the entire thing to creak in protest.

Julia winced and turned to catch a glimpse of Neil again. She caught sight of him and Slag, still near the blazing hearth, just as Slag swung his stick and struck Neil's arm. Neil faltered but didn't go down. He swung with his good arm and his fist collided with Slag's nose. Blood sprayed, a rain of crimson, and Slag raised his walking stick for another strike. Julia closed her eyes. She couldn't stay under the couch until this was over. If Mr. Mostyn and Neil lost the fight—and that looked very likely—she was doomed. She had to find her own way out.

More importantly, she had to save Billy.

She could squeeze out from under the couch and… Her thoughts trailed off as she caught a whiff of smoke. She risked another look at Neil. His head was still round, not caved in as she had feared, and he continued to wrestle with Slag before the hearth. Neil had one end wrapped around the end of the walking stick, and he and Slag played tug-of-war with it. Behind them, the fire burned inside the grate.

And she still smelled smoke. She turned and looked at Mostyn, her eyes widening. She couldn't see much but legs from this angle, but she could see the overturned lamp and the small licks of fire eating at the rug.

"Oh no," she breathed. In this old building, the fire could spread quickly, blazing into an inferno before any of them had a chance to contemplate escape. The patrons in the front room might get out, but anyone upstairs, where Billy was likely hiding, would burn to death.

Julia looked at Neil again. Still fighting for his life. If the shuffling feet on the other side of the couch were any indication, Mostyn was engaged in the same battle. It was up to her. Julia slithered out from under the couch, covering her head when one of Mostyn's attackers looked like he might trip and fall on her. He fell the other way, and she scrambled to her knees. She crawled to the fallen lamp, reaching out to right it and then snatching her hand back at the intense heat. She bent and attempted to blow out the burgeoning fire, but too much of the lamp's oil had soaked into the carpet and her efforts made no difference.

Her last hope was smothering the flames. Fingers fumbling, she ripped off her cloak and threw it over the fire, then lifted and lowered it yet again. But she had missed her chance—when the flames had burned through the oil but not yet found other fuel. The fire had slid its talons into the rug's fibers and held on. She watched the trail of fire snake out along the pattern of the rug and away from her useless cloak.

Julia dropped the garment and did the only other thing she could think to do. "Fire!" she yelled. "Everyone out! Fire!"

The men fighting Mostyn had already taken notice and scrambled to avoid the flames. Julia glanced at Neil in time to see him wrench the walking stick from Slag's hands and swing it at the crime lord's head. Slag blocked the blow with his arm, but even across the room, she imagined she heard the crack and pop as bone splintered.

Her gasp was cut off when she was grabbed about the waist and lifted off the floor. Julia kicked and tried to wrench free.

"It's Mostyn," came the voice of the man holding her. "I'll get you out."

She stopped struggling as Mostyn carried her through the open door of the chamber. Slag's men had fled before them, and she could hear their shouts of "Fire!" as they ran into the taproom. Mostyn made to follow them, but Julia fought him again. "No!"

He could have ignored her. He was strong enough that her struggles didn't impede him, but he paused and set her down. He bent and looked into her face. "My lady, the Warrior will find his own way out."

Julia was suddenly ashamed that she hadn't been thinking of Neil. She'd wanted to go back for Billy. "It's not him," she said. "I want to find Billy. We have to get him out."

Neil stepped into the doorway beside them. Perspiration ran down his face from the heat of the fire, making the spattering of blood run down his cheeks in macabre rivulets.

"I'll get him out," Neil said, his voice hoarse from the smoke that was beginning to burn her throat and lungs. "You go with the Protector."

"No. I'm coming."

Neil bent and took her chin in his cupped hand. "Not this time, and don't fight me on this." He gave her a hard kiss that surprised her not simply because it was unexpected but because of its intensity. Then he looked at Mostyn. "Get her out and keep her out."

"Yes, sir."

She didn't even have the chance to say goodbye before she was lifted again, this time slung over Mostyn's shoulder and carried through the smoke-filled building. Outside, Mostyn didn't pause and lower her to the ground. He continued walking until they were well away from the burning Ox and Bull. Then he set her down, not exactly gently, but carefully at least, and turned to look behind him.

Julia found her balance and followed his gaze. The building was engulfed in flames. The dark sky was lit with a haze of red and orange. All around them men and women rushed toward the building. Some carried buckets of water, but most just wanted to watch. In the rookeries of London, few buildings were insured in case of fire. Even if they had been, the fire brigades were unlikely to venture into those parts of Town. If a building caught fire, it burned. Attempts might be made to save the nearby buildings, but if those caught on fire, the best one could hope for was a dousing rain.

Julia watched the smoke billow up from the burning alehouse in great plumes. Neil was inside. Neil and Billy. Billy was only a child. He had made a poor choice to go to the Ox and Bull, but he did not deserve to die. She would hold herself responsible if Neil died. He hadn't wanted to take responsibility for the orphans and the orphanage, and she had put him in a position that left him no other options. In fact, since she'd met him, he'd done nothing but take care of her and the boys, thinking of her needs before she even thought of them herself.

And then instead of urging him to get out of the burning building, she'd likely sent him to his death. She had made many mistakes in her life, but this was the first she truly wished she could undo.

"Wait here," Mostyn said, his voice low and filled with gravel from the smoke. In fact, even away from the fire, the smell of smoke still rose from her clothing and choked her throat closed.

Or perhaps that was fear and guilt.

She nodded, pressing her lips together and watching the flames lick at the roof through watery eyes. What else could they do but wait?

"I'll go back for him."

Her gaze snapped to Mostyn. "You're going back? You can't!"

"Wait here," he said and walked away, his long legs taking him out of sight before she could think of an argument.

"Idiotic men," she muttered. "Who walks *into* a burning building?"

She would have to spend the rest of her life feeling guilty for the death of three males. She was such a fool. She should have listened to Wraxall in the beginning. She should have brought an army of men into the orphanage to keep the boys safe and Slag out. She didn't know where she would have found the funds for such an army, but that seemed like a paltry concern at the moment.

And now Slag was dead. Neil's blow might not have killed him, but the fire would. Would his cronies come after her? Would they know she had been responsible, indirectly but still responsible, for his demise?

Julia took a deep breath and tried to quiet her mind. A group of men ran past, and she pushed herself into the shadows. She knew where the orphanage was from here, but she dared not go alone, especially now that she'd lost her cloak and her copper hair would be a beacon to anyone looking for her.

But how long should she wait for Mostyn to return? What if he never returned? What if he returned carrying the lifeless body of Neil? *Please let him be alive*, she prayed. She had no right to ask God for anything after the sins she'd committed today. Sins for which she was not even sorry, for the pleasure Neil had given her seemed a small price to pay for a mark against her name, if indeed St. Peter was keeping track.

"Lord," she whispered, "if you save him, I promise to entertain no more impure thoughts and refrain from any further impure behaviors. Just save him."

She opened her eyes and a woman with a scarred face and loose but matted brown hair stared at her. Julia inhaled sharply—immediately wishing she hadn't, for the woman smelled truly rank—and pressed farther back. But she was up against the building and had no room to hide herself more.

"Was you praying?" the woman asked, her accent so thick even Julia could hardly understand her.

"I was." Her voice shook from fear and emotion. "My friends are in that fire."

"Good." The woman stepped forward. "Then they'll be no one to 'elp you." She moved closer, so close that she pressed against Julia, who was forced to turn her head to the side to avoid touching her nose to the woman's as well as the stench.

"What do you want?" Julia asked, trying not to breathe too deeply.

"I want yer blunt." As she spoke, her hands grasped hold of Julia's waist, then skittered like bony beetles all up and down her sides. "Where do ye keep yer purse?" She felt for pockets in the dress and, finding them, delved inside. Julia resented the violation and pushed the woman back.

"Leave me alone. I don't have any coin with me."

"Come, now. Fine lady like you." The woman looked her up and down, then shoved one shoulder into her chest and continued patting Julia. Julia tried to catch her breath even as the woman's hands felt up her arms and over her breasts.

"Remove your hands! I'm no fine lady. I live at Sunnybrooke Home for Boys."

The woman leaned her head back. "Where?"

Julia blew out a breath. "St. Dismas—the orphanage. I don't have any blunt."

The woman pulled an embroidered handkerchief from Julia's bodice. "Maybe not, but I can sell this for a ha'penny."

Julia shoved her back. "Then sell it and be gone."

But the woman was staring at her hair. "Not so fast. Your hair is a fine color."

Julia put her hand to her head. "Get away."

The woman produced a dull knife with the dexterity of a professional. "Might fetch me a crown or more."

"You cannot have it. Go on before I scream."

The woman laughed—or rather cackled. "Scream all you want, dearie. No one will 'ear you." She raised the knife and moved toward Julia.

Julia had two choices at that moment—give up her hair or fight. She'd always been rather proud of her hair. It was vanity, she supposed, and unfounded vanity, as the color was not fashionable. Still, she knew it suited her, and more men than she could count had complimented it. One had even had the audacity to touch it. But her hair was not worth dying for. And yet, if she didn't fight now, when would she fight? She couldn't hide under couches—metaphorical or otherwise—for the rest of her life. She couldn't close her eyes and hope those who wished to harm her—men like Slag—would simply disappear. If she'd fought Slag from the beginning, maybe Neil wouldn't be in a burning building. Maybe Mostyn wouldn't be risking his life to save him. Maybe she wouldn't be on the street being accosted by a foul-smelling hair thief.

"Leave me be," Julia said and took a step toward the woman and—dear God—the knife.

"Stand still or I'll slit yer throat and then take yer 'air." The woman advanced, but Julia didn't cower. She had no room to back away. Instead, she made a grab for the knife. The woman slashed down, and bright pain flared in her arm. But Julia grabbed the woman's wrist anyway, pushing her assailant's arm back. A quick glance showed her the pain in her arm was accompanied by a stream of blood.

"Now look what ye done," the woman said, struggling to wrench free of Julia's hold.

"What I've done?" Julia used her momentum to push the woman a step back. "Who knows what sorts of filth you have on that blade?" She would probably die of some horrible as-yet-undiscovered disease. She forced the woman back another step, but it was a hard-won victory. The woman was tall and Julia was barely medium height. Both women were breathing hard, and Julia was grateful the struggle had forced the woman to stop speaking.

Her muscles burned and blood ran down her arm, but she refused to give in to fatigue. This was life and death. If she failed, Mostyn would find her lifeless body when and if he returned. Her *bald*, lifeless body.

With a growl, the woman pushed back, and Julia stumbled. Her feet scrambled for purchase, and she regained her balance and fought back. She might be small, but she had spent the last few months carrying small children, laundry, and heavy pots. She was strong.

The woman bared her teeth and pushed Julia back again, lowering her knife hand a fraction of an inch. Julia tried to raise the knife, but gravity was not on her side. She was tiring.

The woman pushed her back again, and this time Julia lost ground, her feet sliding backward. She concentrated all her strength on keeping the knife high and away from her face. But as she watched, the knife came closer and closer. The dull blade, red with her blood and black with God knew what, dipped lower and lower.

Julia tried to muster the strength to make one last push, but all she could manage was to keep the knife from plunging into her forehead.

Dear God, she would die this day. She had survived the Ox and Bull, survived Slag, and made it out of a raging fire, only to be killed on the street by a hair thief.

She closed her eyes as the knife moved closer, infinitesimally nearer to her skin. She did not want this woman's face to be the last thing she saw.

And then suddenly, the woman's wrist sprang free of Julia's grip, and the knife clattered to the ground. Julia opened her eyes in time to watch the woman's feet leave the ground as she flew backward. A dark-skinned man had the woman about the waist and shoved her at a pale man streaked with soot.

Julia's gaze flew to the man who'd saved her. It was Neil, his skin covered with soot and ash. Only his sea-blue eyes were recognizable to her. He was alive!

"Mr. Wraxall," she gasped.

"Good God, but can no one leave you alone for even a moment?"

She wanted to tell him if he insisted on being so surly, he could go straight back into the fire, but just then her legs gave way, and she wobbled. His arms caught her around the waist even as she caught herself. But he swept her up anyway, bringing her closer to his chest and the overpowering smell of smoke and fire.

"I can walk," she insisted.

"And step into the middle of a dice game or a street brawl? I think I had better carry you for your own good."

"You are acting like an arse," she said, too tired to care that she'd used language unbecoming a lady.

"Yes, well, watching you almost stabbed through the eye brings out the worst in me."

She looked up at him, hoping to discern something from his face. Was his statement an admission that he cared for her or was he simply angry that she might die and he be blamed for not meeting his responsibilities? But she could not see his features through the black grime. And then she remembered Mostyn. And Billy.

She struggled to look behind her. "Where is Billy? Did you find him?"

"I'm here, my lady," came a voice from somewhere nearby. Wraxall was moving quickly through the dark streets of Spitalfields, and she could not pinpoint the voice. But she knew it.

"Billy." She reached out a hand, and the boy took it. His hand was the same size as hers but rougher. He squeezed it.

"Major found me, he did. Got me out just in time."

"Thank God. I will scold you later for all the trouble you caused, but now I am so thankful to have you alive."

"Could we save the speeches for when we're safely indoors?" Wraxall muttered. "The less attention we draw to ourselves, the better."

"What about Mr. Mostyn?" she asked, ignoring Neil's injunction. "I thought I saw him—"

"Here, my lady." He moved from behind Neil so

she could see him and then back again. He truly did seem to always be at Neil's back.

"Thank you," she said to him. He gave a curt nod and went back to his position. They were all accounted for and safe, or nearly safe, at any rate. Slag was gone. His alehouse was gone. She did not know if Goring had survived or not, but she did not think he would dare show his face again.

But most importantly, Billy and the other boys were safe. She hadn't lost one. She could rest now.

Leaning her head on Neil's chest, she closed her eyes and dreamed of fire.

❧

Neil had felt fear. He had known dread and profound loss, but nothing could compare to the terror he'd felt when he caught sight of Juliana and the street wench struggling with the knife. In that moment, the rank, muddy street in Spitalfields became a battlefield once again, and he was racing against time to save Christopher.

He raced to save Juliana, but in his mind, they had become one and the same. He hadn't been able to reach Christopher in time, and he would not be able to reach Juliana. He would live the rest of his life with the image of her death imprinted in his brainbox—the way he stored the images of the deaths of so many of those who'd trusted their lives to him.

Neil knew if she died, he would not live long. This was one death he could not survive.

He'd begun to run, pushing through the crowd still heading for the Ox and Bull and the spectacle of the fire. When he'd reached the wench with the knife, he was certain he'd been too late. He'd pulled her off Juliana, prepared to rip her to shreds with his bare hands, when he'd heard Juliana's voice.

The woman had been forgotten, and in that moment, there was only Julia.

He held her close and stood in the entryway of the orphanage. When they'd come in—just the three of them, as Mostyn had melted away once they'd reached the building—Jackson had bustled the older boys off to their beds, taking Billy by the shoulders and threatening a bath. Rafe had only glared at him, taking in his soot-stained face and clothing.

"I get all the worst missions," he complained before leaving in a huff. Neil rolled his eyes.

The cook's brows lifted and then she retreated to the kitchen to prepare something soothing, but Mrs. Dunwitty had seemed unperturbed. "She always was a trial, this one. I told her father on many occasions her life—and mine—would have been a great deal easier had she been born male."

Neil supposed that would have made his life easier too, but he couldn't wish for it. Not when he held her soft body in his arms, loving the way her curves pressed against him.

"Don't just stand there, Mr. Wraxall; carry her to her chamber. I don't suppose there's a maid about," she said as she ascended the stairs in front of him. "I imagine I will have to see to that as well. Ah, Jackson, there you are."

Jackson had been shepherding the boys into their room, but he took a few steps into the corridor. "May I be of service, Mrs. Dunwitty?"

"Yes, you may. I need hot water for a bath and clean linen for a bandage. My lady is filthy and injured."

Jackson glanced at Juliana, who looked relatively clean compared to Neil. "I will have Mrs. Koch heat water and bring it personally." He gave Neil a direct look. "While the lady is bathing, sir, perhaps you might do the same downstairs."

Neil frowned. He didn't want to leave Juliana, but Mrs. Dunwitty would hardly allow him to stay while she bathed Juliana, even if he'd already seen far more of her than he ought.

"Very good, Jackson." Neil looked at the former governess. "Shall I hold her until the water arrives? If I set her on the bed, the sheets will need washing."

"No need," came a small, quiet voice. Juliana moved in his arms. "I am awake. I don't know what came over me."

"Shock and exhaustion, I imagine," said her former governess. "Let us just hope you have not caught some dreadful disease of the lower orders whilst you were out and about in those dreadful streets."

"You know I am never sick," she told the woman, pushing out of Neil's arms. He was forced to release her, his body protesting at the loss of her warmth and her softness.

"And I intend to keep it that way. Now, out of those clothes. Jackson will draw you a bath." Mrs. Dunwitty gave Neil a pointed look.

"Excuse me," he said and moved into the hallway. There, he was confronted by four sets of small eyes, each wider than the last. "What's this?" he said. "I thought you were all in bed."

"Will she die?" asked Chester, his dark hair rumpled and his cheeks wet.

"You can't let her die," Charlie said, or something to that effect. His thumb was firmly in his mouth.

"She ain't going to die, is she?" said Jimmy.

"No," said Neil. "She will not die."

"I told you," James broke in, hand swiping at the wetness on his cheeks. "I told you Major would keep our lady safe."

Neil put his hand on James's shoulder. "And so I will. I'll keep all of you safe, and that is a promise." He did not know how he would keep that promise, but he meant it. "Now, back to bed with you."

"Lory?" Charlie asked.

"No story tonight," Neil translated. "My lady or I will read you one tomorrow."

The boys groaned.

"I'll read them a story."

Neil turned and saw Robbie behind him. He also spotted Juliana leaning on the casement in her doorway. Their eyes met—hers shiny with unshed tears—before she closed her door.

"You can read?" Neil asked before glancing back at Robbie. The boy shrugged. "A little. Come on, boys. Climb in bed. Uncle Robbie will tuck ye in tonight."

The boys cheered and raced into their rooms, all fears for Lady Juliana momentarily put to rest. Robbie made to follow, then looked back at Neil. "And if I can't read the words, I can always make them up, right?"

Neil nodded. "A time-honored tradition among storytellers."

"That's what I thought." He wrinkled his nose. "You'd best clean up, Major. You stink."

"Thank you, Robbie."

He moved toward the steps, listening as Robbie said something that made the little boys giggle. For the first time he could remember, Neil felt like he was home.

Eighteen

JULIA CLOSED THE DOOR AND TURNED TO A NARROW-
eyed Mrs. Dunwitty. "You have ideas."

Julia blinked. "No, I don't," she answered quickly.
Denial of all culpability was second nature when it
came to dealing with Mrs. Dunwitty.

"Oh, yes you do. And I know because if I were a
few years younger, I would have the same ideas."

Julia stared at her, hoping she had misunderstood.

Mrs. Dunwitty held out a hand. "Give me your
clothing. I doubt it is salvageable. Why don't you
employ a maid, for goodness' sake? And do not stare
at me so. I was young once."

"I don't have the funds for a maid." Julia pulled off
her gloves and the remnants of her hat. She refused to
imagine Mrs. Dunwitty as young.

Mrs. Dunwitty looked at the proffered articles and
motioned for Julia to drop them on the floor. "I had
plenty of beaux when I was your age, and in my time,
we were far less prudish."

"Oh dear," Julia muttered. This was not at all a

conversation she wished to be part of. She bent to unlace her boots.

"How did the boys' lessons go today?" she asked.

"But when the time came," Mrs. Dunwitty said, ignoring Julia's attempt to change the subject, "I decided marriage was not for me. I wanted my freedom. I think you of all women understand that."

Julia removed her half boots. They were dirty but still serviceable. Those she moved to the side of her discarded garments, then unpinned her bodice and loosed the tapes of her dress, allowing it to fall to the floor. Once her outer garments were removed, Mrs. Dunwitty stepped forward to assist her with her stays. "I can manage," she said.

"You are tired and have been through quite the ordeal, from what I can see. I'll hear no argument."

Julia was tired, and she offered none as her stays were removed, and when the hot water arrived, she wore only her chemise and stockings. She retreated behind a screen to wash. The small hipbath she had bought for the orphanage and insisted the boys use at least once a week was in the older boys' dormitory. She always made do with soap, a cloth, and water from a basin. At least this water was hot.

"It's obvious you feel something for Mr. Wraxall," Mrs. Dunwitty said on the other side of the screen. Julia heard her moving about, probably straightening up Julia's already-straight chambers. "In your absence, I asked his man, Jackson, about his presence here. Apparently, Mr. Wraxall has been living here for several days. Unchaperoned."

Julia paused in the act of sliding the cloth over

her face. "I am hardly in need of a chaperone at this point," she said. "I have been living, more or less, in a house with twelve boys for a quarter of a year."

"Those are boys. Mr. Wraxall is a man."

"He is a gentleman my father sent to take me home. That is all." She rubbed the cloth over her knife wound. It was just a scratch, really, but it still burned.

Mrs. Dunwitty huffed. "Your father might have sent Wraxall, but if he knew the man had taken up residence—"

"Mr. Wraxall has *not* taken up residence. He will be leaving in a day or so, and now that you are here, we are adequately chaperoned, not that anyone will care. Like you, Mrs. Dunwitty, I have chosen not to marry. In time, my father will come to accept that. He will understand that this is the life I want, and I am quite content to live here and help these boys."

"Oh, is that why you came here? To help these boys? I thought it was because you were running away."

"I have never run away from anything in my life."

"You ran away from the situation with Lainesborough."

Julia dropped the cloth and stuck her head around the screen. "I did not run away. I did everything I could to keep Davy. I fought Lainesborough until the end."

Mrs. Dunwitty's eyes held sorrow, but Julia did not want her sorrow. Instead, she focused on the older woman's mouth, which was set in a determined line. Julia wanted determination. "And I lost. The court and the judge and even the bloody regent—"

"Language, Juliana."

"—did not care about the best interests of the child

or what his mother would have wanted or that his father didn't even show the most remote interest in the child until he was half a year old. The law gives the man precedence in this case, as in practically every case. Now, you tell me why I should want to tie myself to a man when men are selfish, manipulative, and cruel at best?"

"Your father was not cruel."

"My father was benignly neglectful, and when I needed him—when Harriett needed him— he would not lift a finger to help," Julia cried, her voice rising to a pitch that heralded tears. "Now I am in a position to help, and I will not walk away. Mrs. Dunwitty, if you have come hoping to persuade me to return home or to abandon these children, then you should know that I will do neither."

Mrs. Dunwitty nodded and said nothing. After a moment, Julia moved back behind the screen. She took a moment to compose herself, then finished washing. When she'd dressed in a clean chemise and come around the screen, Mrs. Dunwitty waited with Julia's robe and some linen she'd torn into bandages. "And yet," she said quietly after she'd bandaged Julia's arm and held out the robe, "you are in love with Wraxall."

Julia started. "I most certainly—"

Mrs. Dunwitty raised her hand. "Do not bother to deny it. I saw him with those children just now. I fell half in love with him. And it was still in your eyes when you closed the door."

"I can't love him. I've only known him a handful of days."

"And you think there are rules to falling in love?" Mrs. Dunwitty laughed. "Even if there were, you would not follow them. But you must hear me in this, Juliana."

At the serious note in her voice, Julia looked up.

"You must not go to bed with him."

Julia thought she would tip over from mortification. This was worse than when her mother had tried to explain where babies come from. "Please stop," she begged.

"Let me say my piece."

"Must you?"

"It is clear to me you want him in your bed, and I have no doubt he wants to be there, but if you sleep with him, it will be that much harder to let him go. The children have already become attached to him. Do not allow yourself to become any more attached or you will not be able to support them in their grief because you will be mired in your own."

Mrs. Dunwitty was correct, of course. She knew this. It had never been her plan to become attached to Neil nor to allow the boys to become attached to him. And yet somehow he had found a way into all of their hearts. But she was not so young and innocent as to delude herself into believing he would stay simply because she wished he would. She was not so foolish as to ask him to stay because even if he desired to stay, she had no room in her life for a man. She might fancy herself in love with him, but that did not mean she trusted him or that she could count on him. He had proven himself to be trustworthy and dependable thus far, but in the end, he would fail her. Every other man in her life had.

"The boys are my sole concern," Julia said. "He has been a good influence on them, but we must all prepare ourselves for his departure. Now that we are safe from some of the more dangerous occupants of Spitalfields, I believe Mr. Wraxall intends to see to the roof repairs and be gone."

"Good. In my opinion, the sooner the better. The last thing you should ever do is allow him too many liberties or an entrée into your bed."

Julia's cheeks flamed. Dear God, she would say her prayers faithfully for a year if Mrs. Dunwitty would only speak of something else. Anything else.

"I see you are tired, so I will leave you to rest. We shall discuss the boys' lessons in the morning. Their arithmetic is not bad, but their reading is very poor indeed. Shockingly poor."

And with that the woman left Julia in peace.

Neil hadn't intended to be standing in the corridor outside Juliana's chamber when Mrs. Dunwitty emerged. He quickly tried to look as though he had some purpose for being there—ostensibly to check on the little boys—but he feared he failed miserably when Mrs. Dunwitty stopped and gave him a pointed look.

"Mr. Wraxall, do not think I do not know what you are doing here."

"I wanted to make certain the boys—"

She dismissed his excuse with a wave. "I have spoken with my former charge and warned her against your charms."

Neil raised a brow. "My charms?"

"Yes. More to the point, I told her specifically not to allow you into her bed. Knowing that girl, the more I tell her not to do something, the more likely she is to do it. And so I will warn you as well to stay away from Lady Juliana. Go back to your rooms and go to sleep."

"Yes, Mrs. Dunwitty."

"Good night, then." And she started for her own rooms at a clipped pace.

Neil was accustomed to following orders, and he almost turned to follow the lady, as they both had chambers in the servants' quarters. But then he paused to wonder why Juliana's former governess would tell her charge not to allow him into her bed if that would only make her more likely to do so. And if she made such a blunder, why would she make her mistake known to him?

Did the lady want him to seduce Juliana? Rather, *further* seduce Juliana? Was she playing matchmaker? If so, this was a rather unorthodox method, since, for all she knew, he might get Juliana with child and then leave her to suffer the consequences.

But if she thought him capable of such behavior, she would have undoubtedly thrown him out on his ear already. He had no doubt she was capable of that and much more.

Which still left him standing in the corridor wondering what he was about. He didn't need to check on the little boys. Robbie had seen to that. Their room was dark and quiet, as was the older boys' dormitory. The boys, even Billy, slept in clean beds under warm blankets. Their bellies were full—or reasonably so, considering young boys were never really full—and they were safe from the likes of Slag and his men. Neil hadn't considered how truly remarkable this orphanage was. He had not spent much time in any orphanage, but even he knew that they were little more than dens of disease and misery. If what he had seen of orphans on the streets of London was any indication, the children were unwashed, practically starving, and dressed in rags.

Of course, there were a few orphans who were left at institutions accompanied by funds to be used for the rearing of the child. But as there was virtually no oversight, those who ran the orphanages were free to use the funds for whatever they liked, which was, more often than not, lining their own pockets.

But here was a place that had likely been as miserable and wretched as any other orphanage in London, and Lady Juliana had come in and made it a haven. She had few funds from the board of directors, and so all the improvements she had done she must have paid for herself. The children were clean, fed, and looked after. Now that Slag was dead, Billy and Walter were safe from being coerced into joining his gang. And Juliana was in part responsible for Slag's demise too.

Neil had walked into the orphanage and seen all the potential dangers for the daughter of an earl. Thus, he had failed to see all the ways she had provided security for these children who would have been out on the streets of London had she not stepped in. No wonder she had resisted his help initially. She did not need one more outsider trying to save her when the real danger was what would happen to the children if she returned to Mayfair.

And he still had not answered his own question as to what he was doing pacing outside her bedchamber. For all intents and purposes, his work here was done. St. Maur could hire men to repair the roof. It wasn't as though Neil knew anything about roof repair. He would have hired men himself. Of course, he'd planned to supervise the work and keep an eye on Juliana at the same time, but now that Slag was no longer a threat, she didn't really need him. He could try and persuade her to go home to her father, but that was a losing battle. Neil didn't make a habit of fighting battles he could not win.

She probably wouldn't care if he told her she still wasn't safe. New threats could come at any time, but he couldn't live here permanently, just in case she needed protection again.

Could he?

Of course not. He had his own life. He was busy mourning his fallen friends, drinking himself into a stupor, and fighting off nightmares. Not to mention, once every two or three months, his father had some small task for him to complete. If Neil stayed at the orphanage, he would give up all those hours sitting alone in his rooms or whiling away the hours at the Draven Club, nursing the what-ifs and flagellating himself for putting Draven's men into deadly situations, which was of course the very idea of a suicide troop.

Neil stopped pacing and stood in front of Juliana's door. If he went inside, if he stayed, he would have to marry her. He couldn't marry her. What kind of husband would he be? He was a bastard and she the daughter of an earl.

The door to Juliana's room opened, and she jumped back when she spotted him. "Wraxall!"

"I didn't mean to startle you, my lady," he said.

"Then what did you mean by standing outside my door?"

"I…" He had no answer, but he knew a few interrogation techniques. "Why did you open it?"

"I… Because. I wanted to check on the boys."

It was a lie if he'd ever heard one, but he'd be damned if he would call her on it. His gaze had dipped from her face to the vee of her robe, which was open slightly to reveal the lacy, white night rail. With her coppery hair down about her shoulders and her cheeks pink from being freshly scrubbed, she looked very much like a dollop of cream with a cherry on top.

And Neil would have liked to lick his way down the cream-covered expanse of her body.

"Tell me," he said, his voice gravelly. "Why does the matron of an orphanage for boys wear a night rail with such a revealing bodice?" He reached out and trailed one finger along the opening of the robe, parting it farther to reveal more of the swell of her breasts. He had been prepared to be slapped away, but she all but leaned into his touch. She had been lying when she'd claimed she'd opened the door to check on the boys. He would have wagered a sovereign that she had planned to go to him.

And though he had no skill at gaming, Neil was certain he would have won this wager.

"It's not mine," she said, her voice little more than a whisper.

"You stole it? More and more intriguing."

"I didn't... No. I..." She looked up and down the corridor. "Should we have this conversation elsewhere? I'm afraid we might wake the boys."

Neil thought a horse race was unlikely to wake the boys after a day of lessons with Mrs. Dunwitty, but he didn't argue. Instead, he took a step forward and then another.

Juliana took a step back, and Neil followed her into her chamber, closing the door behind him and locking it. Her brown eyes darted to the closed door. "This is most inappropriate."

"As is that garment." He wanted to move closer, to push the robe off her shoulders and see what tantalized beneath it more clearly, but he stood rooted in place.

"It was meant for a bride."

Neil lifted a brow. "Were you betrothed?"

"My sister was. She married Viscount Lainesborough. This"—she gestured to the nightgown and robe—"was part of her trousseau, but the valise into which it was packed was left behind. When my lady's maid packed for what was to be a brief stay at Sunnybrooke, she must have thought I'd already packed this valise and sent it with the rest of my things."

Neil did step forward. "It suits you."

"It seems silly to wear it here, surrounded by squalor and shabbiness, but I suppose I like to forget where I am at times and pretend I am still the spoiled, naive earl's daughter."

"I can't picture you as spoiled, though you've held on to a great deal of that naivety."

She narrowed her eyes. "Always quick with compliments, I see. You should have known me before."

"You wouldn't have spoken to me before."

"You wouldn't have spoken to me. I was unbearably stupid and frivolous."

He stood before her and reached one hand to caress the sleeve of her robe. "What changed you?"

"Davy," she said.

Neil stiffened. He hadn't been prepared for the possibility of another man, but now that he considered it, why hadn't he supposed that she would be in love with and loved by someone? She was smart, brave, and beautiful. What man wouldn't want her?

But if she loved another, then why had she allowed him to touch her so intimately earlier that day? Why did she allow his hand on her arm now? Neil dropped his hand. "And who is Davy?"

She shook her head. "I don't think I should talk about this."

"It's too late for that."

She shook her head, making her hair flutter about her shoulders. "You don't want to hear my sad tale."

"Why not? You heard mine." He met her gaze directly. "Why not show me what you're hiding?"

"I'm not hiding."

"But you are." He ran his hand along the sleeve of her robe again but refrained from divesting her of it. Now, there was Davy between them.

"Davy—David—is my nephew, and certainly no secret."

"Your sister's son?"

She looked down. "Yes, and her only child. She died just hours after he was born."

"I'm sorry to hear that." And he was. As a man

who had never known his own mother, he could empathize with this child who would also grow up motherless. However, this child had been born within the realm of matrimony, which meant he would be accepted and wanted. He would have the love of his father and obviously that of his aunt. Unless something had happened to the child.

"Where is Davy now?" he asked.

"With his father."

Neil nodded. "As to be expected, I suppose."

Her eyes flashed fire, and she rounded on him. "Why, pray tell, is that to be expected? Why should a child be reared by his father as a default? Not every father is a suitable guardian."

He had stepped, unwittingly, into a battle zone. He could either make a hasty retreat or fight his way through. He wasn't certain what he was fighting for, but Neil had fought many battles where victory was undefined. Sometimes that was the nature of conflict.

"You have a point," he conceded. "Am I to understand Davy's father was less than desirable?"

"He is much worse than 'less than desirable.' He didn't care a fig for the child until he realized that I wanted him. You see, I opposed his marriage to Harriett and so he has always hated me. He took Davy away simply to spite me and now"—tears glittered in her eyes—"I've lost him forever."

And with those words, Neil finally understood.

Nineteen

HE STOOD LOOKING AT HER AS THOUGH SHE WERE daft. Julia could hardly blame him. Perhaps she was daft. Here she was, months after Davy had been taken away, crying over him as though he'd just been torn from her arms yesterday. But there were moments, many moments, when the wound still felt that raw and tender.

She half expected Neil to make an excuse and get away, but he didn't look as though he was going anywhere. He stood before her, not touching her any longer, but remaining close, offering her the comfort of his arms if she would only step into them. And perhaps she should. She had already said far more than she'd wanted. What was one more mistake?

"And this Lainesborough won't allow you to be part of the child's life?"

She looked away, fighting the tears threatening to spill. "As I said, he hates me."

Neil raised his brows. "I fail to see how anyone could hate you."

She gave a short laugh, glancing at him to see if he

was serious. "I think you know quite well that I have the capacity to be…shall we say stubborn?"

"You?" He shook his head. "Never."

She was smiling, the tears held at bay. "Your charms will not sway me, Mr. Wraxall."

"I have charms?" He pretended innocence. "We shall return to the matter of my charms later. Now, I want to hear the story of this man who is such a bad judge of character."

She felt weary—and no wonder, as she'd destroyed a crime lord and fought off a knife-wielding assailant. And that had been just this afternoon. Julia sat on the bed. "Yes, well, the viscount thought I was a bad judge of character."

"His character?" Neil sat beside her, which she knew was improper—as was his presence in her bedchamber—but she couldn't seem to manage to protest.

"He was all show and no substance. I knew it the first time I met him. He is like an actor on a stage who plays a part with such depth and emotion it brings tears to your eyes, but offstage, he is shallow and vain and cares more for the cut of his coat than the thousands of orphans roaming the streets."

"In all fairness, most of London cares more for the cut of a coat than the plight of orphans."

She waved a hand. "Yes, but you know what I mean. He played a part with my sister, and she believed it."

"And you did not. Did she also care for orphans?"

"Not really. She was a member of several benevolent societies, but all ladies are." It shamed her to say this, but as long as she was spilling her soul… "I didn't always care as much about orphans as I do now."

"Well, this is shocking."

She rolled her eyes, but she could appreciate how he used levity. She was trying quite diligently not to appreciate the feel of his body beside hers. When he'd sat on the bed beside her, the mattress had given, and his thigh rested against hers. She liked the solid heat of him there—too much. Images of earlier that day came to her—of his mouth on her breast and between her legs. She wanted that again, and she knew she should never have allowed it the first time. She should not even be thinking of it now.

"I always wanted to do something, to help as much as I could, which was why I became involved with St. Dismas. I even visited several times, but I was only too happy to allow myself to be convinced that all was as it should be, even though the children were dirty and too thin. I had balls to attend and the theater to dress for."

She was quiet, remembering that life, when she'd been carefree and ignorant. When she and Harriett spent hours primping before mirrors and gossiping about the most eligible men in the *ton*.

"And then Harriett met Lainesborough," Julia whispered, "and everything changed. I tried to like him if only because she liked him so much, but I could not. And I loved my sister and voiced my concerns to her. Of course, she told him, and though he pretended to play the gallant knight who would win me over, I could see he hated me for daring to jeopardize his chance with St. Maur's eldest daughter. We both had substantial dowries. Well, I still have mine. Lainesborough wanted Harriett's, and after they married, it became clear why."

"Gambling debts," Neil said.

"You know him?" But one look at his face told Julia he didn't. She supposed it was not difficult to guess why a man of the upper classes might need blunt. "You know men like him," she said. "Yes, he gambled too much and drank too much, and, well… did everything too much. The day after he married my sister, he disappeared for three nights. We later heard he had spent the time at"—her cheeks blushed—"a house of ill repute," she whispered.

Neil didn't comment, for which Julia was thankful. Nothing he might have said at that moment would have comforted her. Instead, he simply took her hand and held it. She surprised herself by squeezing his hand tightly. She closed her eyes to finish the story.

"After that he was more often away than home. When my sister discovered she was with child, she came home to be with me. Our father did what he could to keep Lainesborough away, but the viscount had little interest in her at any rate. He'd wanted her money, and he had it."

Harriett's confinement had been a mixed blessing. She had grown more beautiful with each passing week as her body ripened with child. The sisters had spent all their time together, something social responsibilities had made all but impossible the past few years. Despite her father's protests, Julia had withdrawn from Society to be with her sister, who also shunned Society and the news she would hear of her husband's infidelities.

"When her time came, there was no reason to think it should be anything out of the ordinary." She could not look at him as she spoke these words. She shouldn't have been in the room when the baby was delivered, much less speak about it to a man, but who else could she tell? And it seemed now that the dam was open, she could not stop it up again. "The delivery seemed normal to me. Difficult, yes, but when we were younger and my mother was still alive, she would tell us about her painful labors to make Harriett and I feel guilty for vexing her."

Neil laughed quietly, and Julia smiled too.

"But then after the baby came, Harriett seemed to become worse, not better. She was too exhausted to hold her son, and she was so pale." Julia swallowed. "And there was so much blood. I took Davy to meet his grandfather, but when I returned, I became alarmed at what I saw. Harriett could not be revived. The midwife was in tears, and when we called for the doctor, he said there was nothing he could do. She was dead before the end of the day."

Neil's hand tightened where it held hers.

"I laid Davy in her arms, but the baby cried when he was away from me. Still, we stayed until the end. And then, when she was gone, I made the mistake of falling in love with Davy, though he'd never been mine to love."

"What did Lainesborough do when he was informed he had a son and heir?"

Julia swiped at her eyes. "Nothing. He did not answer our letters or come to see the child. I think I began to believe Davy might be mine. I can't tell you how I wished he'd been born a girl. If he'd been a girl, Lainesborough wouldn't have ever taken notice of her, no matter how much he wanted to spite me. Girls were not worth his attention. But I suppose because the child was his heir, eventually he had to take an interest. One day he came to the house and demanded to see Davy. The baby was almost six months old at that time and just so beautiful. Lainesborough didn't speak to him or even touch him, but he saw how attached I was to the child and how much the little boy loved me. Maybe if he hadn't seen that—"

Neil lifted her hand to his lips and kissed it. "Shh. None of that now. No what-ifs."

She nodded. She knew the particular hell she entered when she gave into that line of thinking. "He came back the next week with his attorney and his footmen and took the child away. I tried to protest, screaming and crying, but I had no argument. Legally, the child is his. I managed to be calm and feign happiness when I had to hand Davy over. He was scared enough as it was, and I didn't want to add to that." The tears fell unbidden. "But I will never forget the way he held out his chubby arms to me or the way he cried as though his world was ending or the fear in his eyes. I will never forgive myself for abandoning him."

"You did not abandon him. He was taken away. Those are two very different situations."

"And yet I still feel as though I failed him—as though I continue to fail him. Where is he now? Who comforts him when he wakes crying? Who holds him and hugs him?" She sniffed and closed her eyes to stem the flow of tears before they threatened to overwhelm her. When she opened her eyes again, Neil had a determined expression on his face.

"It wouldn't be difficult to discover the answer to those questions."

Julia wanted to hug him. Sweet, sweet man. "I already know the answers. Davy has a nurse and Lainesborough has a house full of servants. Though he may rarely be home, the child is cared for."

Neil's expression turned perplexed. "Then why are you crying?"

"Because it's not me holding him. It's not me comforting him. I loved him as though he were my own, and I think, for a little while, he was."

"And now you have a dozen boys who are your own, a dozen boys who are unlikely ever to be taken away."

She nodded, relieved that he finally seemed to understand. "And I don't want to lose a single one." Not ever again.

To her surprise, he reached over and cupped her cheek. She wanted to lean into his touch, to rub her cheek along the rough pads of his fingers. She wanted him to kiss her again until she forgot all about the leaking roof and the woman with the knife and the image of Davy's scared face when he was torn away from her.

"Listen to me, Juliana. I want what you want, but I know something about boys. In particular, I know something about orphaned boys. I wasn't an orphan, but I know what it is to wonder where you belong and to search for your place."

She tried to draw back, uncertain what he would say and whether she wished to hear it. He took her shoulders and held her so he could look into her face.

"These boys want to belong. Even if it means belonging to a gang of thieves. Even if it means taking orders from a man like Slag."

"But they can belong here. I've made a home for them."

He nodded. "Yes, you have, but all you can do is offer that home. You cannot force them to accept it. Some of these boys have never known what you are offering—warmth, security, and love. They only know fear and intimidation and following a man who would as soon kill them as pat them on the back. You may need to give up some of these boys to save the rest."

"No!" She stood and backed away from him. Why had she thought he understood? He didn't understand anything at all. "I won't give up on Billy or Walter or any of them. I love them." And though she hated him at the moment, she wouldn't give up on Neil either. Because he had found a way into her heart, and she loved him enough to know that she would be devastated when he left.

Neil stood. "And would you allow Billy to stay and corrupt James and Chester and little Charlie?"

Julia's heart thumped quickly. He knew the boys' names. He pretended he did not, but he knew them. He knew all of them.

"Because that's what he will do. Slag is gone, but another will take his place. Men like him are as abundant as fleas in the rookeries. Billy will find another upright man, and one of his first tasks will be to recruit other boys. Because if there's one thing a gang needs, it's a steady stream of thieves to replace the ones who are sent to prison."

Julia wanted to argue again, but she knew he was right. And still she wasn't ready to let Billy go so easily. "What do you want me to do?" she asked quietly.

Neil crossed to her and took her arms in his hands. His touch was so warm, so warm that she wanted to walk forward and put her arms around his waist and just let him hold her, wrap her in that warmth. Instead, she stood completely still. Finally, when the silence had dragged on for some time, she lifted her eyes to his.

"I want you to trust me."

⤙⤚

Neil saw the conflict in her face. She wanted to trust him, but she had not trusted anyone in so long that she rebelled against the idea of putting her faith in him. In many ways, she was like a new soldier—still learning to trust the commanding officer. Unlike a soldier, she had a choice. She was no meek, biddable female who would jump to follow his commands. She had her own mind and her own plans. He could only offer advice and hope she would take it.

At least that was the attitude he should have had. But for whatever reason, gaining her trust meant more to him than he wanted to admit. He'd been trying to gain it since the first day he met her.

And now, they were alone, and all the boys she loved so much were asleep. And he wanted her trust in an entirely different way.

"Do you trust me?" he murmured.

Her eyes widened at the low timbre of his voice. He hadn't bothered to hide his desire in the way he looked at her or in the way he spoke.

"I want to," she whispered.

"Then perhaps all you need is more practice." He slowly lowered his mouth toward her soft, plump lips, giving her ample time to turn her face away. She didn't, and when he brushed his lips over hers, he felt the same charge of heat he'd felt the first time he kissed her. Neil had to resist grasping the back of her neck and taking her mouth the way he wanted. Instead, he kept the kiss slow and light, moving his hands up and down her arms until she stepped closer and wrapped them around his neck.

And still he teased her mouth with his, nipping and licking and suckling her lips. She had such delectable lips and she had cleaned her teeth with tooth powder that tasted faintly of mint. She pushed closer to him, and he needed to touch her skin and to see her in the flimsy night rail he had been fantasizing about since he'd first laid eyes on it.

He ran his hands up her back, then up into her loose hair, brushed until it fairly crackled. His hands stroked down her neck and then pushed into the robe, easing it back and over her shoulders. He was prepared to pause and unknot the sash, but she had not tied it tightly, and the silky garment slid from her shoulders like a cascade of water.

And then his hands were on the bare skin of her shoulders and her neck, and he wanted the soft weight of her breasts in his hands.

But first he wanted a look at her body in the lacy night rail. Reluctantly, he lifted his fingers from her skin and took a step back. Her face was flushed, her hair falling over her shoulders, and her eyes closed. He could have admired that picture of her all day, especially the pinkness of her swollen lips. Those lips needed to be kissed daily.

She opened her eyes, and they were darker than he'd ever seen them, filled with desire for him.

"I want to see you," he said, voice low and husky.

She blinked, slow and uncomprehending.

"Step back. I've been imagining you in that for days. I want to see the real thing."

Her cheeks turned even pinker, red spots staining the centers. "You have seen it."

"Bits and pieces," he said. When she still didn't move back, he ran a hand down her hair. "You are beautiful, Juliana. I only want to see you in all your glory."

"I don't know why I should feel so shy," she said, ducking her head. "You've already seen... That is to say, I've never been overly modest before. You should have seen some of the ball gowns I've worn."

He wished he had seen them and her in them. Though he would never be the sort of man who accompanied her to a Society ball, he wished he had known that part of her. Still, it would be no hardship to content himself with the woman she had become. Neil had known many soldiers who wore fancy dress and gleaming brass buttons. But when all the finery was stripped away and the cannons were firing and the men charging, it was the man underneath who mattered.

"Silks and flounces don't impress me," he told her. "I've already seen what lies beneath them. What is at the heart of who you are."

Her head notched up.

"And I know you are as beautiful inside as you are on the outside."

Her gaze met his, and though her color was still high, she stepped back and twirled around. The garment was made of expensive lace at the bodice. Neil supposed the lace had some sort of name, but he didn't know it. Her sister must have been slightly smaller than she, for the bodice fit her tightly, her breasts swelling over the low neckline. The sides of the garment were held together by pink ribbons—three of them—that had been tied in pretty bows. More ribbons donned the lacy sleeves and the waistline. The skirt of the night rail was not lace, but it had been made of thin, almost-translucent silk. He could see the coppery curls of her womanhood and the outline of her buttocks when she turned.

It was the sort of garment that would make a new husband lose his breath, and Neil felt the air whoosh out of his lungs. He swallowed and attempted to tamp down the lust threatening to overwhelm his judgment, but then she faced him again, and his eyes were drawn to the dark pink of her nipples and aureoles against the white of the lace.

"Come here." His voice was low and husky.

She took a step forward, then paused. "What will you do?"

"Not all I want to do." Though certainly every time he was with her, it became harder and harder to keep his virginity intact. "But I'm certain I can think of something you'll enjoy."

"More nefarious activities?"

He smiled. "If you'll indulge me."

She did, moving close enough that he could wrap a hand around her waist and pull her hard against him.

She gasped, and he took her mouth, swallowing the sound and the moan that followed. He took his time with her mouth again, exploring it and allowing her a turn to explore him, and then he broke the kiss and turned her around, lowering his mouth to kiss her neck. When he looked up, her eyes met his in the cheval glass across the room.

"You look like a medieval warrior."

He liked the image. And he liked the reflection in the mirror even more. "And you are my prize?"

"I'm no man's prize."

"True enough. Then be my partner in this."

Her eyes widened. "How?"

"I'll show you, but first it has been too long since I've seen your perfect breasts. I can't wait any longer." His fingers reached for the first neatly tied pink bow.

Her hand covered his, and Neil paused. He wanted her. He wanted more with her than he'd ever wanted with any woman. With Julia, he dared to think of a future. He wanted her as his wife, the mother of his children, his partner through the good and the bad. But she had every reason to stop this now. He'd made her no promises, and she didn't seem to want or need them from any man. She didn't even need him, though he'd tried hard enough to make her believe she did—as he'd always tried to make anyone believe that he, who had always been the illegitimate one, the one who didn't belong, was worthwhile and valuable.

Neil looked down at her hand. He could accept defeat. He'd lost eighteen men, proving to all the world that he was a failure and as unworthy as his status of bastard implied.

Neil looked up and met her gaze.

"Allow me," she said.

His heart all but stopped. His breath caught in his throat and his hand dropped away. He could not seem to tear his gaze from her long, graceful fingers as they tugged at the ribbon to loosen it.

A small expanse of flesh, the creamy swell of her breast, was exposed. It was the most tantalizing image Neil had ever seen.

"Shall I continue?" she asked.

She wanted this. She wanted to be with him. He had to clear his throat to speak through the lump. "Please," he said.

Her hand reached for another ribbon and she gave it a careless tug. The action allowed him to see more of the curve of her breast, more of the valley in between.

"One more," she whispered.

Thank God or he would have to sink to his knees. He might anyway. She reached for the last bow, her fingers toying with the loops of pink satin. Finally, she caught an end and pulled. The ribbon seemed to hold fast for an eternity as the loop pulled through the knot. Neil's hand clenched as he itched to tug it free and push the night rail from her body. His fingers dug into his palm as the loop finally slipped free and the bodice parted.

And caught on the hard points of her nipples.

Neil's breath hitched. How the devil was he supposed to withstand this sort of torment? He needed a drink. He needed to sit down. He needed to touch her.

Neil sank to his knees before her. She blinked and gave a surprised laugh. "What are you doing?"

He put his hands on her waist and pulled her closer. His mouth was at the soft expanse of her abdomen. "Kissing you," he answered her.

"From there?"

"Right here." He pressed his lips on the skin of her abdomen, and she drew in a sharp breath. He kissed her again slightly to the left and then again on the other side. "And right here."

"Yes," she whispered. "But I think you have left some terrain unmapped."

"Have I?" He would kiss every inch of her before the night was through. "Perhaps right here?" He kissed lower, just above her navel, where a knotted ribbon held the skirt of the night rail in place. He placed his mouth on the ribbon and kissed her. "Or here?"

"Neil," she murmured and swayed. He held her steady and looked up at her.

"Where else have I missed?"

Her eyes seemed to grow impossibly darker, and her mouth opened with indecision. And then her lips set in a familiar determined line. "Here," she said. Her hands inched over the ribbons of the bodice and she slowly drew it open, revealing her full breasts with their dark-pink crowns. The nipples jutted proudly, and his cock jerked at the sight.

But he would take this slowly, savor her and give her pleasure. His mouth brushed up her abdomen, and she trembled as his lips slid over her warm skin. Finally, he reached the soft underside of her breast, and he ran his tongue over the skin, watching it pebble and hearing her breath come in gasps as her fingers bit into his shoulders. He traced the curve of her breast, up one side, over, and down the other. He moved inward, and her nipple hardened in anticipation. He wanted that hard point in his mouth, on his tongue, lightly between his teeth, but he deprived them both and worshipped her other breast as he had the first.

Her head had fallen back at his ministrations, and she trembled from head to toe. Her breath came in short pants, making her chest rise and fall in a motion that made him groan. And then finally, as he nuzzled between those perfect breasts, she grabbed his cheeks and pulled his face back so she could look down at him.

"Your mouth," she said. "I need it here." She touched one nipple, her pale finger sliding over the swollen peak, and Neil almost lost control. With a growl, he took her breast in one hand and captured her nipple with his mouth. He slid the hard point inside, teasing it with his tongue and sucking lightly until she moaned and arched. He sucked harder then, his hand holding her heavy flesh while the fingers of his free hand teased and rubbed at the untended nipple.

She moaned again, her hands thrusting into his hair to hold him to her. "Yes, like that," she said on a half sob. "Exactly like that."

He allowed her to move his head to the other breast, and when he licked that nipple, she shuddered. She knew what she wanted now, and as he served her, she slid her hands out of her hair and to the ribbon on her skirt. With one flick, it was loose, and the fabric fell away.

Her coppery curls brushed against his chest, and he caught the faint scent of woman and arousal. He slid one hand over her belly, then her bottom, so plump and smooth, and then over a hip and between her legs. She was wet and warm, and she bucked when he brushed over her.

"Please," she said.

He slid two fingers into that slick heat, licking her nipple in a motion that mimicked his hands. She tightened around his fingers, only releasing him when he drew out and swiped moisture over her hidden nub.

"Neil," she moaned.

His fingers moved inside her again, gently and deeply, sliding in and out as his palm pressed against her center of pleasure. She ground against him, her hips moving in an instinctual rhythm. She was close to climax. One glance at her flushed face told him that much. He slid out of her, his fingers wet and the scent of her all around him. Without thinking, he lowered himself, placing his lips against her curls. God, her scent was like sweet wine. He was drunk on her arousal and the heat of her.

"Neil," she said again, her voice filled with more urgency. He slid his mouth lower, parting her lips with his tongue, sliding over her bud and making her cry loudly, and then lapping at her wetness.

He loved the taste of her even more than her scent. He would die remembering her sweetness on his tongue. Her hips moved and her cries grew more frantic. His fingers parted her, exposing her small, swollen bud. Red and all but throbbing, he placed the tip of his tongue on it.

She all but screamed, and he pulled back. "You'll wake the children."

She nodded and bit her lip, her hands sliding into his hair and clutching it almost painfully.

"Shh," he said, blowing air where he had exposed her. She gave a choked sob. "Not a sound," he said, putting his mouth on her and using his lips to tease her until her hips moved and she pressed hard against him. And then he touched her lightly, so lightly, with his tongue. Small, tortured sounds came from her lips and her hold on his hair became almost painful, but she did not scream as he flicked and swirled that tight, little bud.

She moved with his tongue, her bottom sliding against his hands as she tried to move closer, unashamed of her need and her reaction. Finally, she stiffened, and he took the bud in his mouth and sucked deeply. She shattered then, her entire body convulsing against him. How he wanted to free his cock and slide inside her. He slid his fingers inside her instead and wished her body clenched his cock and not merely his fingers.

Finally, she was spent, and he moved back to guide her to the bed. He expected her to fall onto it. He expected to join her, kissing her lips again, then her breasts, perhaps turning her over and running his teeth over her buttocks before he pushed her up on her knees and used his mouth and his fingers from that angle.

Instead, she caught herself on her elbows and looked up at him. The slant of her eyes and the tilt of her mouth were coolly seductive, and he paused in the process of joining her on the bed.

"What does that look mean?" he asked warily.

"I'm not ready to sleep."

"Good," he said, putting one knee on the bed beside her. "Because I have other plans for you."

She cocked her head. "Are you content to give me pleasure and take none for yourself?"

He stilled. "We discussed this already."

"I know, and while I want you inside me, I also know the risks."

Neil closed his eyes and swallowed. In his mind, he knew he must remain a virgin, but his body did not always agree. Her words appealed to his body, and he fought the war between desire and duty.

"But do you never take any pleasure? I'm not a complete innocent." The blush on her cheeks belied her words. "I've been touched by men, and I know they never touch me without wanting something in return."

Neil stiffened. "I may be a bastard, but I'm a gentleman enough not to expect anything from you."

"But what if I want to give you something?" She reached for his waistband and tugged him closer. "What if I want to touch you and"— she loosened the fall of his trousers—"see you?"

"I wouldn't argue," he said, voice tight. The placket came loose and his cock sprang free and into her small, warm hand. Dear God but those long, lithe fingers felt good as they curled around him and slid up and then down.

"You're softer than I thought," she said.

He blew out a breath. He felt anything but soft at the moment. "That's not exactly a compliment."

"What I mean is, I didn't expect the skin to feel so much like velvet—velvet over steel. Do I move like this?" She slid her hand up and then down.

"Yes," he managed, clenching his jaw. He swallowed, attempting to regain control. *Think of something benign—long lists of orders, a game of billiards, polishing my boots.* "And here I was thinking you had done this before," he said when he managed to regain his voice.

"No. I've never touched a man skin to skin. I've never put my hand on a man or taken him in my mouth."

"Oh, bloody hell," he said between clenched teeth, squeezing his eyes shut and trying desperately to think of anything but the motion of her hand or the promise of her plump lips. She would be the end of him.

"May I?" she asked.

He opened his eyes and looked down at her. She'd risen to her knees and sat with her mouth poised over the tip of his erection. The image was the most erotic he had ever seen, and yet his first thought had nothing to do with fellatio.

She wanted *him*. Of all the men she might have had, all the men who had wanted her, *she* wanted *him*. Him—Neil Wraxall, bastard of the Marquess of Kensington, failed leader of the Survivors. The man who was responsible for the death of eighteen men.

He didn't deserve her or this.

He began to shake his head, but then her tongue darted out, skating over him. "Please," she said.

And he couldn't say no. For the first time in a long, long time, he took the affection—or perhaps it was love?—offered.

Twenty

Julia watched Neil's face go from a mask of control to soft and vulnerable. He was a beautiful man, and when his eyes darkened to azure blue and his full mouth relaxed, she found him utterly irresistible. She lowered her lips to taste him again, sweeping her tongue over his tip.

He smelled musky and clean, like the gardens in Mayfair after a hard rain. At first she explored him tentatively, learning the shape and feel of him, but gradually also the way he tensed or the hissed exclamations of pleasure he made to let her know what he enjoyed. She closed her mouth over him, taking him inside, and he swore loudly.

She paused and looked up. "You don't like that?"

"I like it," he said between clenched teeth. "You don't have to do this."

"Oh, I want to do this," she said, taking him in her mouth again and sliding her tongue over his length. She understood now why he enjoyed giving her pleasure. She loved the way he reacted to her touch. She loved knowing she could have this effect on him—this man who was so strong and confident, this man who was not afraid to face down even the worst villains of the underworld. He was hers at this moment, completely hers. She loved knowing he wanted her, and that she could make him feel the same pleasure he'd given her.

She loved touching him intimately, and she loved his touch on her.

She loved him.

She hadn't wanted to fall in love. It had been the furthest thing from her mind when she had twelve boys to care for, an orphanage to keep up, and three rats to keep contained, but how could she help falling in love with him? From the moment she'd met him, he'd done nothing but take care of her and the boys. He'd done nothing but protect her. He might have been ridiculously regimented, overprotective, and overly concerned with duty, but she could trust him. She could count on him, and he was the first man she really believed she could rely on.

And that was not taking into account his perfect face or his hard soldier's body. Appearance should not have mattered. She of all people should know that, considering the Viscount of Lainesborough was considered handsome by most ladies of the *ton*, and he'd used his appearance to steal Harriett's heart and then her dowry. But Neil was no rake, and though she knew what she did broke every single rule of her upbringing, she did not care.

She wanted him.

She wanted this.

She wanted more.

"Julia," Neil said with a choked sound. When she

pulled back, he stepped away, his glorious manhood stiff and at the ready. "I can't hold on any longer."

"Then don't," she said. She wanted more. She wanted all of him. She moved back on the bed and held out her arms. "Come here."

Though he breathed heavily and she could see the desire in his eyes, he did not move toward her. "I cannot."

"Neil, I want you. I…" She faltered. If she said the words now, she could not take them back. But if she did not say them, she might suffer her father's curse and spend the rest of her life wishing she had. "I love you," she said quietly.

His eyes widened and lost some of that hazy quality. She thought for a moment, he might turn and bolt. Instead, he merely stood motionless before yanking his shirt over his erection and covering himself.

The action only made her feel more vulnerable. She was still lying naked on the bed. She sat, drawing her knees up to her breasts. "I shouldn't have said anything. You obviously don't feel the same."

"You don't know what you're saying." He moved closer to her, which she wanted to believe was a good sign, but his face looked hard again. The warrior was back. "You don't know me or what I've done."

"I *do* know you," she protested. "And I know exactly what you've done. You've repaired locks, built rat cages, guarded the door, fed hungry children, defeated Mr. Slag—"

"That was my duty, and protecting a beautiful woman and innocent children is no penance. At least, not the penance I deserve after the sins I've committed."

She rose on her knees, taking his hands in hers. "What sins? Defending your country? Safeguarding your men? Killing an enemy who would have killed you if you hadn't acted first?"

"Juliana, I was never supposed to come home. I was sent to die and take as many of the French with me as possible."

"But you did come home, and you're alive." She took his face in her hands. "Act alive. Kiss me, Neil. Make love to me."

He shook his head.

"Neil, I know how you feel. When I lost Davy, nothing else in my life mattered. I'd lost my sister and best friend, and then I lost her child. I wanted to die. But strange as it seems, this pitiful orphanage and the lost boys saved me. They gave me a home and a family. You can be part of that family."

His body went rigid. "What are you saying?"

What was she saying? What was she saying to this man in the middle of the night, as she knelt on her bed, naked and vulnerable? "Marry me," she whispered, wishing for all the world she did not have to be the one to ask him. Praying he would want her as much as she wanted him because she had never wanted anything as much as she wanted him.

He shook his head, and she felt ice slide down her bare back.

"That's not possible."

"I see." She sat back, feeling more naked than ever before. She reached for the coverlet and pulled it up and over her.

"It's not that I don't want you, Juliana."

She moved back and out of his reach when he extended a hand toward her.

"You simply do not want to marry me. I understand. I run an orphanage. No man of my station will ever want to marry me when I won't return home."

"No." He took her shoulders in a firm grip. "That's just it. I'm not of your station. I'm a bastard—"

"You are the acknowledged son of a marquess, Neil. That hardly makes you lowborn."

"But not a legitimate son. My father's legitimate son—the youngest, Christopher—died in the war. I was there that day, and I couldn't save him."

"Neil—"

He released her shoulders and stepped away. "It should have been me lying dead on that battlefield, not Chris."

She shook her head, tears stinging her eyes. "No," she whispered. "Do you think God or fate or whatever you want to call it makes mistakes? You survived and you deserve to live a long, happy life with a family." She could see the word *family* affected him. He swallowed convulsively. "I am sorry about your brother. So sorry. But you are the one who is here. And if you know me at all, you know I wouldn't care if you were a cobbler or a beggar on the street. I love *you*." She should stop saying that. She should stop ripping her armor off, especially when he possessed so many arrows.

"And what kind of husband would I be? I have no fortune, no title, I wake with nightmares."

"You would be the husband I love," she countered. "Do you think I'm perfect? I have a list of flaws as long as Rotten Row."

"No, you don't."

"I do." She held up a finger. "I'm headstrong." Another finger. "I'm impulsive." Another finger. "I don't think before I act."

"That's the same as impulsive."

She scowled at him. "I repeat myself when making lists. I can't keep a servant. I'm a horrible judge of character, if Mr. Goring is any example—I could go on all night. Whatever your imperfections, I love you despite them. The circumstances of your birth matter not a whit. It's the two of us together that matter. Together we are stronger than anything."

He gave her a long look, then shook his head. "I wish things were different." He straightened his clothes and moved toward the door.

"That's it then?" she called out. "You're leaving?"

"I was always leaving. I'll make sure the roof is repaired, and I'll speak to Billy before I go."

Her mind reeled as her body grew ice cold. "You won't even try? You won't even consider giving this…this family a chance?"

"This is the best thing for both of us."

She reached for the closest object and took hold of a pillow, throwing it with all her strength across the room. Unfortunately, he reached up and caught it easily. "Arrogant man! Who are you to tell me what's best for me?"

He tossed the pillow onto the bed. "You needn't worry I'll leave without making certain you're safe."

"Damn your bloody duty, Neil Wraxall," she yelled. "I don't want it."

He went to the door, and she grabbed another

pillow. She threw it, but the cushion thudded uselessly against the closed door.

Neil was gone.

∾

Walking away from her had been the hardest thing Neil had ever had to do. It was also the right thing. She needed a peer—a man with rank and wealth and connections. Not a former soldier and a counterfeit hero. Even the boys at the orphanage deserved better. They needed a man they could emulate, not one who had been born into circumstances little different from theirs.

Neil paced the orphanage, patrolling it and checking to be certain doors and windows were locked. Slag was gone, but that didn't mean Julia wasn't still vulnerable. After his third pass, he found himself in the servants' quarters and the room he'd been given. He stared at the bed. For the first time in memory, he wanted sleep. Tonight he was weary enough to succumb quickly. He stripped and lay down, asleep before his eyes were fully closed.

He knew it was a dream as soon as he saw the battlefield. He stumbled through it, as he had all those years ago, his focus on the fallen infantry, looking for Christopher's golden-blond hair. Men with brown hair, black hair, gray hair, and dark-blond hair lay with unseeing eyes or clutching bleeding arms or legs. One man held a hand over a gash across his middle, keeping his intestines from spilling out. Neil couldn't let himself see this. Couldn't allow himself to believe any of it was real, else he'd lose his breakfast and his faltering courage. Neil trudged through the pools of blood, halting at the bright cap of blond hair lying in one of the bloody puddles.

His breath caught and his belly tightened.

"Chris," he said hoarsely, turning the man over. His heart pounded wildly, his vision dimmed, but when he opened his eyes again, the man he touched was not Christopher, not his brother.

"Water," the man croaked. With shaking fingers, Neil unfastened his canteen and pressed it into the man's hands. He moved on, moved down the hill, his eyes scanning for that crown of bright curls.

Please, God. No.

He almost passed another man with blond hair. This man's cap was still on his head, his face obscured because he lay facedown on the hill. Neil did not want to do this. Did not want to see the dead face. But he had to know. He'd go mad otherwise. Neil got behind the body, dug his heels into the steep slope for purchase, and flipped the man over.

Shock and pain stabbed through him as he stared at the face of Christopher Wraxall.

But in the dream, Chris's eyes were closed. They'd always been open before. They'd been open, seeing nothing, that day on the battlefield. Neil stared at the face of his dead brother and noticed it was not as defined as it had once been. He was forgetting the small details, not only of that day, but of his dead brother. Before he could decide whether this was good or bad, the corpse opened its green eyes.

Neil woke, a scream lodged in his throat. But that was all it was—lodged in his throat. He hadn't made an actual sound. His throat was not raw. No one came running to see what was the matter. His hands still trembled, but he clenched them, and the shaking ceased.

Slowly he became aware of the clink of pots and pans, the shuffling sounds of people moving about, and the pinpoints of light that filtered through the dark curtains.

It was morning. He'd slept the entire night. Without drink. Without waking in a cold sweat from nightmares. He wanted to hope and yet he didn't. He'd had good nights before. One good night didn't mean anything. But his brother's eyes had been closed. What did it mean?

And what did it matter? Today he would leave. He would go home, and if he saw Juliana again, it would be for a moment when he checked on the roof repairs or stopped by to ensure the orphanage's board of directors passed on the funds donated.

He'd never kiss her again, touch her silky skin, make love to her—and perhaps that was for the best. She'd never be his, and he'd be the worst sort of rogue to take her innocence without the promise of marriage.

Neil dressed, and when he stepped out of his room, he met the disapproving look of Jackson. The valet's gaze slid over the haphazard way Neil had yanked the nearest available clothing on, and the man shook his head.

Neil raised a hand. "Before you decide I'm not up to snuff, let me remind you we are in an orphanage."

"That is no excuse for poor—"

"And we are leaving this morning."

That announcement silenced Jackson.

"Pack my things and your own. I want to be off first thing."

"Leaving, sir?" Jackson asked.

"As soon as I speak with Billy, yes."

Jackson's expression was still one of shock. "Does Lady Juliana know this, sir?"

Neil put his hands on his hips. "Not that it matters, as she has no authority over me, but yes, she knows. I believe she will be quite glad to see my back."

"But I thought—"

"Do not think, Jackson. Pack."

"Yes, sir." Jackson trudged into Neil's chamber, shoulders hunched in dejection. Neil blew out a breath. He'd thought at least Jackson was on his side.

Once upstairs, Neil found Billy easily enough. He was in the dining room with the other boys, waiting impatiently for the morning meal.

"Major!" a chorus of voices rang out, surprising Neil. James ran to him and grabbed one of his legs in a fierce hug. Charlie smiled around the thumb in his mouth. George held up a paper where he'd drawn what Neil thought might be a horse—or a ship—and even Ralph nodded at him, his black eye now just a faded yellow.

"Can I sit by you, Major?" Sean asked.

"I get to sit on 'is other side," Angus said.

"He sat on that side of the room yesterday," Michael announced. "He's eaten on that side five times and only four on this side. That is, if we're counting."

"You are always counting," Robbie muttered.

"When do we eat?" Jimmy asked. "I'm starving,

and once Mrs. Dunwitty finds us, we'll be trapped all morning."

"Can I sit on your lap, Major?" Charlie asked around his thumb.

"Actually," Neil said, speaking through the cacophony for the first time, "I haven't time to eat this morning. I need to speak with Billy."

Billy, who had been sitting in a corner, looking down at his hands, raised his head. He was clean of soot and ash, but he had a welt on his forehead and his lip still looked swollen. The boy rose slowly to his feet. "What is it, Major?"

"I'd like to speak in private." Neil motioned to the door. Billy made his way across the now-silent room, and Neil led him into the parlor, where he left the door open slightly. "Sit," Neil ordered, gesturing to the couch. He tried not to remember lying on that couch himself, Juliana wrapped in his arms. He tried not to remember her in his arms, pushed up against the far wall, her lips hot and eager.

"You have a choice to make," Neil said when Billy sat. "About your future."

Billy looked up, his eyes defiant. "What choice? No one ever gave me a choice. I had no choice about living here. No choice about being beaten every day, before Lady Juliana came, no choice about what to eat. What choices do I have?"

"You have to choose between living here or out there," Neil said, crooking his thumb at the street.

"That's no choice. If I don't do what Slag wants, he hurts me."

"Slag is gone now. That means you do have a choice."

"And when another takes his place?"

"Walk away. If you can't, you send for me." Neil reached into his coat and took out a card. "This is the name of my solicitor. He can always find me, and his offices are not far from here."

Billy took the card, looking at it as though it were an exotic piece of fruit.

"You can always come to me for help, but if you want to live here, if you want to stay at Sunnybrooke, you'll have no more dealings with the gangs and the upright men."

Billy pressed his lips together. "I don't see the problem with making a little extra on the side."

"The problem," Neil said levelly, though he wanted to rage at the boy to stop being an idiot, "is that sort of activity leads to the events of last night. Either I have your word you will walk the straight and narrow, or you pack what meager belongings you have and leave right now."

Billy's head came up. "You can't make me leave. Lady Juliana won't make me leave."

"Yes, I will."

Neil's gaze shot to the door where Juliana stood in the small opening. She pushed it wider, the skirts of her green dress swishing against the wood. She looked beautiful with her copper hair in a sleek tail down her back and the tight-fitting bodice of the dress molding to curves he wished he could forget. The contrast between her fragile beauty and the dark squalor of the orphanage was stark, but somehow she managed to look regal all the same.

She did not look rested. Her eyes were puffy, her

mouth a tight line. If he hadn't known her well, he might not have noticed, but he knew her now. Knew he was most likely the cause of her tossing and turning.

"Mr. Wraxall is correct, Billy. You do have a choice to make." She moved into the room, her gaze on Billy and studiously averted from him. "Last night proved to me that every relationship has give-and-take. I can offer you love and safety and a home, but I can't make you take it."

She didn't look at Neil, but he knew she spoke to him as well as to Billy.

"And you cannot have things both ways. You choose this orphanage and me, or you leave. I do not want to give you up, but I have eleven other boys to think about. I won't sacrifice them for you. And I won't risk them for you again either. Make your choice."

Billy looked from Juliana to Neil and back again. The silence in the room was so heavy Neil wished he could push the weight from his shoulders. He wished he could take Juliana in his arms, tell her he'd made his choice for her.

Because he loved her too.

Then Billy lifted a hand and swiped at his eyes, but it wasn't enough to stem the tears. Juliana leaned forward and stopped herself. She wanted to take the child in her arms—and that was what he looked like again, just a child—but she would wait until he made his choice.

"I want to stay with you, my lady," Billy sobbed. "Please let me stay."

And then Billy was in her arms, and she was patting his back and smoothing his hair, and whispering that everything would be okay. Over Billy's shoulder,

Juliana's gaze met Neil's. Neil nodded. Everything was as it should be again. She had her lost chick back under her wing.

She'd saved another boy, but Neil was no child who could be soothed with a pat on the back. She couldn't change the station either of them had been born to.

With a sardonic salute, he walked away—out of the parlor, out of the orphanage, out of her life.

Twenty-one

LIFE WENT ON WITHOUT NEIL WRAXALL. SHE HADN'T
thought it would. She'd thought she'd wither and
close herself off from the world like Harriett had when
Lainesborough had finally shown his true colors.

But Julia wasn't Harriett. Or perhaps she'd learned
from her sister. Or perhaps she just had too much to
do to take the time to indulge her broken heart. She
had workers on the roof to oversee, boys to feed,
wages to pay, and the riffraff of Spitalfields to fend off.

Neil might have gone, but Billy had stayed. The tall,
quiet boy still kept to himself, but once in a while, he
would sit beside her. He might make a face when she
tried to hug him, but he didn't push her away. Billy
and Robbie had declared a truce of sorts, and the two
of them had worked with Walter to build a racetrack
for Matthew, Mark, and Luke. All the children and
Mrs. Dunwitty had gathered in the parlor to watch
the rats race. Although Julia had firmly outlawed any
wagering, she suspected a few of the boys had placed
bets anyway.

"Robbie, I believe we are ready," Julia said when

all the boys had gathered around the track, jostling and nudging each other with excitement. The younger boys had climbed on chairs to see better, and Julia was pretending not to notice.

Robbie rubbed his hands together. "That's it then, lads. Last chance to, er, find a seat."

Julia wanted to roll her eyes. She really would have to lecture the children on the evils of gambling—but she'd pretend, just for tonight, that she didn't know what they were up to. She knew she should have put an end to the wagering, but everyone was so excited and so happy and all together. The boys had been glum since Neil had left, and they needed something happy to bring them all together. She needed something happy because, as she looked around the room, all she could think of was Neil. He would have found Michael with his pencil and notebook and serious expression amusing and she wished he could see that Charlie had finally stopped sucking his thumb (except at bedtime, of course), and she wanted to show Neil that Billy and Robbie were almost standing beside each other.

The room and the orphanage seemed empty without him. She could wish him back for the next decade, but he'd made his choice. He didn't want her. He wanted his life of blame, a life where his status as a bastard would mean he never truly fit in. He had fit in at Sunnybrooke. The boys had loved him, and they didn't care about circumstances of birth or one's past deeds as a soldier. They'd loved Neil because he'd cared for them, given them his attention, given them his time.

She'd loved him because he'd cared for the boys and because no other man she'd ever known would have done the same. She'd loved him for a thousand different reasons, not the least of which was the way he'd kissed her, the way he'd made her feel.

But in the end, he hadn't loved her back. Or at least not enough to stay.

She caught Mrs. Dunwitty's gaze on her from across the room, and Julia gave a watery smile. She blinked her eyes to stem the tears that threatened and focused on Robbie as he placed each rat in his starting box. Each rodent had his own lane, and the race would begin when the block sealing the rat in the box was lifted. At the end of the race were three pieces of cheese—incentives for the rats to run quickly. The first rat to make it to his cheese was the winner. Julia did not wager, but if she had, she would have put her money on Matthew. He was fleet of foot and not quite as rotund as Mark and John.

George, Ralph, and Angus each put a hand on a block, poised to lift it when Robbie said the word. Robbie raised his hand, and the room hushed. "Ready?" Robbie said.

Angus nodded slightly and George and Ralph kept their eyes on their blocks. "Steady," Robbie cautioned. The room took a collective breath.

"And go!"

The blocks were yanked up and the room erupted in cheers. The three rats looked about in surprise, not a one showing any inclination to run.

"Do be quiet, boys," Mrs. Dunwitty said. "All this noise will startle them."

The boys quieted—or at least what was quiet for them—and Julia heard whispers of *Should we nudge them?* and *Come on, Mark!*

Then Luke's nose twitched, and Charlie said, "He smells the cheese!"

He must have because Luke took a few tentative steps forward. The other rats couldn't see Luke, but their noses seemed to twitch, or perhaps Luke sent them some sort of message only rats could decipher, because Matthew and Mark began to scurry forward.

The closer to the cheese the rats came, the faster their feet carried them until they were running full speed and all the boys were once again yelling. Julia yelled too. She couldn't help it. Their enthusiasm was infectious, and when Matthew and Luke reached the cheese at the same time, she cheered.

"It's a tie!" Robbie announced. "We need another race."

"Let them finish their cheese first," Charlie said, always concerned for the rats' welfare.

"We need more cheese," James said.

"I'll get it!" Charlie offered. But just as he ran to the door of the parlor, Mrs. Koch stepped inside. Charlie almost ran into her, but she held out a hand and grabbed his shoulder stopping him.

"Let me guess. You vant more cheese?"

"If you have any to spare, Mrs. Koch," Julia said.

"Cheese for the rats. Vhy not? This is a strange country, yah. Very strange." She held out a parcel wrapped in paper. "This came few minutes ago. You vere making so much noise, I could hardly hear the rap on the door."

"What it is?" several of the boys asked.

Mrs. Koch looked at Julia for permission. She gave a slight nod. "I think in this country you call it black pudding. Yah?" She parted the paper to reveal the long black cylinder resembling a large sausage. The boys gasped in shock, as did Julia. She did not care for black pudding, but she knew it would be a treat for the boys who had grown tired of their daily diet of porridge.

"Where did it come from?" she asked.

"A man delivered it," Mrs. Koch said. "I don't know him, but he said it vas a gift. Vhat do you vant me to do vith it?"

"Can we eat it, my lady?" George begged. "Please, please?"

"Yes, can we cut it and eat it now?" asked Michael. "If my estimate is correct, we can slice it into about fifteen even pieces."

"Can we give some to the rats?" Charlie asked.

Julia tapped her chin. "I don't know if we should eat it. A gift like this—who sent it?"

"I don't know, my lady," Mrs. Koch said. "I asked him, but he said 'a friend.'"

"I bet it's from Major," Sean said. "I bet he sent it! Please can we eat it?"

Julia did not think it was from Neil, but it might have been from someone of the upper classes trying to do a good deed. But why wouldn't the person have left his or her name?

"Please?" James asked. "Please?"

Julia smiled. How was she to hold up against this sort of pressure? "Very well."

The boys cheered.

"We will eat it at breakfast."

The boys groaned.

She clapped her hands. "If we're to have another race before bedtime, someone go with Mrs. Koch to fetch more cheese." She almost smiled as Charlie and Jimmy both all but knocked Mrs. Koch over in their attempts to be the first to the kitchen. She would have smiled if she hadn't seen Billy's white face. The boy hadn't said a word, but he had gone white as a sheet.

"Billy, what's the matter?" she asked.

He blinked as though just remembering where he was. "Nothing, my lady. Nothing at all."

"Are you well?"

"I… Can I go lie down? My head is pounding."

"Of course. Is there anything I can do?"

"No. I'll be fine." He tried to smile, but it didn't reach his eyes.

∽

"I didn't think it possible, but you look even worse tonight than you did last night." Rafe Beaumont slid into the chair opposite Neil. They were alone in the dining room of the Draven Club, although it was well beyond the time when meals were served. Neil had lost all track of time.

"In fact, you look even worse than you did the morning after that skirmish in—"

"Stubble it," Neil said, pouring more gin.

Quick as a cat, Rafe swiped the bottle of gin and Neil's glass, handing it to Porter, who was conveniently passing by.

"What the devil?" Neil roared, rising.

Rafe blocked Neil's path as Porter made his escape. "If you want to hit someone, old boy, hit me. I'm to blame."

Neil stared at Rafe, and Rafe stared right back, refusing to back down.

"I would ask that you confine your blows to the area below my face. Others have found a punch to my breadbasket quite satisfactory."

"I ought to break your nose."

"And face the ire of London's female population? They're far less forgiving than me."

"I don't give a damn about London's female population," Neil said, but he sank back into his chair.

"And with the way you look, they won't give a damn about you." Rafe also sat, slowly, keeping his gaze on Neil. "If it's any consolation, Porter had considered sending for Draven. I asked him to let me have a try first."

"A try at what?" Neil muttered.

"Civilizing you for one. Sobering you up for another. How much have you drunk these past few days?"

"Who are you? My mother?"

"Oh dear God. You can't even think of a clever retort. This is worse than I thought."

Neil almost smiled despite himself.

Rafe leaned his elbow on the table and propped his chin in his hand. "Tell Uncle Rafe all about her."

"Who?"

"Whoever it is that drives you to drink—never a good solution to the annoyances wrought by females, by the way. You had us all running in circles for the chit in Spitalfields. Is it she?"

"Be careful who you call 'chit.'"

"Ah." Rafe steepled his hands. "It is Lady Juliana. What happened? You love her, but she doesn't return the sentiment?"

"What the deuce do you know about love?" Neil grumbled. For all his attempts to drown himself in drink tonight, he was still sober.

"I know all the symptoms," Rafe said. "Hangdog mouth—check. Starry eyes—check. Quick temper, most likely due to sexual frustration—check."

"Fists slamming into the face of the bloody idiot across from me"—Neil swung halfheartedly and Rafe leaned back—"check."

"Fine. You don't want to talk about it, then sit here and wallow, but I will say something before I leave you to it."

Neil raised a brow. Rafe had sounded more serious than Neil could remember him sounding in a long, long time. "So you think to lecture me?"

"Pathetic state of affairs, is it not? Here's the thing, Neil. We all lost friends and brothers-in-arms during the war. We were all part of the Draven's troop, and we each have our cross to bear. You don't have a corner on grief."

Neil leaned back and crossed his arms, anger rising in his chest. "So this isn't to be a lecture on love?"

"I'm getting to that, but you need this lecture too. We let you wallow—"

"You *let* me?"

"—because you were taxed with giving the orders—"

"And I don't wallow."

"—but we all volunteered to serve under Draven. We knew the risks, so stop blaming yourself for our losses. Blame Draven for giving the orders. Blame Napoleon for starting the war. Blame the dashed government for authorizing a suicide troop. Or"—he raised a hand—"here is an even better suggestion: forgive yourself and live your life."

"And exactly how am I supposed to forgive myself?"

"Why don't you begin by honoring our brothers' memories?"

Neil reached across the table and grabbed Rafe by his perfectly tied cravat. "I honor their memories every day."

"Of course you do," Rafe wheezed out. "Sitting here drinking all night is quite a tribute."

Neil let him go, none too gently.

Rafe smoothed his coat and slid a finger under his cravat. "Ask yourself what your men would have wanted. If I'd died on one of our missions, I'd sure as hell want you to be back in London doing all the things I loved doing."

"There's only one thing you love doing."

"You should try it before you criticize."

"I won't honor anyone by fathering bastards."

"Then marry the ch—lady in Spitalfields. I've always known you were the marrying sort, and you're obviously besotted with her. What are you waiting for?"

Neil shook his head. It was one thing to talk about letting go of the past and quite another for his mind to release the memories and give him peace. "And what kind of husband would a bastard be for the daughter of an earl?"

"A damn fine one," Rafe argued. "If I were a chit, I'd marry you."

Neil closed his eyes. "Words I never thought I'd hear. But it's not so sim—"

"Mr. Wraxall, sir!" Porter hobbled into the room as quickly as his wooden leg would allow him. For a moment Neil was shaken. The man always walked so smoothly, but then Neil had never seen him in this much of a frenzy.

Neil and Rafe both stood, legs braced for battle. "What is it?" Neil demanded.

"There's a boy, sir. He's outside the club. He said he must speak with you. It's a matter of life and death. He looks a bit rough, and I started to turn him away, but he said something about Lady Juliana, and I thought—" His gaze slid to Rafe.

Neil didn't wait for any further explanation. He took the steps of the main staircase two at a time and yanked the front door open.

Billy stood in the yellow lamplight.

"What happened?" Neil asked.

"It's Slag, Major. He's back."

Twenty-two

JULIA STOOD WITH HER HANDS ON HER HIPS, HER EYES narrowed at the line of boys in the older boys' dormitory. "Tell me where he is or, so help me God, not a single one of you will have a bit of the black pudding."

The seven boys looked to her and then at each other. A few looked at the floor, shuffling their feet. Billy was conspicuously absent, and Julia was furious. He'd promised to stay out of trouble. Hadn't she made it clear he would have to leave if he did not follow the rules? Her belly felt sick inside, knowing he had snuck out of the orphanage and she would have to evict him for good.

But first she wanted to be certain he was safe.

"I don't want any of that black pudding anyway," Walter mumbled.

"What's that?" Julia asked. "What is wrong with the black pudding?"

Walter's expression turned mulish, and Julia advanced on him.

"Does Billy's absence have something to do with that pudding arriving? What? Tell me."

Walter pressed his lips together. Robbie, who stood on his left, elbowed him hard in the ribs. "Tell her, Walter. Tell her what you told us."

Julia looked from Robbie to the other boys. She saw she'd mistaken their expressions for guilt. What she saw now that she looked closer was fear.

"It's a sign," Walter said, his voice low.

"What sort of sign?" Julia asked.

"From Slag. I seen him send it before. To his enemies."

Julia pressed her fingers to her temples. Her head pounded relentlessly. "Slag is dead. It can't be from him."

"He ain't dead," Walter argued. "Not if he sent the black pudding. He's still alive, and he wants revenge."

"And you think he's taken Billy?"

Walter shook his head. "Billy went to see if he could save you—save us." He made a sour face. "He's probably dead by now. Killed by Slag. And we'll be joining him soon."

His voice hitched at the end, reminding Julia that despite his awful words, he was still a boy.

"I have to go after him. And I won't let Slag do anything to any of you."

Suddenly she heard the thunder of running feet and pounding on the walls. "Fire!" Mrs. Koch yelled. "Help! Fire!"

"It's already too late," Walter said.

✧

A familiar rush of heat and icy cold flooded through Neil at Billy's words. Some men called the feeling battle lust. Neil had never liked to think of himself as a man susceptible to lust.

But at the moment, he wanted nothing more than to slit Slag's throat from ear to ear. He had no weapon, but then he'd honed his fighting skills until his body and brain had become the weapon.

"Lady Juliana?" Neil barked. He must take control of the situation. He must assess it from every angle.

"She's safe. I came to you as soon as I could get away."

"What is Slag planning?"

Billy lifted his shoulder. "I don't know, but it will be bad."

Neil did not need to be told as much. Slag would want revenge for the loss of the Ox and Bull and the loss of his position as the crime lord of Spitalfields. He'd have to make an example of Juliana if he wanted to earn back the respect and fear he'd lost.

"Porter!" Neil called, knowing the Master of the House waited nearby. "Flag a hack for me."

"Yes, sir."

"Could you use my help?"

Neil would have recognized Rafe's slow drawl anywhere. He turned to see his friend leaning negligently in the club's doorway. "You might wrinkle your cravat."

Rafe sighed heavily. "Such is the burden I bear." He pushed away from the door. "I had better come with you despite the danger to my wardrobe. God knows you always forget to watch your back."

"You sure you're ready?" Neil asked, climbing into the hackney that stopped before them.

"I have my dancing shoes on." Rafe clapped him

on the shoulder and took a seat beside him. "I rather fancy a dance with the devil."

This time Neil would make certain Slag was nothing but a pile of bones. If anything had happened to Juliana… If Slag had dared to touch her…

Neil didn't know how he would go on, knowing he'd left her alone and defenseless. What had he been thinking? He'd been so concerned with his own pride, with his fears that he could never be worthy of her, that he'd put her in danger.

Why hadn't he listened when she told him she loved him despite his bastardy? Why didn't he understand that he had the family he'd always wanted right there? A family was stronger together than apart. Together, they'd repaired the orphanage and restored order to the lives of a dozen boys. Together, they'd taken a troubled boy like Billy and taught him to trust them. Together, they had taken down one of the most notorious crime lords in London.

Together, they could do anything.

He had to reach her before it was too late—too late for her and then too late for himself.

❦

Julia took a deep breath. She could not panic. She had to move the boys safely down the stairs and out of the burning building.

"No pushing," Mrs. Dunwitty instructed. "Count them when they reach you, Mrs. Koch."

Mrs. Koch nodded and coughed into her sleeve. The black smoke pouring into the vestibule made it difficult to breathe or see. Her eyes watered and stung, but she would be free soon enough. As soon as Mrs. Koch had sounded the alarm, Juliana had wanted to send the boys down the servants' stairs and out the kitchen door. But Mrs. Koch had seen her moving the boys that way and yelled, "No! No! The fire is in the servants' quarters and the kitchen. Ve must go out this vay!" She'd pointed to the front door.

Juliana hadn't liked that idea. Who knew what, or whom, might be waiting for them right outside the door, but she had little choice if the servants' exit was consumed by fire. She wasn't quite ready to blame this all on Slag, as Walter had done. Fires often began in the kitchen, and the kitchen was close to the servants' quarters. But if Slag was alive and behind the fire, then this might all be a trap.

And very likely, he or his men would be waiting for them outside the door.

"Robbie. Walter." Julia grabbed the boys' hands and stalled them as the remaining children continued down the steps with Mrs. Dunwitty shepherding them. "If Slag is behind this, then we don't know what to expect once we step outside. Be ready, yes?"

"Yes, my lady."

The look of gravity on the boys' faces made her heart clench. She didn't want to give them this responsibility. She wanted them tucked in their beds and fast asleep. She wanted her heart to stop pounding and the fear of losing her boys to disappear. But she couldn't think of that now. She had to act, not think.

Mrs. Dunwitty stood at the bottom of the steps. "I think we're missing someone."

Julia's heart rose in her throat. She counted all the boys again. "Eleven. Yes, we're missing someone."

"Billy went after Slag," Walter reminded her.

Billy. Why hadn't he come to her with his worries? Why had he tried to take Slag on himself? Brave, brave boy. She wished she could hug him and tell him she was the one who was supposed to take care of him.

"Mrs. Koch and I will lead the boys out. Mrs. Dunwitty, you follow." She had meant to say more, but she started coughing again. She had to escape before it was too late. Julia unlocked the door, took a deep breath, and opened it. Men and women had gathered out front, but they were gaping at the building, not lying in wait. Still, she would have to be vigilant.

She stepped outside, pulling Chester and James with her. Next came Walter, his eyes scanning the crowds. He was followed by Angus, Sean, and George. Julia led the boys away from the building and into the shadow of the shop across the street.

"Are you hurt, miss?" a man asked.

"No, I—"

Chester gasped, and Julia turned to see what the matter was. Chester pointed at the orphanage, and Julia gasped. Flames, bright red and orange, shot from the kitchen and into the dark sky. "Oh dear God," she whispered.

"I want my mama," Jimmy said, pulling at her skirts. Julia lifted him and hugged him.

"Shh. I have you. You're safe."

"I'm scared," Chester wailed.

Julia lifted him too, hugging both boys tightly.

Ralph and Michael pressed close, Robbie keeping vigil beside Mrs. Koch.

"Julia!" Mrs. Dunwitty said, rushing toward her.

"Is everyone out safe?" Julia asked.

Mrs. Dunwitty shook her head, her eyes wide with fear. "The little one, Charlie. He was right in front of me, and he wanted to go back for those rodents."

"Oh no!" How could she have forgotten the rats?

"Matthew, Mark, and Luke!" Chester cried.

"I told him to forget them, but as soon as we reached the door, he pulled away from my hand and ran back inside. I tried to go after him—"

Julia shook her head. Mrs. Dunwitty could barely climb the stairs. She couldn't be expected to go back inside a burning building. She handed Chester to Mrs. Koch and Jimmy to Robbie. "I'll go back for him."

"I'll come with you," Robbie protested.

"No! You will stay right here and keep the other boys safe. I am counting on you, Robbie. Promise me."

He nodded. "I promise."

Julia looked at her friend and former governess. "I'll be right back."

"I wish you wouldn't go." Tears streamed down the older lady's face.

"I can't lose him. I'd rather die than lose him."

"I know. Come back to me. To us."

"I will!" Julia called as she rushed back into the burning orphanage.

⁂

Neil jumped from the hackney even before it had come to a stop. He'd seen the flames shooting from the orphanage from a half-mile away. From that moment on, Rafe had to physically restrain Neil to keep him in the hackney.

"It will take longer on foot," Rafe had argued when Neil tried to throw him off. Billy hadn't moved. He'd sat still as a statue, his face as white as marble.

And when the hackney slowed, Neil hadn't given Rafe a chance to hold him back. He'd sprung from the conveyance like a cat, sprinting with all he had for the burning building.

"Major!"

Neil had skidded to a stop and turned at the sound of the child's voice. He scanned the darkness and the unfamiliar faces of the residents of Spitalfields, who had gathered to watch the fire burn and attempt to stop its spread with buckets of water. He lowered his gaze, and that was when he saw James waving wildly at him. James's blond hair caught the light from the fire and shone like a beacon. Immediately, Neil spotted other orphans, plus Mrs. Koch and Mrs. Dunwitty.

But he didn't see Juliana.

He jogged toward the small group, praying he had simply missed her. She would be where he orphans had gathered. She was simply not in view.

Then why did he feel like casting up his accounts and emptying his belly of all the gin he'd consumed tonight?

"Major! Major!" The other boys had spotted him, and they called for him, their voices frantic and their faces mottled with the reflection of the red and gold flames. When Neil reached them, he surprised himself by pulling the closest boys into his arms. Walter looked quite dumbstruck, but James and Michael embraced him back. Neil ran his hands over the boys' heads and his gaze touched on others—Angus and Sean, Chester and Jimmy.

"You're safe," he said. "Where is Lady Juliana?"

James's gaze dropped and Neil inhaled painfully.

Robbie stepped forward. "I'm glad you're here, Major."

"Where is Lady Juliana?"

"She went back inside, sir."

Neil whirled to stare at the burning building again. Juliana was *inside*. Memories of the fire that had left Jasper scarred and Peter dead slammed into Neil. He'd let Jasper and Peter down. He couldn't let Juliana down too.

"Charlie is still inside," Mrs. Dunwitty said, coming forward, tears streaming down her cheeks and Jimmy clinging to her skirts. "He went back for those rodents."

Of course he did, Neil thought. He loved those rats.

"The fire started in the servants' quarters," Mrs. Koch added, "and spread to the kitchen. The lady still has time to escape."

"No, she doesn't," Billy said, coming up behind them.

Neil gave the boy a hard look. "What does that mean?"

"It means I know Slag, and he's probably waiting inside for her. He won't let her out alive."

⌒⌒

Julia covered her mouth and nose with a handkerchief and made her way through the thick smoke toward the stairs. She could hardly see and she stumbled almost blindly, making her way mostly from memory.

"Charlie!" she called, though she doubted he could hear her over the roar of the flames and the crashes of falling debris. "Charlie!"

Her foot struck something hard and elevated, and she realized she'd reached the stairs. She groped for the banister and pulled herself up the steps, coughing and choking. "Charlie," she managed in a hoarse voice.

Was it her imagination or had she heard a cry in response? A small, frightened cry, like one a boy might make if he was scared and alone.

"I'm coming, Charlie!"

She made a renewed effort to climb the stairs, grateful that Neil had repaired the boards that had rotted. She couldn't have avoided them now, and she might have fallen through. She climbed another step, her head spinning and her throat clenching in agony. How she longed for a breath of fresh air or a sip of water. She was so thirsty and so tired.

"Mama!"

Julia's head snapped up. She had not imagined that. It had been Charlie, and the poor child must have been so terrified he was crying for his mother.

"I'm coming, Charlie. I'm coming!" She found a reserve of strength and climbed quickly to the top of the stairs. "Where are you?" she called, but she knew where he must be. The rats were in the older boys' dormitory. That was where Charlie would have gone.

She turned to the right, hoping she was correct, stumbling slightly as the floor beneath her seemed to shift and creak. Dear God. The whole house would collapse soon. She had to find Charlie and get out before escape became impossible.

"Mama!" His voice was closer now, and she knew she'd chosen wisely. The smoke wasn't as thick in this section of the second floor, and she could almost make out the shadowy corridor leading to the older boys' dormitory.

The door was open, and she saw the shadow of a boy in the center of the room. He held a box—the enclosure Neil had built for the rats—and called out for her. "Mama!"

"I'm here, Charlie!" She raced into the room, her short legs eating up the little distance between them. When she reached him, she threw her arms around him. She hugged him fiercely, then pulled back. "What were you thinking?" she asked, tears of relief mixing with tears from the smoke. "I told you to stay together. Give me the rats. I'll carry them out. You hold my hand."

"Oh, Mama," Charlie said, sticking his thumb in his mouth now that his hands were free. He closed his eyes and burrowed his head into her skirts.

"Charlie, we have to go. We have to—"

The dormitory door slammed shut.

"Not so quickly, my lady. You haven't paid the toll."

Julia spun around, pushing Charlie behind her. A large figure loomed before the door. He took a step forward and she saw the burned wreck that was now Mr. Slag.

Twenty-three

"I'M GOING IN," NEIL SAID, PUSHING AWAY FROM THE children and starting toward the building, now almost completely engulfed in flames.

"I'll go with you," Rafe said, walking at his side, no hesitation in his step.

Neil glanced at him. Having Rafe beside him, at his right arm, seemed eerily familiar. He and Rafe had fought together before, Ewan on his left—Neil's weaker side—and Rafe on his right. Rafe was ready for battle again, though he looked much readier to dance a reel in the ballroom.

"Stay here," Neil said, barking the order over his shoulder. "You'll ruin your coat."

"I don't give a fig for my coat."

"Liar."

"Fine. I'll allow you to buy me another."

Neil paused and faced Rafe. "I need you out here," he said quietly. "If Slag didn't come alone, the women and children might be in danger. Stay here and protect them."

Rafe frowned. "I'm never chosen for the dangerous

assignments. It's always, 'Rafe, seduce that woman. Rafe, use your charm to distract those villagers.'"

Neil would have laughed if fear hadn't been clawing a bloody path through his heart.

"Here, take this at least." Rafe pulled a pistol from his coat.

Neil stared at the pistol and then at Rafe. When the devil had Rafe begun to carry a pistol?

"It's loaded and ready."

Neil raised his brows. Correction: When the devil had Rafe begun to carry a *loaded* pistol?

Neil took the pistol.

"Are you ready?" Rafe asked as Neil strode away.

"I have my dancing shoes on."

"Hey, one of these days, I want to dance with the devil, eh what!" Rafe called.

Neil ignored him and stepped into the fire.

Flames licked at the walls and the ancient paper hangings decorating the vestibule. The bones of the house were dry and dusty, perfect tinder for a hungry fire. His instinct was to shout for Juliana, but then he'd alert Slag to his presence. Neil wanted the element of surprise on his side.

The rats were kept in the older boys' dormitory, so that's where Charlie would have gone to fetch them and where Juliana would have followed. If Slag had been lying in wait, he would have cornered them there. Neil started up the creaky stairs, covering his mouth with his sleeve when he coughed. The smoke filled his lungs and burned his throat. The heat from the fire singed at any exposed skin, but he walked through it.

He would come out with Juliana or not at all.

At the top of the stairs, he started toward the boys' dormitory just as a loud crack boomed over the roar of the fire. Neil looked up in time to watch the heavy wooden beam slam through the ceiling and crash onto the floor.

A cloud of dust rose up, making him cough harder and momentarily blinding him. He stumbled back, barely catching himself at the edge of the stairway. Soot and debris rained down on him, and when he finally shook it off and he had a view through the dust again, he realized his path to the boys' dormitory was blocked.

Even worse, Juliana's escape route was gone.

∽

"I sorry, Mama," Charlie said, his voice high and frightened.

"Shh. It's not your fault," Julia said, pushing him behind her and turning to face Slag. What she saw when she looked at him made her belly roil. He hadn't escaped from the blaze at the Ox and Bull unscathed. His face was a mass of red, shiny skin. One side drooped so badly it looked as though it had melted off, the eye completely lost. She couldn't imagine the pain Slag must have been in. She couldn't imagine how he was even on his feet.

He stumbled forward. "For once, Lady Juliana is correct," Slag told Charlie. "It isn't your fault. You broke away from the group and fell right into my plans. I thought I'd have to nab one of you, but you made it easy. And you"—he pointed his walking stick at Julia—"are so predictable. I knew you'd come back."

"You have me," Julia said. "Let Charlie go."

"I don't think so," Slag said, moving away from the door. "I want you to suffer as I've suffered."

"Charlie has done nothing."

"You love him, so he dies."

Julia stood immobile in the center of the room. All around her the fire crackled and hissed. Small tongues of it licked at the door. It had a taste for the orphanage now. It would lick and taste and devour until the building was nothing but ashes. Slag was correct that watching Charlie die would cause her to suffer. But if he'd allowed Charlie to go, then she might have accepted her fate docilely. Now the crime lord gave her no choice but to fight.

She looked down at Charlie. She didn't know anything about fighting. But perhaps she could distract Slag long enough for Charlie to escape. She bent and hugged Charlie, whispering in his ear under the guise of comforting him. "I will attack Slag."

Charlie stiffened. "No." He shook his head.

"While he fights me, you run. Run as fast as you can and straight outside." She prayed he could still get through the fire.

"What about Matthew, Mark, and John?"

Charlie would never make it carrying the rat cage. It was too large and unwieldy for him under the best of circumstances.

"I'll get them out," she promised, knowing it was a lie. Knowing she would die here with Slag.

Charlie nodded.

"Ready?" she asked, hugging him tighter.

"Yes."

And then she released Charlie and ran straight for Slag, screaming like a wild banshee.

⤜⤛

Neil heard the screams and felt the twin emotions of terror and elation rise in his heart. Juliana wasn't dead, but she was in danger. He'd been staring at the fallen beam for a good thirty seconds, and he saw only one way around it—under it. He'd have to lift it and then slide underneath. Unfortunately, the quickness required for the move would mean dropping the beam back into place. And once the beam dropped, more debris would rain down. He wouldn't be able to go back the way he'd come.

He was trying to think of another way—any other way—when he heard Juliana's screams. They were immediately followed by a man's yells. Neil didn't stop to think any longer. He ducked under the charred and steaming beam and used his shoulder to lift it. With one arm, he held it up, then slid through the narrow passage. Just as he was about to drop the beam back into place, the dormitory door opened and a small figure rushed out.

Neil's arm shook from the effort of holding the heavy beam aloft. The heat from the burning wood seared through his gloves. But he held the beam. Squinting, he saw a child had emerged from the room—a child with his thumb in his mouth.

"Charlie!" he called.

Charlie, eyes wide and terrified, looked up. "Major?"

"This way," Neil said. "Through here and down the stairs. Hurry now." He said the last through gritted teeth. Charlie darted through the small opening with little trouble. As soon as the boy was safely through, Neil's strength gave out, and he dropped the beam and rolled clear. A mountain of plaster and wood and rained down, all of it burning with the wrath of the fire.

"Major?" Charlie called.

"I'm fine. Go!" Neil answered. "Hurry!"

He ran for the boys' dormitory and kicked open the door. The sight he came upon would forever haunt him. Slag stood over Juliana, cane raised. Juliana lay on the floor, her hands held up in a defensive posture. But Slag had turned when the door burst open. Neil shrank back at the devastation the fire at the flash ken had wrought on Slag's face. But Juliana had wasted no time at all. She'd kicked up, her foot colliding with the tender flesh between Slag's legs. The crime lord crumpled to the floor.

Neil rushed forward and pulled Juliana up and away from Slag. The man was clutching himself and rolling on the floor, but Neil wanted Juliana far away when Slag regained his strength.

"You came back?" she asked, looking at him as though he were a ghost.

"I should never have left." He pulled her into his arms, holding her tightly, thanking God he'd been in time. He would never let her go again. "You were right," he said stroking her back.

"I know," she answered, her arms coming up to embrace him. "But what specifically are you referring to?"

He smiled. The orphanage was burning all around

them, their only escape cut off, and the man who wanted them both dead lay just a few feet away. Still, she could make him smile. "We are stronger together," he said.

She drew back. "I did say that, didn't I?"

"You did. And now we'd better use that combined strength to get out of here."

"Charlie—"

"Is safe outside." He hoped. But when she started for the door to the dormitory, he grabbed her hand. "Not that way. It's cut off. Charlie made it through, but we won't."

"Then how?" she asked.

Neil pulled her to the window. "There's one latch I fixed three times but mysteriously kept breaking." He pushed on the window latch, and it gave easily. Obviously, the boys had intentionally broken it so they could sneak out of the dormitory without Julia knowing. Neil lifted the window. The escape route the boys had taken was plain to see. A decorative ledge, one of the remnants of the building's finer days, wrapped around the outside of the structure just a few feet below the window. Any of the older boys would have been tall enough to climb out of the window backward and rest his feet on the ledge. From there, he only had to walk around the side of the building to the edge where an old drainpipe ran from the roof to the ground. A nimble boy could shimmy down with little trouble. Neil was not so certain Juliana could manage it. And even after he explained the plan, she looked a bit worried.

He glanced back at Slag. The man had risen to

his knees and appeared to be gathering the last of his strength. There was no time for doubt.

"Juliana, there's no other way," he said.

"I can make it," she said sounding far more confident than she looked. "It's you I'm worried about."

"Me?"

"Yes. You'll have to do it all carrying the rat cage." She pointed to the cage sill sitting in the middle of the floor. Neil wanted to say *hell no*. Those rats had been the bane of his existence since the first day he'd met her. But he also knew she wouldn't leave them behind. She would have made a good soldier, if her superior officer didn't order her hung for insubordination.

Neil knew he couldn't manage the ledge or the drainpipe with the cage, but he could do it with the rats in his pockets. He shuddered, realizing he'd have to touch the creatures again, but he gritted his teeth. This was for Juliana.

She glanced up at him. "Stronger together, right?"

"Right." And he had no time to argue as to which situations that phrase applied to. Slag had begun to crawl toward them—or perhaps he was crawling away from the fire. It had engulfed the doorway now and enveloped the bed closest to the door.

Keeping an eye on Slag, Neil bent, opened the enclosure, and gathered the trembling rats into his hands. One bit him, of course, but he just swore and tucked the little bastard into his pocket. When he had all three, he raced back to Juliana. "Go."

She threw one leg over the ledge, but before she could climb out, he grasped the back of her neck and kissed her. "I love you," he said.

"I didn't hear that," she said. "You'll have to tell me again when we're on the ground." And she slid out of the window, her feet dangling in the air for a long moment before they landed on the ledge. With a wobbly smile for him, she slid away from the window, her sooty fingers clamped tight on the wall of the orphanage. When she was close to the drainpipe, Neil followed her out. He'd never liked heights—a fact about himself he'd learned on a mission for Draven—and he didn't look down. Instead, he scooted one foot and then the other, his progress a bit shakier than Juliana's, as his feet were wider than the ledge. At one point, he almost lost his balance, and he pinwheeled his arms. When he didn't fall, he rested his cheek against the building's wall and stifled the urge to whimper. Opening his eyes, he saw Juliana descending the drainpipe. Her progress wasn't smooth or graceful, but when she landed on the ground with a thud, she stood and gave him a wave.

"Stronger together," Neil muttered to himself, ignoring the feel of the squirming rats inside his clothing. He slid closer to the drainpipe. That was when the first object almost hit him. Neil hadn't seen it coming or he might have tried to avoid it and fallen. When it soared past him, narrowly missing him, he'd looked back at the window. Slag stood there with a wooden toy in his hand. Neil didn't waste time, moving even more quickly toward the drainpipe. Slag threw the toy and it bounced off the building where Neil's head had been a moment before. Slag lifted another toy, but he would have to lean out farther to hit Neil. Neil felt a surge of relief until Slag leaned farther out the window—a bit too far.

Neil saw the horrid loom of realization on the crime lord's face. The streak of black was gone in a moment, barely enough time for Neil to call out, "Don't look!" to Juliana.

The thud was soft, like a boot sinking into mud.

Quickly, Neil made his way to the drainpipe, shimmied down, and when he stepped away, Juliana threw herself into his arms. "Say it now," she said. "Please."

"Can I at least free myself from the rats?"

"No."

Truer words were never spoken. He'd never be free from these rats—or from her—and he liked that idea just fine. "I love you, Juliana," he said, and kissed her.

Twenty-four

NEIL SAID IF SHE'D BEEN BORN A MAN, SHE WOULD have been a general. She'd marshaled her ragged army of boys out of Spitalfields, descending on her father's house in Mayfair. The whole lot of them were dirty, tired, and hungry. When her father had come to the door, she'd said, "Hullo, Papa. I'm finally home!"

To his credit, St. Maur had only raised his eyebrows, gave a long-suffering sigh, and let them all in.

One by one, the boys had filed inside, mouths agog and necks craned to look at the soaring ceilings and winding marble stairs. The housekeeper and Mrs. Dunwitty, who were already acquainted, ushered the boys upstairs to be bathed and put to bed. In silence, the earl watched them file in until Neil walked through the door.

"Wait," her father said, holding up a hand. The diminutive earl narrowed his perceptive, green eyes. "This is not an orphan."

Neil bowed. "Forgive the intrusion, my lord. I wanted to see everyone safely settled."

The earl leaned back on his heels, obviously surprised at Neil's battered and bedraggled appearance.

"Wraxall? But I thought you had completed your work at St. Dismas."

"It's Sunnybrooke, my lord," Neil said before Julia could. "And I did complete my work there, but I haven't completed my acquaintance with your daughter."

Now the earl's brows shot up. "With Julia?"

"I intend to marry Lady Juliana, my lord."

Julia felt her entire body go numb. It was as though someone had just plunged her into a cold bath.

"Marry Julia?" The earl almost laughed. "I don't think so."

Neil stiffened. "Is it because I am a bastard, sir?"

"What? No! I only meant she wouldn't agree to marry you or any man."

"I'll marry him," Julia said, just managing to squeeze the words out of her paralyzed body.

"What?" her father said.

She kept her gaze on Neil, who didn't look surprised in the least. "If he asks me."

Neil gave a crooked smile. "With your permission, my lord?"

St. Maur could only nod, apparently struck speechless.

Neil took Julia's ash-streaked hand in his own sooty one. "Will you marry me, my lady?"

"I think the better question, Mr. Wraxall, is will *you* marry *me*?"

"Come again?" her father said.

Neil just waited for her explanation.

"I come with a large retinue, sir. A teacher, a cook, and a dozen orphans."

"Don't forget the rats," Neil said.

"I was just coming to them, and to the fact that we

have nowhere to live. I fear your accommodations will be too small for all of us."

He squeezed her hand. "Then we find new accommodations."

"In a safer location," the earl added.

"She'll always be safe with me," Neil said.

"And even more so if you use a portion of her dowry to build the orphanage—this Sunnybrooke—in a better area of Town."

Neil raised a brow. "Dowry? I don't know much about this dowry."

Julia smiled. "There's quite a lot you don't know about me, Neil Wraxall."

"Right now, all I want to know is whether you will consent to marry me."

"I will, Mr. Wraxall."

"Shall we ask the lads and the rats if they consent?"

She smiled. "The boys, yes. The rats' opinions don't concern me."

From above came a loud cheer. Julia looked up to see the boys leaning over the stair banister above them. Robbie gave her a nod of his head while Billy crossed his arms and smiled. Charlie jumped up and down, yelling, "Yes! Yes!"

"I think we have our answer," Neil said, then leaned down and kissed her in front of everyone.

❧

Neil didn't know why he should be nervous. Yes, he was a virgin on his wedding night, but wasn't the bride supposed to be the nervous one? The groom was supposed to be eager.

And Neil was definitely eager. He'd been pacing Juliana's bedchamber at her father's house for the better part of an hour. He hadn't been quite so nervous when he'd first come in here, but the longer he waited, the more his hands shook and his insides did loops and tumbles.

It had been two months since the fire—enough time to call the banns, for Juliana to ready her trousseau, and for the both of them to find a location and a building suitable for the new Sunnybrooke Home for Wayward Boys. The building had needed repairs and Neil had hired men to do the work, paying them from his own pocket. Juliana's dowry was far more than he had ever imagined, but he wanted to feel ownership in the orphanage. Her dowry might pay for the boys' upkeep and the monthly expenses, but he'd contributed to the building's foundation.

To *their* foundation.

He was thinking about the best location for the schoolroom when the dressing room door opened and Juliana stepped into her bedchamber.

And then all thoughts of orphans or schoolrooms fled completely.

She wore a lace-and-silk night rail, much like the one he'd admired before, but this one was somehow even more provocative. The lace bodice fit tightly over her breasts, then flared into a silky skirt that was nearly transparent. Neil felt his mouth go dry.

Juliana patted her shiny, copper-colored hair, which fell about her shoulders in a straight shower. "Do you like it?" she asked.

"Come here" was all he could manage.

She walked toward him, her hips swaying slightly in a movement that made him dizzy with desire. At the wedding today, Draven's men had congratulated him on his beautiful bride. Jasper had said he had the luck of the devil. Rafe had said the two of them were too pretty to look at. But Neil could look at Juliana all night.

And he would. They were married now. The papers were signed, the ceremony completed. She was his, and when he took her to bed tonight, he would not have to force himself to stop just when his body wanted more and more. She was his wife. Any off-spring would be legitimate. He would always be born on the wrong side of the blanket, but the shame he felt had lessened over the past weeks. Juliana loved him. The boys looked to him for guidance. He was not a mistake. He deserved a home and a family.

She stopped before him, the scent of roses on her skin light and teasing. "Here I am," she said with a coy smile.

"Are you nervous?" he asked.

She shook her head. "Should I be?"

Of course she wasn't nervous. She was the bravest woman he'd ever known.

"They say it hurts for a woman the first time."

She lifted one pale shoulder. "You'll make it right."

He gave a brief laugh. "I've never done this before either."

"Is that what's troubling you?"

He straightened. "I'm not troubled."

"You look as though your tumbrel just arrived at the guillotine."

"I hope the night doesn't end that badly," he said.

"It won't." And then she leaned forward and brushed her lips over his. The barest touch of her mouth was like a white-hot brand. He forgot his nervousness and gave in to desire, pulling her into his arms. The feel of her body beneath the flimsy silk intrigued him. He knew how soft her skin was, how generous her curves, but the silk sliding over it made it that much more tantalizing.

Her mouth opened slightly, and his tongue slipped into it, stroking her tongue and showing her what he wanted to do to her body. She trembled in his arms—not from fear but pleasure—and his lungs seized. He had to pull away to catch a breath. But his hands did not cease moving—up and over her bottom, around her slender waist, cupping her generous breasts.

"The bow," she said, her voice thick.

Neil frowned. Juliana took his hand and placed it on the small white bow centered in the valley of her breasts. "I want your hands on me. I've been wanting this for weeks."

They'd had only a few stolen minutes together since the fire, when she and the orphans had come to stay at her father's town house in Mayfair. Neil had missed the days at the orphanage when she hadn't been so well chaperoned. The handful of moments they'd had alone since were not nearly enough to satisfy either of them and had left them frustrated and unsatisfied. But that was all at an end now. In a few months, they'd be in their new home—their own home—one they'd share with the twelve boys and, Neil was sure, however many more Juliana took in.

To his surprise, he didn't mind. He'd spent most of

his adult life molding young men into soldiers. Now he would mold boys into honorable young men. Funny how he'd spent his entire life hiding from his status as a bastard, and now he embraced it and others like him. He would offer safety and love to the boys and to Juliana, and together they could make a new family to replace the ones they'd lost.

Neil tugged the bow, and the lace over her breasts parted. He loosed the next bow and the next until the lace fell away, revealing her lovely curves to him. He pushed the silky skirts over her hips and took a shuddering breath when she was naked before him. "I'm afraid this night might be over all too quickly."

"Perhaps the first time," she said, parting the robe he wore to reveal his bare chest.

"The first time?" His mouth felt dry.

"We have a long night ahead of us, Major."

He put his hands on the curve of her hips and drew her close. "Yes, we do."

"And you're wearing too many clothes," she chided.

"That can be easily rectified." He pulled the tie on the robe and let it drop. Then as naked as she, he scooped her up and carried her to the bed. "I've had my fill of couches, parlors, and broom closets," he said, laying her down and then coming down beside her. "I've wanted you in a bed, and now I plan to take full advantage of it."

"Please do." She wrapped her arms around his neck, her mouth lifting to meet his. As soon as their lips touched, it felt as though lightning had struck between them. The urge to take her then was overwhelming, but Neil battled back his impulses and drew their kisses out until they were slow, languid caresses. When he'd explored her mouth to his satisfaction, he pressed his lips to the column of her neck, her rounded shoulder, the curve of her breast, the hard tip of her nipple, and the gentle swell of her belly. He wanted to take his time learning the shape of her silky legs, but he would have to save that for later. His fingers had dipped between her legs, and once he'd felt how wet she was, how ready, his desires could no longer be ignored.

Neil hadn't asked for conjugal advice from his friends at the Draven Club, but they'd given it anyway. The consensus seemed to be that a woman's first time was less painful if she was fully aroused. It had been some time since Neil had done much more than kiss Juliana, and now when his fingers slid between the slippery folds of her sex, raw hunger and longing suffused him. He glanced at her face and saw her watching him with those beautiful eyes. Her lips were red and her cheeks pink.

"I want you," she whispered. "I love you, Neil."

"I love you," he said as he bent to taste her. Her climax seemed to ripple through her without warning. He'd barely touched his tongue to her before she writhed on the bed and cried out, shuddering. Neil liked the sound of that cry and immediately decided they needed thicker walls and doors on their bedchamber at the orphanage. He intended to see that she made many more of those lusty cries.

Now he rose and positioned himself between her legs. His cock seemed to know what to do, even if he didn't, and he was an inch inside her heat before he could stop himself. Juliana didn't help. She bucked against him, urging him, trying to pull him deeper. Gritting his teeth, Neil moved inside her slowly. She was tight and hot, and he wanted to thrust hard and deep. Instead, he recited the names and numbers of every cavalry unit he could think of. He stroked her with his fingers, pausing when he heard her gasp or when her eyes widened in surprise.

"Am I hurting you?" he managed. *Seventh Queen's Own Hussars. Eighth Light Dragoons. Ninth Light Dragoons.*

"A little, but it also feels wonderful," she admitted. "Very strange."

"Yes, that was the effect I wanted," he said through clenched teeth. "Strange and painful." *Tenth Prince of Wales's Hussars. Eleventh Light Dragoons.*

"That's not what I meant. Neil, I—"

She gasped on a moan as his fingers teased her again, sliding up and down over her sensitive flesh and circling that small, sensitive nub. He felt her contract around him, felt his own control slipping, and then she arched her hips, and he couldn't hold back any longer. He thrust inside her. She cried out, even as her body continued to climax. Her muscles gripped him several more times, and he was almost undone.

Fifteenth King's Hussars.

He closed his eyes and remained as still as possible. Finally, what seemed like months later, he felt her fingers stroke his cheek. "Are you hurt?" she asked.

He laughed and opened his eyes. "No. I'm attempting not to hurt you."

"I feel quite wonderful," she said, her gaze hazy and unfocused. "A little strange with you...well, *there.*"

"Could we possibly cease using the word 'strange' for the time being?" he said.

"Of course. Should we—Oh!"

He'd moved, and her eyes widened.

"Did that hurt?" he asked, concerned.

"A little, but it felt"—he gave her a warning look—"pleasant."

He moved again, and she did not cry out in pain. He thrust deeper, and that was when she moaned. "Oh yes. I can see how that will feel lovely next time."

Next time. He could barely fathom what was happening this time. It was both better and worse than he'd ever imagined. She was wet and tight and impossibly irresistible, but he felt like a schoolboy who had no control.

And perhaps that was as it should be—the two of them learning this dance, this new part of their lives together. As Juliana had said, they had a long night ahead of them. They had a long marriage ahead as well.

Later, after Neil had succumbed to the pleasure of his wife's body, he held her against him. Her warmth and scent enveloped him just as his arms surrounded her. This was a new beginning, a new world; together, they would explore it. If they were together, their love could conquer anything.

⤳

Everything had gone as planned. Neil had gathered the surviving members of Draven's troop and given orders like he had in the old days. It had felt damn good, giving an order that wouldn't get anyone killed. It had taken finesse, charm, bribes, and royal intervention, but he had finally prevailed.

"Ready, sir?" Mrs. Dunwitty asked from the other side of the coach. The child slept peacefully in her arms after his long journey.

"Yes. Hand him over, will you?"

Mrs. Dunwitty obliged, and Neil took the baby, surprised at how solid he was for only ten months. He had wispy, dark hair with hints of auburn and chubby, pink cheeks. His eyes were brown, much like his aunt's, and he smiled now in his sleep. Neil wondered what he dreamed of.

The coach's door opened and Neil climbed out and carried the child into the town house. St. Maur was waiting in the vestibule. Silently, he pointed to the parlor, where Juliana liked to see to her correspondence most mornings. The man who had become his father-in-law only a week or so before knocked on the door and opened it.

"Yes, what is it?" Juliana asked, her head bent over the desk.

"We have a new resident of the orphanage," Neil said.

She looked up, her brows furrowed. "What do you mean? Neil!" She rose. "Where did this child come from? How will we find room for—" She put a hand to her heart, and for a moment Neil thought she might scream. Then she ran to him and all but ripped the child from his arms. Davy fussed, then snuggled against her as though coming home.

She stared at the child, then at Neil. "Is it really him? Really Davy?"

"Yes," he said. "It's really him, and he's really yours." He would tell her all the stipulations and legal agreements later. Lainesborough had not relinquished custody of the boy completely. But in the end, money had mattered more to him than a child he would take no interest in for another eighteen years. Neil hadn't had to compromise as much as he'd feared.

"How?" she whispered. "I tried everything."

Neil shrugged. "I'm a war hero. You know that."

She laughed, her voice shaky. "And all this time you have been trying to convince me you were anything but a hero. Thank you." She cradled the little boy, tears running down her cheeks.

Neil caught one. "You are supposed to be happy."

"I am. I'm weeping for joy. He's so beautiful."

Neil looked down at the child, his eyes closed so peacefully, and he thought of the dream he'd had of his brother. In the dream, Christopher's eyes had been closed, his face serene. He was at rest, at peace. Finally, Neil could be at peace too.

"Papa, isn't he beautiful?" Juliana motioned to her father standing in the doorway. "Isn't he the most beautiful boy?"

The earl nodded. "Our family is complete."

Neil couldn't have agreed more.

*Read on for an excerpt from book 3
in Shana Galen's Survivors series*

An Affair with a Spare

Coming soon from Sourcebooks Casablanca

COLLETTE TOOK A SHAKY BREATH AND PASTED A
bright smile on her face.

Do not mention hedgehogs. Do not mention hedgehogs!

Collette Fortier was nervous, and when she was
nervous her English faltered, and she often fell back
upon the books she'd studied when learning the
language. Unfortunately, they had been books on
natural history. The volume on hedgehogs, with

its black-and-white sketches, had been one of her favorites.

This ball had been a nightmare from the moment she'd entered. Not only was she squished in the ballroom like a folding fan, there was no escape from the harsh sound of English voices. Due to the steady rain outside, the hosts had closed the doors and windows. Collette felt more trapped than usual.

"He's coming this way!" Lady Ravensgate hissed, elbowing her in the side. Collette had to restrain herself from elbowing her chaperone right back. Since Lieutenant Colonel Draven was indeed headed their way, Collette held herself in check. She needed an introduction. After almost a month of insinuating herself into the inner sphere of Britain's Foreign Office, she was finally closing in on the men who would have knowledge of the codes she needed.

Lady Ravensgate fluttered her fan wildly as the former soldier approached and then let go so the fan fell directly into the Lieutenant Colonel's path. Lady Ravensgate gasped in a bad imitation of horror as Draven bent to retrieve the fan, as any gentleman would.

"I believe you dropped this." He rose and presented the fan to Lady Ravensgate. He was a robust man with auburn hair and sharp blue eyes. Still in the prime of life, he gave the ladies an easy smile before turning away.

"Lieutenant Colonel Draven, is it not?" Lady Ravensgate said. The soldier raised his eyebrows politely, his gaze traveling from Lady Ravensgate to Collette. Collette felt her cheeks heat and hated herself for it. She had always been shy and averse to attention, and no matter the steps she took to overcome her bashfulness, she could not rid herself of it completely. Especially not around men she found even remotely attractive.

Draven might have been twenty years her senior, but no one would deny he was a handsome and virile man.

"It is," Draven answered. "And you are...?"

"Lady Ravensgate. We met at the theater last Season. You called on Mrs. Fullerton in her box where I was a guest."

"Of course." He bowed graciously, though Collette could tell he had no recollection of meeting her chaperone. "How good to see you again, Mrs....er..."

"Lady Ravensgate." She gestured to Collette. "And this is my cousin, Collette Fournay. She is here visiting me from France."

Collette curtsied, making certain not to bend over too far lest she fall out of the green-and-gold-striped silk dress Lady Ravensgate had convinced her to wear. It was one of several Lady Ravensgate had given her. She'd bought them inexpensively from a modiste who had made them for a woman who could then not afford the bill. Whoever the woman was, she had been less endowed in the bosom and hips than Collette.

"Mademoiselle Fournay." Draven bowed to her. "And how are you liking London?" he asked in perfect French.

"I am enjoying it immensely," she answered in English. She wanted people to forget she was French as much as possible and that meant always speaking in English, though the effort gave her an awful headache some evenings. "The dancers look to be having such a wonderful time." The comment was not subtle, nor did she intend it to be.

"You have not had much opportunity to dance tonight, have you?" Lady Ravensgate said sympathetically.

Collette shook her head, eyeing Draven. He knew he was cornered. He took a fortifying breath. "May I have the honor of the next dance, mademoiselle?"

Collette put a hand to her heart, pretending to be shocked. "Oh, but, sir, you needn't feel obligated."

"Nonsense. It would be my pleasure."

She gave a curtsy, and he bowed. "Excuse me."

He would return to collect her at the beginning of the next set. That would be in about ten minutes. Which meant she had time to think of a strategy.

"Do not mention the codes," Lady Ravensgate said in a hushed voice, offering Collette advice she had not asked for. "Lead him to the topic, but you should not give any indication you know anything about them."

"Of course." She had danced with dozens of men and initiated dozens of conversations she hoped would lead to the information she needed. Lady Ravensgate's tutelage had been wholly ineffective thus far. She always told Collette not to mention the codes. Her only other piece of advice seemed to be—

"And do not mention your father."

Collette nodded stiffly. That was the other. As though she needed to be told not to mention a known French assassin to a member of Britain's Foreign Office. What might have been more helpful were suggestions for encouraging the man to speak of his service during the recent war with Napoleon. Few of the men she had danced with had wanted to discuss the war or their experiences in it. The few she had managed to pry war stories from did not know anything about how the British had cracked the French secret code. And they seemed to know even less about the code the British used to encrypt their own messages.

But she had learned enough to believe that Draven ranked high enough that he would have access to the codes Britain used to encrypt their missives. It had taken a month, but she would finally speak with the man who had what she needed.

She watched the dancers on the floor turn and walk, link arms and turn again. The ladies' dresses belled as they moved, their gloved wrists sparkling in the light of the chandeliers. They laughed, a tinkling carefree sound that carried over the strains of violin and cello. Not so long ago, Collette had danced just as blithely. Paris in the time of Napoleon had been the center of French society, and her father had been invited to every fete, every soiree.

He hadn't attended many—after all, he made people nervous—but when he was required to attend, he brought Collette as his escort. She couldn't have known that, a few years later, she would be doing those same dances in an effort to save his life.

The dance ended and Collette admired the fair-skinned English beauties as they promenaded past her. She had olive-toned skin and dark hair, her figure too curvaceous for the current fashions. Then Draven was before her, hand extended. With a quick look at Lady Ravensgate—that snake in the grass—Collette took his hand and allowed herself to be led to the center of the dance floor. The orchestra began to play a quadrille, and she curtsied to the other dancers in their square. She and Draven danced first, passing the couple opposite as they made their way from one side of the square to the other and back again.

Finally, she and Draven stood while the waiting couples danced, and she knew this was her chance. Before she could speak, Draven nodded to her. "How do you like the dance?"

She'd been unprepared for the question, and the only English response she could think of was *Hedgehog mating rituals are prolonged affairs in which the male and female circle one another.* In truth, the dance did seem like a mating ritual of sorts, but unless she wanted to shock the man, she had to find another comparison.

More importantly, she did not have much time to steer the conversation in the direction she needed. She had not answered yet, and he looked at her curiously. Collette cleared her throat.

"The dance does not remind me of hedgehogs."

His eyes widened.

Merde! Imbécile!

"Oh, that is not right," she said quickly. "Sometimes my words are not correct. I meant...what is the word...soldiers? Yes? The dancers remind me of soldiers as they fight in battle."

She blew out a breath. Draven was looking at her as though she were mad, and she did not blame him.

"You fought in the war, no?"

"I did, yes."

"I live in the countryside with my parents, far from any battles."

"That is most fortunate." His gaze returned to the dancers.

"Did you lead soldiers into battle?" she asked. Most men puffed right up at the opportunity to discuss their own bravery.

"At times. But much of my work was done far from the battle lines."

Just her luck—a modest man.

She knew it was dangerous to press further. A Frenchwoman in England should know better than to bring up the recent war between the two countries, but her father's freedom was at stake. She could not give up yet.

"And what sort of work did you do behind the lines? I imagine you wrote letters and intercepted missives. Oh, but, sir, were you a spy?" Her voice sounded breathless, and it was not an affectation. She was breathless with nerves.

Draven flicked her a glance. "Nothing so exciting, mademoiselle. In fact, were I to tell you of my experiences, you would probably fall asleep. Ah, it is our turn again." And they circled each other and then she met with him only briefly as they came together, separated, and parted again performing the various forms.

When he led her from the dance floor, escorting her back to Lady Ravensgate, she tried once again to engage him in conversation, but he deftly turned the topic back to the rainy weather they'd had. Lady Ravensgate must have seen the defeat on Collette's face because as soon as they reached her, she began to chatter. "Lieutenant Colonel, do tell me your opinion on Caroline Lamb's book. Is *Glenarvon* too scandalous for my dear cousin?"

Draven bowed stiffly. "I could not say, my lady, as I

have not read it. If you will permit me, I see someone I must speak with." And even before he'd been given leave, he was gone.

"I take it things did not go well," Lady Ravensgate muttered.

"No."

The lady sighed in disgust, and not for the first time Collette wondered whose side her "cousin" was on. She'd claimed to be an old friend of her father's, but might she be more of a friend to Louis XVIII and the Bourbons who had imprisoned Collette's father?

"Poor, poor Monsieur Fortier," Lady Ravensgate said.

Collette turned to her, cheeks burning. "Do not bemoan him yet, madam. I *will* free my father. Mark my words. I will free him, even if it's the last thing I do."

She knew better than anyone that love demands sacrifice.

Acknowledgments

Thank you to Michelle Arnold, Pat Viglione, and all my Facebook friends for help with naming Juliana's orphanage.

About the Author

Shana Galen is a three-time RITA Award nominee and the bestselling author of passionate Regency romps, including RT Reviewers' Choice *The Making of a Gentleman*. *Kirkus Reviews* says of her books, "The road to happily ever after is intense, conflicted, suspenseful, and fun," and *RT Book Reviews* calls her books "lighthearted yet poignant, humorous yet touching." She taught English at the middle and high school level off and on for eleven years. Most of those years were spent working in Houston's inner city. Now she writes full time. She's happily married and has a daughter who is most definitely a romance heroine in the making.